FILTHY
RICH
VAMPIRES

For Eternity

FILTHY RICH VAMPIRES

For Eternity

GENEVA LEE

NEW YORK TIMES & INTERNATIONALLY BESTSELLING AUTHOR

Entangled Publishing, LLC
644 Shrewsbury Commons Ave., STE 181
Shrewsbury, PA 17361
rights@entangledpublishing.com

Amara is an imprint of Entangled Publishing, LLC.

Visit our website at www.entangledpublishing.com.

Edited by Yezanira Venecia
Cover art and design by Geneva Lee
Stock art by Gluiki/Adobestock, Alexstar/Adobestock, and James Steidl/Adobestock
Interior design by Britt Marczak

ISBN 978-1-64937-646-6

Manufactured in the United States of America

First Edition May 2024

10 9 8 7 6 5 4 3 2 1

ALSO BY GENEVA LEE

For the queens

At Entangled, we want our readers to be well-informed. If you would like to know if this book contains any elements that might be of concern for you, please check the back of the book for details.

PROLOGUE

My queen.

Past the blood that stained her gown, under her sharp weariness, I saw proof of what I'd always known. She was a queen. No longer only in my eyes but in the eyes of every magical creature in our world. She glowed as if the sun burned inside her, as though the world itself centered around her being. Her hand tightened around mine, and I could feel her magic pulsating through her skin. It was wild and free, like a storm brewing on the horizon.

Tears glistened in her eyes as she looked upon me—as she understood why I knelt before her. Her mate. Her protector. I pledged my allegiance, letting the crowd of onlookers see that I worshipped at her feet and a move against her was a move against me. I could sense the power coursing through both our veins—her light and my dark feeding off of each other—and I knew that together there was nothing we couldn't face. The crown on Thea's head shimmered in the light, a symbol of her power, and I felt a surge of pride.

"Long live the queen." I allowed my voice to carry through the stone chamber.

A few creatures behind us echoed the sentiment.

"Get up," Thea said to me through gritted teeth.

"As you wish." I couldn't help smirking again. I rose to my feet, still holding her hand, never wanting to let go, and faced the crowd of onlookers. They were all silent, their eyes fixed on the two of us, waiting for our next move, waiting to see how the new queen and her mate would take control. A few vampires watched with darting eyes, assessing, *searching* for a hint of weakness in their new queen. But Thea was far from weak, and she would prove herself.

For now, I just needed her in my arms.

My mother approached the dais, her lips curled back in feral rage. "She cannot be queen."

A growl rumbled deep in my chest. No one would touch Thea. Not even my own blood.

"She has been chosen," Mariana called out in response. "Anyone who doesn't agree should leave." I don't think I imagined the slight look she cast at Zina, as if daring her other sister to desert her throne.

Everyone stayed in place until, at last, my mother drew a deep breath and stalked from the room. I waited for my brothers and father to follow. Each of them looked torn, and then Thea spoke to them. "Go after her. She is *our* family."

It was more respect than my mother would have extended her if their situations were reversed. My father inclined his head, relief washing the tension from his shoulders. "My queen."

My brothers followed suit. Lysander and Sebastian barely contained their snickers as they addressed her. After they were gone, Mariana cleared her throat. "There is much to discuss." She looked between us, her features softening. "But it can wait until the morning. You should rest and allow your powers to settle."

A small ball of light formed in her palm. It danced toward us, and she sighed with satisfaction to find her magic working. "This will take you to your new quarters."

Thea blinked with surprise but collected herself quickly. "Thank you."

But even as she spoke, she swayed slightly on her feet. Calling on that powerful magic had drained her. Instinct took over, and I forgot about the crown and her new status. All I cared about was attending to my mate. I swept her into my arms and carried her away, following that ball of light as it led us deeper into the court.

Thea looped her arm around my neck and nuzzled into it. "Where are we going?"

"Somewhere with a lock," I promised her. "And a bath." I needed to get her out of these bloody clothes. My dick twitched, registering its interest in this scheme.

I ignored it until she said, "And a bed?"

"As you wish, Your Majesty," I promised her.

Thea stuck her tongue out, and something primal roared inside me. "That's the idea."

She paused, sucking in a shuddering breath, and when her eyes met mine, they were bright with need. "Stop talking and take me to bed."

CHAPTER ONE

Thea

"This must be it." Julian nodded to the door the ball of light had stopped in front of and reached for its knob. As soon as he did, the magical orb faded away, its purpose fulfilled.

I stared at where it had been. "A spell?"

He nodded, keeping his hand on the door. He didn't open it, as if he, too, was struggling with the reality of what had happened.

The door was made of thick oak and stood at least ten feet high. Other than its impressive size, it was rather boring. Not what I expected from a place with thrones and magical balls of light and queens.

My stomach flipped at the thought—just thinking of queens made me feel like I was being turned inside out. The farther we got from the throne room and everything that had happened, the more out of sorts I felt.

Magic.

Magic was awake. No longer cursed. It no longer slept in our veins. I felt it. Not like I had before in those rare, stolen touches. It was changed, but how different was it? Would it be little party tricks like a floating night light, or were there bigger surprises to come? And why had I been chosen? Why would the throne choose to anoint me?

I pushed my worries aside and focused on this moment—on the male standing before me.

I coiled my arm around his neck more tightly. I didn't want to worry about any of it now—not with my skin touching his, not after being given a second chance. But the truth was that I was growing more tired by the minute. Julian's resurrection seemed to have invigorated him, but all of it had worn me out.

"What are you waiting for?" I purred, battling the exhaustion I refused to give into until I had my fill of him.

"It's just…" He trailed away before shaking his head. "Never mind. It can wait."

Before I could press him on the issue, he swung open the door and carried me inside. Based on the door's simplicity, I wasn't prepared for what we found. The vestibule we stood in was oversized and luxurious. Unlike the rest of the court's brutal elegance and stone facades, these walls were plastered over. Frescoes depicted the celestial movement of the sun and moon. As we entered, the sun rose along the wall, its light falling over plants and fauna. Birds dusted the painted sky, rising in flight to midday. As the mural progressed toward the room, the sun lowered, meeting with stars as twilight fell.

The corridor opened into a room that night had swallowed entirely. The walls were painted in shades of deepest blue that faded to near black where they met the ceiling, and speckled throughout the darkness were stars that seemed to twinkle as we moved. I had no idea if it was a trick of the light created by a skilled artist or magic, but I found myself unable to speak as I took it all in.

Twin orbs hung like full moons overhead, casting the entire room in a warm glow despite the darkness. A fire had been lit in the hearth, its faint, smoky scent welcoming us. On either side of the stone mantle, deep velvet couches piled with jewel-colored pillows sat around a slab of marble. Someone had left a bottle of wine and two glasses for us on the table, like we'd been expected. For a second, I wondered if the room had been prepared for Sabine—Sabine, who had expected to ascend the throne and take the crown. Sabine, who was probably plotting revenge on me from wherever she'd found a place to claim as her own at court. I would have to deal with her. Later. For now, I focused on my surroundings.

Black sheers curtained ten-foot-tall windows, held back with a rayed sun on one side and a silver crescent on the other. Outside, the night sky sparkled on the surface of a canal. The water rippled in the moonlight, its surging dance calling out to me like a thrumming pulse.

"Is that the *Rio Oscuro?*"

Julian nodded as he placed me on my feet, his hand straying to my back as if he wasn't quite ready to let me go. "The source of all magic."

"All?" I repeated, beginning to understand. This wasn't just another magical hotspot like in Paris or Greece. "Is that why..." But I wasn't sure what I wanted to ask. *Is it why we're here? Tonight? Is this why the court still exists in this spot? Was it a coincidence my father waited to kidnap me until we were in Venice?*

"It's why we are alive," he said in a thick voice. I glanced up and saw shadows clinging to his handsome face. I understood what he didn't say: it was also why we had died in the first place. It couldn't be coincidence that we'd been drawn here—that the Mordicum had chosen this location or that Willem had come after me here. Now I was bound to the magic flowing outside the window as surely as I was bound to my own body.

The crown on my head felt heavy. My limbs ached, as if whatever magic I'd called on earlier was leaking from my bones and trying to make its way home to the water outside. I swayed on my feet, and Julian caught me with a steadying hand.

"Are you hungry?" he asked.

My stomach grumbled in response, but I swallowed as memories surfaced. They were hazy, clouded by whatever enchantment Willem had kept over me in my captivity. I could not remember the last time I'd eaten food, and what I could remember...

I nodded, adding in a whisper, "I fed this morning."

There was a heartbeat of silence between us as Julian processed what I meant. I searched his eyes, waiting for his thoughts on that confession. Because that was what it was: a confession. I had no idea how long I'd been under Willem's control, how long I'd been feeding on blood as he attempted to manipulate my vampire genetics.

Finally, Julian shucked off his ruined tuxedo jacket and began to roll up his sleeve.

"What are you doing?" I blurted out.

"You need to feed," he said softly before extending his wrist. "Whatever happened out there, it's obvious you need strength."

I shook my head, tears welling in my eyes. "You shouldn't...not after—"

"I feel fantastic," he cut me off. "I feel like the *Rio Oscuro* itself is running in my veins."

It wasn't just about him, and we both knew it. "I don't want to be a monster," I said, and my voice cracked.

"You will never be a monster," he seethed. "The crown wouldn't have chosen someone who could be easily corrupted."

His words drew attention to the crown's weight, and I ripped it off my head before throwing it onto one of the velvet couches.

Julian picked it up and carried it to the mantel. He held it for just a moment, its stone catching the light overhead. "Thea, *you* wear the crown, and you decide when you want it."

I wished it was that simple, but something told me it wasn't. Still, I understood what he meant. "I don't want to wear it now."

He placed it on the mantel and moved in front of it. I knew he understood what I meant, too. I wasn't a queen now. Not when it was just the two of us. Not after everything that had happened. There was only one thing I wanted to be—his mate—and only one place I wanted to be: in his arms.

He strode toward me, lifting his wrist, and in response, I held out my own. Neither of us spoke as we took the other's offering. As my fangs descended and pierced his vein, a moan spilled out along with his blood.

I barely remembered my time with Willem. My memories of it

seemed hidden behind a veil. But I knew that the blood I'd tasted there could never compare to the sweet taste of my mate on my tongue.

His eyes blackened entirely but stayed on me as he took one slow swallow at a time. He didn't rush, even though I felt his need radiating from him. Maybe he was worried I wasn't ready—that I was too weak—but after everything we'd endured, this was exactly what I needed. His body, *his life*, strengthening me as mine strengthened his. Magic flowed through his veins, perhaps some lingering effect of his resurrection. I tasted its spikes of spiced honey, and as his blood filled me, trickles of the light seemed to dance under my skin until I felt as full of magic as the water outside.

When Julian finally lowered my wrist, he brushed a single kiss over the wound. My eyes tracked the movement, my body remembering what it felt like to have his lips on other parts of my skin.

"Did you feed while…" I let my question trail away, but Julian's head fell, hanging with shame, and I had my answer. I placed a soothing hand over his heart—over the bloodied patch of shirt where it had been pierced through. A shudder racked me, and I forced a tight smile. "I'm glad. I wouldn't want you to go without."

Something else kept his head bowed, something heavier, and I wondered what guilt he carried. And what he'd done to cause that feeling.

"There were no lines I wouldn't cross—no lines I didn't cross," he clarified in a gruff voice that sent a new wave of shivers cascading down my spine. "And I will not apologize."

"I won't ask you to." Someday we might face the memories of the darkness together. We'd both been forced to do things that felt wrong. But in this moment, I refused to share even a piece of him with my guilt.

"You're a mess," I whispered to him.

His lips quirked into a crooked grin that made my heart skip. I forgot how to breathe. "I've got bad news for you," he said. "You look even worse."

"Maybe we should do something about that."

He didn't say another word. Instead, he took my hand and guided me from the living room into the attached bedroom. A king-size bed with an ornately carved headboard held court in its center, covered in so many white pillows I felt like I was walking amongst clouds. Their airy comfort was in direct contrast to the ink-blue walls. There were no stars to break up that darkness. It consumed the space around me, beckoning me to drift away into that starless sea. But over the large bed, a crescent moon hung pointed up at an unnatural angle so that its two sharp points held a smattering of stars. I stared at it a moment before looking more closely at the headboard underneath. It wasn't vines twining along the frame but rather snakes, their mouths swallowing the tails of their brethren. Only one serpent rose higher, its head extended and mouth reared, as if waiting to swallow the oddly placed moon.

"It looks like the throne," I said to him, and he nodded.

"Your seat draws on the magic of change—transformation. It changes with the moon."

I lifted an eyebrow. "That sounds complicated."

"Magic always is." He directed me past the bed into the attached bathroom. A large circular tub, big enough to fit both of us, sat in the center of the room. Its long faucet extended from the ground and arched over its edge. A drain in the corner caught my attention, and I discovered two showerheads over it. There were two sinks that seemed to be carved from moonstone on the far wall, and I guessed the other door led to a toilet.

Julian looked between the shower and the tub and back to me.

"Shower," I said. His blood had revived me, but I didn't trust myself not to fall asleep in that bathtub—and sleep was the last thing on my mind.

Especially as Julian began to unbutton his shirt. I let myself watch his fingers as they nimbly worked, drinking in the sight when he finally shucked it off his shoulders. The first thing I spotted was my engagement ring hanging from a chain he wore around his neck. But as he slid the shirt entirely off, my gaze followed and snagged on a mark, not unlike a tattoo, on his chest over his heart.

"What is that?" Somehow—to my horror—I already knew.

He glanced down, his forehead wrinkling as he took in the snake coiled there with a crescent moon in its mouth. "This was Ginerva's symbol," he told me, smirking a little. "Yours now. It seems you've left your mark on me."

"The bond," I murmured, realizing what it was. "They told me I would have to tie my life to yours. I didn't know they meant literally."

"You did what?" All hint of amusement was gone.

"My life—I offered it to save yours." I bit my lip, aware of his piercing, unblinking stare. "Your life is tied to mine now. It was the only way." I waited for him to respond, but he only stood there. "Do you mind?"

After a moment of silence that seemed to stretch on forever, his throat bobbed. His voice was awed as he answered. "Do I mind?" he repeated. "I'm honored, but I don't want you to make that sacrifice for me. I want you to live."

"How could I live without my heart?" I whispered. "Could you?"

Another beat of silence followed, and then he was striding toward me. When he reached me, his palms cradled my face. "I will never live another day without you," he swore, and I knew that this wasn't about the price I'd paid to save him. It was about what had happened before—it was why we'd found ourselves standing here now. "I am not a perfect male. I've made mistakes." The smirk returned, and I sagged with relief as he added, "I might even make more."

Might? I rolled my eyes but couldn't help but smile.

"But I will face them with you," he finished. "No secrets. You don't need me to protect you from the truth."

I took a deep breath as the full meaning of what he'd said sank in. He had kept things from me, and I'd done the same, both of us thinking we were protecting the other. Instead, we'd found ourselves ripped apart, and why? It was a risk I was unwilling to take, no matter how uncomfortable the situation we found ourselves in.

"No secrets," I vowed, but if there were to be no secrets... "Julian, my father is a vampire."

His gaze hardened into sapphires. "I know."

"Then you know what I might become. What I might already be." Terror welled inside me as I admitted the fear I'd barely corked since the moment I awakened on the throne.

"I don't care." He brushed a tear from my cheek with the rough pad of his thumb.

"You should. What if—" A choked sob cut me off, but he shook his head.

"I love you. I don't care what blood runs in your veins. I don't care about your magic or how powerful it will make you. I love you—all of you. The power and the weakness and the human and the creature. Nothing will change that."

"What if I change?" I forced myself to ask even as my heart pounded inside me.

"If you change, I will love you more just as I do with every minute that passes," he murmured, then paused before smiling. "Now, can I get you out of these bloody clothes?"

I nodded, tears still leaking down my cheeks. He walked to the shower and flipped on the water before turning back to me. My breath hitched as he circled me and found my gown's zipper. He drew it down slowly—so slowly that I felt his worshipful gaze on my bare skin. Expectation rippled across me and pooled in my core until I was molten. His long fingers slipped under its straps and slid it from my shoulders to puddle at my feet.

The gown itself had been too low cut for a bra, so I stood before him in nothing but a scrap of lace masquerading as panties, stockings, and my heels. Julian knelt, his mouth brushing along the column of my spine, and hooked his thumbs around the elastic band at my waist. He took his time removing them, allowing his mouth to explore their wake. It felt as if I was being wound around again and again, each flicker of his tongue, each caress of his lips coiling me tighter until I thought I might explode under the tension.

He removed my heels and then my stockings, at last gripping my hips and urging me to face him. I closed my eyes, my entire being centered on the spots where his fingertips touched me. When his grip tightened, I felt something crackle in the air between us. I opened my eyes to find him staring at my chest—at the blood dried there. The blood I'd spilled as I'd died with him. When he finally looked up at me, his blue eyes were haunted.

He released me and reached behind his neck to undo the chain he wore. When it was off, he slid the emerald ring free and reached for my hand. Neither of us spoke as he slid it onto my finger, but I vowed silently to never take it off again. His palm flattened against mine, and he twined our fingers. Energy crackled between us, proof of the new magic we carried, but neither of us pulled away. And when Julian lowered his head to rest on the center of my rib cage, I knew he was counting my heartbeats, even as magic surged and sparked between us.

I lost track of how long we stood there, each of us cherishing the other. I never wanted it to end. When he finally moved, it was only to stand and lift me into his arms to carry me into the shower. Steam billowed around me as he lowered me to my feet and reached for the soap. He lathered it between his palms before he began to wash me. His touch was so tender, I could hardly breathe. He slowed as he reached between my breasts, his eyes narrowing on the red-tinged water.

His jaw worked for a moment before he brought his scorching gaze to meet mine. "You shouldn't…"

"I don't regret it," I said fiercely, "and I would do it again."

His answering smile was full of sorrowful understanding.

"You are *my* mate," I whispered, my tears mixing with the shower.

Julian growled, a primal hunger twisting his features. In one swift move, he swept me into his arms. He didn't bother with a towel as he carried me to the bed in the adjoining room. He laid me across it, leaving my bare legs to dangle over the edge, but he didn't join me.

"I told you earlier that I would be the first to kneel before you and offer my allegiance, my queen." A smile wrapped itself around his words, but I still made a face. His chuckle slid down me, making my body clench. "But you are my queen. You always have been. Now I just have to share you."

"Will you?" I asked shyly.

"As long as I am the only one who gets to do this." The huskiness in his voice sent a bolt of pleasure through me. It pooled between my legs as he lowered himself to the floor one knee at a time. His palms sent pulses of magic up my sensitive thighs as he pushed them apart. I stopped breathing entirely when he lowered his head between them, his hands spreading me wide open before him. One hot lash of the tongue sent me arching off the bed. He loosed another sinful chuckle as he pinned me to the mattress with one hand.

This time he took his time dragging his tongue all the way down. Lightning followed in its wake, and my hands shot out to grab hold of the sheets. I gripped them more tightly as he continued to pleasure me with long, lazy strokes. He only slowed to circle the ache pulsing at my apex. But as I climbed, climbed, climbed, each tremble of pleasure only reminded me of the hollow need inside me.

"Please," I finally gritted out as I writhed under the palm pinning me to the bed. "I want you."

His response was swift, and I didn't flinch when he stood with midnight-black eyes and moved between my legs. Julian lowered his mouth to my breast and caught my nipple between my teeth. Between the insistent nibble of his teeth and the stretching sensation as he slid inside me, I groaned and gave in to my overwhelming need for him. Releasing the sheets, I sank my fingers into his chest as he finished sliding home.

"I will never get enough of this," he said, then began to rock his hips in and out in languid, teasing thrusts. "There will only be you for the rest of my life."

"For eternity," I echoed our earlier vow.

He nodded. "For eternity."

His magic rose to meet mine, and I felt them embrace—felt

myself become whole again. Julian pinned his blue stare on me as he rolled his hips in undulating strokes that took me closer and closer until finally...

I was falling—falling into him.

Falling in love again and again.

And there was no hard landing, because I shattered around him, only to be carried higher by his darkness as he came with a mighty roar.

For a long time, we stayed like that, my legs hooked around his narrow waist. Our breathing gradually returned to normal, and when I found myself shivering in my sweat-slicked skin, he pushed me onto the bed, then joined me.

His arms wrapped around me, and my body molded against him. His hand drifted lower and paused on my stomach. It stayed there, his fingers splayed protectively over my flesh as if he somehow knew.

Taking a deep breath, I placed my palm over his and twisted my neck so that I could see his face. "There's something I need to tell you."

CHAPTER TWO

Julian

Silence roared around us as I stared into Thea's eyes. The weight of her hand felt heavy, and I braced myself for whatever she was about to say. But she didn't continue. Instead, her teeth sank into her lower lip, and I wondered how bad the news was if she couldn't bring herself to say it.

"Did Willem..." It took effort to dredge up the words, but not as much effort as it took to control the sudden urge to find that monster and rip his head off. "...hurt you? Or have someone hurt you?"

Thea swallowed, her face flinching with disgust. She understood what I meant—what I was implying. She started to roll away, but I refused to release her. She relaxed and turned toward me. "No." She shook her head. "At least, not like that."

I felt no relief from her answer, but I didn't want to pressure her to tell me more. Instead, I waited.

"He told me something." Another heavy pause. She traced her finger down the mark on my chest—the symbol of her ownership. "He told me that if a siren and a vampire breed, their child..."

"I know," I said darkly. Her eyes widened, pain flashing through them, and I explained quickly, "Sabine told me after you were taken."

I couldn't bring myself to tell her more of what my mother had said—about us. About our children. But the joy that had filled her face only moments ago now faded entirely.

"Then you already know." Her lips turned down. "We can't have children."

Anger gripped me with icy fingers. I took a deep breath, forcing myself to remain calm. "We can have whatever *we* want."

I wasn't certain when it had changed: my vision of the future. I think it had started the moment that we met, but it wasn't until she'd been taken that I'd realized how real that vision had begun—and what I stood to lose.

"There's more. If Willem is my father, then I'm not just a siren."

"I know." I'd pieced that together when she'd told me what had happened earlier.

"Does it matter to you?" she asked softly.

"Does it matter?" I repeated, blinking at her. My arms tightened their hold on her. "No. You're my mate. I love you for who you are, and nothing will change that."

"He told me that's why there are no sirens, that we were hunted, and if that's true, our children..." She sighed, shifting her head on the pillow. "We're talking about this like we have kids."

"We're talking about our future. I won't apologize for that." But something new weighed on my mind after what she'd said. "We have a bigger problem to deal with."

She lifted her brow, her eyes distant and preoccupied, and I wondered if she realized what I just had. I felt for her through that new bond we shared, the one linking my life with hers, but I couldn't sense what she was feeling.

"The vampires hunted the sirens," I said through gritted teeth. "If they know what you are..."

I couldn't bring myself to say it. I didn't even want to think it, but I couldn't ignore it. Not without risking everything we'd fought for. If the vampires—if my kind—knew what she was...

They would come for her.

If they didn't know already, if they hadn't guessed that the crown had found a powerful new magic and chosen her, if they hadn't already guessed she was a siren, how long would it take before they realized? She was safe at court.

For now.

"You think they'll come for me?" She blinked, reaching for her head like she felt the weight of that absent crown. "They wouldn't come after me because…"

I waited for her to say it, but she remained silent. Confusion and fear twisted on her face, the last vestiges of that powerful ruler falling away to reveal what she would only show me: her vulnerability.

Because I'm a queen.

She didn't speak, but I heard the words spoken in my own mind. A whisper down this new bond we shared. A smile cracked my mouth. "Yes, you are."

Thea froze as she registered what had happened. "Wait, you heard my thoughts?"

"I did." I tugged her closer, and she melted against me, her softness curling around my hard body. Her hands flattened against my back, desperate to leave no space between us.

Smoke and cinnamon laced with night-blooming flowers. She shuddered in my arms and pressed closer. *Like us. Like home.*

I searched her eyes for how she felt about this new development. Nuzzling into her hair, I breathed her in and planted a kiss before I said, "You smell pretty good, too."

"So you can hear all of my thoughts?" she squeaked. "I'm not sure how I feel about that."

"Because you no longer have the advantage?" I teased, brushing another kiss to her forehead. "I didn't hear them before. I think I have to be…attuned to you."

"Attuned?"

"Right now, you're the only thought I have, and I think it's opened whatever bridge there is between us. Earlier, there were so many people to distract me, but now…"

"I'm just worried that I'm going to think something stupid or cruel or that I will upset you," she said in a small voice.

"I get that," I said. How many times had I worried the same thing when her powers had first manifested? But unlike me, my mate didn't have a cruel bone in her body. "We'll figure it out. And selfishly, I like being able to hear you. I want to know you, *all* of you." I snaked a hand up her back and wove it through her hair, tugging it so I could see her face. "I don't just want to hear what you are thinking. I need to hear you," I murmured, tracing her jawline with my lips. "I've missed you."

She heated beneath me, sending another scent surging. Sweet and ripe and tempting—a scent that belonged only to her. Her head craned, stretching her neck to reveal two crescent-shaped scars. An offering.

"That's right…" I swallowed, the words thick with need, and angled my mouth to those scars. "You *have* missed me."

"Of course I missed you," she whimpered as my fang scraped her skin. "I need you, too."

"You need me…" I shook my head, allowing another slight scrape, enough to draw a single bead of blood, and she moaned. "You are a queen. You need no one."

I need you.

"I need you, Julian," she said as if she needed this to be clear. She needed me to hear it. "You are my king."

"I'm not sure your new sisters will like that." I chuckled, even as my heart strained. There were things she needed to understand about court, things I needed to warn her about. "I'm not sure being a queen is enough to protect you. There are vampires that don't respect the authority of *Le Regine*."

She shook her head. Her hands roved over my skin, seeking a distraction. "I don't want to talk about this."

As much as I wanted to stay in bed with her forever and ignore the reality of our situation, we couldn't. "My love."

She turned her face, displaying her slender neck again, and sent a single command through our bond.

Bite me.

The demand sent blood rocketing to my groin, and I groaned.

She wasn't playing fair. It did the trick. My concerns vanished entirely as she wrapped a leg around my hip and pressed her soft flesh against my erection. An invitation. Not long ago, I'd lived with the fear of never seeing her again.

The world could fucking wait.

My vision darkened, and I lifted black eyes to her. She'd given me an invitation, but I offered her a warning. It had been so long. I craved her. I needed her in ways that might make me feel ashamed later. Ways that might scare her. Ways that scared me. Her fingers sank into my shoulders, urging me closer to those scars, to the veins that pulsed under her fair skin.

All of you.

Danger. The queens. Nothing mattered if we were together.

I lowered my head and kissed those sensitive marks. Thea's breath hitched.

My fangs pierced her skin as I slid inside her, deeper and deeper until I filled her entirely.

Her legs circled my waist as I drew out her pleasure with slow thrusts. Her blood spilled on my tongue was made sweeter by her keening moan.

You belong to me. I want you, my love. I want you as you were meant to be, mine for all eternity. I sent the thoughts between us as I fed.

She cried out, trembling and clinging to me as I plunged in and out.

Her palm found the mark on my chest, and I felt that spark of magic that belonged only to us. Our bodies had changed when we mated, but now I felt that bond even more deeply. We were one, our lives as twined together as our bodies.

I lifted my mouth to capture hers, letting her taste the blood and venom mingling on my tongue.

Her fingers splayed over my tattooed heart as I drove us toward that eternity. With every thrust, my lips found hers, erasing all the fear and pain we'd felt with each kiss. I was hers. I would always be hers. I didn't need words to tell her that. I didn't need my voice to speak to her heart. And as we reached the precipice, I knew she was mine, too.

On the verge, I sank my fangs into her neck once more, and she pressed her hips to meet me. "Take it," she whispered, willing me to wring the last bit of pleasure from us both.

I felt her release build, her body loose and tight as she surrendered. It hummed between us, vibrating in our veins. I had never felt anything like this, not even in her arms. In death, the last bits of her left unchanged had transformed.

My fangs retracted, and I lapped at the pricked wounds to help seal the skin.

She went limp in my arms, but I didn't let her go.

"I will burn down the world before I ever let anyone take you from me again." I buried my face in her hair as I made the vow.

There was a battle ahead of us. I knew she needed to think, to breathe. Just like I did. Our hearts raced together. The blood I had taken from her wasn't enough, and I wondered what would be enough to help soothe the trauma of our separation.

"I won't let anyone hurt you," I said, drawing back to stare into her eyes. I traced the changed lines of her face, now more beautiful than ever. More precious.

Had death transformed me in her eyes?

I needed see her, touch her, prove to myself that she was real.

But we also needed to be practical.

"How can you promise that?" she asked, snuggling deep into my arms.

"Because I'm bigger, stronger, faster, and more vicious than any vampire who doesn't respect my queen." I forced a grin, knowing she could see through it.

"I told you that we're equals," she reminded me. "Whatever happens, we're ride or die."

I inclined my head. "Even as equals, it is my pleasure to serve you *and* to set an example. I will kneel before you at court. They will *all* kneel before you."

"And with the court behind us—with its magic—no one will

dare touch us." I felt our magic thrumming inside me now, rising and ebbing with each breath I took. "Or our family," she added softly.

I snarled in approval.

No one will hurt us or our friends and family—even the family yet to be born.

I nodded in agreement with her unspoken words, a hand slipping between us protectively to the spot where our children would one day grow.

"But, Thea, we need to be prepared," I began.

"We are safe now."

"Are you sure?" Maybe her abduction fueled my fear. Maybe I just needed to hear her say yes.

And as if fate itself had decided to answer, a loud banging sounded through the room, followed by a demand we heard all the way in the bedroom.

"Open this fucking door right now!"

CHAPTER THREE

Jacqueline

Willem hadn't taken a normal residence. He'd moved into a fortress.

The locator spell the local familiar cast had worked. I'd taken a small motor boat from the *Rio* and allowed the spell to lead me out of Venice proper into the open water around it, then finally to a small island that sat only a few thousand feet from the city. I docked the boat on a small pier and climbed out to the craggy shoreline. The island itself was clearly shrouded in some ancient spell to keep it from view, but the magic we'd used had allowed me to see beyond. It was no wonder we hadn't been able to track Willem in the city. I had no doubt he'd been here all along, right under our noses. Fog hung like smoke on the water surrounding me, and I stared at the stone towering before me, my stomach beginning to churn. I'd promised I would find Thea tonight. I'd sworn I would bring her home to Julian. But I wasn't sure I was up to scaling some medieval castle to do it—especially not in these shoes.

"Excuses," I muttered to myself, kicking one heel off.

"You aren't actually going to do what I think you're going to do," Camila said from behind me.

I whipped around, my hair flying across my face, to see her step from the shadows.

"How?" I hadn't seen or heard her following me in the darkness.

"I followed you." She shrugged and stepped next to me, her body achingly close.

"I gathered that." I rolled my eyes. "Why didn't I hear you?"

"I have tricks of my own."

Ones she wasn't going to tell me. Maybe she would if I asked, but after earlier, there was no way I was asking Camila anything. The kiss had been a moment of insanity. So had been admitting that I still loved her. Was that why she was here now? Had she followed me to push things? To mock me for that stolen kiss?

"I don't have time for your bullshit," I informed her coolly. "I need to worry about Thea."

"I'm not here to be in the way." She spoke with unexpected softness, sounding more like the woman I'd known when we were younger, before everything happened. But I didn't trust that softness—kiss or not.

"You thought you'd tag along and watch?" I kicked off my other shoe.

"I'm not completely without skills," she hissed. But she hung back as I surveyed the stone cliffs, looking for a way up. After a few seconds, she sighed. "Seriously, stop."

I turned on her, frustration rising inside me like the fog on the water. "Do you have a better suggestion?"

She gave me that poison-laced smile, and I tried to ignore the slight tremble I felt.

"How about we go in through the front door?"

I narrowed my gaze, debating the merits of throwing her into the frigid water and letting her swim back to Venice. "Do you have a key?"

It wouldn't help much, since there was no door, just unbroken walls of stone.

"Oh, don't look at me like that." She sauntered past me. "I didn't keep anything from you. I just know Willem. There's a door here somewhere. We only have to see it."

"And then? We still need a key."

"You forget one thing." She began pacing the length of the rocky shoreline, checking for some unseen entrance. "I'm still his wife, and he doesn't know I'm not dead."

"So you can theoretically waltz right in?"

"I'm hoping."

I stood back and crossed my arms. I was about to tell her that I would believe it when I saw it when she straightened and placed her hands on a stone. The wall shimmered, and then, as if a curtain had lifted, there was a door. Camila placed a hand on the knob, and it opened.

"I told you I had skills," she said haughtily.

I bit back a retort as I followed her inside.

The inside was as welcoming as the outside, which was to say not much. We found ourselves in a corridor lined with torches that cast dancing shadows on the dreary stone walls. The musty smell of decay bloomed in my nostrils, and I fought the urge to gag. Something else lingered in the air—a scent I recognized. Death. Not the coppery tang of freshly spilled blood but old death that reeked of decay and wormwood. I kept my eyes on the worn carpet that ran the length of the corridor, trying not to wonder whether the woman next to me smelled it, too. If this was what the home she'd shared with him had been like: a cold and desolate grave with towers and walls, a living tomb.

"Okay, since you're the expert, where do we start?"

"That depends on what he wants with her." Her mouth pressed into a line that told me it was as ominous as it sounded.

"Split up or stay together?" I asked, and for a second, I could have sworn she blushed.

"Together. It's safer that way."

I wanted to ask for which one of us, but I didn't. We started down the hallway, walking on tiptoes. "Why did you really come?" I asked.

"Why is it so hard to believe that I want to find my brother's mate?" she asked.

"Because you resent her."

"I don't resent her." Her words were hot, laced with an edge of fire that told me she might be lying to herself. "I resent that everyone wants to help her."

"If *you* want help, you should ask for it."

"No one will help me. That's clear enough."

She was angry because she felt *alone*? "What? What is it? What do you want?" I demanded.

Her eyes skimmed my face for what felt like an eternity, and I knew she was making a decision.

"If you don't trust me, fine." I threw my hands up and continued down the hall.

But she caught up with me and grabbed my hand. I opened my mouth to tell her to back the hell off, but something in the way she looked at me stopped me. "I feel the same way," she whispered. "Like I wish I could hate you. Like it would be easier."

I was not doing this now, not while we stood in her psycho-husband's home. Not while Thea was still missing. "We can argue later."

"Jacqueline." She sighed. "I know I can trust you. I think you're the only person I trust, but it's hard for me after...after everything."

"I would have been there for you," I said a bit too harshly.

"I was tethered," she protested.

My heart broke even more. "After the tether was broken, you could have come to me."

"I know." To her credit, there was infinite sadness in those two words. "I wish I could have come to you, but there was something else I had to do."

"Join an insane vampire rebellion? Get revenge?" I asked coldly.

"No. Those were means to an end." Her eyes met mine, and I nearly stumbled when I saw how they burned. "I think... No, I *know* that I was lied to about the night I died. Jacqueline, I think my children are still alive, and I think my family is hiding them."

"From who?" Dread sluiced like cold canal water through me. "Why?"

"I don't know why." She shook her head. "But they're hiding them from...me."

CHAPTER FOUR

Lysander

There was no whisky to be found in the court. After tonight, I didn't want the wine the Italian vampires loved so much. I needed something stronger, something that would burn away the memories of my brother and his mate lying bloody and broken on the ground. Even now, knowing they were alive, there was a slight tremor in my hand as I took a begrudging sip of rosé.

I nearly gagged on it.

But there was something else preoccupying me, too. Or rather, *someone* else. I took another sip as Sebastian joined me.

"What are you drinking?" He grinned at the face I made.

"Fucking rosé," I grumbled.

"Care for something stronger?" He reached behind him and pulled a small bottle of whisky from the waistband of his pants.

"What will you drink?" I asked drily. He laughed and tossed it to me, and I decided to not ask him why he was carrying around Scotch in his pants.

"Take it." He swiped the open bottle of wine. "I happen to like fucking rosé."

"You like everything. And everyone."

He smirked, his gaze scanning the empty lounge tucked in a hidden corner of the court. It was a little better than a hotel lobby. Bland but expensive furnishings meant for guests. It had none of the comforts of the quarters we'd been given by the queens upon our arrival.

A few lamps with burgundy fabric shades cast the room in muted hues of red. In the dim light, it was easy to mistake the antique tables and chairs for the real thing. But I was an archeologist, and I could spot reproductions. Gold wall coverings brightened the room a little, although the whole lounge had the feel of a chintzy hotel.

But it had one important feature that my bedroom didn't.

A bar.

More importantly, a bar that my mother didn't seem to know existed.

"Has she finished her rampage yet?" I asked him, my mouth pinching as I recalled her actually throwing a vampire twice her size into a wall for calling her *Ma'am*.

Another snort. "*No*."

"She's going to get us kicked out." I sighed. Sabine was accustomed to getting her way—to being the matriarch—and Thea had just claimed *the* throne meant for her.

"So?" My brother shrugged and took a swig. "This place sucks, and not in a good way. I need an orgy."

I ignored him. Sebastian always needed an orgy. "You would think she'd be happier her son was breathing again."

"I think the fact that Thea is breathing is her issue."

He might be right, and it left a bad taste in my mouth. I liked Thea, but it was more than that. I just didn't quite understand it. I felt like I had an itch deep inside me, too far down to scratch but impossible to ignore.

A pair of full lips floated to mind, along with her face, scarred but breathtaking. Something tightened in my chest before descending toward my groin. *Aurelia*.

Why couldn't I shake her?

She was just a mortal, a familiar maybe. That seemed likely, given her inside knowledge of the court, but still a mortal. The scar was proof.

There was something about her, though—something that seemed intent on commanding my every thought. It had been a long day. A long week, if I was being honest. Perhaps it was just a need to escape, but I couldn't help imagining what curves hid behind the cloak Aurelia wore—or how good it would feel to bury myself inside her and watch those full lips part as I…

I shook my head to clear it. I barely knew her, but here I was thinking about claiming her. I couldn't tell if it was because of the strange pull she had on me the moment we met or because I needed a distraction.

It was simply lust—a temporary, albeit annoying, distraction. I'd gone without sex for years at a time when I was focused on work. There was always a willing female waiting when I wanted it. Either way, something told me that Aurelia was more than I might want to take on, especially if she worked for *Le Regine.*

But no matter how I rationalized it, I wondered where she was and what she was up to. She'd disappeared in the chaos following the resurrection. I'd wanted to ask her how she'd known what to do, what she knew about the prophecy tonight. I'd wanted to grab her and—

"Something on your mind?" Sebastian interrupted my wandering thoughts.

I blinked the fantasy away and frowned.

"Nothing." I had four brothers, and if I was going to ask one of them for advice regarding a female, Sebastian would be last on that list. "Maybe we should hunt down our mother before she burns the place down."

His lip curled with distaste. "Do we have to?"

"Don't worry about your mother," a deep voice interrupted.

I turned to find our father. He looked exhausted, as if his thousands of years had caught up with him in just one night.

"She's under control." He grimly eyed the bottle of wine in Sebastian's hand. Then he turned his attention to the nearly empty whisky in my hand.

I passed the rest to him.

"Thanks." He downed the remaining Scotch.

I lowered my voice. "What should we do now?"

We'd been called to Venice for two reasons: to assist in Thea's rescue and to attend our mother's coronation. I suspected Sabine cared more about the latter. Now that neither reason still existed, I wondered if it was time to leave.

So why did I feel the urge to stay?

"Keep a low profile." Dominic rubbed his temples. "Keep our eyes open. Something feels off."

"You mean earthquakes and lightning strikes and raising people from the dead isn't normal?" Sebastian smirked. To his credit, it looked a little forced. Maybe he was more rattled than he was letting on.

"We came to secure the *Rio Oscuro* and rescue Thea," I reminded him, doing my best to ignore the pull I felt to this place. "It might be better if we don't hang around."

"We tend to get in trouble," Sebastian agreed.

"Then be on your best behavior, boys." Dominic's throat slid, his eyes scanning the room like someone might be watching. "Every vampire faction is in this city. I think it's best if we stay."

"Sticking around when my enemies are in town is how I got kicked out of Glasgow," Sebastian said, "and I'm still not allowed in most of Scotland. And I liked Scotland."

None of us were allowed in Scotland. Not unless we wanted to start a war with the werewolves.

"Why don't you find your brother?" our father suggested to him.

Sebastian hitched a finger at me. "I already did."

"Your other brother."

"Which one?" he asked, feigning innocence.

"Any of them," Dominic said through gritted teeth.

Sebastian's eyes narrowed, but he shoved a hand through his shaggy blond hair. Instead of arguing, he leaned over the bar and swiped another bottle of rosé.

"I'm sure somebody in this city is up for a good time," he grumbled.

Dominic shook his head. "Not *too* good of a time."

Neither of us spoke until Sebastian was gone.

"Was there a reason you dismissed him?" I asked. "Other than the fact he's annoying?"

He sighed and nodded once. "Rumors are swirling."

"Two creatures came back from the dead." I lifted a brow. "That's not surprising."

"It's not just that. Magic has awoken."

"You believe that?" I asked. My mouth felt dry, and I wished I'd kept the whisky. I felt it, but somehow I still couldn't come to grips with what had happened. "Seriously?"

His lips pressed into a thin line that told me he was serious. Deadly serious.

"I never thought…"

"None of us did. Not after all this time." Before tonight, I'd never seen my father look shaken. He'd been shaken twice in the last few hours.

"What do you think it means?" I asked.

"That Thea is more powerful than we realized, and if she is, she will be a target. We have to—"

The doors to the room flew open, cutting us off mid-sentence.

When I turned, I froze.

Aurelia had removed her cloak and traded whatever party dress she'd worn under it for a pair of leather pants and a thick black sweater. Her black hair—which had been hidden under her hood before—was plaited into a thick braid that hung over one shoulder, but the full lips that preoccupied me were turned down.

"One of you needs to get Sabine under control," she demanded.

"Here we go," I muttered.

She shot me a sharp look.

"She just beheaded one of our new guards. You have no idea how hard it is to find good help these days."

My father sighed, tossing a long-suffering look my way. "I'll go."

"Thank you," Aurelia said pointedly. The man was a saint as far as I was concerned.

Aurelia swiveled to me when he was out of sight. "Can he rein her in alone?"

"My father can handle Sabine," I said, the words harsher than I intended as I grappled with the magnetic energy she radiated. One only I seemed to feel. Maybe because she was the first person in hundreds of years who'd quoted a random ancient text to me. That was my area of expertise. Few modern vampires bothered with studying the old texts. But as I scanned her body, I knew it was more than that.

Her gray gaze probed me with a curiosity that mirrored my own, and when it met mine, her eyes widened as if she felt the same insistent tug.

She opened her mouth, her breath catching slightly as if she'd forgotten what she was about to say. I zeroed in on those lips, wondering what she would do if I leaned in, if I kissed her. Then I realized it didn't matter. I couldn't stop myself.

I got one step before that curiosity curdled into disdain. "Do you always let someone else do your dirty work?"

She might as well have slapped me in the face. I stopped, scowling. "Let me be clear, princess," I said, a growl lacing my words. "I've never been afraid to get my hands dirty."

She rolled her eyes, but her cheeks colored slightly. I was getting under her skin. *Good.*

"Maybe I should show you just how dirty—"

"Enough," she cut me off.

She snapped her fingers, and an icy numbness shot up my throat. I opened my mouth to speak and found I couldn't. What the hell kind of magic was this?

And with a smile, Aurelia turned and left me there—utterly, *literally* fucking speechless.

CHAPTER FIVE

Julian

Thea bolted up, drawing a sheet hastily over her nude body. It clung to her curves, her body still sticky with sweat from our lovemaking. I sprang out of bed, looking over my shoulder at her. "Wait here."

It was more of a request than an order. I was well aware that my mate would do whatever the fuck she wanted, and when her eyes narrowed, I tacked on a weary, "Please."

Maybe some manners would slow her down, but I doubted it.

I didn't bother grabbing my ruined clothes. I knew exactly who was screaming outside my door, and if my mother was this pissed off, she'd have it off its hinges in the next ten seconds. There had to be wards—old incantations and spells—guarding the quarters, likely strengthened by magic's awakening. My own magic throbbed in my hands, aching to be released.

If that were the case, Sabine's magic was stronger, too, and my mom was an *old* vampire. Ancient. Not that I would ever dare tell her that. That was a surefire way to wind up pinned to the wall and asking for forgiveness.

That was before, though. Things were different now. I was different. My mate was different. There were so many changes at once, but I knew somehow that nothing would be the same after this night, especially with my family.

My mother's fist rattled the door's hinges with the strength of a battering ram. I swung it open a second later and narrowly avoided catching the next knock in my chest.

Her hand froze mid-air, her lip curling as she took in her naked son standing before her. "Did I catch you at a bad time?"

She was in her gown from earlier, but now it was covered in blood. Every strand of her hair was freed from the careful, polished style she'd started the evening with. Dried blood caked her hands and was splattered across her face. Its scent was thick and coppery on the air, almost sweet, and definitely not human. If she'd gone on a killing spree in the court, there would be a mess to clean up. But if she'd come here planning to harm her new queen, I'd be adding her name to the list of bodies to bury.

"We were just working on grandchildren, so you tell me." I leaned against the doorframe. I knew better than to bait her, but I couldn't help myself. Not because I particularly liked her brand of homicidal maternity, but because I needed to wear her down.

I'd always suspected my mother hid whatever lingering powers she'd once had before the curse that had stunted true magic. If they had awoken, it was the last thing I needed to deal with tonight. I felt strong, maybe stronger than I'd ever felt in my previous lifetime, but Thea had drained herself by resurrecting me, and through the new bond we shared, I sensed she remained depleted.

My mother's soft snarl raised my hackles, and I allowed instinct to take over. My eyes blackened, my fangs extended once more, and I shifted to fill the doorway. But she didn't make a move. Instead, she simply stared.

Stared at the magical tattoo on my chest—at the symbol that now represented Thea's power. Her reign.

My queen.

"What have you done?" she murmured.

"There was a price." Thea's voice was soft but strong behind me.

Sabine tried to look past me, but I remained like a wall between her and my mate. *"What price?"*

"His life is bound to mine." I heard her padding toward me, heard the gentle slap of her bare feet on the marble, but I still didn't move. I felt her behind me and heard the steady beat of her heart as she said, "It's okay."

There was no tether locking me into place now—no primal, undeniable instinct to protect and defend. I could move to the side. I knew that. But I found it difficult to do so. She'd been taken from me. She *had died*.

I hadn't been there to save her, and I wouldn't make the same mistake.

I growled.

For my mate.

For my queen.

Thea rested a hand on my shoulder, her magic seeping through her skin into mine. Golden and warm. Familiar but new. A song I'd heard a thousand times played with a new instrument. My own roared inside me as it rose to meet hers. It wasn't like the tether that had been forged between us when I'd claimed her virginity. There was no demand. No push and pull. It was comforting. It was a circle completed. Our new connection was forged in choice and bound by our lives. Our souls had merged when we mated, but now I felt it more deeply. We were one—a single life contained in two bodies.

So when I felt her magic, I felt the last of the wildness fade, and I took a step back.

Taking Thea's hand, I drew her around me to stand beside me. She was wrapped in a sheet—fragile and vulnerable—but I knew that was an illusion. She was strong. She had proven that tonight.

I had to trust her. I had to trust us.

I alone couldn't keep her safe. *We* would keep her safe—me, her, and the bond we'd forged between us when she gave her life for mine. We were Thea's guard. We would protect her with our body and with our wits.

But for now, I watched my mother warily. My life was tied to

Thea's—whatever fate either of us suffered, the other would, too.

While Thea mastered her new magic, I would be her shield. I would face the threats and fight, even if it meant taking on my own mother.

Even if it meant killing her.

Thea's breath was even and soft under my mother's violent stare, and I tightened my hand around hers.

"Whose blood is that?" Thea asked.

A muscle twitched in Sabine's blood-splattered jaw. "Does it matter?"

"I suppose it does if you came here to kill me." Thea blinked once, no sign of distress or fear on her beautiful face but maybe a little surprise. She was light itself. She was a queen rising to take her crown, her throne, *to reign*.

And even though I was not surprised to find my mate was strong and powerful and fearless, I felt a swell of pride as I felt her realize it herself.

Sabine looked at the mark on my chest and then up to my face. "You've chosen her, then. Your allegiance is now to your mate. You are a Rousseaux in name only. I will not protect you." She swallowed. "I *cannot* protect you. You are no longer my son."

"I know," I said without hesitation. Even as her words settled over me, there was no regret.

Cast out. I'd been expecting it from the moment I chose to take Thea as my mate. Not because of the tether, but because of the obvious prejudice my mother held against Thea. I had tried to find a way to make it work. Not wanting to lose my family. As head of our house, it would be Sabine's decision if I was allowed contact with my brothers, my father, even my twin. I hadn't wanted it to come to this.

But if I had to choose between my family and Thea, I would choose her. She was my blood, my soul, the beating of my heart.

Sabine's gaze flicked back to Thea, and she whispered the last thing I expected. "Thank you for saving my son. I can never repay my debt to you."

Confusion doused me like a splash of cold water, and I glanced to Thea, who looked equally perplexed by the stranger standing before us. I had never seen this version of my mother before. It was like she'd reached up and removed an invisible mask to reveal a different face beneath. Though which of the two faces was real?

I think she's having an aneurysm. Thea's voice filled my head.

She's had a rough day.

Sabine's face hardened, her eyes narrowing to slits. "It's rude to talk behind your mother's back."

"You just disowned me," I reminded her, surprise sneaking into my voice. How did she know…

"There's a lot that I know, and you—"

"There you are!"

I looked up as my father started down the corridor. He was still wearing his tuxedo, and of the lot of us, he looked the most put-together, but I smelled the tang of blood on him as I approached. His mouth turned down in a grim frown when he spotted my mother coated in blood. He shook his head, managing to look disappointed with his wife. "I'm told you beheaded a guard."

That wasn't a surprise—unlike the bout of sentimental gratitude. That *was* a surprise. A shock, really.

But before I could process it, she grabbed my arm and hissed, "There isn't a moment to waste."

CHAPTER SIX

Thea

I stumbled to the side as Sabine dragged Julian inside. Dominic followed her swiftly, casting a concerned glance at me. I looked down, remembering that I wore only a sheet, and muttered, "I should put something on."

Dominic nodded once before raising an eyebrow at his completely naked son. His eyes stopped on the tattoo. "Maybe you should find some clothes, too."

Julian's lips pressed into a line. He tugged free of his mother's grip and grabbed my hand.

He wants to talk to her. His voice filled my head.

You mean lecture her, right?

Sabine had killed someone. That wasn't a surprise, but I'd never seen her so...frantic.

Violent, yes. Imperious. Calculating. I expected these things from Sabine. But this was different. She seemed almost anxious, and it didn't feel like it had anything to do with losing the crown. I wasn't really sure what to make of it, but I held Julian's hand tightly and followed him inside the bedroom.

"I'm not sure this is salvageable." I held up the bloodstained dress I'd worn this evening. I hated the sight of it. Not just because it had practically been my funeral gown but because I'd gotten it from Willem. I shook my head, wanting to clear the memories, but my chest tightened. Julian was beside me instantly, his strong arms around me.

"It's not," he agreed. His head bent, and he nuzzled my neck, his lips brushing the scar from his earlier feeding. "I can hear your thoughts—about Willem and what happened—but we don't have to talk about it."

A lump knotted my throat, but I managed a nod. Maybe someday I would be ready to recall the memories of where I'd been and what I'd done, but right now, they were too raw and painful. Plus, there were other things to worry about. "Your mom seems *different*."

"She does." He took a deep breath and released me before striding over to a chest of drawers. Opening one, he fished in it for a moment before producing a nightgown. He passed it to me and opened another drawer. "Ginerva was taller than you, though not by much."

I slipped it over my head, catching a whiff of gardenia and sweet vanilla lingering on the silk. The nightgown was the deep, blue-black of a moonless night, and it glided over my skin with a soft caress. A strange sense of peace settled over me as I slid the straps over my shoulders. It was a little too big for me but beautifully made, its neckline trimmed with delicate lace and the phases of the moon embroidered across its bodice.

Julian stepped away, shaking out a pair of silk pajama pants. He seemed strangely comfortable here—like he knew the place.

"She had a very well-stocked wardrobe," I commented lightly even though something about the words felt heavy.

"She kept a lot of lovers," he explained. My heart stuttered at the soft swooshing sound Julian's pajama pants made when he stepped into them.

Lovers. It wasn't just that he knew that, but he also knew she kept clothing for them. I tried to ignore the pressure swelling inside me.

"This is lovely. She was really into moons, huh?" I said absently.

Moonlight flickered in through an open window and played over the features of his face. The grim set of his jaw was visible. Barefoot and bare-chested, he tied the pants with his back to me, and I watched his muscles shift and flex. His hair shone like polished onyx in the pale light. Each slight movement made my heart beat faster until I couldn't contain the question I hadn't dared to think. "Were you her lover?"

He paused, his shoulders rigid and set. His head turned, catching the shadows. "Yes. A long time ago."

"Oh." I couldn't think of anything else to say.

"Thea." Apology coated his voice.

I shook my head. "I'm sorry. It's none of my business."

It really wasn't. Julian had been alive for centuries before I'd met him. He'd been with other women. Hell, he'd even slept with Jacqueline once, but there was something about this that needled me.

"My mother sent me to the court," he said, reaching for me. "It was a dark time, and when Ginerva set her sights on me—"

"You don't have to tell me." I wasn't sure I wanted to hear this. Maybe it was standing in her room, wearing her clothes, that made this worse than knowing he'd taken others to bed.

"I was young, and she was very powerful." He set his hands on my hips and pulled me gently to him.

"And beautiful?" I guessed.

"In her way." His eyes were haunted, and I wondered if he was seeing her now. Did I pale in comparison to her? He must have heard the thought, because he said, "No. She was nothing like you."

"You don't have to do that." I stopped him. "You don't have to spare my feelings."

Julian lifted a hand to my cheek, guiding my face up to meet his eyes. "I'm not. It was a fling. It meant nothing to me and little to her. She moved on to someone else soon after I left the court."

"Why did your mother send you here?" Had Sabine been angling for the throne even then? Was that why she was so upset with me now?

He shook his head in response to my unspoken questions. "No. She thought of it as an homage—a tribute—to send her son to serve *Le Regine*. The queens were still powerful then, and my mother had a soft spot for them."

"How did you serve them?"

"They called me *il flagello*," he said quietly, and I recalled hearing it earlier. "The Scourge. I was their enforcer."

"So you…"

He nodded, watching my face carefully.

"And your mom sent you to be an assassin?" I said flatly.

"It was a different time."

"Yeah, parenting requires less weaponry today."

He grinned, relaxing a little, and lowered his mouth to kiss me. "I don't know about that."

"Just promise me we won't send our kids off to assassin boarding school."

"Done." He sighed and pressed his forehead to mine. "We should probably get out there before she throws another tantrum."

I thought of her bloodsoaked clothing and shivered. "Yeah, you're probably right."

When we entered the sitting room adjoining the bed chamber, Sabine was pacing. She paused when she saw us.

Her hands twisted together. No trace of blood remained on them. Her face and skin had been washed. Now only her dress held proof of the violence she'd inflicted earlier.

Dominic sat in an armchair, nursing a glass of wine. The fire in the hearth had been stoked into a full blaze. The logs cracked and sparked, but otherwise, the room was utterly silent, as if waiting for her to speak.

"You have to understand why I did what I did," she started, then hesitated.

It wasn't like her to be speechless. Or to offer an explanation for her actions. Not when she was accustomed to commanding any room—and everyone in it. But she was afraid now, and that terrified me.

"We're listening," Julian said coolly. He stood behind me, his dark presence filling the room like an avenging angel.

I leaned into him, doing my best to remain silent. I wasn't sure I trusted myself to speak. My feelings toward Sabine had always fallen into the *mixed* category. Tonight, I felt more conflicted than ever. If she knew more about this situation, why had she waited so long to say anything?

She faced me. "When I *met* you, I knew what you were."

I kept my face blank, but it took effort. The whole time we'd been searching for answers, she had known. Truly known. Not after we had guessed with Lysander's help. Even when she had told me about the sirens, what the vampires had done to them, she had not admitted the truth. She had hinted at it, but somehow it still stung.

"And you didn't tell us?" Disappointment stabbed through me, but Julian remained silent.

"I couldn't tell you." She bit her lower lip and shook her head. "It was complicated."

"But you did try to break us up," he said. His hands closed around my upper arms, as if he needed to anchor himself to me.

"I had to be certain...about your relationship."

"You could have asked," he seethed, "or *listened*, for that matter."

"I watched," she cut in, "and I tested. I won't apologize for it."

"If this is going to be you justifying your—"

"Will you just listen?" she interrupted him. "I don't know where to begin."

She was completely out of sorts. I looked at Dominic, who was studying his wine a little too intensely. Maybe he'd known, too. Her eyes tracked mine and landed on her silent husband.

"Yes, he knew," she said. "He chose to stay out of it. He has never followed the old books."

"Old books?" I repeated.

"Even before the curse, seers wrote about it, and they wrote about the great awakening. I spent the first half of my life trying to prevent the curse from happening. But I never found the threat, and then it was too late. Since then, I've been focused on the time when magic would awaken and who would break the curse."

Her words hollowed out my gut, and I found that now *I* couldn't speak.

"What does any of this have to do with us?" Julian demanded.

"Do you think it was a coincidence I sent you to work for the queens?" she asked. "That I sent you here and now you are mated to one of them?"

What the hell? Was she really going to play it like she'd been on our side the whole time? She had thrown me to the wolves more than once. She'd even wanted to duel to the death. This was the same female who had allowed her daughter to be tethered to an absolute psychopath.

I know that look. Thea. Don't, he warned me.

Don't what? I shifted in his embrace a little.

Let's hear her out.

I bit back a snort. *Now you want to hear her out? She's been screwing with us the whole time. We can't trust her.*

Just trust me. Even if she's messing with us. There's always a little truth in lies. We have to get as much as we can from her.

So now we're going to sort truth and lies out?

He didn't respond. Instead, he stepped around me. "What the hell is going on here?"

She rolled her eyes and moved to the table to pour a glass of wine. "I'm going to have a drink, and then I will explain everything."

"You're going to explain everything?" Julian muttered with disbelief. "I've heard that before."

"When you become head of the house, you'll learn a few things about secrets. And enemies." She held the bottle out to me. "You should have a drink. You're going to need it."

"Don't—" Julian said, but it was too late.

There weren't any glasses, so I just took a swig directly from it.

"That could be poisoned," he told me.

Sabine's lip curled. "You think I would poison your mate?"

"I don't know what you're capable of." He met her glare with the assurance of someone who had survived her before.

"Everything I've ever done has been for you—for this family."

"I'm not a member of this family anymore, remember?"

"I have to disown you. It's the only way to maintain my status with the Vampire Council," she said quickly. "But you will always be my son."

"Even if status is the most important thing to you," Julian accused.

I moved between them, holding out my hands. So much for hearing her out. This was going south fast. "Just stop. If you have something to tell us, say it now or get out."

A faint smile played at her lips. "You are strong. Good. You will need that strength," she told me. "Both of you. I must maintain my status so I know what is going on. There are spies everywhere, even in the Council. The Mordicum aren't the only ones willing to get their hands bloody. Now that you are on your own, you have to be careful who to trust and you must know when to stand on your own. I'll do my best to keep the Council in check, but every sitting member has their own agenda. I wouldn't be surprised if one of them makes a move against you. If they haven't figured out what you are, they can guess after what you did tonight."

"We have the queens," Julian hedged.

Sabine shook her head. "Have I taught you nothing? You can't trust anyone but your family."

"And you?" I held up my head. "We can trust you?"

She nodded. "I don't expect you to trust me, but yes."

Julian looked like he was going to strangle her, but I wanted to know more. Even if I wasn't certain I could ever truly trust her.

"Why can't we trust the queens?" I asked before they could start fighting again.

Her blue eyes met mine, her gaze so icy that I fought a chill as she spoke. "Who do you think killed Ginerva?"

CHAPTER SEVEN

Julian

I t took me a second to process what she was implying. Thea's hand reached for mine and squeezed it tightly, understanding before I did. A log popped in the fire, and she flinched, but I found my eyes turning to watch the flames licking along the wood. I stared at it until my eyes burned.

"You're…" The words jammed in my throat. I cleared it, but it remained raw. "You're saying Mariana or Zina killed their own sister."

"Their sister-queen," my mother corrected me before turning her attention to my mate. "Never forget that they are *not* your blood."

"I won't," Thea said softly.

I laughed, not bothering to hide the bitterness I felt. "Does it matter? Our family—or, I suppose, *your* family now—was made. Few of us share blood."

"We all share blood," Sabine said fiercely. "Your brothers were reborn with our blood—the same blood that flows through your veins as well as Camila's." She turned to stare at the hearth, too, the flames casting a spotlight that deepened the hollows of her eyes and turned the crimson stain on her gown black as death. "And the sooner you get over being disowned, the better. There are more important matters to discuss."

More important? Thea blinked but didn't say it aloud.

I bit back another hollow laugh. *Her maternal instincts only extend so far, and I think I've depleted them tonight.*

"Are you two finished?" Sabine interrupted our private conversation.

Thea's head tilted, and she pulled away from me. I stayed close behind her as she took a step toward my mother. "Can you actually hear us?"

"No, thank the Gods. It's bad enough watching you two screw each other with your eyes." She pushed a strand of hair from her face. "I'd go clinically insane if I had to hear your thoughts."

"But then, how did you…" Thea chewed on her lower lip.

"I saw the way you were looking at him. I've been around a little longer than you. I can guess what you're thinking. As for your private conversations, you two might want to work on covering that up. Anyone could guess you're speaking mind-to-mind," she advised, "and being able to hide that could be a powerful advantage."

"And we're going to need an advantage," I said, steering her back to the problem at hand. "Because the queens are homicidal."

"Queens are always homicidal." She delivered the words casually, but her flat tone carried a hint of menace. "Getting a crown is relatively easy compared to keeping it." She directed the last bit at my mate.

Thea just shrugged. "If they want to kill me, they'll have to get through both of us."

My mate, the smallest of us in the room, commanded it. Even my mother's eyebrow lifted slightly, a sign she was impressed. Thea turned toward a velvet armchair by the fire, claiming it like a throne. And even in her exhaustion, that new power radiated from her. I felt it in my bones, my blood, in every atom of my being.

"I know that," Sabine said, surprising us again. If I wasn't immortal, I wasn't sure my heart could take it. "That's why I sent you to serve the queens. You know this court, and you know them."

And because of that, I could protect Thea. But it didn't make sense. "I served here hundreds of years ago. You can't have known."

"Mothers always know more than you think," she said drily. "Especially *your* mothers."

"Mother*s*? What do you mean *mothers*?" Thea pressed. "Did my mother have something to do with this? Did she know?"

I felt Thea's hope trembling inside me, a baby bird ready to take its first leap into the world on unsteady wings. I moved to stand behind her chair in case she fell out of it. Her search for her mother had brought us here, had started the chain of events that led to this very moment.

"Your mother must have known what you were," Sabine continued. "She hid you from your father to protect you, but she also hid you because she knew what would happen if you were found."

"You would kill her," I snarled, remembering what had happened to the sirens and their offspring.

"The *Council* would kill her," she said.

I held back a groan. "You're on the Council."

"And you were going to duel me to the death," Thea reminded her faintly, half-joking and half-confused.

Sabine glared at her. "Disrespect is disrespect no matter who shows it. I don't care if it's a mortal or a siren or a queen."

"Noted," Thea said without breaking eye contact.

"But why would they kill Ginerva?" I asked. "She was the most powerful of them all. Without her…"

"That is exactly the question you need to be asking," Sabine said, swiftly returning to the situation at hand. "Who benefits the most from getting rid of her?"

"Perhaps," my father interrupted, and we all turned toward him, "it is not the queens who betrayed her."

"Who was it, then?"

"Not who, but *what*." He placed his wineglass on the table. "There is only one force more powerful than ambition, in my experience." He looked between Thea and me. "You two are proof of it."

It took a moment for me to register what he meant.

Love.

It was love that had saved us. The only thing stronger than death itself.

"No, I do not believe that it was love that killed Ginerva, but love has played a powerful role in tonight's events," my mother explained. "Every curse must have its counterbalance. No curse can be permanent."

"What does this have to do with Thea?" I asked.

"She has awoken magic," my father said, "and now she must serve it. The queens protect the magic. They always have. Now Thea protects it." A reverent awe stole over his face.

Thea stared at him. "Protect it from who? What?"

But Sabine answered, "Other creatures that might use it for ill. Those that might not be ready for its power. When magic was cursed, the queens prevented the source from being drained. Now they will take on the task of channeling its power to those deemed worthy."

"That doesn't sound like protection," Thea said, eyes glinting. "It sounds like control."

"It is." Sabine actually looked impressed. "I don't think many on the Council will be happy that the curse has been broken. They will remember before the curse and before the thrones when magic was not only awake but *free*."

"And how do you know all of this?" I asked.

"Before I met your father—before I was made into a vampire—I saw things. Glimpses of possible futures. *Visions.*"

"But you're a pureblood," Thea blurted out.

"I am." My mother said no more.

"How?" Thea pointed at Dominic. "If he turned you, that means…"

"Oh, little bird, *he* did not turn me. I was *made*, as was he. As we all were when the world was new."

I didn't dare interrupt her. Vampires guarded their pasts, especially the oldest of our kind. Even I knew very little about my parents before they met and married. If my mother was trusting us with her memories, maybe she was finally telling us the truth.

Sabine paced across the room as if telling her story was hard even now. "All creatures are descended from the old Gods: humans, vampires, witches, werewolves, even the fae. They loved to create playthings or find ways to curse those who displeased them. My father wanted me to be a priestess and put my magic to good use. I had begun to study with a local oracle who taught me about true magic, but then the Romans came, and everything changed. I prayed to my God—the one I'd promised myself to—to help me fight them. His answer was to give me this gift. The God made me a vampire."

In one night I'd learned more about my mother than in the centuries before. My father remained silent, not offering his own story. I wondered if he would—if a God had made him, too.

A God made her? Thea's voice whispered in my mind.

Her incredulity mirrored my own, but I remained silent. Whatever had motivated my mother to share her history, I knew the openness was unlikely to last.

"What God?" I asked quietly.

My mother hesitated, glancing at her husband, who gave her a subtle nod. "Hades, of course."

The God of Death. The ruler of the Underworld.

"I thought Hades abhorred vampires. Isn't that why we can't enter the Underworld?" I asked.

"Every gift of magic comes with a price. We may walk the earth for eons, but our time is limited to this realm. Even Gods have some restrictions on their powers," she told us. "The God of Death barred us from the afterlife so we could live forever here."

An eternity cuffed to the mortal coil. I wasn't sure that was a gift at all.

"When he made you…" Thea swallowed. "When he made you, the visions stopped?"

"Not exactly." She hesitated, the instinct to protect her magic flaring in her eyes. "But it was different. Harder to control. After the curse, it was faint. Nearly gone. Until my twins were born." She looked at me. "Until *you* were born."

"What happened?"

"I saw you both surrounded by light and shadow—and I knew it was an omen. I spent centuries trying to decipher what it meant. Then one day, after I'd given up, an old grimoire arrived on my doorstep. There were pages and pages written about the curse used to silence magic, how it functioned, but still no answer as to who used it against us."

"And the counter-curse?" Thea mumbled. "Was it in there?"

"It was, but it was a riddle," Sabine explained. "I had no idea what it meant until tonight, but somehow I knew it was connected to that vision. I felt it." She held up her hands as if we might be able to see its magic scarring her palms. "It was connected to you or your sister. When you met Thea, I knew it was you, at last."

"Why allow Camila to marry a psycho?" My jaw clenched, my fingers curling into a fist at my side.

"It was a calculated error." Sabine didn't sound the least apologetic. "I thought the Drakes and I were after the same thing."

"Why would you think that?" Thea asked, her lower lip quivering. More than anyone in this room, she knew the cruelty that came at the hands of that family.

"Because they sent me the grimoire," she said flatly. "I was wrong."

There was a time when I might have celebrated hearing her say that, but not today. There was nothing worth celebrating in that revelation.

"So, why tonight?" Thea pressed. "What undid the counter-curse?"

She turned gentle eyes on my mate. "You did."

A heavy silence descended over all of us.

Thea finally broke it. "Why test us? Why try to force us apart? Isn't it good that magic has woken up?"

Dominic shifted in his seat. "For many it is," he said.

"Many creatures have wanted it back—have missed it," Sabine added wistfully.

"But?" I prompted.

"Our magic isn't the only magic to have awakened."

"You mean, not just vampires but witches?" Thea asked.

"I mean, witches, werewolves, Gods, monsters. Only fae magic was untouched by the curse, but even they will feel its dawning. Every creature that draws on magic just had the scrap of power inside them ignited into an inferno, and the creatures who slept through the curse are awake now, too."

"Slept through it?" Thea repeated. "But the curse lasted for centuries. What creature could survive that?"

"Pray you never find out. The world has forgotten magic, but magic has not forgotten the world. Not all those who were held by the curse should be freed," she warned.

And we had awoken it. "And you knew we would…"

"I tried to stop it," she said, "but that was as pointless as catching air with my hands."

"Why?" Thea blurted. "Why stop it? Why stop us?"

My mother looked down her long nose at her. "Because I knew the price you would pay. The price my son would pay."

"I would pay it again," I murmured, placing a hand on Thea's shoulder.

"Oh, my child, do not delude yourself. You have not paid the full cost yet." She turned away.

I still have questions. Thea's shocked voice sounded in my head. *Me, too.*

"You said earlier that love might be behind Ginerva's death. What would love have to do with it?" Thea asked Dominic. "If the queens loved each other like sisters, why would one of them hurt her?"

"Perhaps it was not the love they shared." He shrugged. "Or maybe I'm wrong. But it's clear the court has suffered without a third queen. If they were behind Ginerva's death, there had to have been a powerful motivation for their actions."

Thea's eyes flashed up to me, her thoughts moving too fast for me to latch onto any single one.

"My point is that you cannot trust them," Sabine interjected. "You must find out what happened to Ginerva. Few could have gotten close enough to her to take her life."

"What about all her lovers?" Thea asked flatly, still preoccupied with that piece of my history.

Apparently, I was going to need to take her to bed and erase any doubt she had about who held my heart.

"Few know how to kill a queen," Sabine said, and something ominous clanged in her words.

She knew how to kill a queen, I realized. She knew how to kill my mate. And I knew with terrible certainty there would be no resurrection if she killed her. There would be no second chance. No miracle. Not even that magic that walked between this life and the next would be enough to save her.

"How?" I demanded, my voice rough.

"The queens' lives are tied to the magic flowing in the water. At court, they are completely protected. We like to think of ourselves as immortal, but vampires can be killed. The queens are untouchable, thanks to the enchantment that binds them. But there is a counter to every spell. A weapon was forged when the first queens ascended. The queen-killer." Thea wrapped her arms around her shoulders as my mother continued. "My sources say Ginerva died at court, and her death was kept a secret. If she died here, it was from the queen-killer's blade."

"Probably not a random lover, then," Thea said in a hollow voice.

"As I've said, it's much more likely it was one of the queens."

"If we can't trust them…" I blew out a long stream of air.

"Trust only each other," my father advised.

"But we need the queens to protect Thea," I snapped. "The Council wants to kill her, remember? What if the Council has the weapon? Or she's taken from the court?" I also wouldn't put it past her father to come snooping around again.

"I didn't say to leave the court," my mother said with a snort. "The queens have few allies outside these walls."

"And inside?" Thea rolled her eyes.

"Figure out who your friends are before you leave here. You'll need them—and that strength of yours."

Thea inhaled sharply but finally nodded once.

"And you?" I asked.

"I need to find out what the Council knows," she explained, "and if they intend to act on any of it."

I wasn't sure I wanted to know. Mostly because I suspected the Council would act—and soon.

"I think I need to lie down," Thea finally said.

Everyone stood as she rose. My father even dipped his head a little.

Did he just...bow?

You'll get used to it. I wasn't sure that was true, but it didn't hurt to believe it. *I'll see them out and then come in and help you fall asleep.*

A wicked grin twitched on her lips as she paused at the door to the bedchamber. "Thank you." She sounded sincere despite the heap of bad news Sabine had brought to our door.

My parents were silent as I saw them out, but as my mother stepped out the door, I found one last question boiling inside me.

"Why did you disown me?" I asked, my hand gripping the doorframe. "The truth, please."

Her lips twitched, but her eyes remained sad. "It will be easier for me to get information if they think I'm on bad terms with you— that I'm upset the throne went to your mate." She gestured to her bloodstained gown. "I threw a fit to sell the lie. No one would expect me to take such a slight without bloodshed."

Notwithstanding how fucked that explanation was, it forced me to ask, "Are you angry that Thea took the throne?"

"Not in the least. I've known for some time that Thea is unique. If I had known of Ginerva's death, I would have suspected that's why Thea was called here."

"Thea came to Venice to look for her mother," I reminded her.

"I wouldn't count that as a coincidence." She shook her head and reached to stroke my hair like she had when I was a young vampire. "Not with Willem here and the Mordicum. I've lived long enough to know when something is too convenient," she warned me. "Someone went through a lot of trouble to make sure you were both here. Someone who knew about that prophecy and wanted to see it fulfilled."

"Because they wanted Thea to be queen," I guessed.

She nodded, her eyes burning like a flame's tip. "Now you need to figure out why."

CHAPTER EIGHT

Jacqueline

'd been gone for a few hours, and all hell had broken loose. So what was new?

"You going to drink that?" Sebastian asked me, nudging me on the shoulder.

I looked down at my glass of Scotch. I had no idea how long I'd been sitting here, clutching it as its wood-smoked scent unfurled in my nostrils. Glancing up, I realized daylight streaked through the windows.

I stood and shoved the glass toward him. "It's all yours."

"Not into day drinking?" He downed it in one swift swallow.

I didn't bother to tell him that I'd been sitting here all night. We'd gotten back to court hours ago empty-handed. Camila had invited me to her room to talk, and before I could decide if that was a bad idea or a *very bad* idea, Lysander had broken the news about Thea and Julian.

Dead. Resurrected. Crowned.

I had no clue where Camila had gone or when she had left. I'd just sat here, numb from shock, waiting for morning to go and see proof for myself that Julian and Thea were both breathing.

"I need to find Julian," I mumbled.

"Yeah." He nodded, no sign of the usual smirk he wore. "Last night was..." Instead of finishing the thought, he reached for the bottle. I couldn't blame him. He'd witnessed it. At least he'd been there to help. I hated that I'd been off on some fool's errand—off thinking about Camila while my best friend lay mortally wounded.

"You okay?" I asked, my voice thick.

"I will be." He took another drink. "It's just..." Sebastian sighed, blond hair falling onto his face as he searched the contents of his cup for what he wanted to say. "They love each other."

"They're mates," I said, shrugging slightly.

He nodded. "I didn't think that existed. Mates. True love."

"You're sounding dangerously sentimental," I warned him.

"Maybe." He finished his drink. "I just can't imagine being loved like that."

I thought of Camila, of everything we'd gone through and all the ways we'd failed each other. "Neither can I," I said in a hollow voice. "I better go find him before he gets himself killed again."

Sebastian smiled at that and raised the bottle. "I'll drink to that."

I left him there with the bottle. The court itself was built to be a maze, much like Venice itself. A wise defense strategy, if slightly claustrophobic. Murals depicting the court's magical history decorated the walls along with unnerving, marble statues stationed like silent guards. With the court in ruins, there were no living sentries in sight. That would have to change if *Le Regine* returned to their former glory. If Thea...

I knew I was heading in the right direction when I turned and found myself facing a woman in a flowing red cloak. A black, mouthless mask protected her face, and she stood as still as those motionless statues.

Her head turned when I paused to look at her, wary eyes staring out at me.

"Sorry," I muttered. "I'm looking for Julian. Is he around here?"

She didn't respond, and I wondered if the mask was more than part of her uniform—if she actually couldn't speak.

"Never mind." I started past her, but I only made it a step before she was in front of me, sword drawn. I froze, hands up in surrender. "Whoa. I'm his best friend. I just want to see if he's okay."

Her vigilant gaze watched me for a moment, as if measuring me up. She must have decided I wasn't a threat, because she stepped to the side, sword still in hand, and pointed to a door down the hall.

"Thanks," I muttered.

I'd lived long enough to know a bodyguard when I saw one. I wondered how Thea was going to feel about that.

Or how she was going to feel about any of it.

Because holy shit, Thea was a queen. That was going to take some getting used to.

I stopped in front of the door and took a moment to collect myself. I licked my dry lips, forcing moisture into my mouth. Swallowing weakly, my stomach in a constant state of revolution, I knocked.

"Go away," Julian barked from somewhere deep inside the quarters. I wondered how many people had interrupted his reunion with his mate that he was defaulting to that greeting.

"Come tell me that to my face, asshole," I called back. I swore I could feel that masked guard staring at me from down the hall, but I did my best to shake it off.

Footsteps padded on the other side of the door, and then it swung open. Julian grunted a hello before heading straight back into the room.

"Hello to you, too," I grumbled. He'd thrown on some silk pajama pants but was otherwise disheveled. I wondered if I'd woken them up as I followed behind him. There were no signs of the injuries I'd been told about on his back. I scanned his arms as I tried to catch up with him to get a better look. "Is this a bad time?"

"Not the greatest," he muttered. "Thea was just pitching the worst idea in history to me, and I was deciding if she'd lost her mind."

Thea's head poked out of an adjoining room, her lips turned down in a frown. Their corners jolted up when she saw me, and she stepped out, tying the sash of a robe around her slight body.

"Don't mind him," she said. "He's grumpy."

"When isn't he?" I could have wept to see them both standing there acting so damn...normal. After Thea was taken, I wasn't certain I would ever see her again. Then after last night...

"I am not the one who just asked me to kill her to see if she was immortal," he growled.

My eyebrows flicked up as I processed what he said. I looked from him to her, the two of them so locked in their argument that they'd already forgotten my existence.

"How else are we going to find out?" she demanded. Turning to me, she gestured for backup. "Tell him, Jacqueline."

"What?" I swallowed, shaking my head. "I happen to agree that it's the worst idea in history—and I've seen some things."

Thea groaned, crossing her arms over her petite chest. "We have to know."

"We'll find another way—one that doesn't involve you and bloodshed," he said darkly.

How long had they been arguing about this?

I swept my eyes over them, surprised to find they looked exactly like the last time I'd seen them. Then my gaze landed on the tattoo on Julian's chest.

"When did you get that?" I asked.

Thea sagged against the wall, looking relieved for a change in conversation. "Last night," she told me, "when...everything happened."

"You mean when you died," I said flatly.

"Not exactly."

I looked more closely at it and realized it was Ginerva's symbol—the mark of her reign. Now it was Thea's, and I could guess why Julian bore it. She had brought him back to life, according to what I'd been told. "Am I correct in assuming your life is bound to his now, Your Majesty?"

Thea flinched, her eyes widening with pain. "Please don't call me that."

"But you're a queen," I pointed out.

"I'm your friend."

I shrugged, leveling a blank stare at her. "Yes, but maybe that title has gone to your head if you're willing to risk both your lives to prove some crazy theory."

"Gods help me." She threw her hands up, her hair tumbling down her back as she looked to the ceiling. "Obviously, we control my death."

"Control it?" Julian said coolly.

"Yes." She looked to him with soft, pleading eyes, and I saw his broad shoulders relax, his whole body responding to the unspoken request in her gaze.

"That might work on him, but I'm going to need more convincing," I said.

Thea turned to me. "A mortal wound," she explained. I raised an eyebrow, and she continued quickly. "Something that would definitely kill an immortal. We just see if it starts to heal, and if it doesn't, one of you heals me."

Julian spoke before I could. "No," he said firmly. "It doesn't work that way, Thea. Anything that could kill us *will* kill us—and besides that, I'm not watching you bleed half to death, not after..." His voice cracked, and he looked away with haunted eyes.

My throat constricted, and I found it difficult to speak. I forced myself to, though. "Maybe we can come up with a different plan. Ask for some help," I suggested softly. "I think we could all use a little time to...heal."

Julian looked to me, gratitude echoing in his eyes.

"You're probably right." Thea forced a smile.

I knew this was far from over, but I'd bought us time to find another way—or talk her out of it, at least.

"Now." I cleared my throat. "Am I supposed to bow or curtsy?"

Her cheeks reddened, but Julian laughed.

"I think you have to kneel and pledge your allegiance," he crowed.

Thea buried her face in her hands. "Stop," she said in a muffled voice. "This is bad enough."

"Bad enough?" I repeated. "Thea, you are a queen."

"I know." She peeked through her hands. "I just wish I knew what that meant."

"Well, for starters." I marched toward her. "It means you're alive, and that is fucking good news."

I threw my arms around her, relieved to feel she was real. Solid. Alive.

Thea made a strangled sound, and then she dissolved into tears. "Sorry," she sobbed. "It's been a crazy night."

"I know." I patted her back in soothing strokes. "Don't worry. I'm well acquainted with crazy nights."

Julian moved to us but didn't interrupt the hug. "Jacqueline has a point. We're all alive. That's all that matters."

I let her go, releasing her to her mate's arms. She burrowed into him, and after a moment, her tears stopped. I sat on the arm of the couch.

Thea gulped deep breaths until her body calmed. Finally managing a smile, she exhaled. "Okay, but what now?"

"We reopen the court, and you take your throne," Julian said. "No one can touch you as a queen, especially if I'm at your side. And when you've won them over, we go after Willem and end him."

"You make that sound simple." Thea chewed on her lip.

We all knew it wasn't going to be that easy.

"Unfortunately, it doesn't work that way," I said. "You go take the throne, Thea. You show your face, and we'll be right there with you. But you need to learn how to protect yourself."

"Protect myself against a bunch of ancient vampires?"

I nodded. "They told me...about your magic and why the crown came to you. Vampires might be strong, but it's been a long time since any of them faced true magic."

"If only I knew what to do with it," she muttered.

"We'll figure everything out," I promised, "but for now, Julian is right. You need to show them you aren't afraid, so we can do what we need to do."

"Which is?"

"Take Willem out, and stop the Mordicum," I said.

"Oh. Just that," she said flatly.

I smiled at her, but it didn't last long. Because now that I knew they were both safe, protected, and *whole*, I had a new cloud hanging over my head.

"What is it?" Julian eyed me suspiciously.

He knew me too well. There was no point in keeping it from him, even if he already had enough problems of his own. "We have a problem with Camila." I took a deep breath. "She knows about her children."

CHAPTER NINE

Thea

My wardrobe consisted of gowns, all perfectly tailored to my petite frame yet somehow from various time periods. I fingered the cap sleeve of a gossamer dress that looked like something out of a Jane Austen novel. It didn't make any sense. Not that a lot made sense around here.

Especially me.

I was sleeping in someone else's bed, wearing her crown, mated to her ex-lover. But I knew next to nothing about Ginerva. It was unnerving because I felt like I'd stepped not into her life but into her very skin. And underneath it all, my magic itched to release itself. It writhed and stretched, looking for a way to break free. The trouble was that I didn't know the first thing about it, and now I was expected to be a queen.

Shoving the gowns apart, I searched for anything that looked like me. There were no jeans or T-shirts, but I finally found a simple pair of black pants and a cropped tweed jacket. I felt silly as I pulled them on, but not as silly as I would have felt wandering the halls in a ballgown.

Julian would be back from speaking with Jacqueline at any moment. I'd been glad for the excuse for a minute alone to collect my thoughts, but as I ran a comb through my hair, a stranger stared back in the mirror.

It was my face, but different. My skin, which had always been pale, now glowed subtly, like the moonstone embedded in the crown waiting in the next room. And I looked...older. Was that even possible? Had dying aged me? Or was my time under Willem's spell to blame? My cheekbones were carved and sharp, my green eyes sparkled with emerald fire, and even my hair seemed to flicker like flames under the lights. I pulled it back, searching through the bathroom until I found a jar of pins to twist it up with.

But wound around my head, it looked like a crown of fire. I was about to give up and take it down when someone knocked on the bathroom door.

I turned, expecting to see Julian, and nearly jumped out of my own skin. Behind me, the cloaked woman removed her mask quickly, and I recognized her immediately. She'd been with Lysander. She was the one who had taken me to my throne.

"Sorry. I didn't mean to frighten you."

"Holy..." I rubbed my chest, my heart pounding frantically. "I didn't know anyone could get in here."

"Only those you allow access and your personal guard." She pointed at herself. "That's me."

"My...personal guard?" I repeated, blinking.

"Aurelia," she said. "It's a lot to get used to."

That was an understatement.

"I'm here to bring you to your throne." She spoke in a matter-of-fact tone.

"Already? I'm not sure that's a good idea." I gave her what I hoped was a charming smile.

"Your sisters await you, as does your court."

"My court?" I repeated, but the words tasted wrong. How was I supposed to face an entire court?

"You have taken Ginerva's place. You now hold the most powerful throne in the world." She paused, as if waiting for a response. When it didn't come, she continued, sounding put out.

"They're expecting you."

"Look, I don't know what I'm doing." Or why I'd been chosen. Regardless of the magic stirring under my skin, I had no idea how to use it. No idea how to tap the source of power underneath Venice's water. And definitely no idea how to be royalty.

"For the first time in decades, the courtiers have returned. They want to meet their new queen—to see who has claimed the throne. This is a day every creature in Venice has hoped for."

"I'm not sure I'm what they expected." Or what they wanted. After what Sabine had told us, I couldn't help wondering how many of them had come, not from curiosity or excitement but to plot how to undermine *Le Regine* once more.

"And yet the crown chose you."

"Only because you dragged me to that throne," I pointed out. I chewed on the inside of my cheek until I tasted iron on my tongue. "Why? There had to have been someone more...qualified."

"There was," Aurelia said breezily. "Sabine."

My throat knotted, and I swallowed. Even if Sabine had finally opened up to me, it was a reminder that I'd stolen her throne.

"Do you want to get changed?" Aurelia asked.

I frowned, glancing down at my outfit. "Is there something wrong with this?"

"It's a riding costume."

"Riding horses?" She nodded, and I flushed. "Why even have that in the closet? Not a lot of horses in Venice."

"No, but there is a wild herd on a nearby island. Ginerva liked to go riding."

"So these *are* her clothes." Something about that made my skin crawl.

"Not exactly. Most of the court is enchanted to provide for the queens," Aurelia explained. "When you took the throne, your quarters made sure you would have everything you needed."

"So it made my clothes?" I asked her. "With what? Magic?"

She shrugged. "Is that so hard to believe?"

"Considering I thought magic was pretty much comatose until

yesterday, I guess so."

"*Le Regine* dismissed their court years ago when Ginerva died to preserve what remained here. The court itself was spelled long before the curse, drawing what it needs from the *Rio Oscuro*."

I relaxed a little. These weren't Ginerva's clothes. I hadn't just literally stepped into her shoes. "How do I tell the magic I want a pair of jeans? I can't wear anything in there without looking like I belong in a historical drama."

Aurelia's mouth twitched like she wanted to smile, but she didn't. "Can I help you find something more suitable?"

I nodded, stepping to the side to give her access to the wardrobe. When she opened its doors, I gasped.

"That's not what was in there before." I moved to her side and stared. No more Jane Austen gowns. No hoop skirts and bodices. The veritable museum of fashion history had been replaced. I rifled through the hangers, sighing when I didn't find a single T-shirt among the dresses there.

"You said you couldn't wear any of it. The magic heard and responded," she said, her fingers dancing over the hangers as she looked through my options.

"Well, it missed the part about wanting a pair of jeans," I said flatly.

"It's spelled for what you need, not what you want." She lifted a dress from the rack.

"What does that mean?"

Aurelia turned to me, her eyes narrowing. "A pair of jeans won't help you at court. They will be watching every move you make."

"Even what I wear?"

"Especially what you wear." When Aurelia held up the gown, it seemed to catch the light of the room and swallow it like a black hole, save for starbursts and sunbeams embroidered with silver thread. As fathomless and mysterious as the celestial throne itself. "You are powerful. Dress like it."

I took a deep breath. "This is going to take some getting used to."

"I'll be here for whatever you need." The promise sounded more like the words of a friend than a bodyguard.

"I'll change." I took the dress into the bathroom, hanging it on a hook near the door. After I peeled off the inappropriate riding clothes, I took it from its hanger and carefully stepped into the gown.

It was light, considering the lovely drape of the velvet, and it glided over me like a second skin. Its sheer sleeves circled my wrists, covering my arms with such delicate softness that it felt like being kissed by air. Even the bodice, which clung to my curves, didn't feel restrictive. I pulled the zipper up easily and took a tentative step. The full skirt floated around me.

"This is the most comfortable thing I've ever worn," I announced as I stepped out of the bathroom. "I feel like I'm wearing pajamas."

"You needed to be comfortable." Aurelia smiled. "The magic knew that."

"The magic can pick out everything I wear from now on."

She laughed as she held up a pair of velvet slippers. "Unless you want to wear heels?"

I shook my head and took them. I wanted to keep the ground under my feet. I wanted to be able to feel it. If only to remind me that this was all real.

"Thank you," I said. "For everything."

Her brows furrowed, as if my words were foreign to her and she didn't quite know how to respond. Finally, she just said, "You're welcome." There was a pause before she gently asked, "Are you ready?"

"I suppose I don't need to wait for Julian." I had no clue how much longer he would be, and it was clear Aurelia thought I should go. But was I really ready to face this without him by my side? "Let me leave him a note."

"Is he very protective?" Each word was so carefully chosen.

"He's my mate." I shrugged, digging around in a nearby desk until I found a pen and paper. I scrawled a quick message to him. "He wants to protect me."

"Is that a mate's job?" she asked as she led me toward the door.

"Sometimes." I hesitated, both preparing myself to walk outside the safety of my quarters and to answer her. "What are you getting at?"

"I wonder if Sabine Rousseaux's son will struggle with seeing his mate rise to power."

If she only knew Sabine, I could understand her concern, but I didn't share it.

"He won't," I said flatly. "We're equals."

"The queens have no equals," she corrected me.

But that wouldn't do, because I didn't want Julian beneath me. I wanted him beside me. "This queen does. Is that a problem?"

"The others won't share that view," she warned me. "They have had lovers." I winced at her choice of words, remembering what Julian had told me about his relationship with Ginerva. I shoved it out of my mind as Aurelia continued. "But they have never married. Never mated. Never allowed their emotions to be entangled with anyone they took to bed. They have always maintained a firm boundary in relationships for fear a male will demand to be king."

"And look where that got them." I shrugged. "Look, if they want the crown back, I'll leave with Julian. I'm not interested in any of this without him."

She studied me for a moment, and then she laughed.

"What?" I asked suspiciously.

Aurelia only smiled. "Just promise to tell them that while I'm with you."

"They're not going to like it, huh?" I guessed.

Her smile widened. "I want very much to see their faces."

"Speaking of…" I looked at the mask she held in her hand. "Do you have to wear that? Does it help with your powers?"

I could sense magic thrumming from Aurelia. It felt different than any magic I'd experienced yet, but maybe that was something I needed to get used to.

Her shoulders tensed slightly under her cloak. "It's an old custom. Most of the court used to wear masks. *Le Vergini*—the order I belong to—wore these. The queens and other courtiers still wear masks on occasion."

"But you wear it all the time because…"

She looked me directly in the eyes. "*Le Regine* prefers that I cover my scar."

"Do they?" Anger flashed inside me. I vaguely recalled wearing a similar mask to the party to hide my identity. It was not only a pain in the ass—it was offensive. But there was something more. I knew it. Another reason that she hid behind that mask. "Do you want to wear it?"

She stilled for a moment before shaking her head.

"Then I wish you to do what makes you feel comfortable."

"Noted." She inclined her head, looking grateful. She considered the mask for a moment before slipping it into the pocket of her cloak.

I hoped I never saw it again.

Now that we'd settled that, I squared my shoulders as I walked alongside her. "Let's go see how else I can piss them off."

CHAPTER TEN

Lysander

Duty to family or not, I was ready to leave the court. I glowered at a group of gossiping familiars blocking the passage into the throne room. A week ago, the whole building had been covered in dust and decay—as forgotten as the ancient ruins where I spent most of my time—but news had spread quickly. The wealthiest witches and vampires had already been in Venice for the ball. They'd arrived expecting to see Sabine crowned. I suspected a few had come only to avoid getting on her bad side, but it was what had happened after that had drawn the rest of the magical world to the city. Overnight, the number of courtiers had quadrupled, half of them eager to see the new queen—the other half likely already plotting against her.

At least I didn't have it as bad as my brother. He couldn't get out of this if he wanted to. I had options.

"Have you seen your brothers?" Dominic approached. He'd traded his tuxedo for a black suit that was cut close, showcasing his broad, warrior frame. "I need to speak with them."

"Thoren and Benedict are somewhere." I waved a hand. Thoren was probably hiding. He wasn't one for crowds. And Benedict? Usually, he would be behind the scenes, greasing wheels and shaking hands. It was his job as the family politician, but he'd been quiet, keeping to himself. "I think they're hiding. Sebastian is in there flirting."

With anything that moved. Sebastian seemed determined to drum up that orgy to combat his boredom.

"Thea will take the throne soon," he told me in a lowered voice. "I'd like to have everyone nearby…just in case."

He had a point. Our kind wasn't exactly known for our self-restraint. Had news spread that Thea was neither a vampire nor a familiar? I doubted it. My father had filled me in on what my mother had hidden from us. When the vampires realized Thea was a siren—or worse, a possible succubus—things might get ugly. Her crown afforded her protection, but that might not be enough. Queens could wear targets as easily as crowns.

"I thought Mother wanted you to stay out of this." She'd been clear about that, too. In order to stay on top of any potential danger, it was best she remained Thea's enemy, publicly.

"She does," he said grimly, "but I want to be here the first time to see that they're both…okay."

He was always the protective parent. I forced a grin. "And after?"

"We will leave." He paused before looking directly at me. "Your mother and I, at least. It will be up to each of you to decide where your loyalties lie."

I didn't ask him if he meant for show or for real. Sabine Rousseaux lived her life like the world was watching because it usually was. But I nodded to show I understood.

I had a choice to make: stay here and become part of Thea's court, or leave with my parents and cut ties for the time being. It should be an easy decision. Julian and Thea would have a small army guarding them, and I wasn't cut out for a life of bowing and scraping, ceremonies and galas. Still, every moment I lingered here, the ground felt like quicksand. One wrong move and I would never leave. It would swallow me whole. It was better I left before I got stuck. "They're expecting me back in Egypt soon. I told my crew I was leaving for the holidays."

He dipped his head, understanding what I meant. I'd rather not take a side. I'd rather get back to the life waiting for me.

"I expect they're planning a party. Sabine wishes to leave this afternoon."

"I'll head out at the same time," I decided. "They party a little too hard for me."

He snorted, but no other glimmer of amusement showed. Maybe someday we would laugh about what happened, but I doubted it. "There is something, though." He searched my face. "We need to know more about this curse and who was behind it, as well as Ginerva's death."

"You suspect foul play?" I said.

He nodded. "There's a weapon—one that can kill a queen. It might be best if we find it before…"

He didn't have to finish the sentence. Before most of the magical world overreacted to discovering a siren now sat on a throne. "Mother has resources. I'm sure…"

"She needs to play the part of ousted queen," he said in a lowered voice. "Everyone expects that, and if we start looking around for this weapon or into the curse, more questions will be raised. And to be honest, I still don't trust Sabine's motivations. She still sits on the Council, and the Council will want that weapon. If she has a change of heart, it could fall into their hands. We need to do this ourselves."

"And what am I supposed to do?"

"No one would blame a male for standing with his brother. If you were here, you could look into the archives, find information. You've always been able to dig up dirt." He waited for me to respond.

I stared at him. It wasn't in my plans to stick around Venice. I was expected back in Egypt already. But unlike my mother, my father wouldn't command me to stay. He was putting it to me as a choice. I swallowed, knowing he wouldn't like my answer. "Let me think about it."

"Your brothers." Dominic nodded across the hall to where Benedict and Thoren had just appeared.

Despite my concerns, Benedict looked at ease, but it easily

could've been an act. His suit fit him like a second skin, or rather a snake's skin. It was impossible to know what he was thinking under the casual smile he offered to those he passed.

At his side, Thoren looked uncomfortable. His light eyes squinted, trapped somewhere between resenting his formal clothing and the tightness of the collar around his neck. He fidgeted with the tie, loosening it slightly, but from his grimace, it wasn't enough. Even in a room full of vampires, he towered above most. His discomfort over being stuffed into a crowd of people with faces he didn't know and conversations he didn't care about showed.

We moved swiftly toward them, cutting our way through the masses with hawk-like precision. Those who bothered to look up and see who was coming toward them moved out of the way.

"There you are," Dominic said when we reached them. "We need to talk. Alone."

"Are we getting lectured?" Sebastian broke in, coming up beside us. He grinned, obviously a little drunk, even this early in the day.

"You might be," I muttered.

It took a minute for us to find a quiet alcove. There was no way to guarantee privacy. Not with magical creatures crowding the halls. Who knew what enchantments the queens had reporting back to them? But we'd all been on one battlefield or another with our father, so we knew how to communicate discreetly.

"Your mother and I will be leaving this afternoon," he informed them.

"You're leaving now?" Benedict asked, his eyes glinting.

Dominic nodded. "We have other engagements in the city, but we will stay to see Thea take her throne publicly."

The message was clear. Sabine and Dominic would offer one show of loyalty to the queens—enough to keep Zina and Mariana from questioning them. But they would not stay or pledge their allegiance to their son's mate, especially with rumors circling that my brother had been disowned.

"If any of you want to leave with us, meet at the dock in an hour," Dominic informed them. He glanced at me. "And consider what I said."

Silence stretched between all of us, my brothers weighing his words and what they meant.

"I need to get back to London," Benedict said at last. "I have matters to attend to."

"Me, too." Thoren nodded, and I knew he meant to go. Although I doubted he would head to London with him. Most of us never knew where he got off to when we were apart.

"What are you doing?" Sebastian directed the question at me, some of the drunken edge gone from his voice. "Leaving?"

"I'm supposed to head to Egypt." I shoved my hands in my pockets, avoiding my father's eyes. "I need to get back to the dig. You?"

"I'm still deciding," he said quietly.

Despite his reputation, I sometimes wondered if Sebastian was the most loyal of all of us. If so, this was a test. Which side would he choose?

In the distance, a murmur ran through the crowd, palpable in its excitement.

"Maybe we should go find a good place to watch," Dominic suggested lightly.

We nodded in unison, knowing an order when we received one.

Marching back toward the throne room, its passage now mercifully clear, we split up. Each of us wove our way through the courtiers gathered to see the new queen and took a defensive position in the throne room. Between the five of us, we would see any threat before it could reach her.

But it wasn't Thea who entered through the queen's private corridor. My heart paused at the cloaked figure that swept a path of safety for her.

Aurelia had removed her mask. With her hood raised, she was still mostly in shadow, but I could picture the curve of her chin, the wideness of her lips, that scar that splintered that full mouth and carved across her neck. Some empty place inside me filled as I saw her, as if I'd been holding space for her return.

The ground beneath me seemed to shift, and I took a steadying step forward, only to find it hard to move.

I needed to get out of here. This afternoon, I would put a stop to this—whatever it was—before it could get started. I had a life to get back to, and it didn't involve this court.

My heart clanged in protest, and I ignored it.

It took effort to tear my eyes from Aurelia as she moved to the side, and Thea came into view. The murmur of the crowd turned to a roar as they saw her for the first time.

I couldn't blame them.

The crown she wore might have once belonged to another, but it looked made for her. Her hair was pulled up to hold it, and even at a distance, it looked like a fire blazing beneath that crown. The morning light was bright, but it cut into her in jagged, savage lines, not delicate or elegant but brutal and demanding like the dark gown she wore.

She did not belong to this world. She was here to command it.

All around me, vampires and familiars seemed to realize the same thing. A few voices rose above the rest.

"What is that thing?"

"This is a mistake."

"She's not a vampire!"

I flinched as the protests grew louder, searching the room for signs of Julian. He had to be nearby. He wouldn't let his mate face this crowd alone. But he was nowhere to be seen. Glancing at my brothers, I saw them doing the same. But then the crowd began to move like a swarm, and I lost sight of them, lost sight of my father.

My battlefield training kicked in. This was why we had stayed. In hindsight, we should have armed ourselves, but weapons weren't technically allowed inside court unless carried by official guards. The good news was that even hand-to-hand, we could take out most of the room.

At least, we could have before magic reawakened. The odds were a little sketchier at the moment.

That only left…

I looked at the throne. Not at my brother's mate, who stood poised to take her seat, but at the woman shadowing her. Aurelia's hand moved, shifting her cloak out of the way as she placed her hand on the hilt of her sword.

Before things could get out of control, more guards appeared. They looked almost bored at the upheaval before them as they circled the dais. And then, from the private corridor, Mariana strode to her place. Her sea-green gown brushed the floor like the tide along the shore. She moved to her throne wordlessly, her arrival causing the crowd to silence for a moment.

Zina appeared next. Daylight glinted off her rich, black skin. Her silver hair hung in a loose braid over her shoulder. She frowned when she saw Thea but didn't speak. There was a moment of hesitation before she stepped up to take her own throne.

"It is so lovely to see our court full again," Mariana called, her words musical but cunning. "To see you have come to pledge allegiance to your new queen."

In the front of the room, someone spat on the ground. "I'm not pledging anything to that."

Mariana's soft smile faded, her eyes churning like a stormy sea. She lifted her hand, and I found myself pushing through the crowd. Things were about to get bloody. Maybe Aurelia could handle herself, but I wasn't going to let her fight alone.

I was steps away when the doors to the throne room flew open. The entire crowd stopped, turning toward the open doors in a ripple of curiosity.

Dread filled me as I looked at the dark figure looming there.

CHAPTER ELEVEN

Julian

My entrance had the intended effect. Silence rippled through the crowd, gossip and protests dying on hundreds of lips. I didn't bother to look at any of them. I'd walked into this throne room before but never quite like this. Even with it full of vampires and familiars, my footsteps echoed on the stone as I strode toward the only person that mattered: my queen.

Whatever magic existed in Thea's quarters had gifted me my ensemble. It was cut in the old style, halfway between finery and a uniform. The jacket was tailored like a tunic with a banded collar that rose high on my neck and fastened at an angle across my chest. It was made of a heavy black silk and devoid of all ornamentation save for the moons and serpents embroidered on its cuffs. I hadn't seen a male wear the style in centuries. It had fallen out of fashion, even though our customs hadn't changed all that much. The uniform of a consort.

Thea's eyes met mine across the crowded room. I missed the chain that once tethered me to her, but through our new bond, I felt her heart beating in my chest, felt her pulse quicken as we gazed at one another.

You look dashing, her amused voice sounded in my head, and I fought a smile.

We need to present a united front, I reminded her through our bond. I had to look the part.

I think you upstaged me. I could almost hear her laugh, although her face remained detached.

Perhaps I should find a mirror. You look delicious, Your Majesty.

I felt her quiver of annoyance and something dangerously enticing. From a distance, I caught her mouth twitch slightly.

I continued to watch her as I passed a group of murmuring vampires. They fell silent except for one.

"Traitor," he muttered like he was spitting on the floor.

He might as well have.

I didn't bother to hold back. Shifting on my feet, I caught the male by the throat and hoisted him in the air. Around us, others, even his companions, scrambled back as I lifted him off his feet.

"My loyalty is to *Le Regine* and our new queen," I hissed at him. "Where does yours lie?"

I already knew, although I hoped it wouldn't be the case. Thea wasn't one of us in the eyes of vampires, nor was she a witch to the familiars. If they had wondered what magic ran in her veins, they would soon know. The oldest vampires present, those the age of my parents, would remember sirens—and what had been done to them.

How many of them could spot a succubus?

And that was why I was here. It was why I'd gone searching for the garments I now wore.

If the court would come to know Thea as a compassionate ruler, I would show the opposite side of the coin. I would be her punisher. I would keep them in line. Until they learned to love and respect her, they would fear me.

"Apologies," he said, half the word inaudible as he struggled to breathe.

"Sir," I prompted him.

"Sir." His eyes were bulging now, his face turning purple.

Strangling him wouldn't kill him. Popping his sorry head from his shoulders would. But neither would send as clear of a message as his apology.

I dropped him to the floor. He crumpled there, but I didn't move.

"On your knees," I ordered him.

He was younger than I'd first thought. A couple hundred years old. That explained his utter stupidity. It didn't forgive it.

Trembling, he rose to his knees. "Please."

I ignored him and turned to Thea. Her face remained composed, coolly disinterested in the scene playing before her. But inside me, I felt my heart racing, felt the panic edging into her blood.

"Do you wish me to punish him, Your Majesty?" I asked.

There was a pause before she lifted her chin. "No. Let him go."

"As you desire." I inclined my head to her before turning back to glare at the reckless vampire. "You should be relieved your new queen is more charitable than I am." I leaned in, lowering my voice so that only those closest to us could hear me as I added, "I should have ripped your throat out and asked *her* forgiveness later."

His face paled as he shrank away from me.

I didn't bother to look back at him.

The eyes of the court tracked me as I continued to her throne, but I ignored them and bowed before her.

"I have come to swear my allegiance to you."

I think you did that several times last night.

Aloud, she said, "You're the first to do that."

It was a loaded statement—one meant to catch the attention of everyone present.

"Then it is an honor," I said loudly enough for everyone gathered to hear. I knelt before her. "I offer you my body to protect you. I offer you my heart to cherish you. I offer you my blood to sustain you."

Behind us, there was a collective gasp. For those who thought her a mere mortal, the fact that she fed from me was going to be a shock. I grinned at her, knowing none of them could see me.

My eyes darted to Mariana, who was watching us with detached amusement. Then they looked at Zina, who remained stone-faced and silent.

"I accept," Thea said, pausing to rein in the tremble in her voice.

"But your place is at my side, mate."

The silence that followed was thunderous.

I glanced at Mariana, who no longer looked amused, and to Zina, whose mouth had fallen open.

Careful, I warned her.

I know what I'm doing. She sounded a little pissy, actually.

"Join me, my love." She extended a hand.

It was dangerous business. I knew it, but I took her hand anyway. Rising, I joined her on the dais.

Sit down.

I froze at her instruction, barely remembering the part I needed to play. *Thea...*

Sit. Down.

You have no idea what this will mean.

I know exactly *what it means. We're equals in all things.* Mates. *Even this.*

I stared at her, waiting for her to change her mind. I searched for the right warning to convey what it would imply if I sat on the throne.

Would you take a throne without me? Her question silenced my confused thoughts.

I sighed. *No.*

Her answering smile was triumphant.

Later, we need to have a talk about springing crazy ideas on me.

She snorted softly, her hand squeezing mine.

So I took the throne, and if the silence was thunderous before, it threatened to swallow us whole now.

I hope you're right about this.

United front, right?

Thea smiled as she lowered herself into my lap, undoing a thousand years of tradition—and starting a riot.

CHAPTER TWELVE

Thea

Shouts rose from the gathered crowd. The mass of people began to shove and swarm, and multiple fights erupted. A couple of dozen pitchforks would complete the scene.

Julian's hands gripped my hips, his whole body tense and alert. But as much as I wanted to lean back into his arms, lean against his solid body, I knew that would send a different message.

So I held my head high, more aware than ever of the crown resting atop it.

"We should get you out of here." Julian's breath tickled my ear as he spoke quietly into it.

"Now?" What message would that send?

"Let's worry about bad publicity later," he said, hearing my thought. "Your sisters already left."

My head whipped to Mariana's throne, finding it empty beside me. Then to where Zina sat. Also empty. They'd abandoned me at the first sign of trouble.

"We'll discuss their loyalty later," he suggested. "For now—"

He was cut off by a sharp snarl.

Turning my head, I caught a flash of movement. A black-eyed vampire rushed to the dais. One second, he was coming right at us.

The next, I was in the air. A shrill scream lodged in my throat as I plunged into Lysander's waiting arms.

He caught me like I was a doll, then swept me around to deposit me next to Aurelia.

"Follow me," she said, sword drawn.

But I refused to budge. "I'm not going anywhere."

Her eyes closed for a moment, her face drawn. "How did I know you would say that?"

A vampire crashed into the wall next to me and slumped to the ground in an unconscious heap. I looked up and met Julian's midnight gaze.

Go.

I ignored his order. There was no way I was going to run from the throne at the first sign of trouble. I'd started this fight for a reason, even if it had turned into a brawl more quickly than expected. So much for centuries of refinement and rationality. In the end, vampires weren't so different than humans.

Thea, go! Julian's scream echoed in my mind. He was surrounded by three other vampires.

I didn't move.

He caught the one closest to him around the middle, lifting him effortlessly, and threw him into one of the others. The third hesitated for a second as he watched his companions fall so easily. Julian lifted a hand and beckoned for him to attack.

The vampire turned and fled into the crowd instead.

Julian shifted, his face a stony mask, as he spotted me still standing beside the throne. In one bound, he was next to me. His hands gripped my shoulders gently for a vampire. It would likely leave bruises, but I knew he was doing his best to rein in his strength. I lifted my head to speak to him, but he pushed me toward Aurelia.

Her cold fingers caught my arm, pulling me along. I fought her grip and stumbled toward the other side of the dais.

"I am not going. I need to stop this," I hissed at her.

Meanwhile, Julian placed himself between me and the thick of the fight.

Aurelia's sword glinted in the light as she swept it through the air. She turned to Julian and pointed a gloved finger at me. "You will get her out of here. Now."

"I won't leave you here to fight alone." Julian's voice was nearly drowned out by the encroaching screams and cries of the vampires below.

"I've been doing it a long time on my own." Aurelia's eyes appeared as hard and cold as her blade as she spoke.

"I need to speak with them."

"You've done enough." Aurelia turned on me, all of her early friendliness gone.

"I thought you wanted to be there when I told them my mate was my equal," I reminded her.

"I assumed it would be a private conversation. Not a means to incite a riot." She held her sword aloft as a group of ambitious familiars moved toward us. One look at her, and they fell back into the fighting below.

Julian and I had made a public spectacle before. I'd expected the crowd to protect me from the other queens' wrath. I hadn't expected it to turn on me.

I scanned the writhing mass below, a stone settling in my stomach. This wasn't what I'd planned. Julian's hand reached for mine. Our fingers twined together, and he tugged me gently away. But as I turned, I spotted a familiar face in the crowd.

Quinn Porter looked like the epitome of glamour, even wearing a torn gown and a determined scowl. She pushed her way toward me, knocking over grown vampires with the slightest touch.

"Get back," Aurelia commanded, brandishing her sword as Quinn closed in on the dais. Julian pulled me away as she reached the base.

"Wait!" I broke free and moved beside Aurelia. "She's my friend."

Aurelia continued to hold her sword out, the blade only a few inches from Quinn's face.

"Let her up," I demanded.

"Your Majesty, are you..." Aurelia trailed off as I reached down and held my hand out to Quinn.

She grabbed it, and I hauled her up next to us.

"Thanks, Your Majesty." Quinn grinned at me.

"Not you, too." I threw my arms around her, grateful to see one friend in the crowd.

"I missed you in Greece," she said.

Before I could respond, a candelabra whizzed past my head.

"Can we catch up later?" Julian suggested. "We need to get out of here."

"We need to stop all this fighting."

"Good luck." Quinn flexed her hands. "This is a tough crowd."

As I watched her work out the lingering aches of using magic, an idea occurred to me. "Wait, what about what you were doing? That was magic, right?"

"You want me to knock everyone over?" She blinked at me and then stared at her hands like she was trying to assess this possibility.

"Can we channel magic to get them to be quiet?" I suggested.

"If I knew how to make someone shut up with magic, I would be a significantly happier person," she said drily. "That's a trick I'd like to learn."

"You're in luck," Lysander's voice boomed over the crowd as he joined us. His dark hair had fallen free of its tie and was now covered, like the rest of him, in blood.

A quick scan told me that it wasn't his blood, but I frowned. Violence was bad enough; I wouldn't allow more lives to be lost.

"We are?" I asked.

"Your new bodyguard has a special set of skills." He raised an eyebrow at Aurelia. She glared at him. "She knows how to shut people up."

"How do you... Oh, never mind." I definitely wanted to hear more about this later. For now, I just needed it to work. I whirled on her. "Can you do what he says?"

Her eyes never left his face. It looked like she was imagining the best way to murder him.

"Not with this many people. At least, not without help," she said through gritted teeth.

"I'll help." Quinn stuck out her hand, but Aurelia only looked at it.

"There's a lot of people here. Give us a boost," Aurelia said to me.

I swallowed. "I don't know how."

"I'll walk you through it, but you better have a plan—a real plan—this time," she warned me. "This will only take away their voices. You have to get their attention before they panic."

"Are we sure this is a good idea?" Lysander asked.

I have to agree with my brother.

It's a terrible idea, I admitted silently to Julian, *but I can't stand by and do nothing. I need everyone to know that I'm not their enemy. Though I'm not sure I'm the best one to speak to them.*

Not with how much they hated me and how little they tried to hide it. Resorting to a magic trick to get their attention was one thing, but putting a stop to this...

You've got this.

I wished that helped.

"Ready, Quinn?" I murmured.

Quinn nodded, and I was glad she could hear me over the shouts of the angry crowd. She moved her hand over Aurelia's.

I waited for something to happen.

"Put your hand on top of ours," Aurelia directed me, "and release your magic."

Those were her instructions?

Just give into the light and shadow inside you. Julian stroked a reassuring hand down my back.

I did as she asked. A jolt shot between where my skin met theirs. Aurelia hissed as soon as our skin touched and pulled back. Quinn didn't, but her eyes went wide.

Aurelia shook her hand, eyeing me warily.

"A little less juice," Quinn suggested.

"Sorry." There had to be an easier way to do this. "Can't you just take what you need from me?"

"It doesn't work that way," Aurelia said as she relaxed and let me position her hand on top of Quinn's again. "You're a queen. You must give it to us freely. We cannot take from you."

Like I'd given life to Julian. It wasn't the same. Then I'd hummed the song of life. I had no idea what to do now, so I listened for music again.

At first, I heard nothing, but just as I was about to give up, I heard it faintly. It wasn't the same enchanting melody that flowed through me. This was hypnotic and pulsing—impossible to resist or ignore. I gave into it, feeling its warmth seep through my palm into their waiting hands. Quinn's magic felt like mine, but Aurelia's was entirely different. Perhaps a product of growing up near such a powerful magical source.

Aurelia smiled at me, and I stepped back, allowing the witches to cast their spell. The shouting stopped, but the fighting continued for a few moments until everyone realized what had happened.

I glanced at Julian, whose eyes had grown wide. Lysander looked fairly smug next to him but didn't say a thing.

It's working. I can't speak.

This was my chance. I only hoped the spell hadn't caught me in its grip.

"Magic is here," I announced to the silenced room. "Each of you knows that. Each of you can feel its grip now. For centuries, our magic has slept, creatures have gone extinct, and we forgot how to wield the powers we once held. That ends now. That era is over. I am not a vampire or a witch. My magic is old and new—like the world we find ourselves in now. Who knows what dangers we will face as magic returns to the world? We must stand united. If you are here to fight, leave. This court doesn't fight amongst itself."

I swore I heard someone laugh at that, but the crowd hadn't moved, and no one had spoken yet. They were all still locked under Aurelia's spell.

"And as we welcome the return of the past, we must embrace the future. I am not a celibate queen. I found my mate before the crown chose me, and I believe the crown intended that. We cannot stay the same and survive in this new world. The crown knew I needed Julian at my side just as it knows we need to stand by each other's sides now."

People began to fidget, and a quick look at Quinn and Aurelia told me they were fighting to hang on to the spell.

"If you choose to leave, do so now with my blessing. If you choose to stay, we welcome you. And if you choose to attack us, know that we will protect the blessing magic has given us against all threats."

I closed my mouth, nodding slightly to Aurelia to release them.

First, there were whispers, then a couple of shouts. A few people made their way to the doors and left. Most looked puzzled or bloodied or some combination of the two. Across the room, my gaze found Dominic's. He tipped his head, a smile of approval on his lips, but Sabine was nowhere to be seen.

"We're going now," Aurelia muttered, moving in front of me.

This time, I didn't argue with her.

"That was eloquent as hell." Quinn grinned at me, following alongside us.

"Are you staying in the city?" I asked her.

"The Council has announced the next rite will take place in Venice during Mardi Gras. I think someone pulled some strings to make sure you two could attend."

"Doesn't being a queen earn me a get-out-of-ancient-rites-free card?"

Next to me, Julian snorted, and I had my answer.

"Okay, so if you're going to be in town, we should have a girls' night. Jacqueline is here." At least, she had been. I hadn't seen her at all this morning. "And Aurelia can come."

"Come to what?" my bodyguard asked.

I ignored her.

"That sounds excellent. I need a night away from shapewear and ballgowns," Quinn agreed.

But before we could make plans, we rounded the private corridor to find Mariana and Zina waiting—along with a small army.

"Maybe I should find my parents," Quinn muttered. "You seem busy."

"Good idea." I hugged her quickly, aware of everyone watching. Julian and Aurelia moved up a step, flanking either side of me.

"I'm trying to decide what to do with you," Mariana seethed, her delicate hands clenched into fists at her sides.

"Well, I was already crowned and announced." I shrugged. "It seems like it's time for champagne or cake."

Julian's dark chuckle filled my mind, followed by, *Careful, pet.*

"This is not a joke," Zina said. "You've committed treason against the crown."

I guess they hadn't heard my speech, but before I could launch into it, Julian spoke. "I have no wish to be king."

"She practically crowned you," Mariana snapped. "There's only one thing that can be done about it."

Judging by the cold violence in her voice, whatever that was, was going to be bad—very, very bad.

CHAPTER THIRTEEN

Julian

I did my best to wedge myself in front of my mate. Thea was powerful. I knew that. I could hear the magic humming in her veins, murmuring in my own. But she didn't know how to wield it. Mariana did. Zina did. Thea might be stronger than both of them, but her power was raw and unhoned, and she had no clue how to use it. She couldn't face them yet.

I knew she would be pissed if I told her that, so I did my best to keep my movements small but precise.

You aren't fooling me.

So much for that plan.

Reading my thoughts, or am I that obvious?

You'd be less obvious if you beat your chest. A smile twitched at her lips, but she held it back. Her gaze stayed locked on Mariana's.

"It's the twenty-first century. I'm sure we have more than one option," Thea said. She didn't smile to soften her words.

Mariana's eyes narrowed into snake-like slits. "That may be, but only one makes sense."

"Is that so?" I let some of my newly freed dark magic loose. Shadows around us lengthened, and the room grew cold enough that we could see our breath. Zina shivered slightly and quickly gathered herself, but I'd spotted the crack in her reserved exterior. Mariana's mouth gaped open before she slammed it shut.

Le Regine was not immune to my power anymore. I wondered if anyone was. I didn't dare look at my mate to see if she'd been affected.

Later, I'll need you to explain what the hell just happened.

"What's this option?" I asked. Now that they had felt a fraction of what I could do, Mariana's judgment might have changed.

She leveled a serious stare at me. "You must be made king consort."

Not what I was expecting her to say.

"No!" Zina's composure dissolved entirely as she gawked at her sister.

Next to Thea, Aurelia started but quickly recovered and returned to standing by in silence.

"King what now?" Thea asked beside me.

Her sister-queens ignored her as they started to bicker.

"There has never been a male in such a position. We are celibate," Zina hissed. "That's not going to change because she let him sit on her throne."

"Times have changed. We must adapt—or what happened to Ginerva will happen to us," Mariana said coolly.

Was that a warning or a threat?

Both.

"This was her plan all along." Zina pointed at me.

"I didn't ask to be queen," Thea said calmly. "The crown chose me, and by choosing me, it chose Julian, too."

"We'll see about that." Zina bunched her skirt in her hands and swept away.

Thea sighed. "That went well."

"Zina needs time." Mariana lifted a corner of her mouth. It wasn't quite a smile, more tired reassurance.

"And everyone else?"

"That was quite a speech you gave." This time Mariana smiled when she saw Thea's surprised expression. "There's little that goes on at court that we are not aware of, even when we are absent."

Another threat.

I nodded slightly.

"Speaking of, I want to check on the situation," Aurelia announced. "If I may?"

I felt Thea's annoyance bubbling inside her like water on the verge of boiling, but she pasted a bland smile on her face. "You don't need my permission. You are free to do your job as you see fit."

"Then I will take my leave." Aurelia bowed slightly to each of us in turn. As she passed me, she leveled a meaningful look at me. She was passing the torch. I was in charge of Thea's safekeeping now.

"You really want to make Julian into king-whatever?" Thea asked when she was gone.

Mariana nodded. "Consort," she said. "It simply means you have equal social standing. It does not give him the same power you hold."

"But—"

"That's fine," I cut Thea off. "I'm not interested in holding political power. I only want to see my mate protected and respected."

"Then you must stay by her side." Her throat slid slightly, her eyes sweeping across the room like we were being watched. "This became a dangerous place after Ginerva's death. It's why we dismissed many of the guards and closed the court to visitors."

I thought of the assassinations and interrogations I had carried out under *Le Regine*'s orders. "It was a dangerous place before."

"Not for us," Mariana said to Thea in a lowered voice. "Ginerva trusted the wrong person, and it cost her everything. It cost the court. Be careful. You never know someone else's motives, even those closest to you." She glanced over to me.

"I trust my mate." Thea pressed closer to me, her stance possessive.

"And so we must learn to do the same." Mariana nodded once toward me in silent apology. "Zina will come around. In the meantime, we will reconsider who is allowed into the throne room."

"Good idea."

"And the rest of the time?" Thea prompted. "Do I stay in my quarters?"

Mariana blinked. "You are a queen. You do as you wish."

Why do I have a feeling that I get to do as I wish as long as I have a dozen bodyguards with me?

I'll handle it.

"In the meantime, we will begin planning your coronation." Mariana grinned, and I wondered if she suspected how Thea would react. "It will be an event to remember."

"This has all been an event to remember," Thea said. "What if we skip the coronation?"

"You'll sooner talk Sabine into letting you elope." Mariana's grin widened. "And to that end, I hear you are expected to participate in The Third Rite next month."

"About that—it seems silly considering that I'm one of you now and Julian is king consort."

Mariana's smile faded into a grim line. "Traditions remind us who we are. There will be a coronation, and you will attend The Third Rite. Then we can discuss the matter of a wedding." Thea stiffened beside me, but before she could speak, Mariana added, "As our new sister-queen and the first king consort, you will want to set an example."

"Naturally," I muttered.

Thea clamped her mouth shut, but I had a feeling her protests were far from over.

"Until then, enjoy the city. Get to know your new home."

"Thank you," I said, steering Thea toward the hall that led to our quarters.

As soon as we reached them, Thea exploded. "Naturally? Ceremonies and rites? What happened to a queen doing as she wishes?"

"I'm afraid that only extends to what she does privately. Ginerva felt the same as you."

"It must come with the crown." Thea plucked said object off her head and slammed it on a marble table before slumping against the wall. "I need to get out of here."

Confusion swirled through our bond, moving like a sandstorm until I didn't know which was mine and which was hers. Too much was happening too fast.

"Let's go out. See the city."

She arched an eyebrow. "Is that a good idea?"

I knew what she meant. The Mordicum was here, Willem, and a lot of bigoted vampires and familiars.

I reached for her. Sliding an arm around her waist, I drew her against me. "I'll keep you safe."

"You'll keep *us* safe." She ran a finger across my shirt, over the tattoo I now bore. Her lashes fluttered as she looked up at me, her heartbeat starting to pick up speed and taking my own with it. "I just want you. I can endure all of this if you're beside me."

"I'm not going anywhere," I vowed.

"What happened to going out?" she teased, some of the tension easing from her now that we were alone.

"I'm not going anywhere without you." I took her hand with my other one, allowing my magic to reach out to hers.

It answered. Dark and light sparked and swirled. Thea gasped as it danced along our skin, circling us both until our magic was twined around our bodies. Our magic was proof of what we already knew—that we were two halves of the same soul.

A deep peacefulness settled over me, the same calmness glowing on Thea's face.

"I'll go anywhere with you," she whispered, changing the promise into an invitation.

I leaned down to accept it with a kiss. "Then let me show you the world."

• • •

Venice was a city trapped in time. Without the noise of traffic, it felt like we were under a spell. It was like we had traveled into the past. But as we sailed out of the mouth of the *Rio Oscuro*, the illusion shattered. Antennas rose from every roof. When we reached the canals that fed into the city's *sestieri*, we spotted clusters of tourists with their cell phones. Another time that might have made me sad, today it was a blessed reminder that we weren't stuck in the sixteenth century.

On the opposite side of the gondola, Thea, bundled up in the warm winter clothes her enchanted wardrobe had provided, drank in Venice. I watched her, my oar slicing easily through the water. Her mind was silent. Still. But somehow I knew if I pushed myself below that calm surface, I would find it churning. Her hair blew around her face, across her distant gaze. A few strands clung to her cheeks, her lips, and I imagined pushing it away so I could kiss her and wake her from this dream.

A hint of salt laced the air, the sea tasting of tears as if it, too, was mourning the normal life we'd lost as soon as we stepped onto Venice's stone streets.

But the farther we sailed from the court, the easier it was to remember our lives before. The veil that covered the *Rio* and its magic fell away until I found it easier to breathe.

"Where are we going?" Thea asked as if she was also coming out of a daze.

"Somewhere special." Though the city held many of my darkest memories, I couldn't deny the beauty that bloomed here, either.

"Does somewhere special involve carbs? Because I'm starving." She pulled the blanket she had over her knees higher and grinned.

"That can be arranged." I angled the gondola toward an empty dock. "There used to be a place around here that served the best *Bolognese*."

"You still think it's here?" There was laughter in her voice.

I couldn't blame her for doubting it. She knew it had been centuries since I'd haunted these streets. "Some things change. Some things don't."

I finished tying up the gondola before offering her my hand.

"Ohhh, playing the mysterious vampire now?" She placed her palm in mine, and I helped her out of the boat.

"Maybe." I smirked as I climbed out beside her. "Playing the mysterious vampire seems to be working for me recently."

"Oh yeah?"

"It got me you, didn't it?"

She blushed, and I could smell her scent, sweet but rich and oozing with earthy magic. It was all I could do not to find the nearest quiet alley and feast on her.

Thea's eyes widened, as if glimpsing my thoughts. Her tongue flicked over her lower lip. "Hungry? Shall we get something to eat?"

"Famished." The suggestion was all I needed. Taking her hand, I led her to a side street occupied only by shadows.

"You've got me all alone. What are you going to do with me?"

"Where do I start?" I raked my eyes down her, allowing my dark magic free. Thea's throat slid as I opened my mouth to reveal my fangs.

"What big teeth you have," she said breathlessly.

Her words decided for me. I smirked as I hitched my thumbs under the waistband of her pants and yanked them down to her ankles.

CHAPTER FOURTEEN

Thea

My breath caught as the bitterly cold air hit my bare skin, but I didn't have long to think about how chilly it was when Julian dropped to his knees. I could only think about him, staring up at me with rapidly darkening eyes. His head dipped, and I moaned as his tongue traced a line between my thighs. Suddenly, I wasn't cold. I was on fire.

"Someone will see," I moaned, already ceding my argument.

"Good." He urged my legs farther apart and continued his oral exploration, sucking and kissing along my thighs and up toward more dangerous territory. Just before his mouth reached the throbbing pulse at my center, he whispered, "Do you want me to stop?"

"Please...*don't.*"

My words unleashed him, and his tongue swept up me. I cried out as his mouth closed over me. Julian growled his approval at my scent, at my taste. I felt his hunger growing inside me until I thrashed against the wall as much from his desire as my own.

I grabbed a fistful of his hair, afraid that my body might give out as pleasure built so rapidly inside me, and I found myself screaming his name.

Julian jerked back with a dark laugh, my hand still fisting his hair. "Louder," was all he said.

I obliged him. There was something terribly erotic about watching my powerful vampire mate on his knees with his face between my legs. It was that sight that pushed me over the edge.

Julian held one hand as I fell, never letting up, even as my other hand pulled his hair, my hips bucking against his face.

When I finally stilled, he gently pulled away. Standing, he ran his tongue over his lower lip, a look of purely male self-satisfaction on his face.

I shivered and reached a trembling hand toward the bulge in his pants, but he brushed it away. Leaning, he drew up my panties and jeans as snow flurries began to fall around us.

"I want more," I whimpered, still trying to reach for him. "I want you."

"Tempting." He brushed his mouth along my earlobe as he zipped me up. "But you're shivering, and I'd rather my mate doesn't freeze to death."

I stuck out a lower lip. "Raincheck?"

"Let's get you some carbs as requested," he murmured, tucking a strand of hair behind my ear, "and then I will show you all the secret places I know in Venice."

"Secret?" I repeated, hopefully.

His answering smile was dark and full of promise. "Come."

I raised an eyebrow, earning a wicked laugh that made my toes curl. Julian tucked me beside him as we left the alley and wandered down a deserted cobbled street. Within a few minutes, we found ourselves surrounded by tourists, all eagerly snapping photos and buying souvenirs. I couldn't help wondering if they'd heard me screaming a few minutes ago. A thrill shot through me as I considered that they might have.

Would you like an audience next time?

"What?" I blurted out, flushing as I realized he'd heard what I was thinking. "No. I just…"

"There's no reason to be ashamed." The arm around my shoulders tightened. "There is nothing more powerful than a woman taking her pleasure. Why wouldn't you want to show the world how powerful you are, my queen?"

"You're giving me some ideas for my next throne room appearance," I said drily. An unbidden image of Julian kneeling again, this time before my throne, appeared in my head. I caught my breath, feeling the familiar tick begin between my legs. It took me a second to realize he'd pictured it himself and allowed me a glimpse.

"You're incorrigible."

He paused, turning molten eyes on me. "Oh, no, when it comes to serving you, I promise I can be taught."

I was about to enquire about finding one of those secret places he'd spoken of when my stomach growled.

"You need to eat," he said, his playfulness vanishing as his tone became protective.

"If I become a vampire, will my stomach stop ruining the moment?" I asked.

Julian flinched, his mind going completely blank before he laughed. "Even vampires get hungry," he said, like nothing had happened.

But I'd caught the reaction. "What was that?"

He shrugged, but his mind stayed studiously blank.

"You're keeping your thoughts from me," I accused.

"It's nothing. Let's enjoy our day together."

But it wasn't nothing. I could feel it. "United front, right?"

Julian hesitated, looking me over before he finally sighed and led me toward an alley off St. Mark's Square. It was a quiet street, mostly owing to a lack of shops and the fact that it ended in a brick wall.

Before we reached it, he stopped and turned to face me.

"I can't make you a vampire, Thea."

I realized then that I'd been clinging to one final thread of hope that things could return to the way they were before Venice, and Julian had just snapped it in two.

"I think I knew that," I said, a tremor shaking my words.

"To be turned into a vampire, you must experience a physical death," he said slowly.

And if I died, he would die, too. A sob broke loose from me when I realized that not only had I taken away our chance at eternity together, but I'd also given him a death sentence. I clapped a hand over my mouth, beginning to shake.

"I would not wish to live a day without you." He gently pried my hand from my mouth.

"I killed you!" I blurted out.

"You gave me a second life." His hands pressed against my cheeks, drawing my tear-soaked eyes up to look into his. "Do you think I lived a day before I met you? A life with you is more than I ever expected. I would trade a hundred years for a single day with you. How lucky that I get to have you for decades, not days."

I tried to smile at him, tried to believe him, but the truth was that I thought we would have more time. That was supposed to be the perk of falling in love with a vampire.

"I'm sorry." I swiped at my tears. "I'm ruining our date."

"You aren't ruining anything," he promised. "But let's get you something to eat."

To my surprise, he guided us toward the dead end.

"I think we need to go the other way," I said.

"I told you I knew all the secret places in Venice," he reminded me. With a wink, he stepped right into the brick wall, dragging me with him. I stumbled over my own feet as we found ourselves in a small corridor. I turned to find the brick wall behind us.

"Magic," I grumbled under my breath as we entered a veiled part of the city.

"Let's see if Claudio is still making noodles." He tugged me toward the brightly colored shops on the hidden street. It was busy here, but not from tourists. Vampires and familiars wandered the street, many carrying baskets of groceries as though they were simply running errands.

Overhead, the sky was cloudy and full of flurries that never reached the ground. Like most of the other secret magical spots he'd taken me to, the weather here was kept free of the snow and wet cold the rest of Venice was currently experiencing.

It all looked far more normal than in Paris or Greece. There was a market selling produce and meat. The only sign that anything was amiss was a large freezer case stocked with blood bags. There was a costume shop on the far corner, filled with exquisite gowns and masks and finery. Although maybe it wasn't costumes so much as everyday clothes for Venice's older vampires. But I knew the moment we arrived at Claudio's.

The scent hit me first, so rich I tasted it rather than smelled it. Garlic and tomatoes and onions. My mouth watered, and my stomach growled as we stepped inside. Overhead, a bell rang out above the clattering dishes and lively conversation inside. The entire place was packed.

I shifted closer to Julian, hoping no one recognized us, but no one seemed to notice us.

That was until a burly vampire, clad in a stained white shirt and apron, barreled out of the kitchen straight for us.

"What are you doing in my restaurant?" he demanded.

My mouth fell open at the rude welcome.

"I can't believe this old shack still exists." Julian kicked a battered, old chair, which rocked precariously on its worn legs. "And that you haven't been run out of town yet, Claudio."

"Not all of us have so many enemies, *il flagello*," Claudio said darkly, but then his face brightened, his mouth widening into a grin. "I personally favor admirers."

"Some things never change," Julian said with a chuckle. I stared at both of them, trying to figure out what was going on. Before I could, Claudio turned his attention to me. His eyes lingered shamelessly as he surveyed me.

"And who have you brought to fall in love with me today?" Claudio asked.

"She has better taste than that." Julian scoffed. "Thea, meet Claudio Forner. Be careful. He thinks he's Casanova."

"I'm wounded." Claudio clutched his chest. Shaking his head, he looked to me with wide, dark eyes. "Julian is being a bastard. I taught Casanova everything he knew."

"And yet you're here." Julian's lips twitched.

"And he's dead." Claudio shrugged. "Clearly, I am the better male—and the better cook. There is something Julian isn't telling you." He waggled his brows at me. "He brought you here because he knows no woman can resist my food. He plans to seduce you."

I couldn't resist laughing at that. "Too late," I told him. "I'm thoroughly seduced."

"By him?" Claudio shot a disappointed look at his old friend. "I think you can do better."

"Stop flirting with my mate." Julian wrapped an arm around my waist.

"Mate?" Claudio exclaimed. He clapped a hand on Julian's shoulder. "It can't be?"

"It can." I held up my ring finger. "And fiancée."

"Your mother must be thrilled." Claudio yanked Julian into an embrace, taking me along for the ride.

"You must not know her," I said drily.

Claudio only laughed, urging us toward a table. "Sit and eat, my friends." He pointed at me. "And you can tell me the sad story of how you got stuck with this grumpy ass."

I was still laughing when he flew back to the kitchen to bring us food.

"Don't tell me you're falling for his charm," Julian said drily.

I smirked back at him. "Nope."

"Then what's so funny?" he asked suspiciously.

"I'm not the only one who thinks you're grumpy."

"Grumpy? I think you mean charming."

"Can't you be both?"

He shook his head, a grin playing on his sculpted lips. "You're still laughing at me."

I just laughed harder.

We both looked up expectantly as Claudio returned with a wooden tray filled with plates of steaming food.

"I took the liberty of ordering your favorite dishes," he said. "A little something to celebrate your engagement."

There was a handmade cheese ravioli in a mushroom sauce that made me feel as if I'd died and woken up in heaven. Next to it was warm bread and butter, finely shaved parmesan cheese, and a decanter of red wine. But the *fritto misto*, fresh seafood fried so delicately I could have cried as soon as I tasted it, was my favorite. It had been so long since I'd had anything remotely this delicious that I couldn't help but lose myself in the moment.

With a sigh, I closed my eyes and let the smell and taste take over.

But when I opened my eyes, I found everyone in the place watching me.

"I think our reputation precedes us." He flashed Claudio an apologetic smile.

"So it seems, *il flagello*." Claudio took the seat across from us, blocking our table with his large body—and giving us a little privacy.

"Great," I grumbled, feeling my appetite wane. "There goes our date."

"Do I want to know why everyone is watching you?" Claudio asked. "Have you returned to your old job, my friend?"

He said it without judgment, but his dark eyes strained as he looked at Julian for an answer.

How many people knew Julian had been an assassin? How many remembered?

"I used to come here when I couldn't sleep," Julian told me. "Even when he was closed, Claudio would come down to the kitchen and make me something. Then he would sit with me until I..."

I felt a flash of loathing, hatred directed inward, and I realized it came from Julian—from his memories. That was how he had felt when he'd come here.

"...didn't feel so lost," he finally finished. "And he never complained about sitting up with me, even when I wouldn't talk."

"Shame is a terrible companion," Claudio said wisely. "It's better to sit with a friend in silence than listen to the lies guilt tells you in solitude."

"You sound like you learned that through experience," I said softly.

He nodded. "I'm afraid I did." He forced a smile. "But now you have a beautiful fiancée to keep you company."

"Indeed. But I have not returned to my old position," Julian said, lowering his voice. "I'm sure there are rumors, though, about the court."

"Only recently. The court had fallen away. No one heard much from *Le Regine*," Claudio said, pouring more wine into my glass. "But now the gossip mill is turning. Most of the stories sound crazy."

"I guess you haven't been following it, then?"

"I followed it enough to learn your mother nearly took the throne." He cleared his throat. "How is Sabine coping?"

"How do you think?" Julian asked with a wry smile.

"And the creature who took the throne. They say she isn't a vampire," Claudio whispered, leaning closer. "That's going to cause trouble."

"She isn't a vampire," Julian said carefully.

Claudio's bushy eyebrows rose. "So you know more about this new queen?"

"I would say we're intimately acquainted." Julian tipped his head toward me.

I nearly choked on the bite of pasta I'd just taken.

"You are..." Claudio fell silently, staring at me as he processed what Julian meant.

"Thea," Julian confirmed.

Claudio blinked rapidly, shifting in his chair so much that its legs groaned under the weight. "Should I bow?"

"Please don't," I squeaked. Lifting my head to look over my shoulder, I breathed a sigh of relief that most of the patrons had returned to their meals. If he started bowing and scraping, that would all be over. "I just want a normal day."

"I'm afraid you won't find much normalcy behind the Venetian veils. The entire magical community is talking."

"I bet they are." I swallowed as I remembered my first day at court.

"Maybe this was a bad idea," Julian said uneasily. "I wanted you to have the best food in the city, but if you feel uncomfortable..."

I considered what he was saying. Maybe I shouldn't have ventured out of court so soon, but what was I supposed to do? Sit around and hope everything blew over? "No," I said firmly. "I'm not hiding behind bodyguards and gates forever. *Le Regine* only reign for part of the year, right? And even when I need to be here, I won't lock myself up. I'm in Venice. I want to see everything."

"I can see why you fell in love with her, *il flagello*." Claudio grinned widely at his old friend. "She is fearless."

I snorted. "Hardly. I'm afraid of everything."

"You're right," Julian agreed, taking my hand. "You are not fearless, but you are never afraid of facing your fears—and that is much smarter, my love."

Claudio sighed. "I suppose there is no sense in flirting with you," he said to me. "It's clear your heart is taken."

"It is." My gaze didn't leave Julian's. The entire city could be burning, and he was all I would see.

"You must come here anytime," Claudio said, placing a hand on Julian's shoulder. "I have a small room in the back where you can have privacy."

I didn't know if it was the way that Julian was squeezing my hand or Claudio's offer, but tears blurred my vision. "Thank you."

"Just remember you have a friend here," Claudio said, his tone darkening. "It will be important to know where you can find allies."

"Thank you," Julian said in a gruff voice that told me this visit was about more than the quality of Claudio's pasta.

We ate our food with Claudio acting as a barricade from curious stares. By the time we finished, I was uncomfortably full and totally content.

"I couldn't eat another bite." I patted my stomach. "Everything was amazing."

"I hope you will come again soon," Claudio said as we rose.

Julian pulled his billfold from his pocket, but Claudio waved it off.

"The meal is on me. How often do I get to celebrate my friend's happiness?" he asked.

"You never let me pay." A smile twitched on Julian's lips. "How are you going to keep the doors open if you let people eat free for centuries?"

"I overcharge the assholes," he promised.

Despite my full stomach, I felt lighter when we stepped out of the café. It was brisk but, thanks to the enchantment surrounding the street, not nearly as cold as the rest of Venice. We'd only made it a few steps when we came face to face with a group of vampires.

Julian took my hand, starting across the street, but they followed.

"You're a long way from your queen's feet, *il flagello*," the tallest of the three called.

"Or is this her?" another yelled. "I heard the new queen is a siren."

"You mean a slut," the third added.

"Don't," I said under my breath, but it was too late.

I blinked and found my hand empty and Julian pinning one of the vampires to the ground.

"There are three of us," his friend snarled as the other two began to circle.

"Not very good odds," Julian said through gritted teeth, "for you."

Out of the corner of my eye, I saw Claudio step out of his restaurant. I knew he would step in and help Julian, but that wasn't the problem. The tussle was already drawing a crowd.

I had to do something, but before I could think, the tall one swung at Julian, hitting him square in the jaw. Julian's head snapped to one side, and in an instant, he was on his feet, fangs bared, eyes black, and then he attacked.

CHAPTER FIFTEEN

Julian

No bloodshed.

I heard Thea's voice in my head, but it was overpowered by the rush of blood rage I felt. They'd threatened my mate and insulted their queen. It was my job to make them pay.

I barreled toward the tall vampire, catching him around the waist and sending us both flying into a nearby cart.

I was dimly aware of the owner's shrieks. Rolling my opponent onto his back, I released my rage fully. My fist collided with his cheek, and his head snapped to the side, smacking the cobblestones with a loud crunch.

I raised my hand to punch him again, but one of his friends caught my wrist and wrenched me off him.

"Oh good, you're going to join. I was worried this wouldn't be fair." I spit a mouthful of blood on the pavement.

We shifted back and forth, each of us trying to find the right moment to lunge.

"You should be ashamed of consorting with that slut," the vampire facing me snarled.

"Didn't your mother teach you any manners?" I growled, my fingernails cutting into the flesh of my palms as I tightened my fists.

"Didn't your mother teach you to take out the garbage instead of fuck it?"

Something inside me snapped, and I flew at him. Dark magic gripped me as I grabbed hold of him and threw him against a nearby building. Plaster crumbled around him as he fell to the ground, but he shook it off and leaped back up.

"She is your queen," I said loudly enough for everyone to hear. "For insulting her, I should kill you. But since she's my mate, you're going to suffer first."

His answering smirk was cold, and as he moved, his glove shifted to reveal a single red slash tattooed on his skin.

Mordicum.

Were they following us?

It was exactly what I was wondering, but it could simply be a case of being in the wrong place at the wrong time.

I should knock him unconscious and take him into custody, send a clear message that any other attacks on Thea or *Le Regine* wouldn't be tolerated.

But killing him would probably send that message, too.

He flew at me, which was exactly what I wanted. He was a young vampire. Given that he was probably turned, he didn't have the centuries or the ancient blood to back him up in a fight against a pureblood. Which was why trying to attack me first was a very stupid move.

My arm hooked around his throat as he passed. Twisting my body, I brought him to his knees. I grabbed hold of his head. One twist and his head would pop right off. But the darkness inside me bayed for blood at the slight to my mate. Taking his head would be too easy. I gave into it, feeling it seep into my palms. I'd been with Thea, so my hands were bare and there was nothing to stifle that terrible power. It rushed through me, and I hated how I loved its raw cruelty. The vampire writhed against my grip, choking as I drained him with my touch. I felt the blood drying in his veins as his skin turned ashen, each ounce of life I stole fueling the horrible rage coursing inside me.

His friends were on their feet, fists raised, but they didn't budge.

They knew I could kill him before they moved an inch.

"Stop."

I paused at the command in Thea's voice. So did the other two vampires. But I didn't let go. The darkness inside me ebbed, though. I heard Thea's light footfall behind me, and a moment later, she was at my side.

"This fight ends now. You three, go home." She pointed at the troublemakers.

More like go back to wherever they'd slithered from.

"We don't take orders from you," one spat.

My magic swelled, and Thea placed a single hand over mine. But before it could soothe me, the air rippled, and I felt the darkness inside me stirring, as if responding to the magic brewing in the wind. But it didn't spill from me.

It found her.

It swirled around Thea, as though she had called it. Dark magic lifted her hair from her shoulders so that it flowed around her like a veil of fire. Her green eyes glittered with unrestrained power.

"Do I need to repeat myself?" she asked.

The vampire hesitated before he squared his shoulders. "You can go and—"

He slammed to his knees, his words cut off by the sound of his bones cracking on the stones, followed by a grisly snap.

Turning, I found Thea staring at the lifeless vampire—at what she'd done.

I glanced at the other vampire, who looked as shocked as I felt.

"Go back to your people and take him with you. When he wakes up, he can send his apologies to my court."

She turned and nodded at me. Reluctantly, I let my captive go. His skin was already returning to its normal pallor, but he was shaken. He hurried to his friend. They didn't bother conferring with each other before they grabbed their friend and took off.

Thea turned to me, and her gaze met mine. "Are you hurt?"

Only my pride. I shook my head, well aware that we had an audience.

Thea cast a look around her, and a few people shrank back as though they were afraid of her. Claudio simply stared from the steps of his café with bland amusement.

"If anyone else needs to talk to me, they can come to court for an audience," she announced coolly. "Are we clear?"

A few people nodded. More bowed their heads in respect. Thea looked away from the crowd, and everyone scattered, eager to get away from the danger. She hadn't hurt the vampire. Not really. He would recover. But healing from a mortal wound was a bitch, and he would have a lingering headache to remind him of how badly he'd messed up.

I swept a concerned look down Thea. No one had touched her. There was hardly a hair out of place. The unearthly magic was that she'd unleashed had settled. Hints of it glowed in her eyes and flickered as the sunlight caught her hair.

Her expression remained composed and neutral as she carefully avoided looking at the street around her.

Get me out of here.

Pain laced her words, and I inhaled sharply. Nodding goodbye to Claudio, I offered her my arm. She took it smoothly, and I guided her down the street.

Venice's winter chill and the sounds of tourists hit us as soon as we stepped beyond the magical veil.

We walked at a swift clip, not slowing until we found ourselves swallowed into the crowds of St. Mark's Square.

Near the basilica, I paused and pulled her into my arms. Thea's body trembled, and I knew it had nothing to do with the cold.

"Are you okay?" I buried my face in her hair.

"I don't know," she admitted in a shaky voice. "I killed him. I didn't even think about it. I just…"

"He's not dead," I reminded her gently. "That bastard will wake up with a headache and a newfound sense of respect."

She didn't smile at the joke. "I can't believe I did that." Her lower lip trembled as she cast her eyes to the stone street. "Is it happening? Am I becoming a monster?"

"No," I said more sharply than I meant to. I tipped her face up. "You acted out of instinct to protect yourself. There is no shame in that."

"I acted to protect you," she whispered, then bit her lip. "Is it wrong that it's easier if I think of it that way?"

There was nothing I wouldn't do to keep Thea safe. No line I wouldn't cross. I shook my head. "It's not, and he had it coming. He started the fight. You finished it. Don't blame yourself." But I knew she would. She'd adjusted too many parts of her new world, but I doubted she would ever get used to the violence. "I should have finished them."

I stroked my palm down her back. "Do you want to go back to the court?"

Thea pulled back, some of the fire she'd shown moments ago blazing in her eyes. "No. You promised to show me secret Venice, right?"

"I did." I smiled.

"Then let's go, old man."

I knew she was forcing herself to sound saucy, to pretend like her guts weren't twisted inside her and she wasn't checking over her shoulder every few seconds. But while I felt her paranoia, I also felt her determination, and I wouldn't take that from her.

"This way."

"Where are we going?" she asked as we made our way down a side street, moving away from the crowds.

"It's a surprise." I'd practiced keeping my mind blank so I wouldn't ruin it. If she noticed, she didn't say anything. Instead, she gripped my hand tightly.

We stopped on the *Ponte de Piscina* bridge to admire the saltwater-bleached buildings with their colorful, peeling shutters and empty flower boxes. Water lapped against the ancient brick as a gondola sailed smoothly beneath us.

"This place is full of magic," Thea said with a sigh, resting her head on my shoulder.

I knew she didn't mean real magic, even if the city was full of it.

There was something about Venice that stirred the soul. When I'd been sent here to serve the queens, I'd found myself falling in love with the city even though I hated what it demanded of me. Now I loved and hated it for entirely different reasons.

Unlike so many cities in the world, it had hardly been touched over the years. It still felt like the city I'd left centuries ago, but it was also just as dangerous as it had been then. How many assassination attempts on the queens had I thwarted? My time serving them had prepared me for this in a way.

I knew Venice. It was a living, breathing part of me. That knowledge might help me keep Thea safe, but was it enough? In the past, I'd been acting out of duty. Now I had something much dearer to protect and more to lose if I failed.

"Come on." I tugged Thea's hand. "We're close now."

We turned the corner, passing a bistro closed for the season, and found a large building with columns that stretched to the sky from its marble steps.

"I think this is it," I told her.

"Think?" she repeated. "I thought you were taking me to all of your old haunts."

"I am," I said, wrapping my arms around her to steal a kiss. "But a lot of my old haunts have burned down over the years."

"Accidentally?" She arched an eyebrow.

"What do you think?" I said with a laugh. "Be glad we're not reliant on candles anymore."

"So you've never been here?"

"Not in its current incarnation, but it used to be the home of one of my favorite courtesans."

"You're taking me to an old girlfriend's house?" she asked.

"Never. She was my friend. Nothing more." I leaned down to kiss her forehead. "You're becoming quite jealous, my queen."

"I'm still processing that I'm sleeping in Ginerva's old bed that you two…" She thrust her index finger between the circled fingers of the opposite hand.

I burst out laughing. "I assume that symbolizes intercourse."

"*Intercourse*?" She shook her head. "Sometimes I forget what an old man you are."

My laughter fell into a smile. Tipping her chin up with my index finger, I looked into her eyes. "Do you mind it that much? My past?"

"No," she said quickly. "Not really, but lately, I feel like your past is catching up with us both. It's just a lot to process."

"Still, I wish you were my only lover," I told her truthfully.

"Nine hundred years with no nookie? I'm glad you didn't wait around."

I needed her to know I wasn't exaggerating. "Would it help to know that everything before I met you is a bit foggy?" I kissed her. "My life began the day we met."

"No, it didn't, but I don't mind." She grinned up at me. "Although maybe you could forget Ginerva."

"Done."

"So why here?" she asked.

"Some of the most famous operas and symphonies in the world premiered here. I thought you might miss…"

Judging by the way she swallowed, I was right. She missed the cello. Music. Performing.

"It was built after you left?" she asked as we climbed the steps.

"Yes, and it's burned down twice," I told her as I paid for our admission, adding a hefty donation to the sum.

The bribe did the trick, and a few minutes later, we were being swept past the velvet ropes where the tour ended into the bowels of the theater. Thanks to the donation, I hardly had to compel our eager tour guide to give us some privacy.

I studied Thea as she walked amongst the ropes and pulleys that lifted and lowered curtains and scenery. As she stepped onto the stage, calm overtook her body.

"I always feel at home here," she told me when I joined her.

"You miss performing?"

"Not exactly." She chewed on her lower lip. "Playing mostly, but there is something about playing for people that's different. I feel like I'm keeping the music alive. It feels selfish when I play for myself. Music is a gift. I play to give it to other people."

"You are a siren," I murmured.

"So it's not a gift so much as luring unsuspecting males to their deaths, right?" she asked drily, looking at me out of the corner of her eye. "I lured you to yours."

Her words were sharp as a knife plunged straight into my heart. "You don't really believe that."

"I don't know what to believe," she admitted, keeping too much distance between us.

I frowned and caught her hand. "We've been over this. I wouldn't change anything."

She swallowed, as if she didn't trust herself to speak.

Our date was on life support, and we both knew it. It was too hard to pretend that nothing was wrong. Too hard to pretend we hadn't been cornered by bigoted vampires. Too hard to forget that we had to return to court tonight and then figure out what was really going on behind the throne.

We needed a distraction.

"Do you remember the first time I took you to the opera?"

Thea bit her lower lip, color blooming on her cheeks as she recalled the night at the Paris Opera.

"I couldn't control myself," I murmured, drawing her to me.

"I remember," she whispered.

The memory flashed through my mind. One look at Thea told me she was recalling it, too. It was the first night I'd fed from her. Her taste was seared into my memory—sweet and rich and utterly irresistible.

She tugged away. "What about you?" she asked. "Have you ever played on stage?"

"I was hoping you'd forgotten that," I admitted.

"I can't believe you never told me you played the cello." Her eyes twinkled despite the accusation in her voice. "Or that you had a Stradivarius."

"I believe that belongs to you now."

"I nearly forgot, with...everything."

"It's being delivered to the court. I brought it with me to Venice.

I thought it might score me some brownie points." I forced myself to grin, trying my best to ignore what had happened when I arrived in the city.

"Will you play for me?" she asked.

Pulling her farther into the shadows, I leaned down and brushed a kiss over her lips. Her eyes burned as I stared into them.

"Why wait?"

Thea blinked, confused by my question, and I took the opportunity to spin her around. My arms coiled around her, tucking her body against mine. Sliding my hand along her stomach, I stroked my thumb under the waistband of her jeans.

"You are my favorite instrument," I told her in a low voice as my hand dipped lower.

Thea released a breathy moan, its sound rocketing straight to my balls. I bit back a groan, already hard and ready.

"I need you," I whispered, bending over her, nosing my way to her neck. Her blood pulsed beneath her pale skin. Venom welled in my mouth as I breathed in her sweet jasmine scent.

"I need you, too," she admitted, twisting her neck to offer her lips.

Our mouths collided, my hand slipping down her pants until my fingers found wet heat. "Fuck," I growled. "You're soaked."

She gasped as I dragged my index finger along her wetness before settling over the point of her need. Then I began to play. My fingertips plucked and strummed, her noises forming a beautiful melody, each note of pleasure rising but never bursting into a crescendo. Soon she was gasping and pleading, but I could think of nothing but erasing all thoughts except those of me and my fingers. Of us. Of our song.

"Tell me what you want," I told her. Leaning down, I scraped my fangs down her neck. "And don't forget to ask nicely."

"Julian." She stretched my name across several syllables, her body tightly wound. "Please. I want you."

"How do you want me?" I brushed my thumb down her swollen seam.

She moaned, the sound so guttural, so primal, that I nearly came. "Inside me. Please. I want you inside me."

"Good girl." I knew what she was asking for, but I wasn't ready to stop my performance. Bringing my mouth to the curve of her neck, I slowly sank my fangs into her skin, right over the scar I'd left there.

Thea cried out, her knees buckling, but I held her upright as I slowly feasted. There was nothing like the taste of my mate's blood, especially with pleasure coursing through her.

"More," she begged, and I drew away only to lift her into my arms.

I carried her a few steps to where the stage curtain hung open. Our mouths collided, tongues tangling together, and we nearly crashed into a wall. Thea's hand shot out, grabbing hold of the curtain's thick rope as I paused long enough to wrench her jeans to her ankles. I unzipped my fly, not bothering with more than freeing my cock before I lifted her and thrust inside her with one smooth stroke.

"Take me," she begged. "Take all of me. Forever."

Her body clenched around me as I claimed her. Thea clawed at my back before yanking on the rope until the curtain began to move. Its thick velvet rustled along the stage floor as I thrust again, harder, harder, until I was coming inside her, our song building to a peak that burst as the curtain fell on our performance.

She drooped in my arms, blood welling from the puncture wound on her neck.

"I want another taste," I whispered, bringing my lips to the wound.

She cried out as my fangs pierced her. Her oxygen-soaked blood tasted of her climax, and I found myself hard again.

Thea's body tensed as I began to rock inside her, her breathing ragged, her hands clawing at the velvet as she swelled with an encore. This time, I held her as the music faded slowly, drawing out each sweet note.

When we finally managed to untangle ourselves, her lips were swollen, and her skin glowed in an undeniably supernatural way.

"Everyone is going to know what we did," she said as she smoothed her clothing into place.

"Good." I dropped my arm around her shoulder and smirked at her.

"You're shameless." She bit back a grin.

"This stage just saw one of its greatest performances ever."

"Greatest ever, huh?" she teased.

"Do you need an encore?" I arched a brow, ready to take her back and torture her until she admitted I was right.

"No!" She held her hands up in surrender. "I won't be able to walk out of here."

I burst out laughing. "Now I have a new goal."

She rolled her eyes.

We continued our tour, pausing to explore each other a few more times. When we finally left the theater, night had fallen.

Venice cloaked in inky blackness was a different world. We navigated its dark corridors, hand in hand, making plans we could only hope to keep. Neither of us spoke of the obligations in front of us or the trials ahead. But even though we'd chased our troubles away for the time being, I knew they would be waiting for us in the morning.

"Maybe we should get a hotel," I said as we passed one of the oldest and grandest in the city.

"They'll send out a search party. My new bodyguard seems a bit overprotective."

"She knows I'm with you." But even I doubted that would mean much.

"I don't want it to end, either," she whispered, her confession disappearing into the night. "Can't we just run away?"

I stopped and turned to her. "Say the word."

"You don't mean that." She chewed on her lip.

Excitement rushed through me before I clamped down on it. But it was her excitement. Not my own. She wanted to leave.

It was absolutely insane, but I found myself considering it. We were already on borrowed time. If Thea was cursed with a mortal lifespan, every moment counted. Did we really want to spend it stuck at court?

As much as I wanted to whisk her away, I couldn't do it. Not before I made sure she understood the consequences. Not just for us. But for every magical thing on the planet. Had she done enough to ensure the source would thrive? Magic was awake, but could it survive without her?

"Thea, there's something you should know." I took a deep breath, prepared to tell her everything—to make sure she really understood the choice we were making.

Her eyes grew wide, and for a moment, I thought she'd heard my thoughts until I realized she was looking over my shoulder into the dark beyond. "Thea, what is it?"

The blood drained from her face as she continued to stare. "It's...it's my mother."

CHAPTER SIXTEEN

Lysander

Thankfully, someone had thought to stock the bar, replacing the dreadful wine with the hard stuff. I didn't know if it was magic or if some servant had noticed. Bottles of it lined the bar, ready to be opened. After today, I needed a drink. Not just because of the brawl but because I'd made an important decision.

One I was certain I'd regret.

"Are you sure?" Sebastian asked, twisting open a new bottle of Scotch. "You really want to stick around?"

I couldn't explain it. This morning I'd been ready to get the hell out of here on the first boat. Now?

"Julian is in over his head," I said quietly. "They both are." I kept our father's request to myself. It wasn't that I didn't trust Sebastian, but somehow I knew that the fewer people who knew what I was up to, the better.

"Sabine is going to be pissed." He shook his head as he poured me a drink. Then he took a swig directly from the bottle. "She wants to make it clear that the family sides with her."

"When isn't she pissed?" I asked sourly.

"You really think you need to stick around, and what? Play bodyguard? They have guards everywhere. Thea even has that chick—"

"I wouldn't call Aurelia a chick unless you want to lose a hand," I stopped him.

"That might be the first intelligent thing either of you has said since we met," a dry voice interrupted us.

"Speak of the devil," Sebastian muttered. He spun on his high-top stool and shot me a knowing grin. "I was just leaving."

That stopped her in her tracks. Her eyes shifted to me. "And you?"

"I'm sticking around," I said, enjoying the fear that flashed over her face.

"We won't be far." Sebastian lounged against the bar top. "We have to come back for The Rites in a few weeks."

I didn't think I imagined the subtle warning in his words. He tilted his head, offering me a look that said, *Don't get comfortable.*

"Thank the Gods," Aurelia said, rolling her eyes. "What would we do without you?"

"I find it always better to ask what to do with me. I have a few ideas if you need inspiration." He licked his lower lip in invitation.

A growl rose in my throat, but I swallowed it back. I wasn't getting in the middle of their flirting. She could handle herself.

Aurelia turned away from him without another word, but she placed her hand on her hip, right on her sword's hilt.

"I'll take that as a raincheck." Sebastian held up his hands and backed toward the day.

"Take it as a no," she said pointedly.

My brother was laughing as he left, and I wondered if he'd ever actually felt the pain of rejection. Or if the sheer number of times he'd been rejected had numbed him to it entirely.

When he was gone, Aurelia crossed to the bar.

She hadn't bothered to change after today's altercation. Her hair was still braided, wisps of it loosened from fighting. I could smell blood on her clothes, especially her cloak. "Is that a sword under your cloak or—"

"Do not finish that sentence," she cut me off.

I propped my arm on the bar and smirked at her. "Or you'll

have to kill me?"

"Are all of your jokes as old as you?" she asked with mocking sweetness.

Why was I even bothering?

As if to answer me, Aurelia swept off her cloak, revealing an almost normal outfit under it. Yes, there was still a sword strapped to her hip, but the rest was black leather that fit her tightly enough to leave little to the imagination.

And what little it left, I found myself imagining *vividly*. Forget Julian and his mate. Forget some broken curse and an old weapon. *This* was why I was bothering. Not that I would admit that to her.

She hated me. Despite the attraction I felt toward her, as far as I was concerned, the feeling was mutual. But some of the best sex of my life was with people who fell firmly into the category of enemy.

She sighed, throwing the cloak over the back of the stool. "Are you just going to stare at me? Or are you going to offer me a drink?"

"I wasn't sure if you were allowed," I told her. Picking up the bottle of Scotch, I poured another round into my glass and passed it to her.

"Do I look like the type to ask permission?" She downed her drink in one go.

No, she didn't. She looked like the type who took what she wanted without worrying about what anyone thought. The type who didn't hesitate when violence broke out. It might be attractive if she didn't spew venom every time we spoke.

"Tell me something, Lysander," she said, refilling her glass. She pinned a hard glare on me as she relaxed into her seat. "Do you stare at everyone? Or am I just lucky?"

"I'm trying to figure you out," I admitted. Settling back onto my stool, I grinned at her. "What's your excuse?"

Her glass paused near her lips. "My excuse?"

"For following me around? Stalking me?" My smile widened as her nostrils flared. "Is it my good looks or my charm?"

"I haven't noticed a surplus of either quality." She threw back her drink and slammed the glass so hard on the counter that it cracked.

I'd gotten under her skin. Did that make us even for her stripping my ability to speak? I wasn't sure, but I certainly enjoyed watching her squirm.

She stood to leave, but I grabbed her arm. Even through the leather of my glove, I felt her magic spark at my touch. It thrummed through her so strongly I swore I could hear it.

"Truce?" I offered, quickly pinning on, "Only for today, of course."

"Are we at war?"

"You rendered me mute the last time we were alone. I wouldn't call that friendly," I said drily.

"You were getting *too* friendly," she informed me, tugging her arm free, but for a moment, I swore she hesitated. "It's been a while since I had to fend off a vampire at court."

"Fend off?" I repeated.

"It's why we wear masks." Her throat slid. "I shouldn't have shown you my face."

Without thinking, I whispered, "I'm glad you did."

"It's considered a breach of my oath, even if Thea told me to stop wearing the fucking thing." She shrugged as she spoke. "She's right, though. It's pointless. I'm the last of my kind. Or I was. Now that the queens have a full court, I'm sure they will demand more of us."

"Us?"

"*Le Vergini*." She flushed a little, her eyes finding the floor.

It was so out of character for what I'd come to expect from her that it took me a second to process what she'd said. It hit me like a blow to the stomach.

A handmaiden served for life. Some came willingly. Others were called for or sent by their families. They all arrived to court at a young age. In the past, babies had even been sent at birth. Most of the women who served in the royal guard had known little to no life outside the court. They all pledged their total loyalty to the *Le Regine*—along with a vow of chastity.

"I didn't realize, Aurelia," I said carefully. Clearly, she took that vow of chastity seriously.

"That's why you're still alive—and it's Lia," she said with a small smile. It fell from her lips quickly.

"Lia." I savored the small concession. "If I had known—"

"If you had known, you would have treated me like every other vampire that's come to this court for the last decade." She tossed her braid over her shoulder, lifting her chin. The flush was gone, and if she was embarrassed by this revelation, she was doing a damn good job of hiding it. "I would either be a conquest or an object of pity. And I am fucking sick of it, so don't go all gooey on me now."

I blinked in surprise but finally managed to nod. "So enemies, then?"

"I prefer it to your pity."

I held out my hand. "War?"

Her lips twitched as she took it. "War," she agreed.

It would be better this way. If I was going to stick around and keep an eye on Julian, I didn't need any distractions.

Especially not in the form of a gorgeous, deadly bodyguard trained to view my dick as a breach of contract.

Hating each other would be easier. But as she drew her hand from mine, our fingers lingered before breaking apart.

"Good evening," I said around the lump in my throat.

Good evening? Was I her enemy or what?

Lia snorted, her dark eyes sparkling with amusement as she leaned down. Her face was a fraction of an inch from mine, close enough that I smelled the liquor on her breath—close enough that I considered how her lips might taste. "We're enemies, Lysander." Her breathless voice caught the attention of my dick. "Don't get soft on me."

That was not going to be a problem. I let my mouth curve into the smile that had dropped plenty of panties over the centuries. "Fine. Go to hell."

"I'll see you there," she murmured. An instant later, she was sashaying out of the room, cloak over her shoulder.

I stared after her, rock hard, wondering what the hell I'd just done.

CHAPTER SEVENTEEN

Thea

I'd dreamed about this moment. At night. While awake. Sometimes it was a nightmare that woke me. Other times, it felt more like a wish. But nothing could have prepared me for what I felt when I saw my mother.

Nothing.

Dressed in all black, she nearly blended in with the night. Any sign of illness was gone. No gaunt cheeks or sallow skin. She showed no sign of weakness. The *piazzo* was quiet, too far from the popular tourist areas for anyone to bother on a night this cold. For a moment, I thought I might be dreaming, but then snowflakes began to fall.

I was numb. In shock. The world around me went gray, dull as if all the color had been sucked away. Not by the night but by the surprise. My tongue couldn't form words. My mouth couldn't form words. My mind couldn't form words. I couldn't think.

But Julian could.

Instantly, he was between us, his back to me as he faced her. Snow fell on his rigid shoulders and melted. His body remained tight, alert, and I felt the rush of adrenaline that swept through him—swept through us. He saw her as a threat. I reached for his arm, but he didn't budge.

"Thea." My mother's voice rang across the pavilion. There was no one else around. No one else to catch the lilting music in her words. No one else to see what, even in the bleached world surrounding us, was so painfully clear. Because the only color here was *her*. Red hair the color of flames, glowing moonstone skin, and beauty that radiated in the dark. She was stunning and vital and more alive than I'd ever seen her. Her glamour was entirely gone, and with it, any lingering doubt I'd clung to since she'd vanished.

She was a siren.

"Kelly," Julian greeted her in a clipped tone when I failed.

She cast a sharp look at my mate as she pulled the lapels of her wool coat against the winter wind. For a moment, none of us moved. Then, finally, she did.

It wasn't the tearful reunion I'd once pictured. She didn't throw her arms around me. She came close enough to speak but kept her distance.

That might have something to do with the brooding six feet of vampire in front of me.

My mother looked me up and down, studying me with glittering interest that sent a chill through me. But I straightened, remembering the mate at my side and the crown that waited for me, even as I wondered what she saw. If I looked as different to her now as she did to me. And even with her beauty fully revealed, everything about her was sharper than before. Her stare sliced through me as her eyebrows knit together at what she found.

Her chin lifted, regal and poised, and she glared at Julian. "So you mated with my daughter despite vampire law."

My jaw unhinged, and it took effort to close it.

"Yes," he said coolly. "We are mated and engaged to be married."

Something sparked in her eyes, but her tone was measured when she spoke. "I assume you've completed The Rites."

"No." I finally found my voice. Moving to Julian's side, I met her eyes. "We will, though."

Her answering snort made me bristle.

Who was this stranger? She looked like my mother, but all the warmth had left her. All the love she'd shown me through the years seemed to be gone.

"Good luck," she said flatly.

My temper flared, melting the numbness that had frozen me earlier. "We will complete The Rites and be married and have children and anything else we choose, regardless of what you or the Vampire Council think."

"At least they haven't broken you. Although there are rumors… disturbing rumors."

I'd had enough of this strange reunion. She didn't get to control the conversation. Not while I was burning with questions, questions I'd been asking myself for months. "Where have you been?" I blurted out. "We looked everywhere for you." Pain split my words. Julian's hand on my back grounded me, but my voice cracked again anyway. "Why didn't you tell us you were alive?"

I heard her breath catch before she spoke. Light from a nearby streetlamp caught her eyes, and I saw a flash of sadness lurking there, as if she was just as haunted as me.

"When you left me, I was forced to come here."

"By whom?" I demanded.

Easy, my love. Hear her out.

I shot a glare at my mate.

"I was dying. I had no choice."

I closed my eyes and tried to focus on what she was telling me. "Who made you come?"

"No one," she said, shaking her head. "I needed to heal. I called on unnatural magic to glamour you. My body couldn't handle that power. That is why I was sick. I needed our magic to heal, and our magic is strongest here, *especially* now." She raised her eyebrows in silent question, giving me a glimpse of the woman who'd raised me. "There are rumors that you…"

I remained silent, trying to process what she was telling me. "No one made you come here?"

"No," she said quietly. "I came because I knew that only being near the *Rio Oscuro* would help me."

It felt as though I was breaking in two. Half of me wanted to collapse with relief. She wasn't dying. But the other half felt like screaming.

She knew about the *Rio Oscuro* and vampires and magic and... everything.

Everything. She knew *everything*.

I should have expected that, but I'd been clinging to the hope that it was all a misunderstanding, that she hadn't been keeping secrets for my entire life.

Julian pressed closer to my side. I knew he could hear my thoughts. I was practically screaming, and if he had thoughts of his own, mine were drowning his out. But his presence soothed me.

"I know what you're thinking," she continued. "You want to know why I kept this from you."

I swallowed, a lump sticking in my throat. "For starters."

"That is a long story, and Venice is always listening," she said.

"Unfortunately, your mother is right, my love," Julian spoke gently, his fingers twining with mine. "We should find somewhere more private."

I squeezed his hand. I was not going to break, even though I might have cracked a bit. "We can return to Court."

"So it is true, then? You have taken the celestial throne?"

I almost didn't answer. Why should she get answer after answer when she'd kept so many secrets from me? "Yes. It was the only way."

"What do you mean?" Her face softened with worry.

I'm not telling her.

Julian nodded, knowing exactly what I meant.

She hadn't earned the truth. Not after everything she'd done. I wouldn't tell her about our death and resurrection. I wouldn't soothe her horror or tell her it would all work out. "You've been following all the gossip." I shrugged. "You probably already know."

"Thea, I—"

"No," I cut her off. "I've given you enough answers. You

disappeared!" I was practically shouting now, but I didn't care. "You just vanished without a word."

"You chose him." Disgust twisted her lovely face.

"I chose my heart, and I will never apologize for choosing love." I gripped Julian's hand more tightly. "And until you treat my mate with respect, we have nothing else to say to each other."

Thea...

I ignored his silent plea.

"You have no idea what his kind is capable of—"

"I know about Willem," I stopped her.

She fell silent, her face plummeting. Evening shadows played across her skin and caught her eyes, illuminating the battle being waged inside her mind. "There is more to fear from vampires than your father."

I'd known it was the truth, but hearing her confirm that such a monster was my father rocked me. It felt as if the ground was being ripped out from under my feet. I was falling, unable to deny the truth.

"Then I'm a succubus," I said numbly.

"No." She seized my hand. In the background, I heard Julian growl, but she didn't let me go. "No, you aren't. Not yet. But there isn't much time."

"Take your hands off her," he demanded in a tone that brooked no argument.

She released me. "You have to come with me. Just you."

"I'm not going anywhere with you." I stepped to Julian's side. "Not without answers and not without Julian."

"You have to," she pleaded. It was snowing harder now, coming down in thick, wet flakes that lingered on my cheeks before melting like tears. "You need to know the truth. I protected you for years. You owe me this."

"Owe you?" I repeated. "I didn't ask you to glamour me. I didn't ask you to hide me. Do you think I wanted my mother to be sick? I've spent most of my adult life thinking you were dying."

"I'm not, and I won't apologize for hiding you. I did what I thought was best."

"So it's all okay because you followed your maternal instinct?"

"I didn't say that, but if you come with me, I will explain."

"Not without my mate," I said firmly. "He's helped me find answers while you hid them from me."

She considered a moment, her face a hard mask and her mouth set in a grim line. The wind picked up, tugging at her hair, fluttering around her stony features. Finally, she leaned closer. Her eyes narrowed, and her nostrils flared with each shallow breath. Then she nodded. "Fine."

CHAPTER EIGHTEEN

Julian

I wasn't sure what I'd expected, but this wasn't it.

Tucked into a quiet corner of the *Cannaregio* district sat an unassuming *palazzo*—by Venetian standards, at least. Its windows were arched in the typical fashion, but the rest of its lines were simple, harshly so, as if it didn't want to draw unwanted attention, unlike the flashier palaces throughout the city.

The snow was falling harder, clumping together mid-air and building up on the streets. Next to me, Thea shivered and brushed the melted remains from her cheeks.

I don't like this.

I know.

That was apparently the end of the discussion.

Kelly approached the austere building and pulled out a set of keys. Her fingers trembled from the cold as she moved to unlock the door. "Shit," she said as her gloved hands fumbled, dropping the keys.

"Let me." Thea pulled away and bent to pick them up, but when she held them out to Kelly, her mother hesitated.

"You don't wear gloves," she said, taking them carefully.

A muscle tensed in my mate's jaw. "Are you afraid I'll steal your magic, Mom?"

"No," she replied quickly as the door's ancient lock opened. "Will you at court?"

"Yes, but I don't wear them around Julian."

Kelly glanced at me, and I knew she was wondering if that was a wise choice.

"I don't wear them, either, if you're wondering," I offered. "Not with Thea. There are no secrets between us."

"So you share magic." She spoke as if this was fact, but I caught the edge of question in her words.

Shit. Thea's voice was panicked in my head. *She doesn't know about us...dying. Do I tell her?*

Up to you. I moved closer to her, placing my hand on the small of her back.

There was no way she was going to allow me to go inside first, but there was no way she was going in without me right behind her.

"We do share magic," Thea murmured as we stepped inside to a dark interior.

Kelly's gaze flicked to me. "That's dangerous."

She could think what she wanted. I certainly wasn't going to be the one to sway her. And I had more important concerns—like whether or not we were walking into a trap.

"You aren't," Kelly scoffed, shrugging off her jacket.

She headed toward the quiet, unlit hearth, but I simply stared after her. Thea started to follow, pausing when I didn't come with her.

"What is it?" Thea whispered. She tugged at my hand to draw me out of my stupor.

She can hear my thoughts.

What?

It makes sense—

Before I could finish that thought, Thea whipped around, planting her hands on her hips. "Are you reading his mind?"

Kelly didn't look up from her work. She lit a match and carefully set a bundle of kindling on fire under a stack of logs. "I can only hear what he thinks of me." She stood and brushed her hands on her pants. "The siren's curse."

I think I'm going to vomit.

Thea did look rather green, in fact. I pulled her to me, wrapping my arms around her, both to warm her in the still-cold house and to protect her.

"I assume you can hear them." Kelly cast a pointed look at her daughter.

Thea nodded, fumbling a little as she clarified, "We can hear each other now. At first, I could only hear his thoughts."

"It must be the mating bond." Kelly was moving again. We tracked behind her, finding ourselves in the kitchen.

Thea didn't speak up. She didn't correct her. She didn't tell her what had happened to allow this change.

I caught Kelly watching me as she filled a kettle with water and placed it on the stovetop to heat as she returned to gleefully ignoring me. She'd heard that thought. She could probably hear everything I was thinking regardless of what she said. I slammed my mental shields into place. I should have done it the moment we met her on the street, but I hated being cut off from Thea.

"Good idea, vampire," Kelly muttered as she took a box of tea down.

"What do you want to talk about?" Thea demanded. "We didn't come over for a tea party."

"You're cold," Kelly said, her emerald eyes glittered with annoyance. "And I'm still your mother."

Now that she was healed, the two of them looked so much alike that it was physically uncomfortable. Kelly pointed to a rickety table surrounded by stools.

"You've been here the whole time?" Thea studied the place, her eyes lingering on the peeling paint and cracking tiles.

"Mostly." Kelly placed a steaming mug in front of her.

Thea's eyes darted to mine and then to the stool beside her. I sat, angling myself between her and the rest of the room, and tracked Kelly's movements. Her icy demeanor didn't thaw, even as she picked up a jar and began to measure tea leaves into another small bag.

I took Thea's hand and stroked my thumb along its back in small, reassuring circles. "What is this place?"

"A safe house." She looked at her daughter as she answered. "I'm afraid it's not what you've grown accustomed to."

I felt the sting of her words through our bond. Every ounce of me wanted to roar at Kelly Melbourne for this: for lying to Thea, for hiding from her, but most of all for treating Thea like she was the one who had changed for the worse.

Thea squeezed my hand, as if she knew what I was thinking past the stone shield I'd erected in my mind.

"How did you find this place?" I asked, doing my best to keep my tone civil. I had no idea sirens had a sanctuary in Venice.

"That's a secret."

So far, she was a well of information.

"Where is everyone?" Thea lifted the tea, eyeing her mother over the cup's rim but not drinking. "I assume there are others."

Kelly took a seat on the opposite side of the worn table, her hands laced around a chipped mug. "They're out. I can't keep you here long. No one will return home if *he's* here."

I bristled at her disgust.

"I guess I don't want to meet them anyway." Thea stood, abandoning her mug. "I'm glad you're okay." Then she turned in the direction we'd come from.

I let my mental shields fall and reached out to her. *What are you doing?*

For months, my mate had sought answers, especially the answer to what had happened to her mother. Now, it seemed she was willing to walk away.

I'm not going to sit here and let anyone—even my mother—treat you like this. We're leaving.

"I'm not sure where to start," Kelly admitted softly, stopping Thea in her tracks.

Thea spun around slowly, lifting her chin and looking as regal as her new title. "How about the beginning?"

"That's a very long story," Kelly hedged.

Thea glanced at me, and I nodded. She'd waited for this moment and deserved any peace clarity would bring. I wouldn't rush it.

We both sat back down. I pulled Thea's stool closer to mine, the scrape of its feet splitting the silence in the empty room.

"Thea, you're a siren," Kelly said solemnly.

My mate snorted, rolling her eyes. "I know that."

"I assumed the longer you stayed with him, the more your powers would manifest." Kelly's mouth pursed into a disapproving arch. She sipped her tea, cupping her now-bare palms around the warm mug.

"They manifested because the glamour you had on me lifted," Thea shot back.

"That is not entirely true." Kelly shook her head and placed the mug on the worn tabletop, which already had several centuries of water rings. "I assume you two have been reckless for a while now." She gestured to our joined hands.

"I'm not sure that's your business." But Thea's cheeks burned so hot it radiated from her. I could smell her embarrassment, and I had to bite back a smile. Humans were so strange about their bodies, especially around their parents.

"We aren't human," Kelly correctly me sternly. "You need to remember that."

"Mortals," I said out loud with a shrug.

"Sirens are the daughters of Demeter," Kelly continued, ignoring me.

"Demeter?" Thea repeated. "I know that's what legends say, but that's just mythology. You don't actually believe that?"

Her mother shook her head. "Not legends. We *are* the descendants of Demeter. When Hades took Persephone into the Underground, Demeter wept for her child, but she grew to hate her tears—hate the winter her child's absence brought—and so she put her grief to use. She gave it life. We are her tears. She gave us her essence so that we could walk between life and death, between this world and the next, and call Persephone home."

There was a moment of stunned silence. Except...it made sense. If we believed what my mother had told us, that all creatures were made by the Gods, it was possible. And if my mother—maybe even my father—was made by Hades... I couldn't bring myself to say it, to even think it.

But Thea shook her head. "You really believe that, don't you? That we were created by some Goddess?"

"I don't believe it, I know," Kelly said silently. "My mother told me as hers told her...and now I am telling you."

"Why?" Thea asked. "Why bother now?"

"It's a tradition in our family to wait until powers manifest." She offered a small smile to her daughter. "You were always too busy with your studies to have a boyfriend, so it wasn't necessary to have *the talk*."

Thea was squirming in her chair now, studiously avoiding my eyes. "You didn't tell me because I was a virgin?" she blurted out. "Don't you think it's the kind of thing I should know before I slept with someone?"

"If you'd taken a man to bed, it wouldn't have mattered. The magic barely stirs when you're with a human, but you chose a vampire," she said flatly.

It was pretty clear how she felt about that.

"So did you," Thea said coldly.

"A decision I can only live with because he gave me you. I thought it was just a stupid mistake."

"What changed?" I dared to ask.

She lifted a brow. "He found out about Thea. I didn't expect him to care that he had a child, but he came around and demanded I give her to him. I knew that if I did, I would never see her again, so I ran."

"And you used a glamour to hide us from him?" Thea guessed. "You made yourself sick. Why?"

It made sense in a warped way. I'd seen how far Willem was

willing to go. What wouldn't I do to keep Thea from harm? And if Kelly's actions had protected Thea until I could, part of me wanted to thank her.

"There was only one way to do it. Being near a source was too risky. What if someone saw us and told him? What if someone knew what we were? Sirens have never lived within the magical community."

"Because they were exterminated."

Kelly nodded. "Very few of our kind survived the vampires' attempt to eradicate us."

"How? How did we make it? What's special about our family? Why did Willem want you? Me?"

"When Demeter gave us life, we had families of our own. Her magic passed into all our children, diluted with each generation as it passed from mother to son, from son to his own children. Our line is different."

No one was moving. Thea had stopped breathing, and even I felt poised on a knife's edge.

"How are we different?"

"We are the first tear that fell. We are the divine wish she had for a daughter to fill the space Persephone had left. As such, our bloodline has only produced females," she whispered. "If you believe our family lore, the Goddess herself blessed us to carry her divine powers from generation to generation. To carry on her bloodline in a way that Persephone would not—could not with the God of Death. It's why sirens abhor vampires because, like Hades, they reign over death—but it seems that fate cannot be denied."

My heart had stopped when Thea finally asked what I was thinking. "What are you saying?"

"Magic has awoken."

"That's what everyone keeps saying," Thea grumbled. "Tell us something we don't know."

Her mother ignored her, turning a searing glare on us. "And you two have found each other, at last."

CHAPTER NINETEEN

Thea

"What the hell are you talking about?" My mother might be healthy again physically, but I was beginning to wonder about her mental state. Gods and ancient bloodlines and...

A year ago, I would have cried and made her an appointment to see a psychiatrist. Now? Things were different. Vampires and witches existed. Werewolves and sirens. At this point, I couldn't discount the existence of any supernatural creature, from Bigfoot to the Loch Ness monster.

Bigfoot is a myth.

I rolled my eyes mentally at Julian. *Finally, something's a myth. Wait, does that mean the Loch Ness Monster is real?*

He didn't have time to answer.

"You carry Demeter and Persephone's divine essence just as he carries Hades." My mother hitched a finger at my mate. "You already knew about him, didn't you?"

I felt numb as what she was saying sank in. Sabine had told us about Hades. Part of me hadn't believed her, but Sabine had known, had said my mother knew, too. And that meant we...

"When you mated, your magic stirred. But when you took the throne, it did something more. I'll admit I didn't know the full extent of your magic. My sisters—*our* sisters," she corrected herself before continuing, "were the ones who told me."

"Sisters?"

"The other sirens calling this place home," she explained. "They are from different bloodlines, but we all descend from Demeter. They heard about a new queen and spoke to some...friends."

I glanced at Julian. The rumors she'd heard only told part of the story. It was up to me to decide how much more I wanted her to know. "So they told you I took the throne?"

"We were told a siren was made queen—a siren with a very protective vampire lover. I assumed it was you," she added with flashing eyes. "Our sources within the Council and your court can be a little reticent."

She really doesn't know about the resurrection.

Julian's face stayed unreadable even as he answered me. *It would seem not.*

What did that change? I wasn't certain I knew.

"I'm mortified. I hid you from the world for so long. I was so afraid that Willem might find you that I never considered another vampire might. I just wanted to keep you safe."

"Safe? Is that how you justify lying to me?" I wanted to understand, but I couldn't. This wasn't the woman who had raised me, who had sacrificed so much to give me cello lessons. Even when she was sick, she'd been adamant that I continue my studies and stay in school. I already knew that was a lie. That she'd pushed me toward music to siphon away any siren tendencies. But even knowing that didn't change the years she'd spent cheering me on or the love I felt when I remembered those times.

It couldn't all be a lie.

"I did what I had to do." There wasn't an ounce of remorse on her face. "Sirens hide—it's what we do. It's better if we are forgotten. But you were always in more danger than the rest of us. If your father had found you, he would have tried to turn you into a succubus—a weapon."

"He did find me," I exploded, "and I think he did succeed."

"He could not. The divine spark inside you cannot be corrupted."

That didn't make sense. "I drink *blood*. I have *fangs*."

"An unfortunate gift from your father, it seems." Her eyes

flickered briefly to Julian before she stood and carried her cup to the sink to dump the remainder of her tea. She kept her back to me as she asked, "Whose blood do you drink?"

This wasn't a conversation I wanted to have with my mother. "That's none of your business."

She swiveled to face me, a finger whipping in Julian's direction. "Does he demand it? Do you drink blood to please your vampire?"

I was going to be sick. My stomach churned as the world tilted. All of this time, she had known. Looking at Julian, I saw his jaw tense. He didn't want to answer that question. I couldn't blame him. And while I had drunk from my mate, I felt no shame. Not about sharing blood with him. Still...

"Willem forced me to consume blood," I whispered.

Her face paled. She gripped the counter behind her like she might collapse. "I should have told you. I should have warned you about him. I thought I could protect you from that monster."

My rage quieted as I beheld her. I'd been angry with her since she forced me to choose between her and Julian. Angrier still when I found out the truth about what I was and that she'd glamoured me. Now, "What did he do to you?"

"Some are born of the Gods. Others were made from them—purposefully or accidentally. But yes, all creatures of *this* world are bound to them in some way or another. Vampires are bound to Hades, the God of Death. That is how your kind has dominion over death, how you use blood to feed your long lives."

But I wasn't listening to her take on vampire biology.

"What do you mean by *this* world?" I asked suspiciously.

"There are other magics, other worlds that exist within our own. The fae, for instance."

The *fae*? Someone, Lysander or Sabine, had mentioned them casually. I hadn't really thought they were real. I'd never met any, and none of Julian's family or friends ever spoke of knowing any. And what the hell did she mean by *exists within our own*?

Julian raked a hand through his hair, instantly looking more disheveled than I'd ever seen him outside the bedroom.

"So what have these Gods been doing?" I demanded. "Just hanging out on Mount Olympus or whatever?" How could she have kept this from me?

I wasn't an expert on vampire history, but this was rewriting everything I thought I'd figured out. I couldn't imagine how Julian felt.

Do you think she's crazy? I asked across the bond.

There was a barely perceptible shake of his head.

Distracted by him, my mother's next words nearly knocked me out of my chair. "The Gods are dead." She paused, her eyes pinching together as she studied us. "Or they were."

"What the fuck does that mean?"

My outburst earned me a withering, maternal glare. She never liked it when I cursed.

"It means that whatever happened when you took that throne changed things. Magic is awake. It grows more powerful every day. What once whispered in my veins now roars. Don't you feel it?"

I felt numb, but I managed a single nod. I not only felt it, but I'd also used it today on that vampire who'd attacked us.

"And if our magic is awakening, perhaps it is because the Gods themselves are returning."

Oh, shit. "Which Gods exactly?" I asked weakly.

"All of them," she added. "There are thousands of Gods in cultures all over the world."

I looked to Julian, but he was staring at her, shadows clinging to his face. "And that's bad?"

"It might be." She leaned against the sink, wringing her hands together. "Since the curse, there's been a delicate balance to this world. You two are proof that the Gods are awakening, too, and if so, everything will change."

"How? How are we proof?" I asked.

"You are the daughter of Demeter as Persephone was. He is the son of Hades. In a way, it is as if Persephone and Hades' doomed love has returned."

That's what she'd meant when she said we'd found each other at last.

"Why?" If she was telling the truth, if there were more sirens, why would I have been chosen? There were millions of vampires in the world. Why Julian? "Why us?"

"Believe me, you are not the only one asking that question. The easiest answer is that our bloodline leads directly back to Demeter and his leads back to Hades. But that doesn't answer other questions, like why your ascension to the throne had such a dramatic effect on magic."

"There's a prophecy." Julian paused and cleared his throat. "Magic to magic, darkness to darkness—"

"I know the prophecy," she snapped, cutting him off. "But prophecies are roadmaps to places the fates have already chosen."

I was finding it hard to breathe. The truth weighed heavily on me, and despite my trepidations about telling her, I couldn't ignore that our resurrection might hold the key to all of this.

"We died," I whispered. I almost didn't expect her to hear me.

Horror twisted across her face, and I knew she had. She stumbled a step, as though her legs might give out. In an instant, Julian was at her side. My mother was too stricken to reject his assistance as he helped her to a seat.

Slowly, I told her about what happened. How Willem had kidnapped me and manipulated my memories, how I'd been drawn to Julian at the party even though my warped mind couldn't remember him, how his tether had responded so violently, and how, even in my confusion, I'd followed him into death. She remained quiet as I recalled waking on the throne with the crown and how I had found the melody that drew him back to life.

"And now our lives are bound together," I finished.

No one spoke for a minute. Julian hovered between us like one of us might faint or make a run for it or attack.

Finally, my mother spoke in a low voice, tears swimming in her eyes. "Then it is true. You were the ones in the prophecy. You are Persephone and Hades reborn."

"I think that's getting a little ahead of ourselves," I said quickly. "Sirens know the song of life and death, right? Demeter granted it to us, so we could move between this world and the Underworld."

"Move between," she repeated gently, then stretched her hand across the table and took mine. "Not return from true death. That is a power only the Gods hold. Even when a vampire turns a mortal, they do so by giving the gift of their blood—their magic—before death. No one can command a soul to return from the Underworld."

"I don't have a soul, right?" Julian said quietly.

"You do now." She swallowed, tears spilling over her cheeks. "Hers. She shared hers to bring you back."

This was enlightening and confusing. I was beginning to need a nap.

"Okay, but none of that makes us reincarnated Gods," I pointed out.

"Persephone was the Goddess of Spring. She created life from winter's barren death." She looked to Julian. "And did you not pass into Oblivion?"

"Limbo," he murmured.

"Limbo exists within the Underworld. Only a vampire with Hades' blood could pass into it." She paused, glancing at each of us in turn. "Together you have turned the wheel, rewritten the rules of life and death, reset the laws of magic to their origin. Your gift is life. His is death. Light and dark. An endless circle."

"Oh." I couldn't think of anything else to say.

A few months ago, I was a college student struggling to graduate and hold down two jobs. Now I was a freaking Goddess? Could the world get any weirder?

"I don't understand," I admitted. "Why are we what reset magic? Why did we break the curse?"

"Our kind was hunted down," she reminded me in a fierce whisper, her eyes whipping to Julian, as if he'd been the vampire to personally do so. "Eradicated, or so they thought. Ask yourself why. A siren was key to breaking the curse. Whoever cursed magic made certain of that—made certain that it would be linked to the divine gifts of Hades and Persephone."

"But if there were no sirens, it couldn't be broken." My stomachache returned as I considered what she was saying. "The vampires didn't want magic to awaken. Why?"

Something like pride shone in her eyes when she said, "Now you're asking the right questions."

CHAPTER TWENTY

Lysander

Why had I decided to stay? A few days had passed since that disastrous day at court, and none of the queens had held an audience after. In fact, Thea had been holed up with Julian ever since. My family had left court but had been forced to stay in Venice as preparations began to join the social season and the last weeks of Carnival in an unholy union. One of my brothers showed up every now and then in direct defiance of our mother's orders.

But nothing was happening, and my research was proving fruitless.

At least when they held court, there was the potential for a fight. Instead, I'd made myself at home in the court library—a considerable, if claustrophobic, resource.

The peppery, welcoming scent of old books hung in the air, and I breathed it in as I settled into my seat, a fresh stack in front of me. A considerable amount of archeology was spent sitting in the library, looking for clues hidden in old books no one had bothered to read for years. It was research that yielded precious few results, but when it did, the information might be invaluable. Despite the archives available at court, I'd found nothing but a few cryptic references to the spell binding the queens to the throne. Nothing about the curse or its origins. Not even a single mention of the queen-killer weapon my father wanted me to find. I couldn't help wondering if the oversight was purposeful—if someone didn't want me to find this information.

The lack of information wasn't the most frustrating problem I faced. It wasn't even that I'd stayed for my brother. Or that I didn't trust anyone at court. I knew they would need allies, but Julian was busy with Thea. Jacqueline was always off on some secret mission. Although Camila was my sister, I definitely didn't trust her. All of that was annoying.

Still, what preoccupied me was wondering when I might have a run-in with the only other person I found remotely interesting here.

As the days passed, I knew one thing: Lia was avoiding me.

It shouldn't matter, especially with our agreement to be enemies. She was a distraction, and she was loyal to the court. That definitely placed her in the off-limits category. The problem was that she seemed to have no trouble showing up in my dreams, usually naked, always commanding the attention of my cock before waking me up. I hadn't been this pathetic since I was a teenager. Not even then.

It wasn't getting me anywhere, because Lia did not feel the same attraction. That much was clear, and even if she did, there was the matter of her oath.

I scooted my ancient chair back, its feet scraping on the marble floor, and stared at what I had managed to accomplish from my reading. I leafed through a few notes I'd made about the prophecy, mentions I'd found in various books. Cryptic scraps I couldn't piece together. The longest of which read like a riddle.

Three crowns to bind.
Three thrones to choose.
Three queens to sacrifice.
Ever as three bound.
Ever as three free.

It wasn't much to go on. I reached to crumple the note—another dead end—when a shadow passed over the table. Looking up, I saw Lia pass by the tall windows. She paused and looked inside.

My fists clenched as if they hoped to prevent the inevitable rush of my blood to my dick. Was that going to happen every time I saw her? It wasn't like I was going to get any relief, given her oath to the queens and her—frankly unnecessary, if you asked me—vow of chastity. Maybe it was the sight of her, or maybe I was over whatever this game was between us, but I was sick and tired of sitting alone in this fucking library, trying to puzzle out the meaning of some ancient prophetic riddle, knowing she was out there.

I stood and walked to the door that led to the exterior courtyard. Lia backed up a step when I opened it, but she didn't leave. We stared at each other for a moment before she made her move. Lia didn't speak, walking into the library with a firm step. My eyes tracked her movement, and despite my efforts to be a gentleman, my gaze kept pausing on her ass—her shapely, leather-clad ass.

When she was inside, she faced me, an eyebrow lifting when she saw my wicked grin. "Is something preoccupying you, Lysander?"

I didn't know what to say, so I opted for the obvious. "You should stop avoiding me."

"Avoiding? Did I hurt your feelings?" Despite the haughty tone of her voice, her eyes swept the room like someone might overhear us. It was pointless. I hadn't seen another soul step foot inside here in the last three days. "Besides, we're supposed to be enemies. I generally don't spend a lot of quality time with my enemies, do you?"

She had me there.

"Then why are you here?" I leaned against a shelf and crossed my arms.

"Checking on you. You've been buried in books for days. What are you looking for?" She lifted one of the ancient tomes and studied it.

"I'm just catching up on my to-be-read list." I smirked at her puzzled expression. "Why are you really here?"

"Someone has to keep an eye on things. No one seems to give a damn about the prophecy or what it means now that magic is back. Mariana wants to plan a fucking coronation ball." From the roll of Lia's eyes, I could tell how she felt about that. "Zina is fuming. The Council has summoned Thea for a meeting."

"A meeting?" I said darkly. "Is she going to go?"

Lia rolled her eyes. "I don't know. She won't leave her room. I have no idea what she's doing in there."

I smirked. "You know what *they're* doing."

"They can't do it *all* the time," she snapped.

"They're mates." I shrugged and straightened up. "I haven't been around other mated pairs, but I hear they all act like this."

"Like what?"

"Animals." I chuckled. I dared to take a step closer to her. With her this near me, I smelled her magic. I breathed her in until my vision darkened along the edges. It had been a long time since I'd experienced the heady rush of bloodlust. I minded it less than I should, but each moment with her took me one step closer to losing control. I forced myself to halt, to maintain some merciful distance between us.

It did nothing to squash the desire burning through me.

Lia's eyes widened slightly, but she didn't move. She wouldn't. No, backing away again might be perceived as weak, but I knew better than to think she would give me any ground. She would always hold her own. "What are you doing?"

"Smelling you," I admitted in a low voice.

"What?" She tensed, and I wondered if it was to keep herself from moving.

"Smelling you," I repeated slowly.

"Why?" she blurted out.

"Usually, you smell like blood—other people's blood." Thea and Julian's. The poor bastards who started a fight at court. Now? She was the lush, bold taste of ripe cherries on my tongue, the blooming intoxication of gardenia, and underneath those, in a place that was almost hidden, an earthy warmth that urged me closer.

Her throat bobbed, catching my attention. My gaze slid to her neck. A vein throbbed, and even from here, I saw the rapid truth of her pulse. I wasn't the only one affected. Not that she would ever admit it.

Unlike so much of her, her skin looked soft. I imagined that underneath the leather she wore and the attitude she clung to like armor, there were other softer parts of her.

"What are you thinking?" she whispered.

"I'm wondering if you taste as good as you smell." There was no point hiding it. She could see my eyes. She'd spent enough time around vampires at court to know bloodlust when she saw it.

"Keep your hands to yourself," she warned me, but still, she didn't move.

Was it pride or curiosity pinning her to the spot? I didn't bother to ask. "I don't need my hands to taste you."

I heard her breath catch. The promising breathless gasp made me groan.

"I don't think enemies do that sort of thing," she whispered, but her tongue swept over her lower lip. Heat radiated from her body, sending her scent surging through the air until the whole world darkened.

Lia stared into my black eyes.

Into the bloodlust building there.

One step and she would be against the wall. Another and my fangs would be in her soft, perfect throat.

"Enemies," I said slowly, circling around so I could enjoy her body from every angle, "do that kind of thing, I promise. It's called a hate fuck."

But even as I spoke, even as I imagined pinning her to the wall and making her moan, I suspected nothing about claiming her could ever be defined that way.

"You're forgetting that I have sworn never to bed a male." Her words were firm but breathless, need flashing in her eyes.

She might have sworn it, but it hadn't been her choice, and we both knew that.

"How fortunate that we're in a library without a bed in sight."

I prowled toward her, walking her back until she was against the shelves.

She stopped breathing for a second, long enough to make me pause. Finally, she spoke. "That's not what I meant... I can't."

Regret colored her words, and it nearly undid me.

She wanted me.

Her whole body called to me, but it was more complicated than that. It always was. "There are a lot of ways for me to taste you that won't breach your vow."

"You aren't sucking my blood, vampire," she snarled softly.

"Who said anything about blood?"

There was no fear in her gaze, only a kind of shocked wonder. I couldn't help but question if she felt the connection between us as clearly as I did. If she knew what even I couldn't admit to myself: that I hadn't stayed for Julian and Thea.

"I stayed for you," I confessed.

"That was stupid." There was no biting sarcasm. No warning. Only more remorse.

"I agree." Daring to move closer, I lifted a finger to her neck, tracing along the pulsing vein beneath her tawny skin. I'd taken my gloves off so I could turn pages more instantly. A jolt of magic passed between us, the touch absolutely forbidden. I shouldn't, but I couldn't stop myself, so I waited for her to stop me. Instead, her teeth caught her lower lip, barely managing to swallow the moan I saw in her eyes.

"We shouldn't," I murmured, almost an entreaty to myself.

She shook her head. "No, we shouldn't."

But neither of us moved.

"If you want to leave," I offered, "go."

"You could leave," she suggested weakly.

I grabbed hold of the bookshelf behind her, my arms bracketing her. "I don't want to."

Her teeth caught her upper lip as she inhaled sharply, eyes searching mine. "Neither do I."

"That is a predicament."

"A real problem," she agreed.

"Or an opportunity. You're supposed to keep your enemies close, right?"

"Closer," she breathed softly.

I didn't know if it was a correction or a request, but my self-restraint snapped. My mouth captured hers, a ragged groan catching in my throat as her taste flooded through me. Her tongue found mine, and I growled in surprised approval. Lia softened in my arms, releasing her caged moan, the sound of it bolting to my groin. I pressed my hips against hers, letting her feel my hardness as my fingers sought bare skin—soft and silky beneath my rough hands.

I kept my touch featherlight, afraid I might leave a mark—evidence that she'd given me a taste of something far more forbidden than her kiss.

Her magic.

I stroked a thumb up the curve of her neck, marveling at the energy thrumming beneath her skin as I traced along her jawline. I wanted to touch every inch of her, map every bit of her magic.

Drawing back, I slipped my finger between her lips. Her tongue circled it and sucked, her inexperience giving way to whatever primal instinct drove us. She molded against me, her eyes burning into mine, begging for more.

My finger slid from her mouth and continued its exploration—down her throat, her breastbone, between the swell of her breasts. I paused at her navel.

Touching her was nothing like I'd imagined. It was better. The fantasy of her body paled in comparison to the reality of how it felt against mine, how her soft curves fit against me. She drew a single ragged breath, her tongue swiping over her lip, over that beautiful scar in invitation.

And as much as I wanted her—and I fucking *wanted* her—I knew I had to stop. I tore myself away, placing several feet of distance between us. Lia panted, her eyes wide with hurt.

"I can't do this," I told her. "I won't."

"Because we're enemies?" she murmured.

That wasn't the reason. It wasn't even on the list. "Because," I admitted in a low voice that made her squirm, "I won't be able to stop."

"I'll stop you," she said huskily.

I didn't try to hide my smirk. Not now that I knew she wanted me as badly as I wanted her. "That's the problem, Lia. You won't."

Maybe she knew I was right. Maybe she hated that I said it, but she didn't so much as look me in the eye before she turned and left me standing there—more wound up than ever.

CHAPTER TWENTY-ONE

Julian

"I don't like it."

A letter summoning Thea to an audience with the Vampire Council had arrived late last night. We'd been debating how to respond ever since. Or rather I'd been debating while she patiently resisted all attempts to convince her it was a bad idea.

"You said that before." Thea rolled out of bed, crossing to the armoire. She took a plum-colored robe from it. Slipping the silky garment onto her slight frame, she tied it loosely. "But I don't think we have a choice. Not if we want answers."

I looked at the paper in my hands, my eyes skimming the scrawling handwriting of the summons. "The Vampire Council has no authority to summon a queen," I reminded her. "Going will set a precedent telling them otherwise."

The letter had arrived by courier just after dawn. I'd been annoyed when I was called from my bed to receive it, but I'd been murderous when I realized what it was about. The Council had demanded an audience with Thea this afternoon.

After what we'd learned from Kelly, I doubted this summons was as simple as a meeting between a new queen and the vampire powers that be. If they suspected what the sirens did—that Thea and

I carried the divine spark of some long-gone, but still pains-in-my-ass, Gods—this was an attempt to confirm their theory. Or worse, a trap. The vampires had killed all the sirens to avoid this very outcome, even if we didn't understand why. Even with my mother on the Council, I knew they wouldn't hesitate to assassinate anyone who stood in their way.

"You don't have to go. You don't answer to them," I said in a strained voice.

She flopped onto the bed and reached out for the letter. I passed it to her, but instead of reading it, she balled it up and tossed it across the room. "I'm going," she said firmly, and I tensed. "I know it's dangerous. Don't think I can't hear you worrying." She tapped her head to remind me my thoughts were always laid bare to her. "I know all the reasons to be careful, but we aren't going into this blindly. You're forgetting that we have one advantage over them."

I lifted an eyebrow.

Thea's lips curved into a dazzling smile. "They don't know that we know about the Gods." She paused, and her smile fell. "Not that I'm sure I'm buying everything my mother told us."

For days, that had been the source of our debate in her quarters. We hadn't bothered to leave them as we discussed and researched until we were exhausted. When we came to that point, we reached for each other and stole moments of peace, our bodies joined. After her disastrous first appointment at court, everyone was lying low, her sister-queens included. That had bought us time but not answers.

"Do you think she lied to us?" I asked.

Thea shook her head and beckoned me closer. I moved toward the bed and kneeled before her. "I think she struggles with the truth. She's been keeping things from me for so long, how couldn't she?" She brushed her fingers down my cheek. "I know this freaks you out, but the Council might hold the key to all of this—and understanding this is the key to our future. They could give us the one piece my mom may have held back. I have to go."

"Fine." Between Jacqueline, Aurelia, and I, we could hold our own, even amongst some of the world's oldest pureblooded vampires. "When do we leave?"

"It's not your job to protect me." She brushed a strand of hair from my forehead. "It's your job to love me, so I need you to stay calm while I'm gone."

"While you're gone?" I repeated. "Thea, you aren't going alone."

"The invitation is for me," she started.

"It's not an invitation," I growled. *You aren't serious.*

"I am. They need to respect me."

"I thought we were equals. Isn't that why you've been avoiding court?" I said, reminding her of the bold move she'd made.

"We are equals, which is exactly why you don't need to go. Both of us going sends the message that we aren't strong enough on our own."

The thought had not occurred to me. I had to admit that wasn't a message I wanted to send. That didn't mean I was willing to risk her safety. Did my mate command the power of the *Rio Oscuro*? Yes. But even powerful queens had bodyguards.

"I never said I was going alone," she said with a soft snort. "Aurelia will come with me."

"We have no idea what powers have awoken in the Council. All of those vampires are fucking ancient, my love." I slid my hands under her, pulling her to the edge of the bed to rest the side of my face on her thigh. The contact soothed some of the ragged panic I felt at this plan, but nothing could soothe it completely until it was over and done with.

"Your mother included," she pointed out, "and she's still on our side."

"But she will not risk her neck publicly. She's made that clear. You can't rely on her aid if shit hits the fan."

"I think she would help me." Thea stroked my hair, her gaze lowering to the mark on my chest—her mark. "Our lives are bound together. She knows that. And you will know if something is wrong. You will feel it."

Would there be enough time to reach her? "Thea," I said her

name quietly, "the night that Willem took you…"

She stilled, her breath catching, her hand hovering over my hair. "Our bond was faint with the distance."

"It's stronger now," she interjected. "I don't think the distance will matter."

"Maybe not," I agreed, but that wasn't the point I was trying to make. "It was faint, and then it was gone. *You* were gone." It had felt like my soul was being shredded, like I'd been left to bleed out as half of my very being had been ripped away. "There was no light then, only darkness. Despair. I can't bear the thought of feeling that way again, of wondering if you are alive. But more than that, that darkness…I feel it now inside me. My magic is death, Thea."

She didn't flinch. "So?"

"Why doesn't that scare you?" I was reminded of the night we'd met. She was still as fearless now as she had been then.

"Death is part of life," she said softly, "even for us."

And maybe it was, but that didn't change how I felt about it.

"How do you feel?" she pressed, reading my thoughts.

"Afraid. There is a price to using my magic. I never missed it after the curse. Now that it's back, I wish it wasn't," I whispered. The monster I had become when she was taken was nothing compared to the power thrumming inside me. Darkness. Death. The vampire I had once been, terrible and feared and bloodthirsty. "I don't want to give into that part of myself, but I will for you."

She gripped my face in her hands. "No. I'll learn to protect myself, to use my magic."

A growl slipped from me. I'd given into my shame, and now she believed she had to do that.

"I want to do that." She pinned her eyes to mine. "I know that when it matters, you will be there. But I also need to learn about my own magic…unless you don't want me to."

"Of course I want you to." How could she think anything else? "And it's not my choice regardless. It's yours."

She was quiet for a moment. Even her mind was blank. "You are still you," she said gently. "And if you have been a monster in the past, you've had your reasons. I know and trust you."

I knew what she meant. If Thea could trust me, I needed to trust myself, even when part of me howled to protect her.

"And I trust you with everything," I whispered, turning my head to press a kiss to her soft thigh. "I trust you with my life, my soul, my magic." I kissed her again, moving higher up her leg. "You are my queen."

"And you are my king," she murmured.

I looked up at her, our eyes met, and I saw the same molten need I felt burning there. I yanked her closer, leaving her ass hovering dangerously close to the edge of the bed. Without breaking eye contact, I shifted, freeing my hands so I could undo the sash of her robe. It fell open to reveal the creamy valley between her breasts, down to the flat plains of her stomach that disappeared where her thighs still pressed together.

"I serve you," I murmured as I placed my hands on her knees and urged her legs open wider. She tangled her hand in my hair, leaning back on her other hand to steady herself as my head dipped lower. Her scent hit me, and I growled as bloodlust rushed through me. I would let her go. I would trust her. But that didn't mean I had to like it. It didn't mean that my instincts weren't roaring at me to fight, to protect, to claim. There was only one way to quiet them.

Shadows deepened as I drank the sight of her, the smell of her, in as deeply as possible. Sliding my palms up her thighs, I savored the heat and the magic seeping between our bare skin, dark and light mixing until it became something entirely ours.

I guided her knee over my shoulder, and her breath hitched. Our eyes locked as I lowered my mouth to taste her. Sliding my hand up, I pinned her to the bed, licking and nipping. She shifted restlessly, her hand tightening in my hair, her teeth biting into her lower lip as my tongue worked itself more deeply inside her.

So beautiful.

"More," she moaned.

I obliged. Not stopping when her thighs clamped around my head. Not stopping when her whimpers turned to begging. When I finally lifted my eyes, the world was dark. Thea pried one eye open languidly, beckoning me with a finger and a languid, wanton smile. I rose, shoving down my loose silk pants. Her eyes hooded at the sight of my erection, and I allowed myself a smug smirk.

"Like what you see?" I asked before lowering my body over hers.

She bit her lip and nodded. My cock fell heavily between her open thighs, and I could feel her wet heat calling to me. She propped herself on one elbow, the room filling with her sweet jasmine scent. "What are you waiting for?"

I smirked at the impatience in her tone.

"Go to the Council without me, but I'll be damned if you leave this room without my scent all over you," I purred as I rolled my hips, brushing my crown along her swollen seam.

Her answering smile was feline. She pushed me onto her back with her palms, twisting to straddle me. Folding my hands behind my head, I let her take charge. Her copper hair fell like a curtain over her shoulders, and if I had any doubt that she was a real fucking Goddess, it vanished as she sank onto me and began to ride.

"Maybe I should mark you," she simpered, tugging her teeth between her teeth as she moved on me.

I grabbed her hips, arching mine to fill her more deeply. "You already have, but by all means…keep going."

She huffed a laugh, and I wondered what I'd done to deserve her—why fate had given me her. Her fingers ghosted down my chest, magic sparking in their wake. I felt it calling to my own, felt it burning through my veins—claiming me just as it had changed me. Sinking my fingers into her hips, I urged her harder, faster, until her hands covered mine and filled me with the source of my life: her.

I threw my head back and growled as her power filled me, as it filled the air around us. My hips bucked up, and I filled her with my own release. Shadows wrapped around the shimmering gold. We were life and death. We were in eternity—a cycle with no beginning and no end.

We collapsed into each other's arms, neither of us speaking as our ragged breath gradually returned to normal.

Thea traced the mark on my chest. "I'll never get enough of you," she murmured.

My arms tightened around her, knowing that soon I would have to let her go, soon she would face the Council without me. Burying my face in her hair, I breathed her in. "Neither will I, my love. Neither will I."

CHAPTER TWENTY-TWO

Thea

"I like this even less," Julian grumbled.

I twisted my hair up, my eyes finding him in the mirror. "I know, but look at it this way: I'll have more allies with me."

His eyes remained shadowed. They'd been that way since we'd finally managed to pull ourselves from our bed in time for me to prepare for my audience with the Vampire Council. His newest annoyance was a message from Jacqueline informing him that she and Camila were coming with me to see to business of their own.

"I wouldn't consider my sister an ally," he warned. His mouth flattened into a grim line, but not before I saw a flash of fang. He was really on edge, but I loved him for fighting it.

"But Jacqueline is," I said firmly, adding, "and Camila is in love with her, so she'll listen to Jacqueline. Everything will be fine."

He didn't look convinced, and if I was being honest, I wasn't entirely certain it would be. Julian arched an eyebrow, and I knew he'd caught that thought.

I wrinkled my nose. "Remind me to learn more about shielding my thoughts."

"Why? I'd rather know what you're thinking," he said, coming up behind me. He wrapped his arms around my waist and leaned to kiss my shoulder. "Even if you're just coddling me."

"I wasn't coddling you," I protested, but I didn't lift my eyes to his as I carefully applied lipstick.

"I'm on edge. You want to soothe my anxiety, but I'm being a baby." He rested his chin on my shoulder.

"I never thought you were a baby!"

"I'm paraphrasing," he admitted, "and I know you're right. It's just..."

"What?" I recapped my lipstick with a sigh and twisted around to face him. "You have your shields up—which is totally unfair, by the way. I can't hear what you're thinking."

"You don't want to know," he said darkly.

"Ride or die," I murmured, brushing the back of my hand down his face. He looked so haunted that I almost didn't want to know, but that would get us nowhere. "You used to trust me more."

"That was before I knew the Council might kill you," he said in a low voice, devoid of the savage sensuality it usually contained. Now he sounded deflated, as though the events of the last week had hollowed him out entirely.

"Why would they kill me now? What's done is done. Magic is awake." I shook my head, still not quite believing it. "It would just be petty to hurt me."

"You don't think the Council is petty?" He barked a harsh laugh. "Come on. You've met my mother. I think we'd be wise to heed her warning."

I didn't need to remind him that things were a bit more complicated where his mother was concerned. She might have been acting in our best interest, but she'd also lied to him for centuries. I didn't blame him for his mistrust. I wasn't certain I trusted her motives myself, but I was warming to the idea that even though Sabine Rousseaux might not like me, she didn't want me dead.

It was a win, if only by a very small margin.

"Exactly. I know what she told us." His gaze seared through me, both searching and absent. "But don't fool yourself into thinking she's your ally when you meet with them. She will play her role well."

"I won't," I promised. "But you forget I'm a queen now. The Council won't move against me."

"You haven't been coronated."

"I've been crowned," I argued.

He sighed and released his hold on me. I instantly felt adrift and reached to clutch his shoulders. His mouth lifted into a sad smile as he brought his hands to cradle my face. "Listen to me. There's one thing I've learned over the centuries: When people are afraid of change, of the facts, they will do everything they can to bury their heads in the sand to avoid seeing the evidence. And if someone threatens that, it's easier to bury that person than admit the truth."

My mouth went dry as I understood what he was saying. I'd seen it myself in human politics and drama. But vampires were centuries older. They had to be a little more self-aware.

"Older and wiser does not always apply where vampires are concerned, my love," he said drily. "You need to be on your guard. There's a reason they didn't invite me, too."

For a moment, I considered asking him to come anyway. Then I remembered the disastrous move I'd made at court. He'd said it himself moments ago. Vampires didn't like change, and I was changing things at breakneck speed. My very existence changed things.

"I'll have Aurelia and Jacqueline. No one will touch me." I believed that. If I didn't, I wouldn't risk going. And somewhere deep down, I knew that if it came to it, Sabine would step in.

"No, they won't," he murmured, but he sounded distant. His mind remained utterly silent, and I resisted the urge to ask what he was thinking about. What haunted him? What made him keep those mental shields so firmly in place?

"You don't want to know," he repeated and bent to kiss me. "I love you."

I sucked in a deep breath, torn between pushing him on whatever he was hiding and letting him work through it on his own. Finally, I smiled up at him. "I love you, too." Pulling away, I turned for him. "How do I look?"

He twirled his finger, and I spun around. I'd opted for something more modern than the gowns my wardrobe had given me for court. The Council, unlike here, wasn't stuck in some bygone fantasy era. It still wasn't the jeans and T-shirts I craved, but I doubted it would go over well if I showed up in my *Bite Me* shirt. Instead, I'd chosen a pair of tight-fitting black pants that rose high on my waist and a matching tailored jacket with a nude-colored camisole. Paired with a ridiculously tall pair of nude heels, I looked more like a CEO than a queen, but that was the point. This was a business meeting, and I wanted them to realize I knew it. If they expected me to walk in and take orders, they were going to be very surprised.

"Perfect," Julian said. This time the rasp of his low voice set my skin tingling as warmth spread through me. It turned me molten when he added, "Delicious."

Before I could act on that particular instinct, someone banged on the door to my quarters loudly enough we could hear it in the bathroom. It wasn't a human knock.

"I think my best friend is here," Julian said drily.

I snorted. "We better not make her wait or she'll break down the door."

We walked, hand-in-hand, to the adjoining living quarters. The fire had been lit for the day by some sort of magic, and part of me longed to stay locked in the cozy room.

That wasn't an option. We needed to know what the Council had learned, and I needed to know if they planned to be my enemy or my ally. But before we reached the door, Julian pinned me to the wall. His hands grabbed my wrists and lifted them over my head. Lowering his face, he brushed his lips down my jaw, his fangs scraping my skin before his mouth found mine. There was a desperate edge to the kiss. Desperate and hungry. The longing in it physically hurt, and I knew whatever he was keeping hidden behind those mental shields was causing him pain. I just had to figure out how to get him to let me in.

When he broke away, we were both breathing heavily. His eyes burned with a need that shook me to the core. "I hate that they wouldn't let me come with you."

"I don't want you to worry," I said, my voice thick with emotion. "I can face them without you there, and it's only for a few hours. They won't try anything."

He raised an eyebrow. *Are you sure about that?*

I brushed a kiss over his lips. "I'm a queen, and they don't want to make enemies of the court. Plus, Aurelia and Jacqueline are with me."

I gave him a reassuring smile and did my best to veil the real fear building inside me. The truth was that I might be a queen, but someone had assassinated Ginerva, and until we knew who, that threat remained. "Don't sit around worrying while I'm gone. Find Lysander. Have a drink or something."

It was both an order and a plea, and he nodded slowly. But his expression remained hard, and I knew he wasn't ready to let me go. "If you're relaxed when I come back, we can start off already... unwound... Wouldn't that be nice for a change?"

The banging on the door sounded again.

Releasing my wrists, he gave me a quick nip on the neck. "Go before Jacqueline breaks down the door and kicks my ass."

I forced a laugh past the knot in my throat and complied.

I opened the door and found Jacqueline grinning at me. "You're late."

Her hair was pulled into a tight bun that showcased her high cheekbones and sparkling eyes. She was dressed in slim black trousers and a tailored jacket, like she knew this was as much a diplomatic meeting as it was business. Her ever-present heels gave her an extra few inches of height that sent her towering over me even with my own stilettos.

"I've been out here five minutes. It seems you two were...busy." She winked.

Camila joined her and leaned against the doorframe. "Gross."

I didn't have time for this. Not when I was about to face the Vampire Council. Not when I felt like I was balancing on the edge of a precipice. One wrong move could spell disaster—and maybe that's exactly what the Council was hoping would happen. I cast one more look at Julian.

I'll be okay.

From the grim set of his jaw, I knew he was telling himself the same thing. In the end, he only nodded and let me go.

CHAPTER TWENTY-THREE

Julian

I wanted to go after her. Every instinct I possessed told me that this was wrong. What if she was walking into a trap? The Council had purposefully snubbed me. I took a step forward, but my best friend blocked my path.

"Don't," Jacqueline advised. "She can handle this."

"I wasn't planning to." I grabbed hold of the frame, the wood splintering in my bare hands as I stopped myself from going after her. "I know she can handle this, but if they try something…"

There was a sharp crack, and half the ancient wood crumbled to the ground just as Aurelia and Lysander turned the corner, already bickering. The argument paused when they met Thea, who muttered something to her personal security guard. I watched as her fiery red hair disappeared around the corner, her footsteps quick on the marble as she took my heart with her. I took a step forward, the separation nearly unbearable—and she was only down the hall. We'd been apart for brief periods since she'd saved me, but never in completely different locations.

Jacqueline placed a restraining hand on my shoulder, her fingers digging in hard enough to make me flinch. "Still don't," she said.

Thea's candied violet and smoke scent faded, and I thought I might actually kill anyone who got between us. Instead, I clamped my eyes shut and fought to get control of myself. Was this the divine gift I'd been granted? Hades had stolen Persephone away, kept her captive, and guarded her jealously.

"No one touches her," I snarled.

Jacqueline bowed her head. "On my life." She paused. "Jules, before when Willem took her, I—"

"You weren't prepared then," I said gruffly. "It wasn't your fault. You know what you're walking into now."

"I do." Her mouth flattened into a grim line. "I'll bring your mate back."

I took a deep breath and nodded. Lately, my mating urges had fallen into two categories: fuck and fight. Anyone who looked at her the wrong way had me on edge, and every moment she was near me, I longed to be buried inside her. It hadn't even been this bad when we'd first mated. It had to be a side effect of our new bond.

"Don't sit around. Get out of here or you'll go crazy," she said, patting my arm.

"What am I supposed to do?"

"Can we go already, or do you want Thea to head into Venice alone?" Camila called, interrupting us.

"You'll think of something," Jacqueline promised swiftly before hurrying to join the other females.

"What a fucking relief. I'll just think of something," I muttered to myself as I watched them go.

"Looks like you aren't happy about this meeting," Lysander said, coming over to inspect the damage I'd done to the door. He whistled as he picked up a broken shard of wood about three feet long. "Are you going to do this every time she's out of your sight?"

I glared at him, and he held up his hands.

"Just asking."

I stalked back inside our quarters, my brother following me. I slumped into a chair by the fire. A log cracked and snapped, and I flinched again as I remembered what I'd done to the wood.

How many more times would something like that happen before I actually lost control? I was glad my brother was here to distract me because I needed a distraction.

"Have you had any luck finding out more about the curse or the queen-killer?" I asked him.

"A few cryptic riddles that smack of divination." He recited one to me.

"Why can't ancient prophecy ever be direct?" I made a mental note to ask my mother if her second sight was really so vague.

"What would us scholarly types do if we didn't have to decipher them?"

"You've been in that library all week." I paused and considered my words carefully. "As much as I appreciate having you here, you can leave...unless there's another reason you're sticking around."

"Right now, I'm wondering the same thing." He went straight to the bar cart, took two glasses, and poured from one of the bottles of Scotch that had been delivered yesterday. "I'm a glutton for punishment."

"Punishment wouldn't happen to carry a sword and think you're a dick?" Despite my worries over Thea, I'd noticed the tension between my brother and Aurelia.

"Punishment does indeed," he said grimly, passing me a glass before taking the seat opposite mine.

I resisted the urge to tell my brother that he looked like shit. I'd seen him at the end of a two-year dig looking more pulled together. He had the wild look of a man driven half-insane by lust, and I wondered how long he would hold out before he gave in to his attraction to Aurelia.

Or what had kept him from already surrendering to it.

I held my glass up. "To the women who drive us crazy. May we at least please them in bed as much as we piss them off the rest of the time."

He nodded in agreement before shaking his head. "I'll have to find another way to please Aurelia."

"Why?" I asked, my mind still mostly focused on Jacqueline's advice.

"Seriously?" Lysander said flatly. "She's one of *Le Vergini*, remember?"

"Fuck." I shot him a sympathetic look. I had forgotten about that, in fact. "That complicates things."

"Yep." He sighed heavily and downed his drink in one gulp. "And even if she hadn't taken a vow or she was willing to break it…"

"You'd be tethered. That is shit luck." I understood exactly how fucked he was. I'd been in the same position when I met Thea.

"It worked out for you," he said, almost like he was giving himself a pep talk.

"Because we died," I reminded him.

Lysander glowered over his empty glass at me. "Thanks. That makes me feel so much better."

I shrugged and took a small sip of my drink. The liquor burned down my throat. Another distraction I desperately needed, but how much would I have to drink before I could ignore the pit in my stomach? "Why don't you just leave? There are other women."

"Are there?" he asked in a hollow voice. Our eyes met, and I recognized the haunted look I found there. I'd worn the same expression many times while I battled my feelings for Thea.

Now we both felt like shit, and there was nothing we could do about it while sitting around.

"We have to get the fuck out of here." I stood and tipped my head toward the door.

"You have anything in mind?" he asked. "Or just general mayhem?"

This was why our mother hesitated to get her sons together too often. We had a penchant for causing trouble. It was also why I loved to see my brothers.

"Let's see. Someone killed Ginerva, according to our mother. We know the Mordicum is holed up like rats somewhere in the city. And the man who kidnapped my mate is out there, too. I think we can find something to do." I cracked my neck, giving in to the part of me that wanted to fight, wanted to fuck things up. The bitter taste of Scotch lingered on my tongue, but all I wanted was blood. To smell it. To feel it in my hands. I wanted to be the scourge I once was, and I wanted everyone in the city to fear me. Maybe it was that divine curse of mine calling for death. Plus, fighting sounded a lot more fun than sitting around and waiting for her to come back. "You in?"

Lysander rose to his feet, rubbing his balled fist with his other hand. "I'm always up for taking out the trash."

"Let's go."

My best friend was right. I could find other ways to protect Thea, and I would start by cleaning up Venice one enemy at a time.

• • •

Back in the day, I never had to go far to find a nest of vampires in Venice. Some things didn't change, especially in *Cannaregio.* Shops gave way to stately *palazzi* and apartments in various states of disrepair. Painted shutters peeled under the saltwater winds, and light glowed from the family-owned *ristoranti* filled with locals. There wasn't much nightlife. No hotels or clubs. So the northernmost district saw the least foot traffic visitors. But if a traveler happened upon *Sangue e Denti,* a bar catering to the supernatural creatures that prowled the city, its grimy exterior and the solid metal door did the work of warding them off. But the vampires, werewolves, and familiars that called the city home knew behind the door lay access to every vice Venice had to offer.

And Venice offered plenty of sin.

"What is our plan exactly?" Lysander asked as we approached the building.

A place like this was where scum like the Mordicum hung out. They had been lying low for a while, but I doubted that would last. "Find one of our terrorist friends. With Thea's coronation coming up, I need to find out if they were planning something."

"Just a thought, but couldn't we ask Camila? I thought she was with them."

"I don't trust Camila." I looked over at him, half expecting shock. But Lysander only nodded grimly. He understood my predicament. It wasn't that I didn't want to trust my twin. I couldn't trust her. Not after everything that had happened.

Not after she'd hidden from us for all those years.

"What are we going to do if we catch one?" he asked.

"I haven't gotten that far." My mouth curved into a wicked smile. "But we'll think of something."

I paused in front of the solid slab door, slid a glove off, and pressed my palm to the cold, rusting metal. The wards protecting the bar lifted, and the door creaked open instantly. That was the last deterrent to humans. Only magic got you inside.

Some things about *Sangue e Denti* were the same, but the interior had changed. The oak bar had been replaced by a polished marble monstrosity that matched the sleek, jet-black furniture that dotted the space. Several absinthe fountains glowed neon green against the bar's dark backdrop, and overhead caged black lights cast a purplish hue over the room. The sharp aroma of whisky mixed with licorice in the air, and somewhere underneath it all was the lingering scent of blood from someone's latest meal. Patrons leaned closely together over chrome tables, trying to keep their conversations private. They might as well try to stop breathing. A vampire bar didn't offer much by way of discretion.

"When was the last time you were here?" Lysander muttered as we entered.

"It's been a while." Honestly, I couldn't remember. I'd blocked my memories of Venice for decades. Now it didn't seem important.

But when the bartender looked up, rag in hand, and froze as she spotted us, I realized I was wrong.

"Fuck," I muttered.

Lysander's eyes followed me to the female, and he whistled. "I didn't think this was the kind of trouble you had in mind."

"It wasn't," I said in a low voice. "I can't believe she's still here."

"Maggie?"

"You remember her?" I asked.

"I met her once. I thought she was one of *Le Vergini*."

"A long time ago. She snuck out one night, broke her vow, and came back and told the queens. They kicked her out. I assumed she left town." That had been hundreds of years ago. "Someone must have turned her. If she stuck around the city, she might be able to help us."

"Will she?"

That was a good question. "It's worth asking."

But Lysander didn't move. He was still watching her, assessing. "The queens didn't punish her for breaking her vow."

"They kicked a kid onto the streets of Venice with nothing to her name. At the time, it was punishment enough. I went looking for her, wanted to help her, but I never found her." No wonder she'd found someone to turn her. Venice hadn't been safe for witches back then.

Maggie smiled at a patron, leaning onto the bar and fluttering her lashes over her almond-shaped eyes. The poor vamp didn't stand a chance against that. I continued watching her as she straightened and went to pour a drink. She didn't look our way again. She'd seen us, but she was doing a damn good job of ignoring me. It's not like I was the most popular guy in Venice.

"Are we going to say hello or get the hell out of here?" Lysander asked, eyeing the other patrons. He shifted on his feet.

I shot him a strained look. "Why are you so nervous? I'm the one she probably hates."

"It's not *her* I'm worried about," he said meaningfully and tipped his head.

I turned, realizing we'd attracted a fair bit of attention since our arrival. Faces scowled at us from the shadows.

"I supposed my reputation precedes me," I muttered.

"It will be a long time before Venice forgets *il flagello*," a cutting voice interjected. My memory pricked at the sound of her voice. Some things changed. Some things stayed the same. And she still sounded like the punk kid I'd known all those years ago. "Or perhaps they've heard the rumors that a king ascended the throne a few days ago. Maybe they want your autograph."

I swiveled slowly toward her. "You know better than to believe gossip, kid."

"I'm not a kid, and it's not gossip. I had people there." Her face was still twenty, but her eyes were older than I remembered. She looked tired, like she had spent too much time hanging out in the dark bar and not enough time in the sun.

I didn't ask her what she meant by people. Judging from this bar, which was full of the wrong kind of people, I already knew.

"They also say you took a *mate*," she continued.

"Maggie," I started, but before we could have that awkward conversation, a beefy vampire cut in.

"It looks like His Majesty came to visit us." He cracked his knuckles, nodding toward a table full of similarly burly companions. "Should we kneel before you?"

Lysander cursed under his breath, but I simply regarded him for a second before picking a piece of dust off my jacket. This was exactly what I'd been looking for—what I needed to quench this blood rage I felt every waking hour. A fight. My new friend just needed a push. "That won't be necessary. A simple bow will do."

Maggie groaned as the vampire's eyes bulged at my glib tone. "Do we have to do this?"

He answered her by taking a swing. I ducked, his fist cutting through the air with a loud *whoosh*. I grinned at her. "Getting soft on me, kid?"

As a trained handmaiden, she could handle herself. Now that she was a vampire, no one stood a chance against her. "You didn't just say that."

I winked at her and threw myself at the vampire just as his friends joined in.

Apparently, I'd been wrong. It hadn't been a table of burly companions. It had been *two* tables of burly companions, and from the looks of it, a few absinthe-doused patrons wanting in on the action, too.

"This ought to take the edge off," Lysander called. He twisted, narrowly avoiding a flying fist. He caught the vampire's arm and wrenched it behind the male's back. "Like old times, eh, Maggie?"

"Unfortunately," she yelled, then jumped clear of a vampire stumbling toward her. Catching him around the waist, she swung him into the heavy metal door. He collapsed to the floor in a heap. Before she could catch her breath, another one was on us. "Do you two start fights for fun?"

"Yes," I grunted as a female jumped on my back. Her arms coiled around my neck, and I caught sight of a red slash tattooed on her wrist.

Mordicum.

I needed to keep her alive, which, given that she was choking me to death, was a lot harder than just killing her. I darted for the nearest wall, twisting at the last second and throwing myself back into it. There was a snap as her ribs cracked. Her arms loosened, but she didn't let go, even as she bellowed out.

"I...can...do...this...all...day," I forced through gritted teeth.

Her nails sank into my neck, slicing through my skin and vanquishing any mercy I might show her. I smashed one more time into the brick, and she went limp, falling to the floor.

I didn't bother to see if she was unconscious or dead. One was as good as the other where vampires were concerned.

Spinning around, I discovered Lysander brandishing the neck of a broken whisky bottle at two males, smiling from ear to ear. He lifted his other hand and beckoned them closer with his index finger.

"I forgot how fucking cocky the Rousseaux brothers are," Maggie yelled, leaning over to spit a mouthful of blood on the floor.

"It's earned," I reminded her, starting over to help Lysander finish them off.

"That's not even fair. Two of you against them?" she called after me.

The bigger of the vampires growled at the insult. He swayed in my direction, swinging his fists. I caught sight of another tattoo peeking out from his rolled-up shirtsleeve. More Mordicum. We'd hit the jackpot.

"You aren't welcome here," he snarled.

Across from him, Lysander knocked his companion's head off his body. It took one lurching step and fell to the floor in a bloody heap.

"Here?" I snorted. "I've been coming here since before your lungs knew air."

He lunged forward, right into my waiting hands. My hand sank into his chest like a knife through soft butter. I'd caught one member. I didn't need another for questioning. Not when I could use the others to send a message.

My fingers closed over his heart, and I wrenched it free. Blood sprayed as his body processed its death. The heart beat once, twice, against my palm. I held it up for the rest of the bar to see.

"Anyone else want to go a round?"

There was utter silence, and then, as if nothing had happened, everyone went back to their drinks. I dropped the heart next to the corpse. Maggie sauntered back to the bar and tossed us both a rag before wiping her hands on one of her own.

"I haven't heard from you in over two centuries, and you show up and wreck my bar." She shook her head and reached for a bottle of vodka.

"*Your* bar?" I repeated.

"Why do you think I stuck around this swamp? It's not for the company," she grumbled. "I bought this place in the forties. It's my longest relationship."

She uncapped the bottle and poured some over her arm.

"You're hurt?" I asked, prowling forward and feeling that old protective instinct kick in. She rolled her eyes, and for a second, she was just a kid again. I blinked, and the moment passed.

Maggie wasn't a child anymore. She hadn't been for a long time, and between her training to protect the queens and being a centuries-old vampire, she could hold her own—a point she'd just violently proven.

"It happens, and I'm not mortal anymore." She took a swig from the bottle and held up her arm to show that it had already healed. "Now, which one of you assholes wants to tell me what's going on?"

CHAPTER TWENTY-FOUR

Thea

"Be on your guard," Aurelia warned me. We'd taken a speedboat to reach the Vampire Council's Venice Embassy, a solitary island on the outskirts of the city.

I nodded. I already was. Upon leaving the court, I'd felt my magic shift. It ached in my veins, wanting to be freed, although I had no idea for what reason. Maybe it missed Julian. I wondered if his magic was bugging him.

Jacqueline helped me onto the dock, the ocean stretching around us in a deep indigo blue that blended into the sky. Waves rolled toward the island's shore in heavy white-capped sheets of foam. I could taste salt in the air as the tide came in. Just like in Venice, there were isolated homes along it, but they were in far worse shape. Even the ground looked like a wasteland of concrete, rocks, and sand. A few other islands dotted the horizon, but they also looked deserted. Maybe it was a trick to keep tourists away. I shivered as I considered what would happen to a human who wandered onto an island occupied solely by vampires.

"You look preoccupied," Jacqueline said as I stared at the desolate world in front of us.

"I could say the same." I tipped my head toward Camila. The

two of them had been whispering in the corner the entire trip. I lowered my voice, hoping the crashing tide would keep Julian's twin from hearing me. "Everything okay there?"

"It's complicated," she said with a sigh, "and it's probably about to get a lot more complicated."

I couldn't help laughing as we followed Aurelia down a neglected stone path. Not because what she said was funny, but because she might as well have read my mind.

She frowned. "Thanks. That really helps my confidence this is going to go well."

We both knew it wouldn't. But Sabine was here, and despite what she'd said, I didn't think she would remain neutral and silent if we found ourselves cornered. "If things go south, how far will Sabine let things go?"

Jacqueline raised an eyebrow. "Do you want the truth?"

"Of course."

"She won't step in." Her lips pressed into a hard line, and she shook her head, blond locks rippling behind her.

"That's what Julian said," I said sourly. "He wanted to come. Maybe I should have let him."

"You'll be fine."

I stopped and turned on her. "Will I? I mean, I graduated from college a few weeks ago, and since then, amongst other things, I found out I'm a siren, died, came back to life, and was given a freaking crown. Nothing about this feels fine."

Jacqueline took a step closer and wrapped her arms around my shoulder.

"Sorry," I muttered, taking deep breaths. "I didn't want him to know how nervous I was."

"So you bottled it up." She pulled back and gave me an understanding smile. "He won't think less of you."

"I know that." I did. "He's been so worried lately. I didn't want to make it worse."

"When you were kidnapped…it screwed him up. I haven't seen him like that in a long time."

"You mean you haven't seen him that *violent* in a long time," I whispered.

Jacqueline nodded, and her eyes slid to the others walking in front of us. Aurelia and Camila were dutifully ignoring each other. I wondered how much of our conversation they'd caught. "Julian has always adapted with the times, but being here…"

Being here was dragging him back to his past, to a version of himself that I'd only seen glimpses of.

"I don't want him to be scared," I said.

"I know, but I've learned a few things from my time on this planet," she said with a wry smile. "The deepest fears are born from love. And I've never seen love as powerful as what you two share."

"Even more than yours?" I instantly wished I could take it back, but she only smiled sadly.

Her eyes strayed to Camila, still walking several paces ahead of us.

"We can talk about it later. Right now, we have an island full of old, powerful, unhappy vampires to deal with," she said, bypassing the question so artfully that I knew she'd asked herself the same and still didn't have an answer.

Ahead of us, the others disappeared around a corner. We picked up our pace, following behind them, but I paused as I saw what waited past the bend. The decayed landscape shifted into manicured grounds that led to a domed building. Roses grew in heavy vines up its sides, their blooms blood-red against the winter sky. Despite the sudden life, it was utterly silent, the only sound that of our footsteps on the stone. Even the scent of salt on the breeze died away, replaced by the cloying scent of roses. A pair of vampire sentries, clad entirely in black, stood on either side of the marble entrance. Neither looked as we approached.

"We're here to see the Council," Aurelia announced loudly.

They didn't budge as they continued to stare past us.

"What do we do—" I started to ask Jacqueline, but Camila cut in.

"We're escorting Thea Melbourne, *the queen*." Each word was a venomous dart, and it did the trick. The males shifted, but their expressions betrayed no curiosity.

One angled his head. "You are expected."

"We know." Aurelia rolled her eyes.

He leveled a harsh glare at her. "You are not."

"These are my personal...guards." It wasn't exactly true, but I was on the spot. "They come with me."

There was a moment of hesitation before he gestured toward the door, nodding to his partner to remain at their post. "This way."

The four of us shared a look as we set foot inside the massive stone building.

We passed through the columns and entered through the enormous oak door.

"Have you been here before?" I asked Aurelia.

"No." Her lips pursed, her hand moving to the hilt of her sword always strapped to her side. I wondered if she slept with it. "The Council and the queens keep a healthy distance. This is all new territory."

"I don't think anyone is going to attack us," Camila said.

We all looked at her like she was crazy, but she shrugged.

"If the Council wanted you dead, they'd do it in the middle of the night."

Well, that was a comforting thought.

"They would never get inside the court." Aurelia lifted her chin.

Camila's mouth quirked into a smirk. "Keep telling yourself that, sister."

"*Cam.*" Warning laced Jacqueline's word. "What have we talked about?"

Camila's jaw tightened, and she looked physically pained by whatever she was holding back. Finally, she smiled sweetly at my bodyguard. "I'm just being a bitch. I'm sure your court will never be breached."

The look they shared told me they were not on their way to becoming friends.

The vampire guard escorting us turned before the bickering

could start again. "Come. They do not like to be kept waiting."

He led us down a vast, dimly lit corridor lined with tall windows that looked out over the ocean. The marble floor was covered in a deep red carpet, and I wondered for one paralyzing second if it was to cover bloodstains. I was walking into one of their oldest embassies. Who knew what had happened here over the years?

Portraits hung in gilded frames between the arched windows. Our guide pointed to them. "These are the vampires that have served over the millennia."

Millennia. Would I ever get used to hearing things like that? My feet dragged. The air felt heavy, like there wasn't quite enough oxygen thanks to whatever magic the Council used to ward their private chambers.

I struggled to keep my face blank and my expression neutral as we entered a vast open room. Beneath a vaulted, stone ceiling, a group of six vampires sat in the room's only chairs, two males and four females. I recognized two of them. One was my future mother-in-law. The other was Selah, the vampire who had overseen my Second Rite—the one who had not been pleased when I passed it. They wore black cloaks that covered them from the neck down. If they were anything like Sabine, it was probably to hide weapons. Lots of weapons. Behind them more vampires in black were lined in a single, intimidating row.

I tried to make eye contact with Sabine, but she looked past me like I was invisible.

So that's how we were going to play this. Well, if she was going to act like a bitch, I would, too.

Breaking free from my companions, I walked right up to the seated vampires and planted my hands on my hips. "You summoned me."

Out of the corner of my eye, I swore I saw Sabine's mouth twitch.

But it was one of the males who spoke, his face drawn with distaste. "We have called you here to see to an important matter. It's been a long time since the Council and the queens have spoken officially."

"I gathered," I said drily. "That's why I deigned to come."

He looked to Sabine. "Is she always so *insolent*?"

"Yes, *she* is," I answered before Sabine could.

Selah glared down at me. "You smell of your mate, but he is not with you."

"He wasn't invited," I said with a sugary smile, "but he sends his greetings."

"That is just as well." The male waved a dismissive hand. "The matter we must discuss is for you alone." He looked to my companions. "Perhaps, they should wait—"

"They stay with me," I said firmly.

"So be it," he said blandly. "The Council summoned you for a reason—"

"Your Majesty," Jacqueline interjected, moving to my side. She shrugged when his mouth went slack with shock at being addressed directly. "It seemed like you nearly forgot that part."

"Along with the bowing," Aurelia added.

I kept my shoulders squared, my gaze directed at them, and hoped that I looked fiercer than I felt.

Selah's lip curled at the suggestion. "We do not bow to *Le Regine*."

"Noted," I said coolly. "Now that we have that sorted...*why* am I here?"

Her face relaxed into a wicked smile, and I caught Sabine straightening in her chair, her own face grim. "We have called you here to discuss your *death*."

But I didn't back down. "I'm not so easy to kill."

Turned out it was easier to face the idea of death now that I'd actually died. Not that I was eager to repeat the experience.

Selah leaned forward, her gloved hands slipping from her robe to grip the chair. "Does death amuse you? We could arrange to see how you like it the second time around."

"Selah," the male said her name quietly. "We didn't call her here to make threats."

That was...surprising. "You didn't? I thought that was all you did."

I expected another annoyed reaction, but instead, he cleared his throat. He nodded to me, his face serious.

"We are not interested in making you our enemy. Rather, we have chosen to warn you." He moved so quickly that I barely had time to blink before he was standing in front of me, holding a sealed envelope.

It had a seal on it—a crescent moon being devoured by a snake.

My heart started to pound.

I stared down at the symbol that represented my throne. "What is this?"

There was no denying the mark.

He shrugged his massive shoulders. "We have held that in safekeeping, tasked with waiting for a new queen to ascend. It is meant for you. We have no idea what's inside."

"What do you mean, tasked? Who tasked you?" I hoped he didn't see my fingers tremble as I took it from him. Magic rippled against my fingertips, as though the paper itself was enchanted.

"Your predecessor," Sabine's lofty voice called from across the room. "Ginerva left it in our care."

That didn't make sense. It was pretty clear the queens and the Council didn't get along. Why would she trust them with it? "With you? Why?" I blurted out.

There was a flash of white teeth, and then Sabine swept toward me. Her cloak dragged across the ground behind her, its stiff fabric swishing ominously. "You aren't asking the right questions, daughter."

It was far from a term of endearment. It felt a lot more like a warning.

My eyes met hers as she neared me, searching for answers as to what the envelope contained. But if she knew, she showed no sign of it. "What are the right questions, *Mother*?"

Her eyes pinched together. "Tell me, is your insolence purposeful or do you hide behind it so no one sees how stupid you are?"

I drew a deep breath, exhaling it shakily. It seemed things were back to normal with Julian's mother and me.

"Sabine," the male called.

"What, Marcus?" She didn't bother to turn toward him.

I saw his jaw tighten, but he looked past her at me. "We have no wish to quarrel with the queens, but this letter has been a source of some interest."

"She left it with you before she died." I nodded, turning it over in my hands. Magic thrummed through my skin wherever the paper touched it. "Why? What's inside it?"

"Now you are asking the right questions," Sabine said, her words as sweet as arsenic. "Like you, Ginerva was young when she ascended the throne and equally impulsive and foolish—"

"We get the point," Aurelia cut in, glaring at her.

"You take offense at how I speak of your queen." Sabine lifted her eyebrow. "Perhaps if you had protected her better—"

"Enough." I wasn't about to let her drag Aurelia into this mess. "She couldn't have been more than a child when Ginerva died. She isn't to blame."

"A child? No." Sabine shook her head, a wicked smile playing on her red lips. "Those who dwell at court do not age like other mortals. Aurelia is much older than you."

I bit back a surprised exclamation, not wanting to feel like an idiot for not expecting something so obvious and common.

"We assume that is why you are staying at court. You have been cursed with mortality."

"So has your son," I whispered. "Our lives are bound."

"That is the other reason you are here," Selah interrupted. "We have fulfilled our duty to the late queen by giving you the letter. Now you will do us a favor."

"I will?" I barely contained my laughter.

"Yes," Selah said, her voice pitched low. "You will become a vampire. We cannot accept a siren sitting on the throne."

"Are you fucking kidding me?" I said, my hand going to my hip. "A favor is watering your plants while you're on vacation. You can't force me to become a vampire."

Sabine was noticeably paler than usual. Her eyes tracked me, seeming to whisper for me to be silent. Was this news to her, too?

"The sirens are a danger to us all," Marcus explained gently. "You will give up your siren magic and become like us. Don't you wish to live forever with your mate?"

"It does not matter what she wishes." Selah rose from her throne, her voice filling the room. "There can be no mortal queen. It endangers the source of all magic. Perhaps you should remember we can still prevent your marriage to Julian. It would be a shame if that happened…or if something happened to *him*."

My magic rose, white hot in my veins at her words—at the threat to my mate. Veiled or not. I curled my fists, trying to decide between unleashing my power or ripping her throat out with my bare hands.

"Don't," Aurelia said softly, taking a step closer as if to stop me. "We are outnumbered."

I'd forgotten about the silent Council members and their bodyguards. I might make it to Selah, but I doubted I would get a single strike in before I was stopped.

"I cannot become a vampire," I said coldly, looking from Marcus to Sabine and ignoring everyone else. "My life is linked to my mate's life. There is every possibility that if I die, he will die, too. But more importantly, I will not be forced to change to suit your prejudice."

A few of the Council members gasped. Selah gazed at me, her eyes twin daggers drawn and ready for a fight. Marcus sighed, the sound weighted with centuries of regret and frustration.

But I could have sworn Sabine was holding back a smile.

"*Le Regine* has enjoyed freedom over their own affairs because we allowed it, but it seems you are unwilling to carry on this tradition." Selah sniffed.

"The tradition of being bullied into doing whatever you say?" I asked. "Yep, I'm unwilling to carry that on."

To my surprise, Marcus moved forward, extending a gloved hand. "Please reconsider. Vampires face more enemies than ever before, and with the return of magic, there are other creatures—powerful creatures—that will hunt all of us. We must be strong. We must show a united front."

"Or maybe you could show them all that you aren't elite pricks," I told him. "Having other magical creatures on the thrones will unite us, if you allow it."

"Next, she'll tell us we should give thrones to werewolves or fae."

Aurelia flinched at the disgust in her tone. I was equally appalled. I'd seen vampires belittle the witches, but it seemed their prejudice wasn't limited to just the familiars.

I didn't back down an inch. "Why not? Vampires aren't the only ones with magic."

"Of course the *siren*"—she spit the word toward me—"wants to change *our* traditions."

I shook my head. "It's the twenty-first century. Act like it. We might have different magic, but sharing it will only make us stronger."

"She makes a good point." Jacqueline stepped to my side. "With magic awake—"

"We didn't ask your opinion." Sabine brandished a long finger in her direction. "And there are many reasons why we should never allow other creatures on the throne, *especially* a fae."

"Maybe that's your problem." Jacqueline crossed her arms. She didn't even blink under Sabine's withering stare. "The Vampire Council thinks it knows what our kind needs, but maybe you don't."

"Treachery!" one of the seated vampires yelled.

"It's common sense!" Jacqueline shouted back. "The world has changed. We have to change with it. Adapt or die."

"She's right." Camila moved to her side.

Selah's eyes narrowed as we marched toward Sabine's daughter. "Your opinion is not welcome here. Not after you aligned with those terrorists."

"The Mordicum aren't terrorists." Camila shrugged. "They simply want to even the playing field."

Selah recoiled, as if she wanted to put space between her and Camila. "By killing pureblood vampires."

"How else are they supposed to get your attention?" Camila

tipped her head and smiled.

"Sabine, your daughter is treading dangerous ground," Marcus warned her.

Sabine inclined her head before turning toward Camila. "You aren't here to accompany Thea, are you?"

We all looked at Camila. My stomach churned as I finally considered all the reasons she might have chosen to come along. I couldn't help worrying that Jacqueline's feelings had kept her from seeing the possibility that Camila might be working against us.

"No, I came to see you." Camila looked her mother directly in the eyes.

"I'm your mother. You can see me anytime," she said tightly.

I braced myself when I spotted the malevolent gleam in Camila's eyes. "This is a matter requiring the attention of the entire Council."

"What do you seek from the Council?" Marcus asked.

Camila's lips curled into a triumphant smile. "I've come to demand the right of *primus sanguis*."

There was a collective gasp followed by furious murmuring.

"*Primus whatis*?" I muttered to Aurelia.

Camila continued before she could answer. "I'm a married woman with my own children. It is my right to demand first blood."

"But your children—" Marcus began gently.

"Are alive," Camila cut them off. "Were they dead, I would have no right to make this demand."

"Your children died in the fire," Sabine hissed.

"No, they didn't." Camila lifted her chin, her eyes blazing. "You are hiding them, and I will know where they are, Mother. By *any* means necessary."

Arguments erupted all around me.

"She's challenging her mother to be the matriarch of her bloodline: *primus sanguis*," Aurelia told me under her breath.

"But to do that..." I recalled how Sabine had risen to become the Rousseaux matriarch. She'd fought and killed Dominic's mother. But it wouldn't go that far. Not between a mother and her own child.

"Remember when you slapped Sabine?" Jacqueline murmured

under her breath. "If Camila wins, she will take charge of the family."

And even if Julian was disowned, this would rip the rest of his family apart. Apparently, things *could* get worse. Much, much worse.

"And one of them will be dead?" I didn't know why I asked. I already knew that Rousseaux women were fully capable of killing each other. Hell, I felt increasingly homicidal the more time I spent with them.

But I couldn't let it come to this. If we could get both of them alone, we could reason with them. I could make Sabine see that Camila had every right to see her children and make Camila promise not to do anything too crazy. The last part might prove a little bit hard, but I had faith.

"Yes." Her eyes scanned the room like she was looking for exit routes.

I looked at Camila. She was gazing at her mother, Camila's face unreadable but her eyes hard. A flurry of activity in the corner caught my eye, and I turned to find several vampires in black cloaks bringing a small trove of weapons, from daggers and swords to pistols and bows, into the room.

"They aren't going to do it here and now, right?" This was happening too fast.

"A challenge before the Council must be resolved before them." Aurelia grabbed my elbow and began to steer me away from the action.

I yanked free. There was no way I was going back to my mate and telling him that I'd permitted his mother and sister to kill each other. "I can't allow this. We need a way to stop Camila. We have to find some way to make her realize that killing Sabine will not help her cause."

Before I could come up with anything, Selah's voice rang through the Council chamber. "Camila Drake—"

"Rousseaux," Camila interrupted. She stood, unflinching in her resolve, before them. "I reclaim my family surname as is my right as eldest female."

Jacqueline edged closer to us, shaking her head. Her face was pinched with worry. "She never should have agreed to change her name. It's not how things are done, but Willem…"

She didn't need to finish that thought. My father didn't have a strong respect for vampire tradition. In fact, he seemed to want to fuck with it as much as possible. Of course, he would have demanded she become a Drake and not the other way around.

"Wait." A thought occurred to me. "Does that mean that Julian will take my name when we marry?"

Jacqueline and Aurelia both swiveled toward me, twin looks of disbelief on their face.

"You're asking that *now*?" Aurelia said.

I held my hands up in surrender. "Not the time. Got it."

"Camila," Selah repeated her first name and continued without acknowledging her wishes, "you have demanded the rite of *primus sanguis*. Before the Council recognizes your request, you must give cause to why your mother is no longer fit for her role."

Whatever glimpses of affection I thought I'd witnessed between Camila and her mother fell away. A look of pure hatred twisted on Camila's face. *This* was why she had returned. It had nothing to do with regaining her freedom or reconnecting with her family. It wasn't just about finding her children.

It was about Sabine.

"She's really going to kill her," I said under my breath.

Next to me, Jacqueline nodded, her face white.

I had to do something fast.

"Where should I begin?" Camila addressed the Council. "I could start with the fact that I was kept locked away during my youth, forced to marry as a virgin."

"There was no law against that then," Sabine reminded the room.

"It's my turn to speak, Mother," Camila snapped. "Not that you've ever cared. She knew I was tethered to Willem Drake before our marriage—"

"I did not!"

"Silence," Selah demanded. "The challenger speaks. You will have your chance, Sabine."

Camila continued her litany of grievances against Sabine, her voice low and dangerous. She told them of her marriage and her mother's failure to step in to help her. Then she told them of how she'd been abandoned by her family, how they'd lied about her death and stolen her children. The room was silent as she spoke, all eyes trained on Camila, as if they were transfixed by her words.

I knew a very different story. The one my mate had told me. I believed Julian's version, but as I listened to Camila speak, I wondered if there wasn't as much truth to hers. At least from her perspective. Maybe neither of them had it right.

But even if there was truth to Camila's accusation, I'd seen a different side to Sabine; she had been genuinely grateful when I'd saved her son's life. Camila's tale was compelling to those who knew the Sabine I'd first met, but what of the female I'd glimpsed in the insanity following my resurrection? The mother who had thanked me. What about what she claimed then? That she had been acting one way to protect her children?

I couldn't decide which version of Sabine was the real one.

When Camila finished, Sabine's lips were pursed into a thin line, but she remained silent.

"Do you have any evidence to support your claims?" Selah asked Camila.

Camila opened her mouth to answer, but before she could speak, Jacqueline stepped forward. "I can provide witness testimony," she said quietly but firmly.

"What are you doing?" I hissed, grabbing her hand. "We should be stopping this, not participating!"

Jacqueline squeezed it and shot me a tight smile. "What I have to do for her."

Selah nodded in approval and gestured for Jacqueline to take the floor.

Jacqueline stepped in front of the Council members and began to relate what she had seen during countless visits to the Rousseaux estate over the years: Sabine's sharp words; how she'd isolated her daughter from society; how Camila had changed after being presented to society and meeting Willem; and how thrilled Sabine had been about all of it. None of it was damning, though. It was merely a balanced picture of what Camila's life had been like. It would be up to the Council to draw their own conclusions.

Jacqueline spoke for nearly an hour before finally finishing her testimony and returning to my side.

I wished I had a cell phone. Some way to contact Julian. He would know what to do in this scenario.

"Sabine, you may now share your side of the story," Selah told her, a glimmer in her eyes.

"Is there a point?" Sabine asked, glancing at each of her fellow Council members in turn. "You've known me for millennia. If you believe her after a few minutes, I'm not going to convince you otherwise."

Selah inclined her head, but the rest of the Council whispered amongst themselves.

"We will confer."

"Now they're conferring?" I asked in disbelief. "But they already got out the swords."

"This part is the formality. They're going to let them fight," Aurelia told me. "We need to get you out of here before they do."

I shook my head. "That's my mate's mother and his twin. I'm not going anywhere. I'm going to stop this."

"I knew you were going to say that," Aurelia groaned. "If they're both willing to fight, let them."

"We can't," Jacqueline said next to me.

"*Now* you're on my side?" I asked her. "Five minutes ago, you were testifying for Camila."

A muscle tensed in her jaw, and she told me in a low voice, "I promised her. I have my reasons for what I did. Please trust me."

Our eyes met, and I knew I had a choice to make. Jacqueline wasn't just Julian's best friend and Camila's lover; she was like my sister.

"How do we stop the fight?"

"I don't know," she said honestly. "There has to be a loophole."

Aurelia released a heavy sigh. "There is, but you won't like it, and neither will Camila."

"Do it," I said. What other choice did we have?

Aurelia stepped forward and cleared her throat loudly. All eyes in the room turned to her. "According to vampire custom, only two positions are to be revered above all others—the queens and the Council. To demand action that might endanger the lives of any bearing those titles would undermine that respect to lower vampires. It will send the wrong message to any seeking to challenge the authority of either group. Therefore Sabine cannot duel."

The Council members seemed taken aback by this point, and murmuring broke out amongst them once more as they discussed it fervently.

Finally, Selah stepped forward and declared, "The Council agrees with this assessment."

What a shock. No one sitting up there wanted to give up their holier-than-thou standing. I had to hand it to Aurelia. It wasn't going to resolve the feud between Camila and Sabine, but at least no one had to die.

"But," Selah continued, "the Council must allow a challenge to proceed. Camila will duel with a champion of Sabine's choosing."

"What?" I shrieked.

"I told you that you wouldn't like it," Aurelia said.

This wasn't a real solution. It was a bandage. Turning to Jacqueline, I said, "Any other ideas?"

Her eyes stayed pinned on Camila as she shook her head.

"If Sabine's champion loses, then what?" I asked Aurelia.

"She is no longer the Rousseaux matriarch. She will be under Camila's authority, and Camila will decide her fate."

That wouldn't be good. Not with Camila standing proudly, looking at her mother with pure loathing. How had she hidden that much hate from all of us? Or had we been too preoccupied with our own shit to see?

"And the others might decide she is no longer fit to sit on the Council," Aurelia added.

I studied Sabine from across the room.

"Who will be your champion?" Selah asked her.

She spoke in a hiss, as if she were a snake, but the words she uttered were as sharp and cutting as glass, as cold and as dangerous as ice. "My champion will be Jacqueline DuBois."

CHAPTER TWENTY-FIVE

Julian

Half an hour later, the bar was dead along with some of its patrons. The creatures that Maggie hadn't kicked out had taken off of their own accord. I took a seat on a worn barstool, rolling up my sleeves until I couldn't see the bloodstains.

Maggie leaned against the bar and arched an eyebrow. "Back in the game, I see, *il flagello*."

"Yes." I tried to keep the disgust off my face. What was the point of fighting it? I'd stepped into my old life to save Thea. I'd have to stay there to protect her now that she was a queen.

"You took his heart." She kept her eyes trained on me as she poured two fingers of vodka and pounded it back. "That might cause trouble."

"Isn't there always when we're around?" Lysander asked, dropping onto the stool next to mine.

"Then maybe don't come around again," she said flatly, but there was a sparkle in her eyes that hadn't been there when we first arrived.

"He was Mordicum. Most of the vampires in the bar were." I ran a hand through my hair and sighed. "Maggie, what do you know about this group?"

"More than I'd like." She pulled the bottle back and poured another shot. Her hand shook slightly as she drank. "They got started in the late eighties. At first, it was just rebellious punks who didn't like the Council's rules. Now, well, I'm guessing you know what they are now."

"Terrorists. Murderers."

"And you aren't?" she pointed out coolly. "You just walked into my bar and picked a fight that ended in death. How are you better than them?"

"She makes a good point," Lysander muttered.

I ignored him. "I'm fighting for someone—someone innocent."

"Let me guess." She rolled her dark eyes. "You're fighting for your mate. Males are so predictable."

"You don't approve." That didn't surprise me.

"Women can fight their own battles. That is unless your mate is too precious to get her hands bloody." She poured herself another drink but didn't offer any to us.

"She's not," I snarled.

"Then why are you doing it for her?"

I clenched my jaw to keep myself from growling. "Because she's not here."

"She can hold her own." She shrugged and took her shot. "Maybe I'll end up liking her after all."

"You will." Lysander smiled, his eyes lighting up as he spoke of her. A soft growl slipped from me, and he drew away with his hands up. "What? I like Thea."

"It's the mating instinct," I said through gritted teeth. "It's not easy to control."

"*Try*," Maggie said with false sweetness, "before you wreck the bar again."

"What about you?" Lysander jumped in. "Why are the Mordicum hanging out here?"

It was the question I didn't want to ask her, because I was afraid of the answer. She studied me for a second, as if she guessed what I was thinking. Finally, she leaned onto the bar. "They're everywhere.

You rich boys are too busy attending your balls and orgies to know what it's like for those of us in the lower classes. The Council doesn't care what we say. The second a Switch steps out of line, they're punished if they're lucky. Executed if they're not. We're expected to live by the same rules without any say in them."

"It sounds like you sympathize with them," I said softly.

"I understand them just like I understand you, but I'm not taking sides. This bar is a neutral zone." Her eyes scanned the trashed room. "Or it was until you showed up. Purebloods don't bother coming in here. The Council and those rich assholes don't bother with us unless it's to cause trouble."

"We're rich assholes," I reminded her.

She didn't deny it as she met my eyes. "And you caused trouble. What a surprise. What you are is a reflection of the Council. You're just as bad as they are."

"I don't believe that." I slammed my fist on the counter, making the glasses shake. "And neither do you."

The Maggie I remembered wouldn't feel that way, but time had a way of coloring one's opinions.

She moved to wipe the counter with a rag, mopping up blood spatter. "If you'd been around, you would know. Things are different."

That I *did* know. "Different how?"

"First you wreck my bar, and now you're interrogating me?"

"Let's not pick a fight with a friend," Lysander muttered.

My eyes met Maggie's, and I saw the same question I was asking myself reflected there. Were we still friends?

"We didn't come for trouble," I lied. It wasn't my finest moment, but admitting to her that we'd shown up with violent aspirations seemed a tad suicidal. "At least, not on purpose."

"Sure." She rolled her eyes. "What did you come looking for?"

"I need information." If Maggie had been running this bar for all these years, she would have the inside scoop on everything happening in Venice and who was behind it. "I need to know what happened to Ginerva."

"Didn't she die?" Maggie asked.

"Not of natural causes," I said drily. "But no one seems interested in telling me what happened."

"Why would I know?" she hedged, but her eyes flickered away from me.

"I'm guessing people spoke of her death."

"I heard it was a surprise to the Council," she said slyly. "They didn't know that the *Rio Oscuro* was in jeopardy."

I leaned closer. She definitely knew something. "What else have you heard?"

"I heard"—she lowered her voice like we weren't alone—"that you're paying for all the damage you did to my bar."

Next to me, Lysander chuckled. "Some things don't change."

"No, they don't." She straightened up.

"Like the cost of information?" I asked, taking out my wallet and throwing bills down on the bar.

"Oh no, that has changed. The price has gone up." She grinned at me. "Blame it on inflation."

I emptied my wallet and waited.

Maggie plucked up the bills, counting under her breath. When she was satisfied, she shoved them into her bra. "You want to know what happened to Ginerva?"

I nodded, hoping she wasn't just fucking with me.

"Ask her sisters."

"The queens?" Lysander blurted out, and I felt my blood run cold.

"They wouldn't jeopardize the source without knowing there was someone who could replace her," I said.

Maggie smiled and tapped her nose like I'd hit on something crucial. "Now you've got it."

"You're saying she was killed to clear her throne," I repeated, my ears buzzing. "But she was killed decades ago before Thea ever came here—before she was even born. They couldn't have known."

Could they? I thought of Mariana's vision the night Thea took the throne. She'd clearly seen her then. But Mariana had been the one to demand my mother return. The queens had dangled that throne over my mother's nose. Why? They had demanded my mother ascend the throne before they ever met Thea. It didn't make sense.

"One more thing." Maggie slid the bottle of vodka toward me, and I braced myself. "I'd stop asking yourself who your enemies are and start asking yourself who they aren't."

"And what are you?" I asked gruffly.

"I don't take sides, remember?" she said just as the door banged open, and a dozen vampires raced inside. "But I do take bribes."

Apparently, we weren't friends anymore, because Maggie had sold us out.

If there were rules to being a vampire, the first one would be not to trust anyone who wasn't your own flesh and blood. Or, in my case, not to trust anyone. Somehow I always managed to fuck up and do it anyway. Vampires poured into the bar, rapidly surrounding every possible exit. Lysander was already on his feet, but I didn't move.

There wasn't a point. We'd been ambushed, and until I knew who had bribed Maggie into selling us out, I couldn't be sure if we needed to fight or talk our way out.

A female, clad in black from head to toe, approached us. Her boots struck the stone floor of the bar with an echoing clack. She stopped a mere foot from Lysander. Her icy blond hair was pulled into a tight knot at the back of her head. That was a mistake I could use against her if this turned violent. It was practically a handle. She surveyed me, her milky blue eyes narrowing as if she knew what I was thinking.

Judging by her rigid posture and the close-fitting black pants tucked into her boots, she'd been trained like a soldier. She certainly carried herself like one. But there were no weapons strapped to her slender, muscled form. Something told me that made her deadlier than if she had bothered to arm herself.

"You two made this mess?" The blonde looked around the bar, her eyes stopping on the unconscious female before moving on to the body parts of the less-fortunate vampires. Her nose wrinkled at the iron scent of blood hanging in the air.

"We had help." I hitched a thumb at Maggie.

The blonde glanced at her, slightly surprised.

"Your guys started it, Berit," Maggie said coolly. "I couldn't let them destroy the whole place, and you know my number one rule."

The blonde I now knew was named Berit sighed deeply. "Yes. Yes. You break it, you buy it. I don't think it's meant that literally, Maggie."

"So you two are on a first-name basis," I said, wondering if this was about more than a bribe. I turned to my old friend, waiting for an explanation.

"We have an arrangement," she told me. "They drink here without causing trouble, and we're golden."

"That doesn't explain why you sold us out, kid."

"That's the other part of the deal. They keep this place nice and quiet and off Council radar, and I let them know if any persons of interest pop by." She shrugged. Her time in Venice had hardened her. It would do that to anyone.

"I didn't know you got into bed with terrorists."

She grinned at me. "Julian, I get into bed with whomever I please."

"I need a drink." Lysander groaned next to me. Turning, he stretched himself across the bar and grabbed a random bottle from below.

"Excellent idea," Berit said, and I blinked. I looked to Lysander, who stood with his fingers still gripping the bottle cap. "That will give us time to chat."

"Chat?" he repeated. "We just killed your men."

"You aren't the first, and it sounds like they started it." Berit crossed to us and perched on a stool. "They should have known better."

"How sentimental of you," I said with a hollow laugh.

"We can't afford to be sentimental, Mr. Rousseaux." She tapped the marble counter twice. "Or should I say, Your Majesty?"

"You shouldn't," I warned her. "I'm not royalty."

"But you are mated to a queen, if the rumors are true."

I remained silent. She was baiting me, and until I knew what she was after, I refused to give her anything.

Maggie placed a wineglass in front of her before producing a bottle of Syrah.

"What do you want to talk about?" I asked.

"These aren't the first of our people that you've killed." It wasn't quite a question, since she already knew the answer.

"Do you want me to say I'm sorry?"

Her nostrils flared as she lifted her wineglass to her lips. "I want you to stop killing us."

"You first," I said with mock sweetness.

She swallowed with a loud gulp. "Easier said than done. Your people have pissed off a lot of vampires."

"My people? What does that mean?"

Berit's jaw tensed for a moment, and I knew whatever came next was key to understanding not only her demand but the Mordicum itself. "I think you know, but in case you're as stupid as you're acting, I'll tell you. The purebloods and their elite families, the Council, even the queens."

"And what makes them my people?" I pressed.

"You were born into one of the oldest pure bloodlines in vampire history. You're one of them, even if you don't want to admit it. You protect them all. Their enemies are your enemies, and since they see us as a threat, I suppose that means we're enemies, too. But I would like to change that."

This wasn't going exactly how I expected it would. I glanced at Lysander and found his face shadowed but his eyes alert. Our first direct contact with the Mordicum wasn't what either of us had thought it would be, but we weren't about to drop our guard.

"That's fair, I guess," I said. "But why do you care who I'm fighting for?"

Berit smiled, her white teeth stained with red wine. "Because if we're ever going to change things, we need more allies and less enemies."

"Maybe you should kill fewer vampires," I suggested. I didn't buy any of it. I had been there that night at the opera. I'd seen exactly what the Mordicum wanted to do to vampire families like mine.

"You first." She smirked and took a sip of wine.

"I'm not as easy to buy as some." I kept my tone light, but Maggie stilled behind the bar. She didn't say anything, but I knew the barb had struck its target.

"What if I told you that we want the same thing?" Berit asked.

"I doubt that." I snagged the bottle from Lysander's hand.

"Hey! Get your own."

I ignored my brother. "You seem to want to kill innocent people."

"And you don't, *il flagello*?"

"I said in-no-cent."

"That's where you are wrong," she told me. "We aren't interested in killing innocent vampires."

"The vampires at the opera—"

"Were not innocent," she cut me off.

"And the familiars you killed?"

"Unfortunate casualties. That happens in war."

"Are we at war?" I asked slowly.

"We will be," she said, her eyes pinned to mine.

"Is that a threat?" I muttered.

"It's a warning—and one I hope you heed before it's too late."

"Now that definitely sounds like a threat," Lysander interjected. "Why should we listen to anything you have to say?"

I leaned against the bar and waited for her answer. My brother did the same, but Berit paused.

"We are all vampires," she murmured, her eyes swept over the floor, searching for the words she needed to explain. "The Mordicum only wants to see that all vampires are treated equally."

"Equally?" I repeated. "Good luck." It wasn't in a vampire's nature to worry about things like that. That was especially true the older a vampire was.

"Things have to change," she hissed, abandoning her wineglass to lean closer. "Especially now that magic has awoken."

"I don't see how that affects you."

"Why, because I'm a Switch?" she asked coldly.

I lifted one shoulder. "Like it or not, magic is diluted from generation to generation, especially if you've been turned."

"And that's your problem." She jumped to her feet, her shoulders shaking slightly, as if her rage might consume her entirely. "You want to tell us what to do, how to live, but as far as purebloods are concerned, we're not even real vampires."

"I never said that."

"You might as well have," she hissed. "Magic has awoken, but it is not free to all of us. Not while the *Rio Oscuro* is controlled by the queens. Magic is still being throttled by their thrones. Switches may have little magic, but it is ours and it is being controlled. Now more than ever, vampires need to be united."

"That's what you're trying to do?" I asked.

"You might want to rethink your tactics," Lysander added.

"We haven't had a choice. The Council ignores us. The queens have hidden away. And we've been left to die."

I sat up, staring at her. "Die? What do you mean?"

"As if you would care," Berit spat back. Her eyes slanted, twin shards of blue glass that sliced through me.

I gritted my teeth. My hands clenched into fists, digging into my palm and drawing blood. "Tell me."

"Something is hunting us. Something even worse than you." She lifted her glassy gaze to mine, and beneath the cool blue, I saw the storm raging inside her.

"What?" I asked. "How do you know this?"

"The body count," she said grimly.

"Vampires die," I reminded her.

"Not like this," she said, her tone cautious. "Whatever is killing us is a monster."

"I've heard nothing about this." I turned to my brother and found his face as puzzled as mine. He shook his head.

"The Council knows," Berit told me. "Ask Maggie."

We both looked at her, and she took a deep breath. "It's true. The streets are not safe for Switches." Maggie shot an apologetic look at Berit. "No offense."

"I don't care what you call our people," she said. "I care that we're being murdered and no one is doing a damn thing."

"And what would you have us do?"

Maggie sighed heavily, the sound echoing in my ears. This wasn't about a bribe at all. She sympathized with them, but could I trust what Berit was saying?

Berit's face twisted with disgust, but she answered me. "Listen to us. Join with us before it's too late."

"If there was a threat—" Lysander started.

"There is," Berit stopped him, "and when this monster finishes with us, it will come for you."

"You can't know that," I said.

"It will come for him." She tilted her head to my brother. "And all vampires that were turned, and when it's through with us, it will come after the rest of you. The monster is insatiable, and now that magic is awake..."

I waited, already knowing what she was about to say.

"No creature is safe." Her lips twisted into a mocking grin. "Not even your beautiful mate."

I swallowed but refused to give in to the swell of fear that surged through me at the threat. "And what would you have me do?"

"What you do best." She looked directly at me, her piercing gaze cold and unyielding. "Find this monster *and kill it*."

CHAPTER TWENTY-SIX

Jacqueline

Sabine's smile was a crimson slash on white snow as deadly as the whisper of a knife across skin. A loud buzz grew in my ears, the world dimming around me, as I processed what she had said—what she had *done.*

She had chosen me.

"No." Camila's voice cut through the blur in my head.

"You have no say in your mother's choice of champion." Selah clicked her tongue like she was shaming a small child. And I realized that was how they saw her. *Because* Sabine had coddled and confined her. Even now as she stood before the Council, demanding her retribution, they only saw Sabine's daughter.

I saw *Camila.*

I saw her rights and her wrongs. I saw her anger and rage and vulnerability and madness. Why couldn't they? I saw how her shoulders squared, not in challenge but to hold the weight of her past. I saw a million questions when I looked at her. I saw a stranger that I'd once known. And I saw the answer to every question I'd ever asked myself.

I also knew why Sabine had chosen me. Not because she wanted to hurt her daughter. It was a test.

One that Camila would fail.

Because despite everything that had happened to her, Camila still had goodness inside her.

She wouldn't allow me to fight. Camila would drop her challenge. She would walk away because she loved me. She had always loved me. I didn't know what that meant for us in the future. I wasn't sure we could ever heal the wounds that threatened our relationship. I wasn't certain I could be in love with this version of her—that I could make it work.

Or if she even wanted me back.

But she wouldn't kill me.

And that was the problem.

I started forward, but Thea stopped me. "You can't do this. Please."

"Trust me." It was the second time I'd asked this of her since we'd arrived.

Thea froze before nodding slowly. Julian's poor mate had been thrust into this world, and it had shaken her up. But I had lived my whole life dealing with vampire bullshit, and I knew one thing that Thea didn't.

There was always a loophole.

I carefully avoided Camila's eyes as I approached the Council. Bile rose to the back of my throat, my stomach roiling as I walked. I was going to vomit everywhere and give away my true feelings.

It was one thing to bluff, but I was playing a much more dangerous game. I was toying with not only my life but the life of the woman I loved.

Sabine blinked, the only sign she hadn't expected me to acquiesce to her demand. Still, she held her ground. Her form was elegant, tall, and proud—a lioness who didn't need to pounce, because it was obvious how deadly she truly was.

"I challenged my mother, not Jacqueline," Camila cut in, her voice sharper than it had been a few moments ago.

"And we have been clear about the rules." Selah bowed her head, her curls falling over her black cloak in a swirling wave.

"Sabine will not fight. She has chosen her champion. But if you wish to withdraw your challenge…"

The implication of her words hung in the air, and I couldn't stop myself from turning toward Camila. Our gaze locked, lingering in an unspoken conversation as the invisible connection built between us. The deep blue of her eyes was captivating, yet raging in its depths was a vast and tumultuous sea of grief. I wanted to reach out, to offer her comfort, but I could sense her walls, built out of years of hurt, blocking me from getting close. They would never come down. I would never reach her. Not until she was free of this.

There was only one choice. She had to fight.

"You should withdraw," I said, mustering and masking the fear I felt into icy coldness. "You can't beat me. You spent your life hiding, not fighting."

Camila's mouth dropped open, and behind me, I heard a gasp that I knew came from Thea.

It wasn't enough. I needed to make sure that Camila believed it. I needed her to want to kill me.

"She's too scared to fight me." I turned my head to Selah. "You might as well be signing her death warrant. She's weak. Even her mother knows it. Sabine has always known it, which is why she controlled her. She knew that she would just get herself killed and now—"

"Only the challenger may withdraw the challenge," Selah interrupted me. "Do you wish to do so, Camila?"

Camila's face contorted in a mixture of pain and rage, her eyes desperately seeking mine, yet I refused to meet her gaze, turning away with a disdainful roll of my eyes. It stung that she believed me, but I pushed down the rising mixture of emotions that threatened to overtake me.

"I do not," she said, her voice ringing in the silent room like a hollow bell.

Relief mixed with my horror that I had forced her hand—that she believed I would fight her to the death. Now I had to do just that. There was no other choice.

Selah's lips curled into a smirk that made me want to grab the nearest sword and slice her cruel head from her neck, but that wouldn't help the situation.

"*Primus sanguis* will be awarded to the champion of the duel. Once the challenge is accepted by both parties, only surrender or death ends it. In the event of death, the victor will claim the head of the fallen party."

I wondered how many of those heads had been mounted like trophies over the years. My stomach flipped at the thought, and I nearly threw up my breakfast.

"And how do they surrender?" Thea asked loudly, pure panic racing in her voice.

"No party has ever surrendered," Selah said with a shrug. "But we allow the option."

It wasn't the vampire way. Not with so much at stake, and the shame of losing was too much for any female to bear. Our pride was both our greatest strength and our undoing. Was that why Sabine had chosen me?

Or was it because she believed I was no match for her daughter? Aurelia was a trained warrior. Most of the other vampires bearing witness were eons older than us, with centuries of battlefield experience. I was the least likely to win, but the choice that would hurt Camila most.

Everyone here knew the real reason that I'd been selected: Sabine assumed her daughter would withdraw the challenge. Or I would refuse to be Sabine's champion. It was the only way out of this. It was my only choice in the matter. If I said yes, Sabine would choose my weapon, dictate my stance, and watch as I fought her daughter to the death.

But I didn't want to get out of this. I wanted to get it over with.

"I will be her champion," I said in a low voice.

The room descended into silence; even Sabine stared at me, her composure collapsing under the weight of her own outrage that I'd called her bluff. For a moment, her lips parted as if to speak, and then she pressed them together into a thin line. Her nostrils flared as she looked away.

"There will be no mercy. No person may intervene," Selah continued. "The winner will hold the title of *primus sanguis* when she claims the other party's head or her pride."

I knew which was more important to most vampires, but this was different. Sabine and I were different. At least, we used to be. Now? I wasn't so sure that I wouldn't leave here without bloody hands.

Selah stepped to the side, flourishing an arm toward the weapons cache. "Sabine, as head of house, you may choose your weapon."

Sabine tipped her head graciously, gesturing for me to join her. The vampires surrounding the cache moved away, allowing us a moment of privacy. We met at a stone table strewn with weapons of every type. Swords and maces, daggers with jeweled hilts, single-shot pistols, even a crossbow.

"What are you doing?" Sabine's fingers closed over the ruby hilt of one of the swords.

"You chose me to be your champion," I reminded her in a low hiss. "What did you expect me to do?"

"Refuse," she told me. "Force me to demand more time to choose someone else so that Camila will see reason."

"Do you honestly think she will?" I asked. "You have a choice, too. Surrender. Tell her where her children are."

"Why would I do that?"

"Because you're her mother." I snorted, half amazed at my own stupidity. I knew better than to expect so much from her. My own mother would never do the same for me. I really had to stop being so fucking optimistic.

"This one." She handed me a short sword, the blade honed and razor-sharp. Lightweight but lethal, its handle fit into my palm so perfectly that it could have been made for me. Sabine was a warrior. She knew her weapons. My stomach plummeted. This wasn't a sword chosen for losing a duel.

It was one meant for winning one.

"No mercy, then?" My voice trembled a little, but I recovered quickly. I would not allow her to see my doubt.

Her answering smile sent shivers slithering down my spine. "Do you have to ask? I *am* head of this household."

I swallowed and forced myself to smile. "Good."

Sabine paused, her calculating eyes scanning me. "You will fight to the death, then?"

I knew the real question she was asking.

"You overestimate my feelings for your daughter," I told her, allowing my smile to crack open wider. She stared for a moment.

I took the sword and moved to the side. She followed without another word. At least I didn't have to sit through her instructions on how to fight. I could handle myself.

"No surrender," she reminded me, and I realized the game she was playing.

"You think she'll surrender rather than kill me, don't you?" I asked, shaking my head. Maybe I wasn't the only one playing a dangerous game, but I had something worth fighting for. Sabine? She didn't know how to lose, especially when it came to her status. How far would she go to cling to that power? We were about to find out. I couldn't help but laugh.

Her eyes widened, and I knew I'd managed to get under her skin. She thought she could play us both. Save her daughter and her power.

"Why are you laughing?" she demanded through gritted teeth.

"Because I know something you don't." I chuckled again, even though I was half sick over what was about to happen. "You're overestimating your daughter's feelings for me. She stopped caring what happened to me a long time ago."

And this duel would prove it.

CHAPTER TWENTY-SEVEN

Camila

Jacqueline wouldn't look at me. It wasn't the first time I'd pissed her off, but it might be the last. She moved away from the table, sword in hand, and continued to whisper with my mother. Panic seized me, and for a moment, I couldn't move, couldn't think, couldn't breathe.

"Your turn," Selah said in that bossy tone that made her so easy to hate. I'd always hated her, even when I was a little girl and she would stop by for afternoon tea. It was something in her eyes— something predatory—that I had never quite trusted. She had joined the Council not long after my mother, and like my mother, she would do anything to keep her position.

"Thanks for the update," I said drily, knocking my shoulder into hers as I passed.

Sarcasm was my only friend. It didn't surprise me that Thea hadn't bothered to intercede in my challenge. My brother's mate hated me. Not that I could blame her. I wasn't overly fond of anyone who had tried to kill me, either. Her indifference hadn't stung, but Jacqueline's had. Not that I was about to show that to her.

I'd been stupid to think we could forgive and forget. Even the testimony she'd promised to give the Council was cold and disinterested.

I stopped in front of the weapons and leaned down, placing my palms on the stone table. Its chill seeped into my skin and made me shiver. I stood quickly and hoped no one saw that small tremble. It was a sign of frailty I couldn't afford, especially after Jacqueline had proclaimed I was too weak to fight her. The worst part was that she was partially right. I wasn't weak, but I was scared. Not of facing an opponent, but facing *her*.

I looked over the weapons, not really taking in any of the details but instead focusing on the task before me. This was it. My challenge had been accepted. If I won, Sabine would have no choice but to reveal what she'd done with Hadrian and Laurel.

All I had to do to finally reach my children was kill the love of my life.

No big deal.

At least, it shouldn't be. Not when Jacqueline seemed eager to be done with me. Not if it was the price I had to pay to see my children again. So why did it all feel *wrong*?

I'd returned to my family for one reason: to destroy them and take back what was mine. It had been easy to keep hating them. None of them were sorry. None of them cared about what they'd done to me. But I had not counted on Jacqueline… I had not expected to find I still loved her after…everything.

I looked over at where she stood with my mother. Jacqueline's face was stony, an expression I'd grown familiar with over the years. Her fingers flexed around the hilt of her sword like she was ready to fight.

My gaze dropped to a long, polished blade. It had no jewel-encrusted hilt or fancy engraving like most of the others. It was simple, like death itself, and there was something beautiful about that. What was death but a transaction—an exchange of souls between this world and the Underworld?

I reached out and touched its hilt, feeling its balance and savoring the weight of its steel. It stirred the rage in my blood. They thought I was weak because of my mother and Willem, but I had walked through hell and lived. I would not go back there easily. Not while my children walked this earth. Not even if it meant choosing my life over someone I loved.

I raised the sword, pointing it at Jacqueline.

"No mercy," I said. I'd slipped earlier, when my mother had chosen Jacqueline as her champion. I wouldn't make that mistake again.

Lifting my eyes, I found Thea watching me as she whispered frantically with Aurelia. She was probably trying to find a way to save her bestie from me. I offered her one cruel smile, and she blanched.

Selah swept into the center of the room and nodded to us. Slowly, I made my way to join her, Jacqueline doing the same. With each step I took, the blade felt heavier in my hand, as if my body was at war with my mind, with my heart. I knew what I had to do. There was no choice. I had to kill Jacqueline. It was my only chance to finally be free of the past. It was the only way I would have a future with my own family.

My eyes caught Jacqueline's as we faced each other. Neither of us looked away this time. My heart protested, speeding up with each beat, but I refused to turn away. I refused to be the one to surrender.

"You may not expect mercy," Selah reminded us. "The victor has the right to claim the loser's head, even in the unlikely event one of you surrenders."

Blood thundered in my veins, and my hand clenched around the cold hilt of my weapon. I wanted my mother's head, not Jacqueline's. I would have taken Mother's, too—after I forced her to tell me where my children were.

"Any final words?" Selah asked.

I shook my head, but Jacqueline smirked.

"Good luck," she said, the words dripping with sweet venom.

Good luck? Good fucking luck? The room went black, and I reacted on instinct. My blade sliced through the air with a metallic whoosh. Jacqueline leaped backward, raising her own weapon to block my next strike.

And so the fight began.

Every reason I had to stop this fell away as I realized the truth. Neither of us would win this fight.

But one of us had to, and for the sake of my children, it had to be me.

They'd been in *my mother's* care this whole time.

When I'd joined the Modicum, I was weak, but they had trained me—honed me into something sharp and lethal. I focused on that instead of my opponent. This was all a dance. She slashed. I parried. I lunged forward, and she faded with ease.

Pivot.

Retreat.

Thrust.

Jab.

Children—my children—I fought for them. Each movement, I reminded myself of that, reminded myself of what I had lost and what I stood to gain, even if it meant giving up the person I wanted most. Somehow it was easier that it was her fighting me.

Maybe because it had always been Jacqueline.

I'd been fighting my feelings for her for years, at first hiding our relationship. Then, forbidden by Willem to see her, I tried to stop loving her. I'd waged this battle so long that now everything fell away. There was only her. Only me. Only the music we made—the whisper of our blades slicing air, the sharp ringing as our steel met—and this beautiful, deadly dance.

Our bodies spun, and my head turned toward hers just long enough to spot something unexpected in her eyes.

Dread.

Not determination. Not the cruelty she'd spewed before. My foot caught on an uneven stone, and I stumbled. My sword twisted up and away from me as it slipped through my fingers. It spun away from me and landed with a deafening, hollow clang on the floor. I scrambled for it and found her blade at my throat.

The tip of it pressed into my skin, and I forgot how to breathe.

I had died once, but this time would be different. This time I would die looking into the eyes of my best friend. I wasn't certain if that made it better or worse.

The world zoomed back into focus and balanced on the tip of her blade. Murmurs grew louder around me and turned to shouts.

"End it!"

"Kill her!"

Jacqueline held her position. She didn't look away.

"Do it," I said softly enough that only she could hear.

I took a step forward, and the blade fully pierced my skin. Searing pain shot through me, but before I could take another step, Jacqueline spun. She caught my arm, pinning it behind my back as she brought the sword's edge to my throat.

She was close enough that I felt her heat against me, smelled her sweet scent. Despite the futility of my position, my body responded, pressing against hers, searching for contact. Maybe it was always going to end like this. I'd never been able to resist her before. How could I in my final moments?

"Do it," I said again.

"Shut up," she snarled softly in my ear. "You made this choice. Do you regret it?"

I started to shake my head but, considering the sword at my throat, decided against it.

"No," I murmured.

"You would kill me, then?"

"For my children?" I asked. "Yes."

My heart splintered even more as I admitted it, but I owed them that.

"Why?" she whispered.

"Because I failed them." Pain cracked my words. "And I will not fail them again."

"And would you die for them?"

"Yes," I said without hesitation. "And I will not live another day without them." Reaching up, I grabbed the blade, barely processing the sting as it cut through my flesh. I pushed it into my own throat and felt my warm blood spill. Jacqueline's grip faltered.

"Camila." My name whispered from her lips like a prayer. "Don't."

I opened my mouth to speak, but there was only the gurgling, hideous sound of wet violence.

The hand pinning my arm behind my back moved, and her fingers clasped mine. I finally knew this was how I wanted death to come to me—in her arms. It didn't hurt. Not with her here. I wondered what this death might bring.

I hoped it would be peace.

"No mercy," Selah shouted.

"Trust me," Jacqueline whispered, her lips brushing my ear as she pushed the blade deeper.

I do, I wanted to say. I always had. I always would. And if she was my death, I welcomed her with open arms. I closed my eyes.

"Stop!" Sabine's scream shattered my peace. "Stop! I surrender."

CHAPTER TWENTY-EIGHT

Julian

We were alive, despite finding the Mordicum. But for how much longer? The day faded into night. Stars winked on in the deep, midnight blue sky overhead. In the dimming light, rose vines turned into shadowy tendrils that reached above us like a warning.

"What now?" Lysander asked as we trudged through the court. A few vampires turned to stare at us, and I glared at them. I wasn't sure what it said about these particular courtiers that they were shocked over seeing one of their kind post-fight.

Maybe Berit had been right when she'd said that my kind did nothing. There was a time when every pureblood vampire had seen a dozen battlefields. Now, not so much, and many seemed content to forget it ever happened.

A young vampire in a well-fitted suit, his skin smooth alabaster, stared as we walked toward our private quarters. His gloved hands clenched and relaxed nervously. I didn't know if it was my bloody clothes or notoriety. I also didn't care. I bared my fangs at him, and he shrank away, backing toward a nearby group of vampires.

"We need to get out of Venice," I muttered.

"And how the hell are we going to do that?" Lysander laughed at the idea. "The Third Rite is coming up and, well…"

My mate's duty was bound to this city. More than ever, I wished I could go back in time and stop her from ever coming here.

He didn't offer any suggestions, and we both remained trapped by our thoughts as we walked.

"We need to get to the bottom of this monster bullshit," I said, breaking the silence as we entered the private residence of the queens. It would never be home to me, but at least there was no one here to stare at us.

Lysander nodded. "We do."

"But what is this monster, and why is it targeting Switches?" I'd never heard of a monster that preyed on vampires. Usually, *we* were on top of the food chain.

"Whatever it is, if it's targeting vampires, we're screwed," he said, his words echoing my thoughts.

"*If* Berit is telling the truth," I said.

"Why would she lie about it? They could have just killed us. We were outnumbered," he pointed out.

I groaned, throwing an arm over his shoulder. "When did you lose faith? We totally could have taken them."

"Were you willing to risk Thea's life to prove it?" he asked in a low voice, like the oil-painted portraits might be able to hear us.

Anger swirled inside me as I considered the question. Not for the first time, I wondered if I was following my heart or if I was merely doing the right thing. I didn't bother to answer. Instead, my eyes narrowed and focused on the four women standing by a large stone hearth in the great room. I'd forced myself to keep my mind off Thea as we made our way home, refusing to give in to the panic I'd felt when Berit had warned me that my mate wasn't safe. Now her warning rang in my head.

No creature is safe. Not even your beautiful mate.

But Thea was right here. Safe. Whole. I scanned her quickly, looking for anything that might warrant concern. There wasn't a scratch on her. Still, my pulse picked up speed as we approached. I wouldn't be satisfied until she was in my arms—until I could touch her.

I tore my eyes from her and glanced at the others, nearly coming to a halt when I saw Camila. Blood coated her entire upper body, and nervous energy seemed to radiate from her. Jacqueline paced the length of the fireplace, her eyes flickering to Camila every few seconds and looking away as soon as my twin caught her.

"Why is my sister covered in blood?" I asked slowly.

"Why are you covered in blood?" Camila shot back.

Thea spun around, a strangled cry escaping her when she spotted me. Tears welled in her eyes, falling down her cheeks as she scanned me with a look of absolute horror. It was that look that stopped me.

"Not important," I muttered to my twin, not tearing my eyes from Thea.

"I could say the same." But the dark edge of Camila's words and the obvious pain on Thea's face told another story.

"Whose blood is this?" Thea asked, not moving a single step in my direction. Exhaustion etched lines around her eyes, and I felt a wordless plea to save us from this conversation.

I wanted to go to her—wanted to gather her in my arms and kiss her—but Lysander stepped between us.

"We ran into some Mordi-*scum*," he said.

That got everyone's attention, but I shrugged. It was the least of my worries. The facts that Thea was tired and Camila looked like she'd seen at least as much action as we had were both much higher on my list of concerns. My mate turned, waiting for me to explain.

"Don't worry about it."

Thea's lip trembled, and she turned away. I wasn't sure if she was waiting for an explanation or upset that I'd shown up in my barroom brawl attire.

"You?" I tipped my head at my sister.

"Don't worry about it," she parroted me with a mocking smile.

Aurelia stepped forward. "She challenged your mother for *primus sanguis*."

"You what?" I whirled on Camila, my stomach plummeting like a stone.

11252943527387

"And she won," Aurelia continued. For a brief second, I couldn't move, couldn't think, as I processed this information. If Camila had challenged our mother to a duel…

My brain refused to do the rest of the work.

"She's dead?" Lysander asked, his words coated in disbelief.

It couldn't be true. Our mother couldn't be…not at the hands of my sister. Camila hated her for what she'd done, but my twin also loved our mother in her own way. Just as I did. I took one stumbling step forward, and Thea rushed toward me. Maybe she wasn't as tired as I thought, which would be a relief. Especially with the news I had to deliver to her.

"She's alive," Aurelia said, "but she is pissed."

"But if she's alive…" Lysander blinked a few times, his confusion mirroring my own. We all knew the rules of a *primus sanguis* challenge. There were two ways to lose: die or… "She *surrendered*?"

"Crazy, right?" Camila rubbed her hands together in front of the fire.

"I can't believe you got our mother to surrender," I repeated.

Her nose wrinkled, and she shot a frustrated glance at Jacqueline. "Jacqueline did it."

"I did what I had to do." Jacqueline held her hands up, and I sensed we'd walked into a much bigger argument. One that needed some privacy.

"It sounds like you two have some things to talk about," I said smoothly, reaching for Thea's hand. I held down a moan of relief when my skin met hers. I didn't know why her gloves were off, but I was glad about it. "I should change."

I tugged Thea gently by the hand back toward our quarters.

"We need to talk," Lysander called after us. "Can't that wait?"

"No!" I yelled back.

Despite her annoyance with me, Thea giggled as we dashed toward our rooms. As soon as we were inside, I hauled her over my shoulder and locked the door behind us.

"Where are you taking me?" she demanded, wriggling to escape.

I held her firmly. "To bed."

Instantly, she stopped fighting. At least we were on the same page about that. She didn't say anything as I continued in that direction, but as we reached the bedroom, her voice sounded in my head.

I need you, too.

It was the first good news I'd had all day. My blood rage had nearly gotten out of control at the bar. Tamping it down had taken a considerable amount of effort. The second I'd spotted Thea outside, my fragile grip on it had given way to full-blown bloodlust.

The bedroom was dark as we entered, but I didn't stop to turn on the lights. Later, I would inspect her with them on, but for now, I would take her word that no one had touched her. It was everything I could do to keep myself from going to my knees and devouring her.

But something held me back, and I paused, studying her in the dark.

Thea reached to stroke my face. "Are you hurt?"

"Not even a scratch."

"We need to talk," she said.

"We will," I promised, my voice strained as I continued. "But right now, I need my mate."

There was a lot to deal with, but I was also increasingly aware of how painfully hard my dick was becoming with each second that passed. Knowing what I did now, I needed to touch her, feel her, remind myself that she was real, that she was safe.

"Then claim me," she whispered.

Tears salted her lips as I claimed her parting mouth, welcoming me, and I deepened the kiss. I would never get enough of her, but this was different. Though she hadn't been directly threatened, I wasn't stupid enough to ignore the danger she was in.

For a moment, there was only the rustle and whisper of clothing as we undressed each other, as she shucked my bloody clothing from me. Her fingers coasting along the ridges of my abdomen, reaching lower to wrap around my cock. I groaned as she pumped her fist, leaning to kiss her bare shoulder. My tongue lashed down her neck, nipping at the pulsing veins in her pale skin.

Claim me.

It wasn't a demand. Instead, the thought was edged in desperation. I had no idea what drove her need, but I felt the same raw hunger. Pulling back, I looked into her eyes and gave in to the darkness inside me. Thea's throat slid as she watched my eyes go black. Then she turned her head, offering me her neck.

I wanted her blood nearly as much as I needed her body. Somehow she knew.

A growl tore through me as I lifted her and carried her to the bed. Giving into that hunger growing between us, I pushed in an inch, pausing to enjoy the tight stretch and her accompanying moan before I buried myself in her. My fangs protracted, and I sank them into the pearly scar tissue on her fair skin, beginning to move.

Thea wrapped her arms around my neck, holding me there as I fed and fucked. Her hips rose to meet each thrust as if she, too, wanted me deeper, needed me to fill any lingering atom left untouched.

It was primal and raw, driven by a need I knew neither of us quite understood but both felt. I gave in to it.

The world disappeared as we crested together, and I spilled inside her.

I rolled us on our sides, still connected, and held her. Neither of us spoke, and I lost track of time. It could have been hours or days or years. It didn't matter. The only thing I cared about was wrapped half naked around me.

We lay there for a long time, our bodies fused together, unwilling and unable to let go of this moment.

Finally, I spoke. "So my mother surrendered?"

"For now." Thea sighed as we found our way back to the real world together. "It's a long story."

"Since I plan to be buried inside you forever, you might as well tell me."

"Not yet." She nuzzled into my neck. "I just need a minute.

What about the Mordicum? Did you learn anything?"

"Maybe." I shook my head, stroking my palm down her bare back. "It's hard to know who to trust."

Instantly, Thea bolted up as if my words had triggered her. "The letter!"

"What letter?" I reached for her, determined to steal a few more moments before we faced the world again.

Thea was already on her feet. She disappeared from sight for a moment. I pushed myself up to find her digging in the pockets of her pants. Finally, she held up an envelope, sealed with a familiar crest. Ginerva's symbol. Now Thea's.

"What is that?" I asked suspiciously.

Thea's eyes widened, and she swallowed before forcing a grim smile onto her face. "That's what we're about to find out."

CHAPTER TWENTY-NINE

Thea

"I don't understand." My fingers shook as I read the letter again, but no matter how many times I read it, I couldn't make sense of it.

Julian held out one hand, his other pressed reassuringly to the small of my back, and I passed him the yellowed piece of paper. "It doesn't," he agreed, his eyes flashing as he skimmed its contents.

Thea, it began. How did she know my name?

You will have questions, and I wish I had more answers. As I write this, my death draws nearer. I feel it coming for me, and it will come for you, too, if you do not heed my warnings. The queen-killer is gone but not lost. Do not trust the other queens. One moves against our throne. Neither will accept what you are.

But you must. Vampire blood runs in your veins, but that is not why the crown chose you. You must not give in to the Frenzy. The Gods chose you as they chose your mate. It is only together that you can face what is coming. Trust Julian, but choose the rest of your friends carefully. One will betray you. I can see that much, but I do not know who it is. Just as I see my own betrayal looming and do not know whom to trust.

That is my blessing and my curse. I hope knowing will be enough to save you.

And don't be too angry at Julian for what he must do. He's really a simple creature.

Julian huffed, shaking his head. "A simple creature?"

"You were in a bar fight a few hours ago," I reminded him, wishing I could find it in myself to laugh.

He shrugged, a cocky grin hanging on his lips. "In fairness, I didn't start it."

Not really.

"You aren't charming your way out of it," I warned him. "We don't need any more trouble." I took the letter back and folded it carefully.

About that… It was a bit more than a brawl.

"Do I want to know?"

"Probably not."

I sighed as the crushing weight on my chest grew heavier. "Sometimes I think we should have listened to Celia."

"Oh?" His lips twitched. "She'd love to hear that."

"I mean it." I dropped onto the bed and grabbed a pillow. "We should have run off to some private island and just waited for everyone to forget about us."

He lifted a brow, and I didn't need to hear his thoughts to know what he was thinking.

"We still could," he said after a moment.

I started to roll my eyes, but he pressed a finger to my chin. "We could go to my place near the Keys."

"The Keys?" I repeated. This was the first time I was hearing about this.

"Remind me to send you a list of our homes," he said breezily as though having a real estate portfolio with multiple properties on every continent was no big deal. "I have an island in international waters."

Despite everything that was happening, I found myself smiling at how casual he made it sound. "Of course you do."

"It was my sanctuary before…" His gaze ghosted over me, and

I knew what he was thinking. Before we had met. Before we had become each other's safe harbor. "It's where I was for the last few decades."

I swallowed as that information formed a knot in my throat. "Is it a good idea to go back?"

"That depends." A slow smile that promised his mind was currently in the gutter spread over his beautiful face. "I wouldn't mind spending another thirty years in bed if you were there."

"Napping?" I said drily.

"I suspect we would get very little sleep." His thumb traced my jawline, his tongue darting over his lower lip, and I knew he was already planning those thirty years.

Every ounce of me ached to go—to leave all of this behind—and be selfish. We deserved that. Neither of us had asked to be tasked with protecting magic and fighting nefarious vampire factions. Why couldn't we just walk away? We probably couldn't save magic anyway. Not with everyone around us hell-bent on destroying one another. Staying here might be a death sentence. Hadn't Ginerva's letter warned me as much? Compared to that fate, thirty years in bed with Julian sounded like an excellent use of what time we had left.

"What do you say, my queen?" he asked softly.

"I want to go," I whispered, not daring to look into his eyes. "But we can't."

I know.

The sadness in his words squeezed my heart, settling there and adding more weight to my already heavy load.

"Hey, remember when I was just your fake girlfriend?" I tried to sound light before that heaviness broke us.

"That feels like a lifetime ago." He smiled.

"And now, look at us." I forced a grin on my face. "I'm a queen with death threats of my very own, and you're hanging out with the Mordicum."

"I would hardly call it hanging out." He wagged a finger at me. "But you're wrong. You were already a queen when I met you."

"A queen directs her own empire." I recalled the words he'd spoken to me once in Paris. Back then, our lives felt so complicated as we struggled with our feelings for each other. Now? I shook myself free of the thought. It wouldn't get us anywhere to relive the past. I pointed to the letter, choosing to focus on Ginerva's warning instead. "Too bad I can't trust my empire."

"We have people we can trust. Jacqueline. Lysander. Sebastian."

"Camila?" I said with a snort.

"I wouldn't put her on the list," he admitted. He took a deep breath and shifted onto his back, staring up at the ceiling. "The Mordicum wants my help."

"Your help?" I repeated. I hadn't heard him correctly. They wouldn't come to a pureblood vampire for assistance, especially if that vampire's mother was Sabine Rousseaux. "Are they suicidal?"

He chuckled softly. "That's pretty much what I said. They claim a monster is coming after vampires."

"Coming after how?"

"You don't want to know the details," he said darkly.

I lay down next to him, placing my head on his chest. "Why come to you, though? Why not Camila or someone sympathetic to their cause?"

"I think that's why they need me." He absently brushed a hand over my hair. "They need a pureblood. They need the Council. If they're telling the truth, all vampires are in danger."

"Maybe they should have considered that before they started attacking innocent vampires."

His hand stilled. "No vampires are innocent. Sometimes you forget what I am."

But I wasn't having it. "I think vampires are so obsessed with their own superiority that they forget they share plenty of mortal traits," I told him, turning my face to meet his downturned eyes. When he didn't respond, I continued. "Humans are just as capable of being homicidal maniacs, you know? Humans act out of love, fear, desperation, and I think that's true of vampires. All creatures do, and in all species there are good apples and rotten ones."

Julian inhaled sharply before sighing. "You're right, but..."

"I'm not trying to justify the actions of the Mordicum, though." I pulled away slightly, propping myself up on an elbow. "I think they're rotten apples, but maybe..."

Julian didn't speak. He waited, letting me work through my own complicated feelings.

"Maybe they're just up against a wall."

"Purebloods have treated most turned vampires as inferior for ages." He brushed a hand lazily down my shoulder. "Even me. Part of me understands where they are coming from, but I will never condone their actions."

Sometimes I still dreamed of that night at the opera—the bloody horror of it all. Those nights I woke up drenched in sweat, my stomach churning. "Me neither."

"And if they're right?" he asked, his expression serious. "What if there is a monster attacking vampires?"

I shuddered at the thought. Not only because most of my friends—most of my family—were vampires, but because I knew we were vulnerable. Between the threat of the queens, the Vampire Council's constant interference, and everything else, the last thing we needed was another enemy. "We have to be prepared, and we might have to work with them, but we still have to hold the Mordicum accountable." I believed that, but I couldn't just instantly accept allying with them, either. "There's just one more thing. How are we going to do all of this? A coronation? Figuring out who betrayed Ginerva? Dealing with Willem? Your family's new matriarch?"

"Don't forget the Third Rite and the season coming to Venice," he added in a flat voice that told me he'd been asking himself the same thing, "and the wedding."

The wedding. In the midst of all the chaos, I'd forgotten completely we were even engaged. Given that we were mated and our lives were bound together, it hardly seemed necessary.

"We could just skip it." I dared a look at his face and found it stony. "Or elope."

"We aren't skipping the wedding," he said firmly.

"It's just a chance for Sabine to show off her—"

"It's a chance for me to show off my mate," he cut me off. Pushing up, he brought his eyes level with mine. "I've waited lifetimes for you, and no matter what else is going on in our lives, I will never take our love for granted. I want to marry you. I want to kiss my bride and dance with her and cut cake and make love to my wife."

For one moment, the rest of the world fell away, and I saw what he'd done. We'd been so wrapped up in darkness and drama I'd almost lost sight of what was really important. Us. We'd fought to get here, and there were more battles ahead, but why we were fighting was important, too. I wanted that day, too, even if only to give me a taste of what we might find at the end of all of this.

"Okay," I said softly. "Let's get married."

"Soon?" The corner of his mouth tugged up, and warmth spread through me.

"I hear most of the important vampires are going to be in town shortly," I whispered.

"They are." He hooked an arm around me and dragged me into his arms. "What do you say? Surprise last-minute wedding?"

"It's not like we have anything else to do," I teased. Despite everything we were facing, I felt light for the first time in weeks.

His mouth found mine. The kiss started slowly, his lips soft but demanding as he claimed me, claimed us, claimed our love. My arms coiled around his neck, my fingers digging into his taut shoulders. I tasted forever in his kiss, the promise that no matter what we faced, we would do it together.

When we finally broke apart, our foreheads still pressed together, I lifted my fingers to trace the contours of his lips. This was what I wanted. This male. My mate. The family we might make if the world allowed it. Our own bit of eternity.

And I knew one thing: I couldn't have any of it until I faced the truth—the dark fear that woke me at night and the terrible, selfish thoughts that consumed my days.

"Julian," I whispered, hoping he would understand—needing him to understand. "I don't want to be queen."

CHAPTER THIRTY

Lysander

Everyone was fucking or fighting except me. My brother and his mate were definitely doing the former. I suspected Camila and Jacqueline were doing the latter. Although they might be better served by just giving into whatever there was between them. I couldn't imagine wanting someone for centuries. I'd had blue balls for a week thanks to Lia, and I felt like ripping off some heads.

I was in the library in the name of research, or maybe because I'd hoped to find Lia here again, but it was dark—not even the fireplaces were lit. I switched on a bronze lamp and found the pile of books I'd pulled the other day was still waiting for me. Given that the court had just bothered to bring in new guards, I supposed a new librarian was a long way off. I picked up a book on Sumerian prophecies and settled into a chair. The Mordicum might want us focused on some boogeyman, but I couldn't shake the sense that all of it was connected. But how?

Two sentences in, the door to the library creaked open. The scent of sun-ripened cherries soaked in jasmine drifted toward me, and I cursed under my breath.

I didn't bother to look up from my book as she approached.

"How can you even see that?" Lia moved behind the chair,

peering over my shoulder at the text. "On second thought, how can you even read it?"

"Don't speak Sumerian?" I kept my eyes on the pages, determined to keep her presence from affecting me. The truth was that I hadn't processed a damn word since I'd opened the book. First, I'd been thinking of Lia. Now she was bothering me in person. I caught another wave of her aroma and decided being bugged by her in person was a clear upgrade.

"I didn't take you for a snob. Then again, you are a Rousseaux." She settled in the opposite chair, propping her feet on a stack of books. She was still in her leathers, right down to the platform boots she wore. Her clothes hugged her body in tempting ways, but it was the damn boots and their crisscrossing straps and buckles that caught my attention. And she hid it all behind that old-fashioned cloak. How could someone with so little experience in the world be so fucking sexy?

"What are you researching?"

"Nothing you'll care about." I forced myself to look back at the book. If I didn't, we were going to find ourselves in trouble again, and this time I might not be able to stop myself. Not with her scent assaulting me.

"Try me." She swung her feet down and leaned forward, bracing her elbows on her knees, sending another wave of sweet cherry in my direction.

My eyes shuttered momentarily as I tried to remember that she was a handmaiden and a virgin, and a self-proclaimed enemy. But while my brain got the memo, my dick seemed less interested in it. It was much more interested in those boots and her scent and…

I needed to avoid her, not mind-fuck her in the same room. I glanced up, trying to keep my voice as bored as possible. "The prophecy."

Lia's brows pinched together. "The one that foretold breaking the curse? Why? It's done. Magic is awake."

"I'm more interested in why magic was cursed in the first place, and I have a theory." I shut the book. I wasn't going to find the answers I needed in it, and its usefulness as a distraction with her present was about as helpful as using a sieve as a cup. "They believed in anthropomorphic polytheism."

"Gods taking human form?" Lia said, nodding her head.

I dropped the book in my lap, my head tilting. She was full of surprises. "You know what anthropomorphic polytheism is?"

"Is it that shocking?" Her mouth twisted in a rueful smile. "Just because I don't speak Sumerian doesn't mean I'm an idiot."

"I never said you were an idiot. I just asked if you spoke Sumerian."

"Not all of us have had centuries to waste on dead languages."

She looked up at me, and something clenched my heart in a tight grip. The trouble was that it wasn't just about keeping my hands off Lia. Every time she opened her mouth and reminded me that she wasn't just beautiful and brave but intelligent, I wondered what would happen if I crossed the line again.

If I kissed her again.

"What the hell does that have to do with anything?" she asked. "Or are you working on your doctoral thesis between bar fights?"

"I already have my doctorate." I had a couple of them actually, but I kept that to myself. "It's a hunch. Might be nothing. But I need something to do while everyone fights and fucks around here."

Lia huffed. "That makes two of us."

Our eyes darted to each other at the same moment, as if the same thought had occurred to both of us at the same time, and we both quickly looked away. We could be doing what the others were doing. Maybe even at the same time. I dragged my tongue over my lower lip, imagining her nails tearing at me as our bodies fought. When I dared to glance at her again and found her watching me, the look in her eyes made me swallow.

I wasn't the only one wondering if there were better ways to spend our time. Off-limits ways. Forbidden ways. Up-against-the-stacks-and-knocking-books-off-the-shelves ways. I still remembered how she tasted. How could I forget with her scent filling my nostrils?

But every stolen touch was a risk, and Lia would be the one to face the consequences. I buried that need for her, determined not to cross the line, and exchanged the book for another.

"About that bar fight," she said, clearing her throat as if she was trying to get the memory of my taste out of her mouth, too. "What happened with the Mordicum?"

I shifted in my chair and tossed the book on the table. It landed with a puff of dust, earning me a look of reproach. Of course she didn't approve of treating library books that way. Lia followed the rules. That's why she was a handmaiden.

"A lot of talk." I needed to speak with Julian before I clued anyone else into what we had learned from the renegade vampires.

"Do you always wind up so bloody tightly when you're just talking?"

I glanced down at my clothes. I'd forgotten the state I was in. The blood had dried a long time ago. I couldn't even smell it now. "Are my clothes bothering you?" I smirked at her. "I could take them off."

"Do you interpret everything a female says to you as a sexual invitation?"

"If I can." I lounged back in the chair and crossed my hands behind my head.

"Charming," she said flatly. Getting to her feet, she forced a smile. "I'll leave you to your Sumerian."

"So we're really not going to talk about it?" I blurted out.

She lurched to a stop, but when she turned, her face was blank. "About what?"

For a second, I wondered if I'd dreamed the whole kiss. It wouldn't be the first time Lia'd starred in one of my nocturnal fantasies, but I knew it was real. Her scent had lingered on my skin for days. I could still taste her in my mouth.

"The kiss," I said, rising to my feet and taking a step closer to her. She might want to pretend it never happened, but that might be more dangerous than just facing it. Trying to keep a lid on this might make it boil over, and we couldn't afford that.

Lia shrugged, glancing over her shoulder at me. "I've been

kissed before."

"Maybe." I stepped behind her and lowered my face to whisper in her ear, "But you haven't been kissed like that."

"Why are you whispering?" She tried to sound haughty, but her swallow told an entirely different story. The movement drew my gaze to her neck, to the veins visible under her brown skin.

I wondered what her blood tasted like. "We're in a library. You're supposed to whisper."

"We're the only ones here."

"I'm not sure that's an excuse to break the rules." I brushed the back of my hand along her arm. "But by all means, I am open to it."

Lia turned to face me and leaned forward so that her face was inches from mine. Her eyes were darker in the dim room, but I saw the same need churning in them. "We can't do this, remember?"

"We can't," I agreed, even as my hand found its way to her waist.

Her breath caught in her throat. "Then why are you touching me?"

"Because I can't help myself." I angled my head lower, closer to her mouth, closer to the promise of how she tasted. "Because I've been thinking about that kiss for days."

Lia kept staring at me softly as she lightly touched my chest, then tentatively slid her palms over my pecs and up to my shoulders.

We were going to cross the line, and there would be no coming back from it. But in that moment, I didn't care. All I cared about was the promise of how her lips would feel against mine, of how much I wanted to press her against the wall and remind myself of her sweet cherry taste mixed with something infinitely sweeter.

"Don't you need to read your old books?" she asked breathlessly, her fingers studying my triceps.

"They've been around for thousands of years. They can wait." I couldn't decide between pinning her to the nearest wall or laying her across one of the disused tables surrounding us and studying her.

Before I could decide, the door to the library banged open. We startled apart, quickly putting distance between ourselves. A moment later, Zina, dressed like she was on her way to court, swept in, her gown rustling behind her. "There you are," she snapped at Lia. "I've been looking everywhere for you."

"You found me," Lia said tightly.

"Yes, I have." Zina's eyes narrowed like a hawk about to swoop in on its prey. "Where is Thea?"

Lia's shoulders squared slightly, but she kept her composure. "In her quarters, I presume."

"You really are useless," Zina said, and I found myself moving at her, snarling softly. She looked at me as if I was an insect. "Call off your dog."

"Lysander isn't—" Lia started, her cheeks burning.

"I don't have time for this," Zina interrupted. "Thea is gone."

"She probably went out with Julian," Lia said calmly.

Zina shook her head, her dark skin glinting in the room's dim lamplight. "All of her things are gone."

"What?" I stepped forward. "That doesn't make sense. I'll find Julian."

"Her mate is gone, too."

"That's impossible," I stammered. My brother hadn't just left. He wouldn't. Not after what the Mordicum had told us. Not after everything that had happened. He wouldn't abandon his family any more than Thea would abandon her own duty.

Zina's grim smile widened as if hearing my thoughts. "You're far too trusting," she spat at me. "My sources say they left Venice an hour ago."

CHAPTER THIRTY-ONE

Julian

Cuba in January was a welcome break. Anywhere outside of Venice and its heavy responsibilities was welcome, even if I knew we were on borrowed time. We wandered under the unbroken blue sky, hand-in-hand, enjoying the warm kiss of the sun. It was a far cry from Venice's rain and snow, and maybe the clear sky would unclog our muddled brains. It was also the height of tourist season, and despite borrowing Jacqueline's private jet for the flight over, we had to brave the crowds to reach the dock where my yacht was kept. I maintained a careful eye on Thea as we wove our way through the crowd, trying to be patient when she stopped to look at a souvenir cart or to admire the elegant Cuban architecture.

She picked up a straw hat and dropped it on her head. "What do you think? Will I need it for the beach?"

"I think I made myself clear about that, my love," I purred, moving behind her to whisper in her ear. "I don't want you wearing anything on the beach."

"I didn't think you meant a hat. What if I get a sunburn? Not all of us have instant healing abilities," she said drily.

I flinched at the reminder that my mate was not a vampire and likely would never be one, thanks to the magic that bound our lives together. She was mortal, which meant she was burnable...and breakable. Thea twisted in my arms, searching my face for a clue as to my silence.

"What did I say?" she whispered, biting into her lower lip.

Even the surge of desire I felt seeing that wasn't enough to combat the sadness I felt. I shook my head. "It doesn't matter."

"You're upset."

"I'll get over it." I kissed her forehead. "Let's buy you the hat."

More than anything, I wanted our impromptu vacation to be a break from, well, everything. Especially thinking about things like our mortality or the court or family drama.

Thea slipped her hand back into mine after we paid. "Do you really think we'll get away with this?"

"It's not like we ran away permanently. Everyone can chill for a few days. Let Jacqueline handle them."

"Poor Jacqueline. I'm going to have to take her shopping when we get back to make up for it." Thea sighed. "Maybe Paris?"

It probably wasn't a good sign she was already planning to leave Venice again. She had meant what she'd said about not wanting to be queen. The trouble was that I wasn't sure she had a choice. Not with magic on the line and enemies everywhere. I kept these thoughts to myself.

"Wherever you want," I said smoothly, guiding her toward the dock where my yacht was waiting.

We hadn't even stepped onto the dock when Thea pulled away. She tapped her forehead. "Why are you so quiet?"

"Tired."

Her head tilted, her eyes narrowing to show she didn't believe my lie. "You've been shielding your thoughts since we left Venice. Was this a bad idea? Did you not want to come?"

I took a deep breath before holding out my hand. "I'm just trying to help you relax."

"And hearing your thoughts would ruin that?" she guessed, lifting an eyebrow.

"Definitely." I lowered my outstretched hand when I realized she wasn't going to take it.

"I want to know what's going on," she demanded, crossing her arms over her chest.

"Nothing. I just don't want anything to ruin this trip." I tried to sound convincing, but while I could shield my thoughts, I couldn't keep her from feeling my emotions. We shared those. It was the problem with the only two bodies, one soul thing.

Sad frustration overtook me until my heart ached. It took me a second to realize that was what she was feeling. "I won't enjoy this trip at all if you don't talk to me. Are you sure it's nothing?" Her tone was gentle, but the concern in her eyes was palpable. "We can talk about this. If you regret coming…"

"I don't regret it," I said. I could at least put a stop to that line of thinking. The thought of having her entirely to myself—naked on a beach—was all I wanted. It might be the closest we got to a honeymoon, even if we hadn't actually gotten married yet.

"Then tell me what's weighing on you," she pleaded. "I can feel all your anxiety. You might as well tell me what's behind it."

Since Venice, I'd had my mental shields up. I hadn't want to add to her worries, but was keeping it inside any better—especially when she had a direct line to my emotions? Plus, she made a fucking good point about the anxiety.

"I'm your mate," she added softly, and I wondered if I'd let those thoughts slip through to her. "For better or worse, right? Talk to me."

"It's just…" Where did I begin? The fears that gnawed at me every waking moment and sometimes sent me startling awake with nightmares? The responsibility that hung around me like a lead weight? Telling her might send the wrong message. I would shoulder all of it for her, but that didn't make the load any lighter to bear.

"Just what?" She reached for my hand.

"I worry about everything. The court, the enemies, the magic… losing you."

She laughed so softly that I found myself looking up in surprise. "Maybe I can hear your thoughts and I'm just mistaking them for my own. That's all I think about, too."

I yanked her toward me, wrapping her in my arms. "I don't think we're doing this vacation thing right."

"What do vampires usually do on vacation?" She pushed onto her tiptoes expectantly, and I knew she wanted a kiss. I smiled and humored her, the touch of her lips instantly soothing the ragged edges I felt inside me.

"I'll show you later," I said darkly. My mouth cruised along her jawline. "What about you? What do you do on vacation?"

"I've only been on vacation once, and I was a kid," she admitted to me, her eyes lowering. Embarrassment flooded through me in a cold wave, and I knew this was a sensitive subject for her. Not only because she now knew why her mother didn't take her places but because she seemed disinclined to believe I didn't care that she'd had less experience of the world.

"Good." I let my hand slide down to grab her rear. "Then we'll do it the vampire way."

"Oh yeah?" She lit up.

"Unless there's an objection." I let my mind conjure up a series of increasingly filthy images of exactly how I planned to spend the time we had together.

Thea swallowed, her cheeks turning pink in ways that gave me entirely new ideas. "No objection," she whimpered.

"Maybe we should get on the boat and get this vacation started."

She yanked free of my arms, grabbed my hand, and proceeded to haul me toward the dock.

"Careful, pet." I couldn't keep myself from laughing. "You'll hurt yourself."

"Then move your ancient butt," she demanded, not slowing down in the least. "We only have a few days."

I decided not to let that reminder sour my mood. When we reached the end of the dock, Thea stopped. "Where's the boat?"

"That is the boat." I pointed to the yacht that was docked at the end of the pier.

Her mouth fell open, and I had to bite back a chuckle.

"That's not a boat. That's a floating hotel." She continued to stare at it like it might transform into something more reasonably sized.

"It's tame by vampire standards." I pulled her toward it. She stumbled along beside me as she took it all in. I wasn't lying. With only fifteen bedrooms and room for twenty or so crew members, most vampires would turn their noses up at my little boat. But I liked the yacht's sleek white exterior with its soft hint of silver running along the edges of the deck and its polished chrome railings. The sun reflected off the deck, making the white leather seats glitter in the light. My mother had been on me to get a better one for years, claiming it was too small to host a proper party. That's exactly why I hadn't listened to her.

But as Thea stepped on board, grinning from ear to ear, I was reminded of how lucky I was to have a mate who wasn't a vampire.

Even if she was mortal.

CHAPTER THIRTY-TWO

Thea

We reached the island in half an hour, but I could have sailed longer. My cheeks hurt from smiling as we docked and made our way ashore. I stepped one wobbly foot onto dry land and found myself face-to-face with someone familiar.

"Welcome." Celia looked to the two of us, her eyes sparkling at whatever changes she saw there since we'd last seen her in San Francisco a month ago.

Julian greeted her with a smile, but I lunged forward and hugged her.

"It's good to see you, too," I said brightly before pulling back with a grin. Celia blinked a few times, glancing at my mate, who shrugged as if to say, *What do you expect*?

"Everything is ready," she told us as we walked down the dock.

"I hope it wasn't too much trouble," I said, earning an eye roll from both her and Julian. "I know it was last minute."

"You two have been busy." Celia smiled at me, her eyes skirting my waistline. She looked away quickly and continued. "The staff wish to greet you. I will bring the golf cart around."

I stared after her, trying to process what exactly that look was all about. "Um, did she just check for a baby bump?"

"Anything you want to tell me, pet?" The arm around my waist tightened, and he brushed a hopeful hand over my middle.

I choked in surprise, turning it quickly into a cough. The question of children was still very much open, and we'd been dealing with far too much drama to make a firm decision, especially with everything we had learned, but we'd also been at it like rabbits, so... "Not that I'm aware of."

It couldn't be, right? It's not like Celia would be able to tell if I was pregnant. I must have broadcast that thought unintentionally to him because he leaned to whisper in my ear as we reached the staff.

"Vampires have supernatural senses, remember? Maybe she can sense something."

I turned an incredulous look on him. "You're a vampire! You tell me."

He just smirked in response.

What did that mean?

Any relaxation I felt from our boat ride or arriving on the private island frayed, leaving a bundle of nerves in its place. Julian's hand disappeared from my waist, and I found myself reaching for my belly like I might discover something. But he grabbed my hand and led me toward the row of people in crisp white uniforms waiting to greet us. Julian stopped to speak to the first man.

"Lord Rousseaux, we're pleased you are back with us." He bowed at the waist, and I had to bite back a laugh.

I would never get used to watching people prostrate themselves in front of Julian, even though seeing my mate, standing tall and sure, showed me exactly why he commanded the attention.

"Richard." He offered a gloved hand, and the man shook it. "Allow me to introduce you to my mate and your new mistress. This is Thea."

Mistress? I raised an eyebrow.

Would you prefer I tell him you're his new queen? I can. Richard has served me for the last four hundred years.

I blanched and shook my head just a little. That was the last thing I wanted, and he knew it, even if Julian had been avoiding the topic of me refusing the coronation.

"I heard congratulations were in order." Richard bowed his head slightly to me. "Welcome, Lady Thea. It is an honor to meet you."

His gaze lingered, and I wondered what he saw when he looked at me. Was he putting those supernatural vampire senses to use? Was I measuring up?

I forced a smile, feeling like every inch of me was being put under a microscope. "Thank you, Richard. It's a pleasure to meet you, and it's just Thea, please."

He inclined his head, but I suspected that he'd continue to call me "Lady" for the rest of our trip.

"He will," Julian murmured as we moved away. "I've been begging him to call me Julian for centuries. You'll become accustomed to it."

If only I would have that long to get used to it.

But with each introduction, my nerves frayed more. There were too many faces and too many names. Did they know what I was? Could they sense something was different about me? Did they even care? Julian had known some of them for centuries. I was sure they had an opinion on his mate. Between the boat ride and that realization, I felt queasy.

"You okay?" he whispered, even though we were finally alone.

"That was a lot." I tried to smile and failed. "I'm afraid I'll forget someone's name or that they're all wondering what you see in me."

He barked a laugh and squeezed my hand. "If you forget someone's name, ask them. They won't be offended. As for the second, I guarantee they all see exactly what I do."

My cheeks warmed, but I finally smiled. "Exactly? I'm not sure about that."

"If they're asking anything, it's how a grumpy bastard like me landed an actual queen." He drew me to him and kissed me. "But seriously, you're the boss. Don't worry too much about what they think."

"That's supposed to be helpful?" I shook my head. "I'll never get used to having servants." I hadn't been born into this world. I'd been born into the human world, and even if I'd begun to see my place was with him—and always had been—I doubted I'd ever quite fit in as easily as the vampires around me.

"It will get easier." He sounded almost apologetic.

"Or we could just, you know, get our own place and not have servants. We don't need them," I suggested as Celia drove up in a golf cart.

Julian stopped and studied me for a moment. "It is not about whether we need them," he said gently. "They need us. I employ them, care for them, house them, and protect them, whether they are vampires or humans. They are part of my family." He cleared his throat and offered me a sheepish smile. "I mean, our family."

I felt my toes curl as I took in that boyish grin that made him look more human than vampire for a minute. "I didn't think of it that way." I paused as a dark memory took hold of me. "When Willem captured me, he had servants…"

Servants was too generous a word for how he treated the vampires and humans beholden to him.

"Not all vampires value life." Julian's jaw tightened. "Many see anyone weaker than them as a slave."

"I feel like some of your family falls into the category."

"I wish you were wrong." He guided me toward the golf cart and helped me step into it. "I suppose it doesn't help to tell you that my mother is quite generous to those she employs and enthralls."

I snorted, but his face remained serious as he took the seat next to me.

"Perhaps you are right about vampires, pet." Darkness shadowed his face, his eyes, and I wished I hadn't brought it up. "No," he said, hearing my thought, "it's too easy when you've lived as long as I have to grow blind to such things. You've given me something to think about."

"But not for the next few days," I ordered him.

"Of course." He nodded to Celia, who had turned to watch us with interest. "We should go before it gets dark."

Celia spent the drive updating Julian on issues and concerns regarding the island. I half listened, more interested in taking in the beauty as we traveled along the island's only road. The sun was a fiery swatch on the horizon, its fading light painting the palm trees and ferns in shades of vivid jewels. Waves crashed onto the shore and palm fronds rustled in a hypnotic, soothing rhythm. Soon, I'd nearly forgotten about the stress of our arrival. The wind swept my hair into my eyes, but I didn't care. The air carried the salty taste of the ocean to my lips, and I found myself dreaming of walking along the beach as the sun rose in the morning.

"Security has been tightened," I heard Celia say, and I tore myself away from my fantasies and paid attention. "No one will be able to get onto the island."

"Good." Julian's hand rested on my knee, and he gave it a soft squeeze when he realized I was listening. "It was already safe before, but it has been breached. It won't be now."

"I trust you," I said simply. As long as he was here, I was safe. I knew that.

His eyes darkened slightly, and I wondered if it was the fading light or the topic.

"I also saw to the other request," Celia added cryptically.

My anxiety jumped again and landed in a knot in my throat, but Julian brushed soothing circles on my thigh.

"What request?" I murmured.

"Thank you," he said to her before turning a smirk on me. "You'll see, my love."

I wasn't sure how he managed to pack those four words with so much insinuation, but I went molten. His nostrils flared, and his eyes darkened as he took a deep, lingering breath.

You smell far too tempting. I'm not sure we'll make it to the house.

Oh my...

More warmth pooled in my core, and he looked away, his jaw tightening slightly. I caught a flash of fang as he clamped his mouth shut. How was I supposed to not react when his whole body reminded me of what was waiting at the end of this drive?

I squirmed in my seat a little. I wasn't sure how much longer I could keep myself under control.

"We're here. Welcome home," he said thickly, and somehow I knew it meant a lot to him to bring me here. This place felt different than his other houses.

Maybe because it wasn't a house, it was more like a compound comprised of sleek lines and windows. Half of it sat over the ocean, supported by black beams that blended seamlessly with the modern lines of the structure. This was a house like his yacht was a canoe.

"We might need to work on your vocabulary," I muttered. "This isn't a house."

"Home," he corrected me softly, taking my hand and guiding me out of the vehicle. "I said welcome home, mate."

A primal desire ran through his words, and I knew I was right. This was different than his place in San Francisco or the house in Paris. I didn't know quite why yet, but I sensed it. Maybe that's why I realized he was right as he led me toward it. He wasn't just taking me away. He was taking me home.

We reached a stone walkway that led into the gardens surrounding it, and I stopped with a tiny, "Oh!"

White petals had been strewn along it. Candles glowed in glass hurricanes nearly as tall as me. I opened my mouth to tell Celia it was lovely, but as I turned, I discovered we were alone.

"As I was saying," Julian said huskily, "welcome home."

Then he swept me off my feet and into his arms.

CHAPTER THIRTY-THREE

Julian

Thea nuzzled into my neck, and I caught a whiff of honey-drenched lilac. Her scent bolted through me and settled in my groin, but the unusual sweetness of it—combined with a growl from her stomach—told me she needed to eat. That meant keeping my hands to myself.

For now.

Stones crunched below my feet as I carried her through the rapidly fading twilight. This felt right. Being here with her, holding her in my arms. I'd barely thought about this place since I'd left to go to San Francisco. Not since the night I'd met Thea. Not since she'd come to occupy my every waking thought.

"You're quiet again," she murmured, lifting a hand to brush a bare finger down my cheek. Even with the slight touch, her magic sparked as her skin met mine. I couldn't find words quickly enough—Thea started to draw away.

"Don't." I stopped her and turned my face toward her hand—toward the power I knew was there—the power that she feared.

Her breath hitched, her body tensing, as she gently placed her palm on my cheek. Golden magic seeped into my skin, and overhead the stars seemed to sparkle brighter. I felt her magic filtering into my veins. It didn't drive away the darkness I carried in my blood. Instead, it caressed it, soothed it, on its way to the creature hidden deep inside me. My magic stirred, waking up as hers sang to it, and when her magic reached that hidden place, it found the bit of her I'd carried since we became mates.

Warmth flared inside me as this new magic wove with the old. I stopped in the middle of a field of seagrass and met Thea's hard gaze. She gasped, her breath turning to shallow pants, and I knew she felt it, too. Her magic continued to flow, as if it meant to drive out the darkness that haunted me.

But I knew what would come of that.

"Stop," I said quietly. "Thea, take back your magic."

She recoiled, her hand jerking away from my face, hers as pale as the moon overhead as she stared at me.

"I'm sorry," she squeaked.

I shook my head. "There's no need to apologize."

"Did I hurt you?" Her eyes filled with confused tears.

"No. Your magic could never hurt me, but I'm afraid you were giving me too much of it."

"Giving?" she repeated, blinking a few times, sending tears dribbling down her pale cheeks. "I didn't mean to..."

"I know." I brushed a kiss over her forehead, holding her tighter. "I should not have asked for such an intimate touch. Not while you're so..."

I stopped myself from saying vulnerable.

She must have heard it anyway. "You think I'm weak?"

"Not weak. Never weak." That was the last way I'd ever characterize my mate.

"But I am vulnerable? How is that different?" She squirmed in my arms, and I relinquished my hold on her, placing her on her feet.

"Weakness shows one's lack of strength," I told her, searching her eyes for proof she was listening—that she understood. "Vulnerability is an acceptance of it."

She stared at me for a moment before rolling her eyes. "I don't see how."

"Strong people allow themselves to be vulnerable." I reached out and placed my palm against her cheek, allowing the darkness inside me to call to her. "Strong people know they need other people."

She took a deep breath. "Isn't this the island where you came to be alone for decades?"

I knew what she was saying, and I didn't blame her for calling me out. "I'm a hypocrite, right?"

"That's not exactly what I'm saying," she said quickly.

I smiled and drew my hand away before I overwhelmed her with my own magic. She seemed to settle as it found its way through her. "I was not strong before I met you."

"I've seen you in action. I doubt that very much," she pointed out. "You've killed, like, thousands of vampires."

"Never mistake violence for strength, my love," I said, letting that darkness inside me show. "I never mastered my magic. There was too little of it before to bother. At best, I ignored it. That's not strength."

"And now? I feel your magic," she whispered. "It's not weak. It vibrates through you. It calls to me, and it's getting louder."

"So is yours." Her *cantatio*, her blood song, was no longer a whisper in her veins heard only by vampires. Other creatures would hear it when they met. Each day it grew louder and more devastating in its beauty.

"We balance each other. Magic to magic..." She trailed away as she recalled the prophecy.

"Darkness to darkness." I drew my thumb across her bottom lip, and she shuddered, leaning into me. "Does it scare you?"

She peeked up at me through her lashes before nodding slightly. "A little."

I heard the apology in her words, and I knew another sorry was poised on her lips.

"Thank you for being vulnerable," I said before she could speak.

"I guess I could say the same," she said, biting her lower lip.

My eyes snagged on the gesture and watched her mouth intently.

Thea's cheeks flamed under the intensity of my gaze, but I didn't rein it in. I could show her all of me, even the hungry beast that prowled inside me. The one that wanted to claim her now without any regard for romance. But I forced myself to look away and held out my hand instead. "Come on."

She took it, her breathing as jagged as my self-control. "Where are we going?"

"You'll see."

We only had to walk a few more feet before the seagrass gave way to a sandy beach. I paused at the edge of the path and knelt.

"What are you doing?" she asked with a laugh as she looked down at me.

I reached for her ankle and undid the strap of her espadrille. "The sand here is soft and warm. It will feel good on your feet," I promised her as I took off her shoes one at a time, "and I don't want you to break your neck trying to walk in it in these."

I stood, hooking her shoes around my index finger, and kicked off my own. I took a second to toe off my socks. Thea shook with barely contained laughter as she watched me. "What's so funny, pet?"

"I've never seen a big, scary vampire wiggle out of his socks before." She giggled, easing some of the tension in the air.

"Glad I amuse you," I said drily. I grabbed her hand, still holding her shoes in my other, and started toward the beach.

"What about your shoes?" she called as she scrambled to keep up with me.

I slowed down and shrugged. "I have more."

"But—" Whatever she was about to say died on her lips as my surprise came into view.

I made a mental note to give Celia a raise.

A linen-covered table with bone china and crystal had been set near the water's edge, just where the tide was on the way out. The water surged, breaking and retreating back to the ocean. The white petals scattered around the table tumbled in the breeze, some washing out to sea with the tide and tinging the salty air with the scent of roses. Wind swept across the beach and tugged at the linen cloth, rippling it like a sail. Lanterns were lit, adding to the mood without taking away from the stars twinkling above us.

"This is perfect," Thea murmured, looking up at me with shining eyes.

"It's beautiful," I corrected her. "You're perfect."

I tugged her toward our dinner. Thea groaned when her feet sank into the sand.

"Was I right about the shoes?" I asked, grinning as she nodded enthusiastically.

"Bare feet the rest of the trip." She grinned back, and the sight of it seized my heart.

"Bare everything would be even better."

She laughed. "I saw how many people work on this island. I'm not sure I want to prance around naked."

"They won't bother us." I'd already seen to that. "The staff are heading back to Cuba."

"Oh." She swallowed. "And Celia?"

I nodded. "Security will circle the perimeter. I already arranged for food. We have this place entirely to ourselves."

Her eyes hooded, her sweet scent rising on the wind around us. "What are we going to do out here all alone?"

She dangled the bait, and I forced myself to resist lunging for it. I needed to take care of her first. "Let's eat, and I'll tell you, my love."

"I'm not hungry."

I raised an eyebrow, calling her bluff, and she groaned.

"That's so not fair." But she didn't resist being led to the table.

I pulled out her chair for her, helping her into it. Thea wriggled her toes in the warm sand and sighed happily as she took in the feast before us. It was island fare at its best thanks to my private chef: a ceviche of fresh gulf shrimp and avocado in lime juice, platters of ripe melon, oysters on the half shell, and champagne on ice. I piled her plate full of food before pouring her a glass of Dom Pérignon.

"What are we celebrating?" she asked as I sat down across from her.

"Being alone," I admitted, and she howled with laughter.

"I'll drink to that." She lifted her flute to me. Taking a sip, she looked around. "It's so peaceful here. I feel like I'm in a different world."

"That's why I like it," I told her as she began to eat with an impressive amount of gusto. Maybe Celia was onto something. But I would sense it if Thea was with child. I was sure of it. "I bought the island a long time ago."

"What's it called?" she asked between bites of shrimp.

I smiled at the way her eyes rolled back as she savored the meal. "I don't remember. I meant to give it a name, but it never seemed very important."

"What?" She put her fork down. "It doesn't have a name. How do your boats find it?"

"Coordinates." I laughed.

She stuck her tongue out at me. "Okay, duh. But it should have a name."

"Isla Thea?" I suggested.

She gagged and shook her head. "You are not naming it after me."

"Well, then, I have no idea." I steepled my fingers and smirked at her. "I guess you'll have to name it."

"Me?"

"It's yours anyway," I pointed out.

"Half mine."

"Yours," I corrected. "It's all yours. Everything I have. Everything I am. It's yours."

We stared across the candlelight at each other, lingering on the promise of those words. Finally, she glanced away. Looking at the table, she frowned.

"What's wrong?" I asked darkly. What had I overlooked?

"Dessert." She shook her head, dropping her napkin on the table as she stood.

"That is an oversight," I agreed as she circled the table. "Shall I call someone? There are still a few people on the island who can bring something sweet."

Thea's teeth sank into her lower lip as she bunched up the skirt of her sundress and climbed onto my lap. "No need. I know what I want."

"And what is that?" I purred.

She smiled, flashing me a little *fang*.

CHAPTER THIRTY-FOUR

Thea

I sank onto Julian's lap and grinned as his hands swept over my ass, finding it bare. He groaned, his eyes immediately darkening to the same inky black as the sky above us. His palms coasted to my thighs, and he sank his fingers into their soft flesh.

"I might have forgotten to pack underwear," I said, fluttering my lashes.

"It seems I'm overdressed," he purred, "or are you only planning to feed?"

I licked a tongue over my fangs, allowing my smile to widen. I'd stopped feeding in Venice—not that I needed to feed at all, really—but there it had felt especially dangerous. Here? I could think of nothing I wanted more than to share my mate's blood. "I want you inside me..." I leaned closer, brushing my lips over the shell of his ear. "...in every way possible."

He turned his face to mine, keeping it a fraction of an inch from kissing me, as he reached for his belt. Undoing it swiftly, he freed his cock and began to pump it with his fist. Julian swallowed, drawing his lower lip into his teeth, giving me a glimpse of an elongated canine. "May I join you?"

My core turned molten at the suggestion. The only thing more tempting than sinking my fangs into him was the thought of his venom coursing through me as I did.

"Of course," I breathed, eyelids lowering as I leaned forward to kiss him. Our lips brushed softly, even the slight contact sending a jolt of need quivering through me. He shifted me in his lap, allowing the broad tip of his cock to drag across my weeping sex.

"Yes…" I murmured against his lips as I felt him continue his slow slide. I inhaled deeply, lingering in the moment before we claimed each other. His scent drove every thought but him from my mind. Julian pressed inside me, and I gasped, clinging to his shoulders as our magics surged together.

Darkness shaded his eyes as he turned his head, offering his neck, and I bent forward, sinking my fangs into him. Julian roared, which only made the rich blood on my tongue taste sweeter. After a moment, he joined me, and I paused long enough to savor the delicious sting of his bite. My hips bucked, wanting him deeper as he sucked.

Julian's hands moved from my back to the straps of my dress, shucking them off my shoulders. Night air caressed my nipples as he fed. His hands covered my breasts, circling with the sharp tips of his fingernails. My whole body was alive. With the venom coursing through my system, I felt every touch like I'd been set on fire. He was shadows and eternal magic, and I gave in to him, letting his darkness swallow me entirely.

Our bodies moved in a desperate rhythm, in a fervent push and pull, as we tried to sate our need for each other. But even as pleasure crested inside me, I knew we would never have our fill. Not just of each other's body or blood but of our magic.

I needed his magic like I needed him. It was the other half of me. The light to my darkness. The moon to my sun. We were the beginning and the end and every moment between.

And as we rose together, we both drew back, continuing to ride out our pleasure as we stared at each other. His eyes were onyx, and blood dripped from the corner of his mouth. He swiped it with his tongue as he grabbed hold of my hips to rock me faster and harder.

I let my head fall back to look at the stars as I savored the exquisite, agonizing fullness of him.

"You are a Goddess," he said through clenched teeth. "You have no idea what you do to me."

I moaned, clutching his shoulders, as he bent his face to take my breast into his mouth. Its heat threatened to undo me, and I cried out, clinging to him as he chuckled softly.

"These are very sensitive." The tip of his tongue circled my nipple, and I felt my entire body tense under that singular touch. "Very sensitive."

I arched my back to grant him better access, and he laughed again. "So greedy, even after you fed."

But I wouldn't be satisfied until I felt his pleasure spill inside me. I couldn't find the words to tell him, but I rolled my hips faster.

"Take your time," he whispered, his lips moving along my skin back to the puncture wounds he'd left on my neck, but he didn't bite me again. That only made me want him more. No, *need* him more.

I needed this.

I needed him.

I tried to increase our rhythm, but his hands gripped my hips tightly, slowing the pace of my body until we found a new tempo, one that lingered on every note, one that found places inside me I didn't know even existed.

When I finally found release, he went with me with a roar that filled the night air.

I collapsed against him, my arms coiling around his neck as we remained entwined as one.

Maybe it was foolish to need the physical connection when our souls were as bound as our lives. Even so, I found myself unable to let him go. I only wanted to stay here as long as possible, in his arms, where no one else could touch me. When I finally managed to pry away, his arms tightened possessively.

"Don't," he said softly. "Let me hold you."

I went limp in his arms. Maybe the tether was still intact. Maybe part of it had survived and found its way into our bond, because that was all I wanted.

I buried my face into his shoulder. How was it possible to love another creature this much? So much that it hurt when we were apart and ached when we were together? Maybe it was the island—maybe it was knowing that, for once, no one could touch us—that we could just be.

"It's not just you," he murmured. "I feel it, too. Something's different."

I smiled, turning my face up to his shining eyes. "We've never done that before—fed at the same time. It was…"

Words failed me. Julian's mouth hooked into a smirk that told me he was completely satisfied to leave it that way. Then his head tilted, a puzzled expression ghosting across his face. A moment later, he brushed his thumb over my nipple.

"Oh!" I jolted up, laughing. "I think they're still under the influence of your venom."

"No, it's not that…" He blinked twice before a grin split his face. Whatever he found so deeply amusing, his thoughts remained entirely blank. I waited for him to finish what he was saying, but he fell silent as he continued to study me.

"Julian?" I stilled in his arms. "What is it?"

Finally, he lifted his eyes to mine, and I felt a new emotion swell inside me.

An emotion I had never felt before. An emotion that could only be coming from him. An emotion that shook me to my very core.

CHAPTER THIRTY-FIVE

Thea

"What is it?" I demanded again. I grabbed the straps of my dress and yanked it back up to cover myself, suddenly feeling too exposed under his awestruck gaze. Wiggling, I tried to untangle myself from him, but his arms snaked around me and held me firmly in place.

His tongue licked slowly over his lip as he shook his head. "I'm not sure. It's just…"

His emotions pounded inside me, overwhelming me to the point that I thought I might burst. I placed my palm on my chest as I tried to catch my breath. Normally, our hearts beat at the same rate. His was slightly fast for a vampire, and mine was much slower than a typical mortal. Right now, it felt like my heart was trying to escape. Could a vampire have a heart attack? Was that a thing? Did I need to be worried?

Julian covered the hand on my chest with his own and took a deep, unsteady breath. "You taste…different."

"Different?" I repeated, my eyebrows jumping up. "Different bad or different good?"

"Different," he echoed.

"That's helpful," I snapped, now feeling more vulnerable

than ever. I had no idea why, or what it was about his reaction that spooked me. Pulling out of his arms, I scrambled to my feet. But as soon as I took one step in the sand, I lost my balance and careened forward. Julian caught me before I landed face-first on the beach.

"Careful," he said uneasily as he shoved his cock back into his pants. "I think you should sit down."

I didn't move. "Tell me what you mean by *different*."

"It's probably my imagination." He shrugged, taking one cautious step toward me like I was about to bolt.

"You're acting weird." I crossed my arms over my chest. "And that is *not* in my imagination."

We locked eyes in the soft, silvery moonlight. As Julian's gaze shifted from dark to his usual bright blue, he continued to study me. His expression had a knowing wonder about it that was making me more uneasy by the second. Neither of us spoke for what felt like an eternity, and then I slowly turned away.

He was at my side instantly. "Where are you going?"

"To clean up. Is that allowed?"

"I should go with you."

"To the bathroom?" Okay, what was going on? He hadn't acted this off since the night we'd met in San Francisco. That night I'd thought he was crazy.

"You don't know where it is," he pointed out.

He had me there. I flourished a hand toward the path we'd taken to the beach. "Tell me."

"Actually, it's this way." He pointed to another path that led through the beach grass. This one wasn't strewn with rose petals. It felt like a sign the romantic portion of the evening was over. Julian gestured toward it, and I sighed as I started in the other direction.

He walked beside me, his gaze darting between me and the path ahead and occasionally over his shoulder at the beach we'd just left. As we walked, his hand coasted over the small of my back protectively.

"I thought this island was safe," I said softly.

"What?" His eyebrows knitted together. "It is."

"Is it?" I stopped and turned on him. "Because you look like you're going to jump out of your skin. Is there something to be worried about, or is it because I taste different?" I still didn't know what that was supposed to mean.

He opened his mouth to answer and closed it again, shaking his head. "It's probably nothing. Let's get you cleaned up."

My stomach dropped, and more of that strange, new emotion flowed through me. Did he just not want to tell me the truth? Still? Taking a breath to steady myself, I nodded and walked faster before he saw the tears threatening to spill down my cheeks. I wasn't sure if the confusion inside me was his or my own, but the hurt I felt? That definitely belonged to me.

We were supposed to be on holiday, free from the drama waiting for us in Venice, safe from the threat of rival vampires. But here we were, making new problems all by ourselves.

"Careful. Watch your step," he urged me as the grassy dune rose higher. I was glad I'd left my shoes behind on the beach as my toes sought purchase in the shifting sand. "Why don't I carry you?"

"Why don't you chill?" I snapped, moving away from him. Just like that, our evening had gone from blissfully romantic to bickering.

And I had no idea why.

Julian turned in front of me, blocking the path. "I don't want you to fall."

"It's sand. I think I'll survive," I said sourly. If he thought he could hide his odd behavior behind chivalry, he needed to think again. The ocean breeze swept around us, making the beach grass ripple and me shiver. I clutched my shoulders tightly, wincing slightly as my arms brushed over my breasts, which were still sensitive from Julian's attention.

Julian's eyes narrowed, catching my reaction. Before he could comment on that, too, I brushed past him and continued up the dune, aware that he was following me as closely as possible.

Was this his security plan? To keep me within arm's reach at all times while pretending we were safe?

"Hardly," he said, sounding amused—which only annoyed me more.

"Get out of my head."

"You're practically shouting at me, my love." There was no trace of bemusement in his voice now.

"And you are radio silent," I muttered. "It's not fair."

He sighed again, grabbing my elbow as I slid a few feet down the steep dune. "Just let me help you, please."

"Tell me why you're acting this way," I countered.

We returned to our staring contest. Finally, he hung his head. When he lifted it, he wore a cautious smile. "What if you just trusted me?"

My mouth fell open. Was he serious? He was shielding his thoughts from me, but not his emotions. Nope. Those were completely out of control and getting worse by the second. It wasn't just the deep, soul-changing swell from earlier when we were making love. That was there, but they were fighting with emotions that I did recognize. Apprehension. Worry. Fear. Frustration.

I didn't bother to respond. Instead, I pushed ahead. We were close enough to the house that I could see inside its windows. I rushed toward it, not realizing I'd reached the top of the dune. My foot met with air instead of sand, and then everything blurred as I toppled several feet down the other side of the hill.

"Thea!" Julian's panic sliced through the night air as he raced to me. Of course, he didn't fall. He was a vampire. Tripping over his own feet wasn't in his repertoire.

It was, however, in mine.

I tried to push onto my feet as he reached me, but white-hot pain shot through my ankle, and I screamed as I nearly went down again.

"Thea," Julian dropped to the ground beside me. "Let me see."

"Twisted. It's probably nothing," I parroted his words back to him.

His mouth flattened into a line that told me—argument or

not—I wasn't going anywhere until I let him check me out. I lounged back in the sand, allowing him to inspect my foot but refusing to look at him.

When I dared to glance at him, apology shone in his eyes. He brushed a finger down my ankle. "You have my blood in my system. It will heal quickly, but you shouldn't walk on it for a few minutes."

I swallowed. "I guess you have to carry me, then."

This was his fault. If he would just be honest with me…

"I know," he said softly, but he didn't stand up. Instead, he reached for my hand. "I should have just told you. It's just… I didn't want to…"

Want to what? I waited for him to finish, but he just watched me with that same restless confusion.

"And the award for most annoying vampire boyfriend goes to…"

"Boyfriend?" His eyebrow tipped up. "I'm your fiancé—and your mate."

"I'll make sure they change the inscription on the trophy," I grumbled. Huffing, I forced myself to look him in the eyes. "Can we go now?"

The hand clasping mine tightened, and he took a deep breath. "I didn't want you to get your hopes up," he finally finished.

A cloud moved across the moon overhead. For a moment, we fell into shadows, darkness obscuring his face.

And as the moon broke free of the clouds, his eyes shuttered, and then he spoke. "Thea, I think you're pregnant."

CHAPTER THIRTY-SIX

Julian

"Nope."

It wasn't the reaction I was expecting. I blinked a few times, waiting for her to fully process what I'd just said.

"Thea, I said—"

"No," she cut me off. Moonlight glimmered in her eyes, and the distance in her voice felt as far away as the night sky over our heads. "I am not. There's no way."

"No way?" I repeated. Did she need a refresher on the birds and the bees? I managed to keep myself from saying it out loud.

Not that it mattered, because her eyes instantly narrowed. "I know how babies are made, Julian."

"Then you know you could be pregnant." I dialed back my certainty for her sake. Maybe she just needed a minute to wrap her head around this.

"But I'm not." She wrenched her hand from mine and got up, dusting sand off her lower half. She limped along, fiercely ignoring her ankle.

I joined her but kept a close distance. It was an exercise in restraint not to pick her up and carry her into the house, especially with her slight injury. If I was right and Thea was carrying my child, it was going to be a long nine months if I gave in to my protective urges all the time. She might have let me have a few minutes, though.

She planted a hand on her hip. "Do vampires really think you can just sniff a woman and find out she's pregnant? Watch out, Clearblue Easy!"

I stared at her. "I did a little more than sniff you. Your blood—"

"Maybe it was something I ate!" She whipped a finger through the air triumphantly. "Did you ever think about that?"

This was ridiculous. Thea's eyes flashed, and I knew she'd caught that thought, too. I needed to get my shit together and keep my thoughts shielded unless I wanted this to be worse.

"I need to pee," she announced.

I forced a smile, albeit a grim one, and offered her my hand. She glared at it like it was a trick.

"I don't want you to fall again," I said as carefully as possible, but she didn't budge. Dark magic blossomed inside my chest, the beast there howling to be set free. I could only imagine how she would react if I gave in and let him take charge. Something told me that if I pushed this too far, I'd have hell to pay. But was I really supposed to just stand back and wait for her to come around? Regardless of what she believed, it was still my job to look out for her. That left only one choice. I swallowed. "Please. Just let me see you inside."

Her nostrils flared as she considered my request. Then she dropped her hand in mine.

It was hardly a win, but I would take what I could get. At least until I could convince her that I was right.

I led Thea toward the house, my eyes sweeping across the dunes for signs of any potential threat as I monitored her for signs that she shouldn't be walking on her ankle. I'd been satisfied with the security situation when we arrived, but that was before. Now I needed to consider both Thea's safety and that of my child.

My child.

I tamped down on the wave of emotions the thought produced. Thankfully, Thea seemed lost in her own thoughts. Part of me hoped she would slip and broadcast them at me. I wanted to know what she was thinking, but now more than ever, she deserved her privacy.

Especially since she seemed not only resistant to the idea of being pregnant, but downright hostile. I wasn't sure what to do about that. Maybe a pregnancy test would convince her, but it wouldn't soothe her jagged feelings on the matter.

When we reached the door, I held my hand over the barometric reader to unlock it. Thea watched me with wide eyes as I held it open for her.

"It's already been coded to you," I murmured. "I had Celia use the scans from our place in San Francisco."

Thea nodded, but she didn't look at me as she stepped inside.

"How's your ankle?" I asked cautiously.

"Fine," she muttered. "I barely feel it." She scanned the three-story foyer that opened into the living area without comment. There were unbroken views of the water from three sides, but given the hour, she likely only saw darkness stretching ahead of her. She finally turned to me. "Bathroom?"

"Third door on the left." I pointed down the hall that led to the ground floor's bedrooms. "I'll, uh, wait out here."

I couldn't tear my eyes from her as she started down the dark hallway. When she finally disappeared behind the door, I smacked myself in the head. "Fuck."

I had fucked everything up. Not by getting Thea pregnant. We'd both actively been taking that risk for weeks. No, I'd fucked up by letting my stupid vampire senses off their leash. If I'd had better control of myself—and my emotions—none of this would have happened. Well, the pregnancy bit would have, but she deserved to find out on her own terms.

She deserved to find out first.

Was that why she was so upset? Had I overstepped by telling her, even though she'd demanded the truth?

I needed to understand. Not only to support her but also because part of me was...hurt.

The part of me that had fallen in love the moment I sensed the subtle change in her blood. I was going to be a father. It was the last thing I had ever wanted until about ten minutes ago. Now? I would fucking slaughter anyone who touched Thea, anyone who looked at her *wrong*.

It was a good thing we were alone on an island because I was going to need to get myself into check—and quickly. My thoughts raced even faster than my feet as I paced the room. Every time I thought about Thea's reaction, my chest tightened, and the longer she took in the bathroom, the worse it got. I'd overstepped by sensing the pregnancy, even unintentionally, so I tuned her out, refusing to feel out her emotions. Given her emotional state, she might not want me sharing her thoughts at the moment.

Relief washed through me when the bathroom door opened. It vanished as soon as I turned to her and spotted the redness in her eyes, the slight puffiness of her face, both of which told me that she'd been crying.

I opened my mouth, but she held up a hand.

"I will take a pregnancy test, but there is no way I'm pregnant," she said firmly.

I wasn't about to argue with her. Instead, I nodded.

"I have no symptoms," she continued, "and I'm going to need a little more proof than vampire tastebuds."

"That is perfectly fair."

"We came here to escape, not add more to our plate. We can deal with this later—but it's nothing," she added.

Her resistance puzzled me, but I didn't argue, and I didn't dare intrude on her thoughts. Although I couldn't be sure if the jumble of emotions I felt came from me or her. Maybe she didn't want to get her hopes up without knowing for certain. How soon could I have someone bring us a test? There were a few souls lingering on the island. I could probably reach Celia. Given her hint earlier, she'd probably be thrilled to run that errand.

"You look like you're plotting," Thea interrupted my thoughts, her voice full of suspicion.

"Just listening," I said, beginning to cross to her.

She shook her head. "There's just no way. I had my period…"

I waited, but her forehead drew together as she tried to remember. I bit down on my lip to keep myself from smiling. That would definitely not go over well.

She let out a frustrated squeak. "I can't remember with everything that has been going on, but," she added swiftly, "I'm sure it was just a few weeks ago."

I refrained from telling her that as far as we knew, she could have gotten pregnant yesterday. Between my vampire senses and the mating bond, I'd notice the slightest change in her body.

"I doubt it." She crossed her arms, hearing the thought anyway. I was so focused on not eavesdropping on her thoughts, my own nerves frayed entirely, that I'd left my shields down. "There's no way that we would know this soon."

"Magical pregnancies are different than human pregnancies." I hated to point that out, but it was probably better for her to start adjusting her expectations now.

"Exactly." She began to pace around the living room. My eyes tracked her every movement. "I mean, how did this even happen?"

I paused. "Is that a serious question?"

"We weren't even sure I had enough magic to get pregnant." She rubbed her stomach absently, then froze with horror. She looked down at her hand like it was a traitor and dropped it to her side. "I still don't even know if I have any magic."

I stared at her. Her power was well established, and if she was questioning it…things were really going off the rails now. Maybe it was related to her pregnancy. Not that I would ever say that to her. Instead, I focused on the facts, hoping that would help her come around.

"You brought me back from the dead, my love," I reminded her gently.

"Yeah, well, I thought that might have been a fluke."

"A *fluke* resurrection?"

"It's not as stupid as it sounds." She threw her hands up. "It's not like I knew what I was doing. I still don't know what I'm doing. I have all this magic, supposedly, but…" She dissolved into tears and flopped onto the leather couch. "You've had almost a thousand years to get ready for kids," she croaked. "I've had a couple of weeks."

"Until the day I met you, I never even considered being a father." I covered her hand with mine as I knelt before her. "Not once in all my centuries...until I met you."

"And now you're suddenly ready?"

"No." I laughed at the thought. "I'm terrified."

She rubbed her chest. "You don't feel terrified."

That was the problem with our bond. Thea might feel most of my emotions and even hear my thoughts, but sometimes she missed the nuance. I couldn't blame her for that. My own feelings were everywhere, and even worse, trying to give her boundaries left me feeling out of balance. No sooner did I think I had a grip on myself than some new consideration overwhelmed me again.

I sat back on my heels, still clutching her hand. I needed to get control of myself. I couldn't care for Thea like this, and if I was right, that was now my primary job.

"I am fucking scared," I whispered. "Scared that I'm going to fuck this up. Scared I won't be male enough to be a good mate—a good father." The word even felt funny on my lips. "I'm scared that I'll lose you again. I'm scared that I'll be like my parents." She laughed softly at this despite her tears. "I'm scared about what happens when everyone finds out, but there is one thing that I'm not scared of."

"What is that?" she asked, her shoulders trembling, tears soaking her cheeks.

"Of us." I leaned forward and carefully rested a hand over her abdomen. "Of this love I feel for *both* of you. Because I know that it's worth all the fear. I *know* that no matter what happens nothing can change how I feel about you, except maybe I'll love you even more."

"What if I can't do this?" she whispered.

I released her hand so I could brush her tears away. "You can."

"How can you be so sure?" It wasn't a question. It was a plea—for proof, for assurance. Not just that she could carry our child but that she could be a mother. I understood where it came from, even though I knew her fear was unwarranted.

"Because you are strong and brave and full of magic, but also because you are kind and good." I paused and drew a deep breath. She might not believe anything I said, but I would spend the rest of our lives proving it was true. "I never thought I would find someone like you, because I never dreamed someone like you could exist in this fucked-up world."

"I know what you mean." She sniffed. "But, Julian, I need to understand my magic before..."

She placed her hand over mine, and I smiled, understanding what she couldn't say. "I understand. We'll find someone to help you with it."

Her head bobbed a little. "And I still want to take a pregnancy test."

"Deal." I couldn't help but smile. Pushing to my feet, I whipped out my phone, buoyed by her abrupt lack of resistance.

"What are you doing?" she asked as I punched out a text.

"Getting that test."

"Now? It's the middle of the night!" She jumped to her feet and grabbed for my phone.

"We're vampires, pet. We like the middle of the night." I finished sending the text before grabbing her around the waist and lifting her off her feet. "It will probably take a while for Celia to bring it. What do you want to do?"

"Well, I haven't seen the rest of the house." She laughed, nuzzling into me. "Where do we sleep?"

"Sleep? Are you tired?"

Thea rolled her eyes. "Just take me to bed, old man."

She didn't have to ask twice.

CHAPTER THIRTY-SEVEN

Jacqueline

I hoped Julian and Thea were enjoying their impromptu holiday because I was not enjoying dealing with, well, *everyone* else.

"This is my job. I took a vow to protect her!" Aurelia glowered at me. She paced the length of my sitting room. Moonlight caught her face as she passed under the large windows overlooking the garden.

It had taken all of three days before they traced Julian and Thea's outgoing flight to my private jet. Since I'd compelled the pilot to take a vacation of his own after dropping them in Cuba, no one knew exactly where they'd gone.

No one but me.

My best friend owed me big time. It was going to take an extraordinary amount of groveling to make it up to me—and probably a diamond or two.

"I promised I wouldn't say anything." I offered an apologetic smile instead, but Aurelia's nostrils flared.

"A few days away can't hurt," Lysander said, reaching for her hand as she passed him. She jerked away, glaring at him with blazing eyes. "Lia…"

"If this is the behavior I can expect from a mated queen, I can see why everyone at court is pissed at your brother. Julian will have to answer for what he's done."

I raised an eyebrow. "And what has Julian done?"

Aurelia lifted her brows and stared at me. "Everything. He's making a mockery of the court. Sitting on a throne. Running off with our queen. He needs to learn his place before I'm forced to put him in it."

I winced. I'd been afraid it would come to this. Aurelia's loyalty to Thea kept her from seeing the truth. Julian hadn't dragged Thea away. They'd gone together. "It was as much Thea's choice to leave as his. Blame them both."

"I will," she promised. "She is a queen, and she abandoned her court."

"Not permanently. Thea belongs to herself first. Not you or your court," I said coldly.

"And she has a duty to her mate," Lysander added.

Aurelia threw a sharp look in his direction. It was a miracle neither of them had killed the other yet. I'd seen wars start over less tension. "You aren't helping. I thought you came..."

"My duty is to my family." His eyes never left hers.

"And mine is to my queens," she gritted.

They were still locked in their battle of wills when Geoffrey entered, carrying a silver tray. He paused in the doorway, assessing whether or not to proceed.

"Mademoiselle," he said tentatively. "If I could have a moment..."

My shoulders slumped, relieved that he needed me. I was going to give him a raise. Or maybe once the lovebirds were back, I'd run away with Geoffrey to somewhere sunny and let the chips fall where they may. I could use a break from all the drama, too.

I left Lysander and Aurelia arguing and walked over to Geoffrey.

"You have visitors." He glanced down at the tray, and my gaze followed to discover a single calling card.

"Better tell Camila to join us," I said tightly, "and show her in."

I was wrong. Julian wasn't going to owe me a diamond; he might have to give me that stupid private island to make up for dealing with this. Since my duel with Camila, things had gone from strained to tortured. Rumors swirled that Sabine's surrender had endangered her standing with the Vampire Council. Camila, meanwhile, seemed disinterested in her new role as matriarch. She'd challenged her mother for answers about her children, but Sabine refused to talk. Despite the real possibility of bloodshed by having them in the same room, I wasn't going to miss the chance to force them to talk. They needed to work this out. I walked back to the other two.

"If you two are done," I interjected, cutting Lysander off mid-sentence, "I'm afraid we have company. Your mother's arrived."

He groaned, but Aurelia's eyes widened. "I need to go."

"I'll come with you," he said, and I wondered if he was being a gentleman or if he was just a glutton for punishment.

"No." She stopped him. "I must see the queens and tell them what I learned—or rather didn't learn. You'll only make it worse."

I smiled as she swept out of the room, but Lysander frowned, his gaze following her as she left. "I always make it worse," he muttered.

"Is something going on between you two?" I asked him.

He shook his head as footsteps approached. Camila rounded the corner and stopped when she saw us standing there. She was already wearing her red silk pajamas. She hadn't said good night, so I was surprised at the state of her undress—not that we'd been speaking much. She was only staying here because she didn't trust her mother not to take back her position by killing her in her sleep. I stared at the way the silk draped over her curves, and she lifted a brow. I looked away quickly.

"Don't let me interrupt, brother," she said sweetly. "I've been wondering the same thing about the two of you."

"She's a handmaiden," he growled with such sudden ferocity that I took a step back.

Across from me, Camila laughed. "I suppose that answers the question," she teased.

Before either of us could pry more info from him, Geoffrey reappeared. "Madame Sabine Rousseaux."

"Gird your loins," Lysander muttered as Geoffrey stepped to the side to allow his mother to enter the room.

Sabine glanced around the room, her eyes landing on each of us in turn. Unlike the rest of us, she was dressed formally. The black hair she shared with her daughter was twisted in a graceful chignon and pinned with amethyst hair clips. Her aubergine gown flowed to the floor, and a fur stole was wrapped around her arms like she'd just come from a party that none of us were invited to.

She inclined her head to me. "Jacqueline—"

"What are you doing here?" Camila cut her off. "I thought I was quite clear. I don't wish to speak with you. As head of—"

"I'm not here to speak with you," Sabine snarled, any semblance of civility vanishing. "I have been trying to reach my son."

"What do you need?" Lysander stepped forward, hands shoved into his pockets.

Her eyes flickered over him. "What are you doing here? Or are you planning to betray me like this one?" She heaved a wounded sigh toward her daughter.

Camila only laughed again.

"I'm just here." Lysander didn't bother to explain he'd come with Aurelia, because that would raise more questions that no one wanted to answer.

"Don't make it a habit," she warned him, sniffing slightly, "but I came looking for Julian. I tried to reach him at court, but he's not returning my messages. I assume he's avoiding me. I'd like to know why."

"He's not avoiding you." I braced myself for Sabine's usual brand of theatrics. She might not be head of her household anymore, and Julian might have his own bloodline in the works, but Sabine wouldn't be pleased to learn the reason he wasn't returning her calls. "He took Thea away on holiday."

"On holiday? What do you mean?" Sabine's face blanched, and she grabbed ahold of the nearest chair.

Lysander shot to her, offering support to keep her steady on her feet. He aimed a questioning look at me over her shoulder. "They'll be back in a few days," he said in a calm voice.

Sabine shook her head, her eyes growing wild with panic. "Tell me they're in Venice, at least."

"They aren't…" It was the most I was willing to share, especially with Sabine. Julian would never forgive me if his mom broke down his door and interrupted his sex-cation. "But they will be back."

"What have they done?" she murmured, her chest rising and falling in deep pants. "Who else knows they've gone?"

"The queens and the guards." Lysander shrugged a shoulder, looking as tired as I felt. "The queens aren't too happy about it, either."

I suspected Aurelia was pissed, too. Maybe that's why Lysander looked like he'd been burning the candle at both ends since they'd left three days ago.

Sabine's eyes closed, and she pushed Lysander gently away. When she opened them, the wildness remained, but she held her head up. "We must contact them immediately. Lysander, you will go to your brother. Take that guard of Thea's and—"

"Wait!" I jumped in as she made plans. It was a good thing I hadn't told her where they were. "I'm not going to tell you where they are."

"Yes, you will," she hissed, "or I will rip your useless tongue out of your smart little mouth."

Camila lunged forward, trying to get between us. My heart jumped at the protective gesture—at what it signaled—but now wasn't the time to analyze Camila's feelings. I held up my hand. I could handle Sabine Rousseaux. "I definitely can't tell you if you do that."

Sabine's mouth fell open, and she looked to her daughter. "You! Tell her she has to tell you."

"No." Camila crossed her arms over her chest and smirked. "I don't take orders from you, remember? I'm head of this household now. Or did you forget, Mother?"

Sabine grabbed her daughter by the shoulders, pinning her with her frantic eyes. "This is not about you or me. If you care about your twin—if you love him, as I know you do—you will convince her to tell you. This is a matter of life and death."

Camila studied her for a second, her face unreadable. Finally, she lifted her eyes to mine. I saw the question there. Not the one Sabine demanded my answer, but the one I couldn't stop myself from asking.

"What do you mean by life and death?" I asked softly.

Sabine released her daughter, her head dropping as she gathered the remnants of her pride. Sabine was accustomed to making orders, not answering questions. When she finally drew herself together, she looked at each of us in turn. "There is a price on their heads. Even telling you puts one on mine. We must warn them before it's too late."

"What?" Camila shouted. "Who would do that?"

"The Council. They know she's a siren," she said grimly. "Thea was safe in Venice. The Council would never move against a queen here, and even if they did, the city's magic would protect her. As long as she is in Venice, she's damn near immortal. I've been trying to undo the mess those two made, trying to convince the Council to have mercy. But Selah wants Thea's head on a platter as well as anyone caught protecting her. She'll see this as her opportunity. They'll do whatever they can to kill a siren regardless of her mate or her position."

I didn't have to ask why the Council wanted Thea dead. It hadn't occurred to me that being in Venice was keeping them safe. But was telling Sabine more dangerous than contacting them myself? She was on the Council. She hated Thea. It could be a trick. I wouldn't put it past her to feign concern only to make her own strike against her unwanted daughter-in-law.

Before I could process this, Sabine had me by the throat. I hadn't even seen her move. Camila and Lysander charged toward her, but she held up a hand. "This is between the two of us, but please believe me when I say, I will rip her pretty little head off her body if she doesn't answer me in the next ten seconds. *Where are they?*"

CHAPTER THIRTY-EIGHT

Thea

I t turned out that it didn't matter what hours Celia kept. Despite delivering the test within hours of Julian's message, it was still sitting in the bag on the bathroom counter.

Three *days* later.

I just hadn't been able to face it yet.

Julian stalked into the bathroom, stretching his arms over his head and giving me a view of his sharply hewn abs. My eyes flickered up to the mark that he bore on his chest—the symbol of my throne and a reminder that our lives were now bound as one. It was also a harsh reminder of the duty I was currently shirking—one I'd decided I didn't want. A grin hooked his face as he caught me staring, and I quickly looked away before he realized I wasn't just ogling him. I was doing something worse.

I was thinking.

Something that had been expressly forbidden for the remainder of our trip.

Unfortunately, given the circumstances, I found myself thinking a lot. About our future and babies and my crown and babies. Mostly babies. As far as my mate was concerned, I was knocked up. I wouldn't be convinced until I took the test.

"Planning to stop torturing me this morning?" He wrapped his strong arms around me, instantly undoing the towel I had knotted around myself after my shower. I grabbed it before it fell to the ground. My eyes found him in the mirror's reflection, and I tried to look innocent.

"Torturing?" I blinked.

"I can hear what you're thinking." He nipped the shell of my ear softly. "If you aren't ready to take it, don't."

It was what he'd said the last two mornings. He was being both frustratingly understanding—because he was perfect—and annoyingly smug—because he was convinced he knew what that "unnecessary" test would reveal.

"If you're so desperate to see what it says, why don't you pee on it?" I forced a smile.

His eyes narrowed as he shook his head. "I don't think that's how it works."

"I guess you'll have to wait, then." I pulled away from him and gathered my wet hair into a loose bun. As soon as it was up, he spun me around and back into his arms. I sighed, content to be where I belonged, despite everything. "There's plenty of time to worry about that later."

That was what I'd told him every time he asked. Considering he'd conveniently stopped opening new bottles of wine and kept within arm's reach of me at all times, I wasn't exactly sure why I was waiting, either. Like it or not, Julian was already acting like I was pregnant.

"What do we have planned for the day?" I asked, eager to steer the conversation away from the status of my womb.

"Well, we could stay here," he said, sliding his hands under the towel to grip my hips. His bare palms sent a shiver of dark magic coursing through me. "What was yesterday's record?"

"I lost count." We'd gone away to be alone, and we hadn't wasted that time. If I didn't think he was so sure that I was already carrying his child, I would suspect he was trying to get pregnant.

He lifted a brow that told me he'd caught that thought. "And if I am?"

My eyes shuttered as he angled his head lower, his mouth cruising along my jaw toward my throat. "I'm not stopping you."

I pressed closer to him, my body responding to the one thing I was certain of. Julian tugged the towel from me and dropped it on the tile floor. His hands drifted up my body to cradle my neck. His lips were soft and searching, and I was lost in a blissful moment, no longer worrying about the future. My fingers tangled in his hair, dragging him closer, wanting to feel the hardness of his body against mine.

Suddenly, he pulled back, and I moaned. His lips moved, smiling against mine. "But I actually have plans for us today," he said, his voice low and husky.

My eyes popped open. "Plans? Real plans or 'beat the record you set for number of orgasms you give me in a single day' plans?"

"I fear I've been a bad influence on you." He propped my chin on his finger. "It's up to you: a surprise, or stay here and finish what we started?"

I thought about it for a second, a grin creeping onto my face. "What are the chances we can keep working on that record during these plans of yours?"

"I would say extremely high."

Well, that settled it.

I pulled free from his arms and headed into the bedroom. "What should I wear?"

"You don't have to change." He followed behind me.

I shot a look over my shoulder. "I'm naked."

"Exactly," he purred, prowling my direction. I didn't try to stop him as he pounced.

• • •

By the time we managed to get dressed, it was already noon. I checked my wrap dress in the mirror before fussing with the tie of the bikini I wore underneath.

"You really don't need that," he said, taking my hand and

dragging me out of the bedroom.

"You said we'd be near the water," I pointed out to him. "What if I want to swim?"

"It's a private island. You don't need a swimsuit for that."

"Taking it off will give you something to do," I said drily.

"How thoughtful of you." He paused in the foyer to grab my sunhat and plopped it onto my head.

"Do I need anything else?" I asked.

"I took care of everything," he said mysteriously, but as we walked out the door, he headed toward the golf cart rather than the beach.

"Where are we going?" I asked as he helped me inside—a bit over-protectively. How was I going to survive nine months of vampire hovering?

"I guess we'll find out." He kissed the tip of my nose, leaving me to wonder if he was answering my question or my thought.

The winds were stronger today, and I held onto the floppy-brimmed hat to keep it from flying off my head and being swept away by the Atlantic. I raised my face up to the sunny sky overhead as my stomach growled.

The golf cart slowed. "Food is waiting," Julian promised, eyeing me with concern. His nostrils flared slightly, and I knew he was checking my scent for signs that he needed to intervene immediately.

"Human food or vampire food?" I asked lightly. It had not escaped my attention that Julian had not stolen so much as a drop of my blood since that fateful night on the beach.

"Whichever you prefer."

He, however, didn't seem to mind that I kept nipping him every time we made love, which only made me feel worse. "You're going to have to feed eventually."

"A worry for another day."

Our worries were beginning to stack up. Julian steered the golf cart to the edge of the dock where his yacht was moored.

"The boat?" I said, surprised.

"I thought we might visit a few of the smaller islands. There's a white sand beach on one of them," he explained as we started toward it.

I caught sight of one of the crew members. "I'm glad I wore something."

Julian only laughed. "I'm not. They're all in thrall. No one will bother us." He leaned closer. "I intend to break yesterday's record."

My toes curled in my sandals, the insinuation in his voice sending a shock of longing through me. "You're insatiable."

His grin widened, but it fell when my stomach growled again. "Let's feed you…"

I didn't miss the way he trailed away, and I suspected there was a word he wanted to add to that statement. Both. I shoved down the thrill that surged through me, the same one I felt whenever he hinted that he was thinking about a family. Our family.

The truth was that other than being hungry all the time, I didn't feel pregnant. Not even a little bit. I just felt like me. It wasn't possible that I was carrying our child and felt entirely the same. I wasn't sure what it would be, but I was certain I would feel something.

If Julian caught any of my thoughts, he didn't say anything. He was picking his battles, and as he led me inside to an already laid dining table, it was clear what one of them was. Ripe apples, grapes, and bananas spilled from a bowl. Next to it was a platter of fresh vegetables arranged into a pretty pattern. There was chicken and fish. It was enough to feed a dozen people.

"This is overkill," I muttered as I took a bottle from a silver ice bucket, frowning when I discovered it was nonalcoholic cider.

"Just in case," he said gently, his eyes tracking me as I dished up, like he was logging my food intake. I lifted an eyebrow, and he held up his hands in surrender.

"I'll go tell them we're ready to head out."

"Good idea." As soon as he disappeared to find the captain, I sank onto one of the couches and popped a grape into my mouth, annoyed to find they tasted especially good. He was probably flying them in from some private vineyard just for me. Silly, overprotective billionaire vampire.

I'd moved on to chicken when he came back and announced we were all clear.

I nodded absently, knowing that I couldn't avoid the truth any longer. "Julian, there's something I need—"

The boat swayed infinitesimally, and my stomach lurched in protest.

Julian was by my side instantly. "What is it?" He pressed a hand to my forehead, and I moaned at the coolness of his touch.

I shook my head, my insides threatening revolt. I didn't dare answer him. Instead, I choked back the contents of my stomach and managed one word: "Bathroom?"

Julian swept me into his arms and raced me to the nearest toilet. As soon as he placed me on my feet, I launched myself at the bowl, barely making it in time.

His strong hands gathered my hair and held it for me as I continued to retch. By the time it stopped, I felt hollowed out. Sitting back on my heels, I shook my head, feeling a little dizzy. "So much for a day out," I muttered apologetically. "I didn't get seasick last time."

He remained silent, watching me, his eyes glinting with a curious mixture of concern and amusement.

"What?" I demanded, but he still didn't speak. I frowned, trying to listen for what he was thinking but found his mind silent.

Finally, he released a deep sigh. "Thea, maybe we should take that pregnancy test now."

I stared at him, my mouth forming a small *O* shape. After a second, I shook myself free of the haze. "Too bad it's at the house."

He smiled in answer and pulled the box out of his pocket. "I told you I would take care of everything."

CHAPTER THIRTY-NINE

Julian

I had no idea what was going on with my mate. I'd thought we were on the same page about our future, about our lives, but as she clutched the toilet, I wondered if I was wrong. If I'd known she wasn't ready, I never would have pushed it. Even if we were bound to a mortal lifespan, we had years ahead of us to start a family. We'd rushed things, and now I had to face the possibility she regretted that.

Regretted me.

Her eyes softened, tears swimming in them from her retching. "It's not you," she said softly, reading my thoughts. "It's all happening so fast."

That was something I actually agreed with her about. It felt like I'd met Thea yesterday, but somehow it also felt like she'd always been there. Always would be there. Maybe it was the conflict between my vampire nature and the mortal part of her I carried within me, but it was somehow both. She had been mine forever, and I'd only known her for the blink of an eye.

"Maybe it's just love," she said, "because that's how I feel about you, and I'm much, much younger than you are, old man."

My lips pressed into a bemused smile, pleased that she was at least joking. That was a good sign.

"If you don't want to take it, I can respect that." I waved the test at her. "But we will have to deal with this eventually."

"I know." She shifted toward the wall, tucking her knees against her chest.

Or maybe I was getting this all wrong. "Thea, if you don't want... I'm sure something can be done."

Her eyebrows nudged together as she considered this. "What do you mean?"

I sucked in a deep breath, allowing it to fill my chest, hoping I could tamp down my emotions enough to say what needed to be said. "If you've changed your mind, I will support you. If you don't want to have a baby—"

"What?" She bolted unsteadily to her feet. "Why would you say that?"

Okay, maybe I had read her wrong. The trouble was that I was having a hard time reading her at all. Even our mating bond felt fuzzy, as though the changes happening to her were fucking it up. In the end, all I had was the truth. "I don't know what to say," I murmured, not daring to move closer to her. "Tell me what to say, Thea."

Her eyes closed. "Just tell me you love me."

"I love you." I took a step toward her.

"I love you, too." She opened her eyes one at a time and gave me a brittle smile. "Tell me that it will all be okay."

"It will—"

But she cut me off. "Tell me that the Vampire Council won't try to assassinate me the minute they find out about us. Tell me my father won't try to kidnap me again. Tell me that I'm not powerless to protect our..."

I closed the space between us. Wrapping her in my arms, I vowed, "No one will touch you."

"How can you be sure?" Her face peeked up at me, searching my eyes for an answer. "If you can sense changes in me, if Celia can sense them...we can't hide it. What are we supposed to do? Stay here forever? They'll come for us. You know that!"

"And I will be ready. The Scourge, remember?" I forced a tight smile, knowing I would become that monster again if that's what it took.

"That's not a solution. You forget that I feel everything you feel. I know what it does to you when they call you *il flagello*. I won't let you become a monster for me," she argued, showcasing the willfulness that I'd fallen for when we met.

I loved her for knowing that and seeing what others could not—for what others refused to. But for her... "Then we find a nice private island with a lot of security. Oh, wait, we have one."

"We can't just disappear."

"We could with a glamour."

"A glamour?" she repeated, tearing free of my arms. "I spent my whole life glamoured!"

"I know." I reached for her, but she stepped farther away.

"And what am I supposed to do? Hide behind magic, and then what? Send it away? Maybe you can ship our child off to be with Camila's children, wherever they are."

I flinched. "We will not do that to our children."

"We can't just hide this." She took a shaky breath. "If..."

There it was again: *if.*

"We will find a way to keep you both safe." I had not endured nine centuries without her to lose her. I would do whatever it took to keep her safe. Damn the consequences. "If there is danger, we will face it together," I swore to her. "No one will touch you. No one will touch our child."

"I feel selfish." Her voice was small. "How can I bring a child into this mess?"

And there it was. The reason she'd been holding back. The reason she'd fought the joy I felt flickering and vanishing through our bond. I wished I had a better answer for her, but once again, I could only be open. Vulnerable. "As you are always pointing out, I am much older than you," I said drily. "But with age comes wisdom, so believe me when I say that life is always a mess."

She choked back a little sob. "Still, maybe we should have waited."

I shook my head. "To be happy? You can't wait for that. Happiness has to be seized. It's in short supply most of the time. We can't waste it."

Thea swiped at her eyes and nodded, but she bit her lip, digesting what I'd said. Finally, she swallowed, and a fresh tear rolled down her cheek. "Okay. Now tell me that test will be positive and that I have not spent the last two days trying and failing not to fall in love with our child, only to find out..."

There was still fear in her voice, but there was also love. Fierce love. The kind of love I knew she would give unconditionally as a mother. I couldn't stop myself. Hooking an arm around her, I drew her to me. As our lips met, I could feel the tension leave her body, and with it, the veil between us lifted. Golden warmth flooded through me—her magic—and I groaned against her mouth, relieved at its return. My hand reached for hers, and I pressed our palms together, answering with my own. As long as we had this, as long as we had each other, we could face anything that came our way. We were two halves of the same soul, and through our love, we'd made a miracle.

When we finally broke apart, she took a deep breath. "I guess I should take that test."

"About that..." She was either about to be very pissed at me or relieved. I couldn't be sure which. Thea lifted an eyebrow, but I pressed on. "You asked me to tell you that the test will be positive."

Her breath caught, but she managed a nod.

"It will be," I confessed, moving our joined hands to her stomach. "This morning..."

"What?" she gasped, clutching my fingers so tightly I thought she might actually break them.

"I heard it. I heard the baby's heartbeat."

Her eyes widened, her mouth hanging open slightly.

I continued quickly. "If you still want to take—"

"You heard the baby's heart?" she said, her face going from dazed to awestruck. Then her eyes narrowed. "So you planned to take me out *on a boat* because you knew?"

"Actually, I took you out because I needed to get my mind off it before I went crazy," I admitted with a harsh laugh. "I was trying to respect your needs, pet."

Her lips curled into a faint smile. "I know." She held out her hand. "Give me the test."

"You don't trust my superior vampire senses?" I feigned outrage.

"Magic is great, but I'm a mortal, remember? I want to see it for myself."

I rolled my eyes and handed it to her, but she didn't move.

"Julian," she pressed, shooing me away with her hand. "A little privacy."

"Seriously?" I stared at her. "We share a soul."

"Not a toilet. Let's keep a little mystery alive."

She continued to squawk at me as she pushed me toward the door. I took my time, perhaps enjoying being the one to drag this out for once. When I finally had both feet out the door, she locked it behind me.

I can break the door down.

I heard her laugh on the other side of it, and whatever lingering worry I felt eased. I couldn't blame her for being anxious. Fuck, I understood that. I leaned against the wall, closing my eyes, and tuned out her movements. She wanted her privacy. But that sent my thoughts drifting to the future—to those fears about the safety of her and our child and whether I would be a good father. I shook free of them. Together, we could face anything. And nothing and no one would come between us.

The door opened, and Thea appeared, the test in her hand, as heavy footsteps pounded overhead. I lunged in front of her, knowing instantly it wasn't the sound of my own security team.

"We have company," I said through clenched teeth.

"Maybe the queens sent—" The thought cut off as vampires streamed down the stairs into the cabin. Their black clothing bore the insignia of the Vampire Council.

"Stay back," I warned her as they leveled guns at us.

"We're here for the siren," the one in the lead shouted.

"You'll have to come through me," I snarled. I'd take on every one of them and rip them to shreds for daring to breathe the same air as my mate.

"No!" Thea shouted, trying to move around me.

We're outnumbered.

I didn't take my eyes off those guns or the vampires holding them. *I'm a little hurt that you think I can't take them.*

I thrust an arm out to keep her behind me, but she ducked under it. "Promise us safe passage and we'll go with you. We can sort this out with the Council."

What are you doing?

"Keeping us alive," she muttered.

"Our orders are to bring you in—only you."

"Over my dead body," I said in a cold voice.

The vampire lowered her gun. "You know, now that you mention it..."

There was movement next to her, followed by whipping air as a glint of metal sliced through the air. I braced for impact. Even as a mortal, I could handle one knife, but Thea jumped first. Not away from the blade.

In front of me.

CHAPTER FORTY

Thea

Darkness crept along the edges of my vision as I continued to stare at Julian. I was dimly aware of my arms going slack, the pregnancy test dropping to the ground with a distant clatter, the knife lodged so deeply in my chest that I couldn't even feel it.

Julian was saying something, but I could barely understand him.

"Don't come any closer," he roared as black-clad figures stormed inside the cabin. His eyes returned to me, frantic, pleading as he tried to staunch the bleeding around the knife.

He wasn't wearing gloves. He never did anymore. There had been a time when I'd thought he would never touch me with bare hands. Now, despite the warmth of his touch, I felt so cold. It reminded me of being a child and going out on a winter's day, the wind sucking all the heat from my bones.

I was finding it difficult to stand up. I tried to take a step toward him and fell in a boneless heap into his arms. He helped me gently to the ground, keeping his body angled between me and the threat.

No one approached. I couldn't understand why. They'd had no problem throwing a knife at my heart.

My heart.

"Thea, stay with me." His face contorted with pain, and I

recalled the bond that sealed our lives as one.

I was dying. I'd doomed us both.

"I'm sorry," I mumbled. I would never get to tell him that he was right. That I was pregnant.

I gasped raggedly, trying to find the other words I needed to say, but darkness closed in around me. Julian leaned over me, placing his forehead against mine, panting, panicked.

"Gods!" a familiar voice cried. *Jacqueline.*

What was she doing here?

"Let me help." Lysander appeared over me, crouching beside his brother.

It took effort, but I managed to lift my head. Bodies lay scattered around me, and standing over them, each wearing looks of horror, were my friends. My family.

"What should we do with them? The Council is bound to come looking for them." Sebastian huddled next to Thoren, discussing options.

"Throw them overboard and hope they can swim."

My mouth tried to lift into a smile. It was such a vampire solution to the predicament.

"We need to get this knife out," Lysander said. "But if we're not careful…"

Julian nodded grimly.

"Listen to me," Julian hissed. His bloody fingers gripped my chin and forced me to look at him. "I need you to be still. We can't risk the blade hitting your heart."

I couldn't manage more than a blink.

"Stay with me," he ordered, his voice full of dark magic, as if he was trying to find the end of the tether he'd once held.

I wished it was still there because I would have obeyed him. I would stay with him. I wanted that more than anything.

But the world was fading at the edges, and it was so hard to stay awake.

"I'm cold." I wasn't sure if he could understand me.

Julian's face contorted, despair ravaging him. Did he feel it, too? Could he see that endless night before us? Was he slipping toward that oblivion?

"Fuck," Lysander cursed. Metal clanged as it hit the ground.

"I need you to drink, pet," Julian begged, bringing his wrist to my mouth. Blood welled from an open vein as he smashed it against my lips.

But I couldn't. Too cold. Too tired.

Then everything went black.

CHAPTER FORTY-ONE

Julian

"Thea, open your eyes." I touched her face, but she didn't move. "Thea!"

Her mouth was slack, her body limp as her heart thumped once. Twice. Then nothing.

No heartbeat. No pulse.

"No, *no*." I gathered her in my arms, cradling her lifeless form against mine. "You can't leave me here." I closed my eyes, drinking in her scent, pressing my lips to her hair. "I'm supposed to go with you."

Our lives were bound, our souls forged together when she sang the song of life. I was not supposed to be without her. I would not. I *could not* live without her.

"Julian," Lysander said softly. "We should get out of here."

"I'm not leaving her." My eyes snapped open, and I crushed her against me.

"We won't," he promised. "But we can't stay here. There may be others. The Council will be waiting for the team to report back..."

But I couldn't move. I'd failed her. Minutes ago, I'd vowed to protect her. I told her that no one would touch her. No one would touch...

My eyes scattered across the floor, searching, searching, searching until they found the pregnancy test. Jacqueline moved into view, dropping down to pick up the object of my sudden interest. She gasped, her hand covering her mouth as if to hold back reality.

"She was," I mumbled as I started to grow cold. Numb. Just like her blood now cooling against my skin.

I'd lost them both. In the blink of the eyes, in one unguarded, preoccupied moment, I'd lost *them*.

Jacqueline shoved the test in her pocket and moved to me. "Let me help you."

I almost couldn't bear the sorrow I found staring back at me. The grief. The sadness. The evidence that my worst fucking nightmare had finally come true.

Thea was gone.

I'd spent nine hundred years restless, purposeless, until she'd stumbled into my life and given me a reason to live. And now she was gone. The baby was gone. It was all gone.

It was too much, and so I did the only thing I could. I released Thea into Jacqueline's arms and stood, only to take my mate's body once more. I carried her out of the cabin. My brothers were on the deck, throwing the Council guards overboard. I was glad. If they'd been left to me, I would have shredded all of them to pieces. I would not have let them live, let them wake up to their failure and the consequences of it.

Lysander placed a hand on my shoulder, and I flinched. He backed up a step, holding his hands up to show he wasn't a threat.

"They killed your crew," he explained. "We think they were tracking your yacht. We should leave on ours."

Ours? I lifted my head and found a smaller vessel anchored nearby. A dark head of hair ducked out of its cabin and walked slowly onto the deck. I snarled when I saw her.

My mother.

"I'm not going anywhere with her," I gritted. She could have stopped this. "She's Council."

"She tried to warn you," Jacqueline explained, then tugged her lower lip between her teeth. "She was the one who got us here."

I didn't move.

"Julian, we have to go," Lysander said firmly.

I continued to stare at my mother across the distance before I finally started walking toward her. Thoren and Sebastian ran ahead, leaping from the yacht onto the smaller boat.

"I'll catch her," Sebastian called, waiting there.

But I couldn't release Thea. Instead, I shook my head. "I can do it."

This time my vampire senses didn't fail. I made the jump easily, landing softly on my feet with her still in my arms.

Jacqueline and Lysander followed, each moving quickly to my side. I knew why they were flanking me. I stalked forward anyway.

"Thea is dead." I spit the words at my mother. "You finally got your wish."

"I did not wish for this," she said softly, her eyes dimming slightly as she stepped to the side. "Take her inside."

I took the steps into the hull slowly. Below I found a tiny compartment with a double bed. No one followed after me. I placed Thea across the white sheets, trying to look past the blood soaking through her summer dress.

And then I fell to my knees.

This was wrong. She was life. I was death. It should be me lying there. Not her. I'd lived lifetimes and hers had just begun.

I couldn't bear to consider our child. I couldn't bear to think of how happy I'd been only hours ago.

Soft footsteps fell behind me, but I didn't look up. I didn't need to. I recognized my mother's scent.

Her hand was gentle on my shoulder, but I felt no comfort.

"I'm sorry we were too late." She sounded small, uncertain, and I knew she meant it.

"You disobeyed the Council." It wasn't a question, more of a realization.

"What's one more enemy?"

"They will pay for this." This vow I would keep. I'd failed Thea.

I'd failed our child. But I would not rest until I slaughtered every last person responsible for this.

"As they should," she murmured in agreement. She gasped slightly, and her hand tightened on my shoulder. She released it and moved to the edge of the bed, ignoring my soft snarl of warning.

"No one touches her," I growled.

She held a hand up to silence me, her face contorting with concentration, and then...shock widened her eyes. She turned and grabbed me by the shoulders. I started to protest, but she cut me off with one sharp word. "Listen."

I closed my eyes, trying to ignore the swell of sorrow I felt, and did as she said. Water lapped against the side of the boat. My family spoke in hushed, anguished tones, one of them tapping their feet against the deck above. My mother breathed in shallow, darting pants. But underneath it all, there was something else.

Faint and racing and precious.

"The baby's heartbeat," I muttered, new tears spilling down my cheeks. "How?"

It wasn't possible. She was only a few weeks along. The child couldn't have survived her death.

"Your lives are bound." My mother sounded amazed.

I knew that sound—I'd heard it only this morning, but I would never forget that soft whooshing, racing heartbeat. And if I lived and...

Thea gasped for air, her body jolting awake.

CHAPTER FORTY-TWO

Thea

I couldn't get enough air. I drank down giant gulps of it, my fingers splaying over the bloodspot on my chest. I had died. Again.

Julian, pale with shock, stared at me from the foot of the bed. He didn't move as our eyes met. The world rushed back to me as my senses flared to life.

The lap of water against the side of the boat.

The salty smell and taste of the ocean.

The buttery light flooding in from the porthole.

"I'll leave you two," someone murmured. Out of the corner of my eye, Sabine moved toward the door with a lethal grace. She paused when she reached it. "Or should I say, you *three*?"

My hand shifted lower, eyes widening as I processed what had happened. But if I had died... "Is the baby...?"

My unfinished question snapped Julian from his stupor. He rose to his feet, nearly filling the small cabin with his massive frame. "Its heartbeat is strong," he said thickly. His throat bobbed as he took one step toward me. "You were..."

"Dead," I finished when he couldn't.

Julian nodded, his gaze never straying from me, as if he expected I might vanish if he looked away.

"Dying twice? I'm a regular Buffy." I tried to make the words sound light, but they were coated in the same heaviness I felt.

Julian blinked. "What's a buffy?"

"The vampire slayer," I prompted. His face remained blank, and I tried to smile. "I forget how much pop culture you missed."

His mouth twisted, a hint of amusement slipping through. "I'm not sure vampire slayers are my thing."

He made a really good point.

I started to swing my legs over the side of the bed, but he moved in a blur toward me. "You should rest."

"I feel fine. Great, actually." Which made absolutely no sense. I stretched my arms over my head as if demonstrating this fact. But even though there was no physical pain, something dark tapped against my mind. Thoughts. Questions. I should ask them, but I didn't want to, not after emerging from that shrouded oblivion so recently.

Julian's brows furrowed, watching me intently. Even in his weary state, he was so beautiful. Maybe a little more beautiful on the other side of death. He hesitated, then spoke softly. "Thea, you…died."

I tore my eyes from his to a snag on the quilt. "I know," I said softly. "But it's too much…"

I can't.

He nodded, and we both continued to stare.

"You look afraid of me," I finally said. "Did I miss something?"

It was as if my words broke him. Julian dropped to his knees before me, his head falling into his hands. His body trembled, but his mind was blank. When he lifted his face, bloody tears stained his cheeks. "I…lost…you…"

Each word hit me with the force of a blow to my stomach. I stretched out a hand to him. "I'm right here."

He didn't take it. Instead, he stared at it.

"Julian?" I pressed.

"I failed you," he whispered.

I started to shake my head, soothing words poised on my lips, but he continued. "I said I would protect you. Both of you. I swore it."

"Julian, there's always going to be danger," I said softly, and perhaps later when I let the full weight of those emotions bear down on me, I would be scared. Right now, I could only feel one thing. Leaning forward, I grabbed hold of his hand and placed it on my stomach. "You saved us."

"None of this would have happened if you had never—"

"Never what?" I cut him off.

"Met me," he said.

I moved my hand over his, holding it against me. "Then I wouldn't have this." This time I found my smile easily. "I wouldn't have you. Or my magic."

"And you wouldn't have died," he snarled, "again."

"Apparently, with me, you get more than one shot at proving how much you love me. I'm alive." I pushed myself off the bed and dropped to the ground, knee to knee with him. "Because of you. The baby is alive because of *you*."

"Because I'm a vampire. Not because *I* protected *you*."

You protected *me*. His words were bleak in my mind.

I shifted away, blinking. "You're angry with me."

"No," he bit out the word, his nostrils flaring. "Fuck, of course not... Okay, maybe a little. I'm not worth it. Not worth your lives."

I grabbed hold of his shoulders, resisting the urge to shake him. "Yes, you are." I angled my head until our eyes met. He lifted them slightly, but a dark edge remained in them. "You are worth *everything*. And while we're on the topic, I'm a little pissed at you."

His whole head rose at my proclamation, surprise smoothing away some of the shadows.

"We protect each other. It's not just your job to throw yourself in front of me. You are my mate. I will protect you, too." Gripping his hand, I moved it to rest on my abdomen. "And *we* will protect our family."

I understood why he was upset. Later we needed to talk. After the shock wore off. After we regrouped. But before we decided what to do next.

"I thought you were gone," he whispered, his eyes wild with pain.

I shook my head. "I'm not gone, and now we know how our lives are bound."

My words were quiet, but I felt the truth of them reverberate through me. The song of life had woven our souls as one, not to my fleeting body but to his immortal one. What would have killed me as a siren, as a mortal, could no longer touch me. Not even death could come between us. He stared at me with an intensity that made my heart race.

Together we were immortal. Together we were forever.

"I'm not invincible," he said quietly. "There are ways that I can still be killed and if I die—"

"You won't," I cut him off. I didn't want to think about the danger that always seemed to creep up on us, the fact that death was always lurking around the corner. All I wanted was this moment to cherish the bond between us. The hope of a future with so much love.

"Vampires can die, my love," he said quietly.

I swallowed. "But you won't."

His eyes pinched at the edges, as if he wanted to say more but knew he shouldn't.

One of his thoughts strayed into my mind, and I could have wept with relief to hear him there inside my head after his own mind had been so quiet. "I know everything dies, Julian. But for the last few weeks, I've lived with the fear that by binding my life to yours—"

"—to save me," he pointed out.

"—I stole our future. I stole your future."

"There is no future for me without you," he vowed, and I knew he meant it.

"You might change your mind after a few centuries. I hear vampires often do," I teased, trying to lighten the mood.

Julian growled, lunging forward to capture my lips in a fierce kiss that told me exactly what he thought of my joke. After a moment, his mouth softened into something more like a promise, as though he needed to not only erase any doubt I had but also replace it with the truth.

When we finally broke apart, he rested his forehead against mine. "Forever with you would not be long enough for me."

"Good thing we have eternity," I murmured.

For a moment, we stayed like that, lost in each other's embrace, lost in the realization that we had forever—so long as one of us drew breath.

Finally, Julian pulled away and stood up, offering me his hand. "If we've got forever, we should probably start sorting our shit out now." His small grin made my heart leap. Guilt still shadowed his eyes, but it was a start. "I guess we need to talk to my family."

I nodded, my fingers tightening around his, but I only made it one step when something hit me. "Your mother."

Julian went absolutely still.

"She knows." I'd been too overwhelmed to process that earlier.

"The others will, too," he told me gently. "They'll be able to smell it. Maybe hear the heartbeat."

"I guess eternity doesn't come with any privacy," I grumbled. This time he actually laughed, and the last of the heaviness between us lifted.

He followed behind me on the stairs, still protective despite what we'd learned. As soon as we reached the deck, we heard raised voices.

"Oh good, they're fighting. How novel."

Julian didn't say anything; rather he stayed close to my side. A wary energy pulsed from him, stronger than ever before as he tried to check it. "If things get violent." He paused to draw in a deep breath before turning to face me. "I don't want to tell you what to do."

"But the baby," I voiced what he didn't say, and he nodded. Pushing up on my tiptoes, I offered him my lips one more time before we joined the others. His mouth slanted over mine, the kiss swift but scorching. I sighed as he straightened back up.

"Something wrong?" he asked.

"Just wondering if it's normal to be this turned on by you acting like a badass daddy."

A low growl rumbled through him, and my knees went weak. "I apologize in advance if I act a little…"

"It's okay," I said, pressing one hand to my stomach. "I feel the same way. If someone tried to hurt…" I practically choked on the words just thinking about it.

His head bowed once in solemn agreement. "When I find out who gave those orders, they're dead," he said, the words barely a whisper despite their lethal promise.

I didn't try to change his mind.

"Do they know who it was?" I asked as we finally made our way to the large sitting area on the outer deck. Wind battered us as the boat sped toward some unknown destination. Before he could answer me, we were surrounded.

"Thank the Gods!" Jacqueline rushed us, throwing her arms around my neck. She pulled away just far enough to clasp my forearms with her gloved hands. "Thea, are you…" She trailed away in wonder, looking to both of us in turn.

I lifted my eyes to Sabine, surprised she hadn't spilled the news. Her face remained completely unreadable.

"What?" Sebastian ambled over, a bottle of whisky in one hand. But as soon as he got nearer, a wide grin split his face. "I guess it's official. You're off the market."

"I've been off the market for months," Julian said sourly.

Sebastian elbowed him, the gesture one of purely masculine posturing. "I meant Thea."

Julian snarled, but his brother only laughed.

"Then it's true." Jacqueline hugged me again as the others joined us, each taking their turn to express their surprise—and congratulations. Even Thoren, usually so quiet, had a goofy smile on his handsome face.

Only one person didn't approach us, and after a moment, she cleared her throat loudly. "While a baby is good news," she said, her voice as cutting as the wind around us, "there's something we have to discuss."

"Is now the time—" Lysander started.

"Time is a luxury we no longer have. The Council came after her because she's a siren. Even with Thea's new immortality, she can still be killed, just like the rest of us, so it's time we did something." Sabine's eyes sparkled like the sun-dappled water surrounding us. "It's time to go to war."

CHAPTER FORTY-THREE

Julian

"No." The single word flew from my lips like an arrow, but if it struck my mother, she showed no sign of impact.

"This isn't up for discussion," she said coldly, "or have you forgiven the knife they lodged in your mate's heart?"

"You disowned me," I reminded her, "and the last I recall hearing, you were no longer the family matriarch."

Everyone stilled around us as I looked at my twin sister. The entire family was here, even her. She didn't move from her seat where she'd isolated herself from the rest of us. Out of the way. Noncommittal. Her feet were up, her head tilted toward the sky like she was sunning herself. As if nothing particularly exciting was happening. She could play the prodigal daughter all she wanted, but the time for remaining neutral—for swaying with the prevailing wind—was over.

At our mother's words, Camila held up a hand. "Don't drag me into this."

"You dragged yourself into this when you dueled our mother— or was that only for show?" Thea moved next to me, her hand finding mine. Calming magic flowed from her as our fingers entwined. But it wasn't enough. "I will not risk my mate or my child."

"Julian," Thea said softly, "we can't run from this. The Council took the first opportunity they had to attack."

"Attack a queen," my mother added, venom dripping in her words.

But I turned on her, tugging free from Thea's grasp. "Did you know? Were you there when they gave the order? Is that how you got here in time?"

For a moment, it was only us, staring one another down under the beating sun overhead.

"Perhaps if you had bothered to tell me you were leaving, I could have had time." She shook her head. "No. To answer your question, I did not know the Council planned to attack."

"Do they know you came here?" I demanded.

Her nostrils flared once. Twice. "No. I am…I am no longer a sitting member of the Council."

Behind me, I heard Sebastian curse, the others barely choking back their own surprise. My father appeared instantly from whatever he'd been seeing to in the captain's cabin and placed one hand on his wife's shoulder. She looked like she might slap it away but didn't.

"When your sister claimed *primus sanguis*"—her eyes flashed to Camila, who had the decency to drop her gaze—"I was given the choice between stepping down or enduring a Council vote regarding my membership. It was past time for me to tell them to go fuck themselves, so I did."

A breathy gasp escaped Thea, but she didn't say anything else.

I swallowed. "I'm sorry." I meant it.

"You aren't the one who should apologize." Sabine's words were even, measured, and although they were spoken to me, I felt every head turn to Camila. Even I found myself looking to her.

"Apologize?" Camila swung her feet down from the seat, rising gracefully to her feet. "I won, and you still refuse to give me what I demand." She sauntered toward us. "I never wanted to run this shit show. I only want to know where my children are. Whoever tells me can be matriarch, patriarch." She shrugged her slight shoulders. "I don't really care."

And that was her problem. It was always her problem. Even in our youth, Camila had followed rather than led. She obeyed instead of questioned.

"How like you," I seethed, "to take the easy way. I'm surprised you had it in you to duel. You were never a fighter."

This time my words hit their mark, and pain flickered in her eyes. She recovered quickly. "I burned your house down."

"Enough." Thea stepped between us all. I flinched to see the dried blood on her top. "This is getting us nowhere."

"Agreed." Camila's voice was icy as she looked down at my mate. "Perhaps you can command my mother to speak, Your Majesty."

White-hot anger barreled through me just as my mother exploded.

"You stupid, selfish child," she hissed at Camila. "Do you think I chose to hide my grandchildren away for spite?"

"I have no idea why you do anything. You don't bother to clue the rest of us in on your grand plans," she shot back.

"She has a point," Sebastian offered, earning a harsh glare from our father. But Sebastian walked over anyway, shoving his still-bloodied hands in his pockets. "You don't tell us anything. You just expect us to go along with it, and that's not really working anymore."

There was a moment of stunned silence, each of us too shocked to speak. It wasn't like Sebastian to be the reasonable one in the group, but...he had a point.

"Why did you hide them?" Thea asked. A simple question but one I didn't expect Sabine to answer.

Sabine drew herself up and dragged a deep breath through her lungs. "The Drakes. I knew they would demand your children."

"By law—" Sebastian started.

"The Drakes have never cared about the law," Sabine cut in, "and I was not about to let them steal away my flesh and blood. Not again. Not after I lost..." Her voice cracked, her head turning from us toward the ocean as a single crimson drop spilled down her smooth cheek.

Before I could process my mother's unexpected vulnerability,

Thea moved to her side and wrapped her in a hug.

Wide-eyed, my mother accepted it, peering over Thea's shoulders with a look of utter bewilderment that slowly softened.

"And why now?" Camila's question cleaved the tender moment in two. "Why keep them from me?"

Thea backed away to give her room to respond.

"Your behavior has not proven it was worth the risk," Sabine admitted far more gently than any of us might have expected. Maybe my mate had granted her some of the golden, peaceful magic she possessed. Or maybe my mother knew that she was running out of time to explain herself.

"I would never harm my children," Camila snarled.

"*You* might not, but I cannot say the same for your husband. Until Willem is dealt with, it's better that they stay hidden."

"A plan I can get behind," Benedict said, finally joining the conversation, "but you aren't declaring war against him or the Council."

"Still playing the part of the diplomat, I see." My mother's lips curled, her fangs bared. "No matter. It is for your sister to decide."

Camila considered for a moment. "I never wanted to be matriarch. I wanted… It doesn't matter. You can go back to ruling the entire family as soon as my children are with me. We won't rest until my husband is dead." She swiveled to face me. "Is that a problem?"

"I take no issue with ending Willem Drake. In fact, it would be my pleasure to do it myself." After what he'd done to my family, to Thea…he was dead, and while my sister might want it over and done with, I found myself inclined to take my time carving him into so many pieces that no magic could ever resurrect him. Thea paled, catching either my emotions or my thoughts.

Is that a problem, my queen?

She swallowed before granting a slight shake of her head.

Good.

"Without the Council backing us, is that wise?" Thoren said carefully.

A cold spark of surprise bolted through me. Not my own. Thea's. Her beautiful voice filled my head. *He's usually so quiet...*

That's his gift. Thoren chooses his words carefully. He never speaks unless he wants to be heard.

She blinked up at me, a little confused, before watching my family. *No one is jumping down his throat.*

Exactly. We all learned a long time ago to listen.

"What would you suggest?" Dominic asked.

Thoren looked around the boat. "Willem has no idea that his children are alive," he reminded us. "He's only shown his ugly face because he's after one thing."

Thea stepped closer to me as everyone looked to her. I wrapped an arm around her.

"We aren't using her as bait," I said with deathly calm.

"Why not?" he countered without blinking. "From what I've seen, she can hold her own."

"She's pregnant!" I roared.

"We know," Jacqueline started to say, but it was Thea who cut her off.

"And I will do whatever it takes to protect our child. We will never be safe as long as my father is alive." She leveled a stare at me, her mind totally blank.

I knew what she was doing. I sucked in a ragged breath, searching for that piece of her I carried in my soul—the spark of pure light that guided me. Finally, I nodded. "You're right." I swallowed. "But what if he's in Venice? We aren't returning to the season."

She held my gaze. "We have to. I cannot abandon the throne. Not until..." She trailed away, knowing I would understand the condition she had on her reign. We'd spent enough time talking about it that her desires were completely clear to me. Thea wouldn't abandon her seat of power until things were righted, until we knew who had murdered Ginerva, until we were certain the throne would not fall into the wrong hands.

"We can't go back there," Camila sputtered, uncharacteristically shaken. "They tried to kill you."

A cruel smile spread over our mother's face as she cast a look of approval at Thea. "The Council won't expect it. They'll expect you to run, to hide."

Thea lifted her chin, looking every bit the queen as she spoke. "I am through with hiding."

"Will you fight?" Sabine asked.

"In my own way."

Thea...

But she turned in a circle, taking us each in in turn. "You've all seen battlefields. War." She paused and lingered on Camila, who had the decency not to correct her. My sister was the only other creature present who had never gone to war. "And there may be a time when that violence is unavoidable, but what if...what if we just outsmarted them? Benedict." She turned and looked at him. "You have been spinning things for the family for years. All that time dealing with politicians has to be useful." Her eyes swept to Thoren, who stood next to him. "Am I right to assume you question the intelligence of fighting?" A pause before he nodded. "Lysander knows more than the rest of you have forgotten over the centuries. Sebastian has friends everywhere." Next she pointed to Jacqueline. "Who couldn't she charm?" My best friend tilted her head, as if to say, *True.*

Thea's eyes met mine for a brief second before she turned to my parents. "And you have seen enough battles to know how an enemy thinks, or am I wrong?"

My mother stared at her, but my father's mouth twisted into a smirk. "You are not."

"Lovely sentiment," Camila interjected, "but what about you? The Council tried to assassinate you."

Thea didn't shy away from her searing glare. "I have magic."

"Magic you don't know how to use."

Thea simply smiled. "Then I learn."

CHAPTER FORTY-FOUR

Thea

"That was quite the speech," Julian said when we were finally alone.

We'd taken the boat back to the island to pack, and most of his family had come along. Dominic and Thoren had volunteered to return the yacht to its dock in Cuba as a matter of precaution. Since the Vampire Council had tracked it once, it seemed prudent. I doubted any of us believed they couldn't find us here, even with Julian's increased security.

I swept my hanging clothes into my arms and carried them to the suitcase on the bed. It felt like I'd just unpacked. "Someone had to stop the bickering," I said lightly. "Was I out of line?"

He came up behind me and wrapped his arms around my waist. So far he hadn't packed a single item. "Thea, you're a queen." He pressed a kiss to my shoulder. "They bow to you."

"Sabine doesn't." I snorted.

"She didn't argue with you."

That was probably as close as I was going to come.

He tucked his chin on my shoulder, watching as I folded shirts into neat stacks. "You want to learn how to use magic."

"I don't really have a choice." Were the knots in my stomach mine or his?

"Mine," he answered for me.

I paused. "You don't think it's a good idea."

"It's not that." He dropped his hold on me and sprawled onto the bed, watching me. "Who are you going to find to teach you? I'm not sure I trust…"

Anyone. He didn't have to say it at this point.

"Every familiar I know is connected to the Council, and even if we found one who wasn't, how many of them will be able to help?"

I bit my lower lip. He was either going to love my idea or hate it. "I had a thought, but I'm not sure she'll help me."

"Who?" His eyes narrowed.

"Diana Jones. The witch who was on my performance committee for graduation—"

"I know who she is, pet."

"She was very clear that she was not a familiar." I decided not to remind him that she'd also been fairly anti-vampire. "She recognized that there was magic in my music. Maybe she can help."

He considered this for a moment, his eyes tracking my movements as I crossed to the chest of drawers. "It's not a terrible idea."

I released a breath I hadn't known I was holding. It wasn't that I'd expected him to be against it. It was that I had mixed feelings about the plan. Seeing Diana meant confronting the fact I'd stopped playing.

Julian's lips twisted, as if he was thinking the same, but he didn't push.

"I looked her up. She's in London right now, preparing for a performance with the city symphony. I know we're supposed to go back to Venice…" I said.

"We have a week before The Third Rite." He pushed off the bed in one graceful motion. "It's not much time, but it's a start."

I nodded. It was better than nothing. "She might be too busy."

"She won't be."

"Julian, she's an internationally renowned musician," I reminded him. "I'm not going to demand she clear her schedule for me."

He stalked toward me, and I swallowed when I saw the darkness seeping into his eyes. "I can be very persuasive."

I put my hands on my hips, even as his nearness sent a heady rush of hormones jolting through me. "You are not going to compel her."

"No." He placed his hands over mine, dragging me closer. "I am going to ask her. *Nicely.*"

I lifted my brow.

"She'll help you because she wants to," he promised. "Even an anti-Council witch will feel indebted to *you.*"

"What? Why?"

"You've given them back their magic. If you think she might help you, I suspect she will." He brushed a soft kiss over my lips, and I felt my core melt. "But if we're going to London, I need to talk to Benedict."

"Going to crash at his place?" I teased, trying to think past the need ticking between my legs.

Julian shook his head. "He has permission to live in London."

"Permission?" I repeated.

"Technically, any visiting dignitary has to clear it with the court before they step foot in the city, and you, my queen, definitely fall into that category."

My cheeks warmed. "What court? Like the royal family?"

If he told me he knew Alexander, I might actually faint.

"Bit of a crush?" he asked, reading my thoughts. His lips twitched.

"Not anymore." It came out more defensively than I'd intended.

But that hint of a smile didn't materialize. Instead, his mouth pressed into a thin line. "The *fae* court."

• • •

An hour later, we were entirely packed, and I'd sent an email to Diana asking if she'd be willing to talk. Julian had thrown his clothes into his baggage with the abandon of a centuries-old vampire and gone out to talk to his brother about our plans while I finally showered.

I tried not to think about the blood crusting my skin, about what had happened. Instead, I scrubbed myself clean quickly and changed into fresh clothes, dumping my ruined ones into the trash rather than the hamper. Even if someone could get the stains out, I never wanted to see them again. When I emerged, toweling my hair dry, Jacqueline was on the bed, a tray of food next to her.

"I thought you should eat," she said brightly, but her cheerful tone didn't match the shadows swimming in her eyes.

My stomach growled in agreement. "Thanks. Dying really takes it out of you."

She didn't smile. "I imagine being pregnant does as well."

The strawberry I'd just popped into my mouth became difficult to chew.

"I know what you said about being clever instead of fighting."

I forced myself to swallow and nodded.

"And while you're probably right, I don't like the idea of you returning to Venice," she continued, pinning her eyes on me. "Maybe that's not fair, but it's clear that the Council wants you dead."

"Good thing I'm hard to kill."

"We can handle this."

"I know you can," I said slowly, letting my thoughts catch up to the conversation. "But I have to see this through. The crown chose me. I can't just turn my back on the throne."

"Even if that's what you want?"

"Julian told you?" I guessed.

She nodded. "Don't be angry with him."

"I'm not." I sighed and plopped onto the bed, making the bone china rattle. Facing my own death—again—had made a few things clear to me. As much as part of me longed for a quiet, uncomplicated life, longed for the friends I'd left behind, I would never trade who I was now. I would not be silent. I would not allow fear to control me. Because of Julian, because of our child, because of the future that lay before us if we only seized it. And if I had to fight for that, I would fight—in my own way. I would not hide. Not anymore. "Wanting and doing are two different beasts. Even if I want to walk away, I can't.

Not yet." Reaching over, I squeezed her gloved hand. If she minded that my own was bare, she didn't say anything. "I have to see this through, because if I don't, we'll never be safe."

Her eyes flickered to where my other hand now rested on my stomach. "Then I will be right next to you," she vowed. Tears welled in my eyes at the solemn tone of her voice until she tilted her head and winked. "Have you given any thought to godmothers?"

I swiped at my tears, rolling my eyes. "We haven't gotten that far, but I promise you're top of my list."

I ate a few more bites while Jacqueline mused about whether or not the baby would be male or female. She'd just asked me what I would prefer when voices rose outside the room.

"You can't have this many vampires under one roof without a fight breaking out," she muttered, rising to her feet.

I followed her to the living room to see what the trouble was. We found Julian and Benedict shouting at each other, their chests a breath apart, as if any minute, they might smash into each other like actual cavemen. Lysander, Sebastian, and Camila stood by, casually taking bets on which one of them would win.

"Absolutely not," Julian growled.

A muscle beat in Benedict's jaw. "I do not make the rules."

"Find another way." Each word was as sharp as a dagger tip.

"What is going on?" I demanded, striding up to them.

"Your mate is getting in touch with his primitive side," Camila informed me.

I spun around, stepping close enough that I could shove an arm between them if necessary. Julian loosed a warning snarl, but I sighed. "Is this about London?"

Benedict took a step back, his eyes never leaving his brother. Their relationship had yet to recover from Benedict's involvement with The Second Rite.

"The fae court demands an audience," he said to me, those eyes still tracking Julian.

I put my hand on Julian's shoulder. "Then they'll have it."

His gaze tore from his brother and snagged on me. *The fae are dangerous.*

"So what's new?" I shrugged, forcing a smile onto my lips. "If that's what it takes to get into London, we'll do it." *They can't be more dangerous than the Council.*

I don't like it.

I don't like any of this, I reminded him silently, focusing on the magic thrumming inside me, willing it to reach out to soothe the darkness swirling inside him. *But we can handle it.*

Julian turned very, very slowly to me and pressed a kiss to my forehead. His eyes remained haunted, and I knew the cause of those ghosts.

We'll talk about it later.

I nodded once.

"What is this about London?" Sabine demanded as she entered with Dominic and Thoren trailing behind her.

"Thea found someone to help her with her magic," Julian said through gritted teeth.

"A fae?" Her eyes widened with surprise.

"No, calling upon Bain and his court is an unexpected *treat*." The final word snapped against his teeth.

Sabine instantly relaxed. "The important thing is that she gets help."

Would she feel that way if I were getting help from a fae?

His low snort was enough of an answer.

"And it will give the rest of us time to assess the situation in Venice," she continued.

Sebastian started, "We can't sit around—"

"We won't," she said sharply. "Do you think we've been sunning ourselves for the last hour?"

Thoren stepped forward and cleared his throat. "We need to ascertain more about the curse. We've been so worried about magic awakening, we haven't considered who wanted to put it to sleep. There has to be something, somewhere."

"I'll look," Lysander volunteered, earning him a bob of approval.

"In the meantime, we need to keep an eye on our enemies."

Thoren looked at Sebastian. "We know the Mordicum are meeting in the city's underground. I need you to watch for signs they're making a move."

"Hang out in seedy bars and clubs?" Sebastian shoved his hands in his pockets with a roguish grin. "Sounds terrible. When can I start?"

"And Willem?" Camila demanded. "Until he is dealt with, I am still head of this family."

"Someone needs to draw him out—someone who knows him."

Thoren shot her a meaningful look.

I didn't think I imagined Jacqueline's flinch.

"It would be my pleasure," Camila purred.

"And you?" Julian asked, not looking at his brothers but toward his parents.

They glanced at each other, and my heart stuttered when Sabine flashed an icy smile. "The Council will know you aren't dead soon, so if you aren't in Venice, we need to distract them. We need them to think Thea is there while we move everyone into place."

"And how are you going to do that?" I asked breathlessly.

Her eyes skipped to mine, and a chill raced down my spine. "By making them believe you are too busy to show your lovely face."

I'd expected Sabine to have a better strategy than this. "What would keep me that busy?"

Her smile widened. "Wedding plans."

"Our engagement is old news," I said with a shrug. "I'm not certain anyone will care."

"They will care," she promised as Julian's shadow fell beside me, "when they receive the invitations."

His hand went to the small of my back as I spluttered, "Invitations? We haven't picked a date."

"I took care of that for you," she said with a breezy wave of her hand that made my stomach clench. "You're getting married in two weeks."

CHAPTER FORTY-FIVE

Thea

"This is the right address." I checked the message again before staring at the house. Black lacquered steps led to a glossy red door with a brass knocker in the shape of a lion's head and the number three hanging above it. Despite the wintery chill, ivy tumbled from baskets hung over the portico, tendrils curling around the sun-washed columns. A wrought-iron railing ran along the path, curving around to keep oblivious pedestrians from falling down the steps that likely led to a basement flat. It was exactly how I'd pictured a London home.

I turned to find Julian staring at the ivy, his lip slightly curled. "Yes, it is."

He reached for my hand and our fingers entwined. Despite how much I hated wearing them, we'd both worn gloves, which seemed a necessary precaution given that we were entering a witch's residence. But as his hand tightened around my own, I felt my magic flare through the leather damper.

"The ivy is a sign of respect to the fae," he explained as we climbed the stairs. "It signals there is magic within but that they defer to the local Court."

I lifted my brows. "I only met Diana once, but I have a hard time imagining she *defers* to anyone."

"There's no choice in London." His voice was tight as he lifted the knocker and struck the brass plate beneath it twice. He'd been on edge since our arrival. "The Infernal Court demands it."

"*Infernal*?" That painted quite the picture, but before I could ask him more, the door opened.

Diana James looked every bit the *impresario* in her loosely flowing rainbow kaftan, regal and composed. Her long braids were coiled in an elegant mass at the top of her head, showcasing her high cheekbones and rich skin. She smiled warmly at me, her hand hovering on the door. No gloves.

"Thea, welcome." The warmth radiating from her cooled as she shifted her attention to my mate, but her gaze wasn't assessing. It was wary. "Julian."

I looked between the two of them. "Do you two know each other?"

When I'd met Diana in San Francisco, she'd spoken knowingly of the Rousseaux family. I'd assumed it was a matter of his family's reputation, especially given that Diana didn't look a day over forty.

"Our family has always patronized the San Francisco Symphony. Diana was once First Violin Chair."

I held back a snort. His family had probably founded the San Francisco Symphony given their ties to the city.

"That was decades ago."

"1984," Julian said, and I knew why he remembered the date, knew that the events of that year were seared into his memory.

Still, it didn't make sense. "But you can't be…"

"Sixty." Her fuchsia-stained lips widened. "One of the few family spells that's never stopped working," she whispered with a wink.

No wonder Julian had been certain she would agree to meet with me, even before I'd heard back from her. They'd known each other. Of course, considering the tension stretching between them, I wondered if she'd agreed despite my connection to him rather than because of it.

"Did you plan to join us for the lesson?" she asked him.

A muscle beat in his jaw, his voice cold as he replied. "Am I invited?"

"She'll do better without you looming over her shoulder." Diana shrugged, her dress rippling in response, the movement as graceful as a perfect note. "But you are welcome to come in."

"Thank you." Julian swiped his tongue over his teeth, unmistakably baring a fang at her, but instead of walking inside, he turned to me. "I will only be a phone call away. Call when you are ready for me to pick you up."

I blinked, both pleased and surprised that he was leaving me in her care. Since the baby and the attack, he'd been sticking close. But Diana was right. I might do better without him distracting me.

Her residence is spelled against vampires, he explained. *Inviting me allows me entrance. It's a show of...trust.*

What did you do to earn that?

His mouth twisted at my dry response. *I believe* you *earned it, not me, but it makes me feel comfortable leaving you here while I see to other matters.*

Julian stepped forward and gave me a swift kiss that despite its brevity left me breathless. Would I ever get used to the ache I felt for him? Even eternity seemed too short a time to want him.

"She is safe with me," Diana promised as I stepped into her home.

Julian lingered for a moment, shadows battling in his eyes, before he nodded and—very stiffly—turned to head down the steps. I watched him go, each step sending a throb through me.

"You're a good influence on him," she said as she closed the door, blocking me from staring at his retreating figure.

I managed a smile. "Was he terrible before?"

Her lips pursed, but she only inclined her head as she gestured for me to follow her.

The attached sitting room with its southwest-facing windows was filled with afternoon light that flooded the cream-colored walls. Books, mostly titles relating to music theory and composers, were stacked in disorderly piles around the space, a few novels scattered along with them. A small, iron stove blazed, filling the space with a comforting warmth. Diana took a seat in an oversize linen chair, and I took the one opposite.

"You've come to me because magic has awoken." It wasn't a question.

I nodded. I hadn't gone into details over email, but now I found myself launching into the story. I told her about the throne and the Council, about my death.

"The Council wants you dead." She shook her head, a sigh shuddering through her body.

"The Council does not wish a siren to carry a vampire's offspring."

"And they know?" She glanced at the hand I kept protectively over the still-flat plane of my stomach.

"Not yet. We think their attack was...preventative."

"It's equally likely that they saw their opportunity to undermine *Le Regine*. There are plenty of vampires who want to control your seat of power," she warned me.

"Tell me something I don't know."

Diana huffed a laugh, her eyes softening. "What can I do?"

"My magic... I need to know how to use it, control it so it doesn't control me."

"And your mother? Her people? Why not go to them?"

I sucked in a shaky breath. "I don't trust them. Not after..." Squaring my shoulders, I met her eyes. "And I can't trust anyone affiliated with my Court or the Council."

"And I'm the only witch you know?" Her lips twitched.

"It's not that," I said quickly. "You understand music."

The twitch widened into a smile, amused but not unkind. "And siren magic is musical. Fair enough."

It was an effort not to dissolve into the chair with relief at her words. "Do you think you can help me?"

"I can try. Sirens are old magic, mostly forgotten. Even if you could convince your mother's people to help you, they might not be able to." Any relief I'd felt a moment ago evaporated. "Magic is largely intuitive. That is how some of us managed to hold on to more of it despite the curse." She winked at me. "Although it is much easier now that you've freed us."

"I wish I found it intuitive," I grumbled.

"But you have used it. Tell me about those times."

I told her of calling Julian back to this world through the Song of Life. About the vampires who'd attacked us in Venice and how I'd handled them. "But there have been plenty of times when I couldn't call upon it. Times when it might have made all the difference."

"It sounds as if you can summon it emotionally," she mused, strumming her fingers against her knee.

"But not all the time." Apparently, my emotions were as fickle as my magic.

"And the times when you've felt it...Julian was present?"

"Every time," I said slowly.

"And the times when you commanded it, controlled it?"

My voice sounded hollow, even to my own ears as I answered, "He was in danger, hurt."

Dying. I couldn't bring myself to say the final word.

"Then that is your problem." She leaned back in her chair.

"Julian?" I began to shake my head. "He awakened my magic."

"But he did not free it," she stopped me. "You did that. Your magic might respond to him, it might protect him, but it is still *your* magic."

I bit my lip. "But there is some of his magic inside me, too, since we..."

She grinned at the color now flushing my cheeks. "That is to be expected, but it doesn't change facts. How much have you practiced using your magic?"

"Practiced? Never." I wouldn't even know where to begin.

"And your music? Are you playing?"

Tension coiled inside me. "I've been busy."

Her eyebrow arched. She didn't say anything, but I knew what she was thinking.

"Ever since I found out what I am, I haven't wanted to play."
I twisted my gloved fingers together as I confessed. "When I have
thought about it, I can't shake this feeling that it was all a lie. My
music. My training. I used to feel accomplished, and now I feel...
like a fraud."

I'd yet to say those words aloud to anyone, even Julian. I
suspected he knew, though.

"Does Julian keep you from the cello?" she asked carefully.

"No." I couldn't help laughing. "He gave me a Stradivarius for
Christmas."

Diana snorted. "Of course he did." She rose to her feet and
crossed the room. I watched as she took her violin from its case.
Before I could ask what she was doing, she began to play.

Music sliced through the air with aching, throbbing beauty,
each note calling to me. Without thinking, I allowed my eyes to
shutter, letting the music consume me. I didn't just hear it. I *felt* it,
felt each golden note, the rise and fall of its power, the primal lovely
urgency of it. When the final note faded, I opened my eyes to find
her watching me.

"I...I..." I couldn't find the words.

"You haven't played since magic awoke," she guessed, carefully
placing the instrument back in its case. "If you had, you might have
discovered what I have. The magic I felt before is nothing—*nothing*—
compared to what I feel when I play now. I can only imagine how it
affects a siren..."

I'd had no idea. None. Because I'd been too afraid, too angry
over the secrets that had been kept from me, and in doing so, I'd
only punished myself, depriving myself of the comfort of music.

"It is good that Julian encourages the music," she said as she
returned to her chair, "but he is not the one who has to embrace it.
You must do that."

"But I need to learn about my magic," I pressed. "I need to
know how to use it."

"I suspect there is no difference between music and magic for
you, Thea," she explained.

There was one problem with my "weapon" of choice, though. "So I should keep a cello on me in case I need to use my magic?"

"I doubt that will be necessary." Laughter glinted in her eyes. "Playing will allow you to find that power within yourself. You felt it when I played, didn't you?"

I nodded.

"Then that is where to begin. That is how you will tap into your magic, how you will begin to understand it, control it, mold it." Diana folded her hands in her lap, triumph on her face as the last of my resistance eddied away. "Find yourself again where you've always found yourself. Find yourself in the music."

CHAPTER FORTY-SIX

Julian

London was as noisy as I remembered, and the traffic was even worse. A thick fog hung over the city, and every driver seemed to trust their horn more than their eyes to help them through the hazy February morning. After the relative calm of Venice, the people and the cars and the chaos threatened to give me a headache.

When we reached the hotel, I slid smoothly from the backseat, thanking the driver—one of Benedict's men—and headed toward the hotel. Staying at the Westminster Royal was my stipulation regarding this trip. My brother had offered to let us stay with him, but I'd never quite gotten past his role in The Second Rite. Even if it has been a necessary evil. Someday I would forgive him, but it might take a few decades.

Or a few centuries.

Once inside, I paused at the reception desk. The woman behind the counter glanced at me, then straightened up and purred, "May I help you?"

"Did a package arrive for me? Rousseaux."

A flirtatious smile curved her mouth. "Yes, I had it sent up." She tucked a strand of hair behind her ear. "Can I help you with *anything* else?"

"That will be all." I turned and left her there, still fluttering her eyelashes.

I made it two feet before a male fell into step beside me. I didn't have to look over to know exactly who was now by my side.

Fae magic simmered under his glamour, but I sensed it, smelled the slight tang of brimstone that wafted from him.

"I've never seen a vampire turn down a willing human." There was a smirk in his voice. "She would have let you suck her dry."

"Bain," I greeted the fae prince without breaking my stride. "It's been too long."

"Such a liar," he crooned, "but it has been a long while. The last I heard, you'd vanished from public life. Imagine my delight to hear that you intended to pay me a visit."

"I had business in London." The less he knew about why we were here, the better. We reached the lift, and I stopped, finally turning to face him. Like most immortals, Bain hadn't changed in years, and that had nothing to do with the glamour he'd cast to blend into the human world.

Not that Bain would ever truly blend in. Not with his pale blue eyes that skirted an unnaturally silver hue or his platinum-white hair that felt at odds with his youthful face.

"And where is the companion I'm told came with you?" He leaned against the wall, blocking me from pushing the button to call the elevator. "I've heard such interesting things about the new queen. I'm eager to learn more."

I barely suppressed a growl, but he only laughed, the sound of it like the warning peals of an emergency siren.

"So possessive, and I always thought you were more cultured than your brethren." He dusted off the sleeve of his tailored jacket. "We aren't going to have problems during your visit, are we?"

Not a question but a threat.

"That is entirely up to you," I said, keeping my words calm. Lethally so.

"How long will you be staying?"

"Not long. We're due back in Venice in a few days."

"Pity." The flash of his eyes said it was anything but. "But you will come to court tomorrow. We're all eager to meet your friend."

I dared nothing more than a grim smile.

"Excellent." He straightened, tugging at his gold cufflinks. "There have been rumors…"

"You know better than to listen to rumors."

He gave an acknowledging tip of his head. "Still, it seems the fist holding your magic has been released."

There was another pause before I nodded. "It's true. Our magic has awoken from the curse." I waited for him to ask me more.

Questions bottled up in those silver-blue eyes, but his lips smashed into a thin line. "My father will ask about it."

"I will endeavor to answer." I'd promise him no more than that.

"Good, and I will entertain your beautiful friend while you speak to him." He smirked at the snarl that slipped from me. "Until then."

And with a snap of his fingers, he vanished.

• • •

I was still waiting for Thea's call when the door to our suite opened two hours later. I shot to my feet, panic seizing my chest when Thea trudged inside, looking utterly exhausted. Instantly, I was at her side. "Are you okay? You didn't call." I searched her for signs that she'd been hurt, but she wrapped an arm around my neck and yanked me down for a kiss.

It soothed the ragged edge of my concern, and she smiled up at me. "I'm fine. I just needed to clear my head, so I went for a walk."

I went utterly still. "You…walked?"

She tilted her head, challenge written in her emerald eyes. "You said the fae control London. I assumed no vampire would have the balls to attack me."

"A vampire wouldn't." My voice was wooden, even to my own ears. "But a fae might." I tried to ignore the crushing fear that rushed through me. She'd been walking through London. Alone. If she had run into Bain or one of his people…

Thea planted her hands on my shoulders. "I'm fine," she repeated, releasing a sigh, "and we think we had a breakthrough regarding my magic."

"Tell me about it." I took her hand, coaxing her toward the living space.

We were halfway to the sofa when she stopped, her eyes snagging on the tall case propped by the bedroom door.

"Is that…" Her words fell away, and I sensed her heart thundering. Whipping to me, her eyes flashed. "Did you know?"

"What?" I spread my hands, wondering how much control she'd gotten of her magic.

"Don't look at me like that," she snapped.

"Like what?"

"Like I might detonate." She rubbed the palm of her hand against her forehead.

"You need to eat something." When she opened her mouth to protest, I gave her a pointed look. "I'll order something. Any requests?"

She shook her head. I went to the phone to call for room service, tracking her as she made her way to the cello case. She didn't open it. She didn't touch it. I was only dimly aware of ordering us both dinner as I waited for her to make a move.

She didn't.

"It will be here soon." I placed the phone back on the cradle. "I bribed them to bring it as soon as they could cook it."

Thea moved to the couch and sank into it with a groan. "Thank you." I approached her slowly, and she frowned. "I'm not going to bite."

"I like it when you bite," I reminded her, but I took it as a sign to sit. Dropping beside her, I leaned down and lifted her feet into my lap. She didn't say a word as I slipped off her shoes and began to massage her feet.

"That feels amazing," she moaned, and I had to tamp down the surge of arousal the sound spiked inside me.

I'd been going crazy since I'd left her with Diana, and now that primitive mated part of me wanted nothing more than to throw her over my shoulder, carry her to the bedroom, and pin her beneath me until I was satisfied that she was *indeed* fine, as she put it. But that would only satisfy me. Not her.

I don't know, I might like it. Her eyes hooded as she watched my hands rub circles on her sore feet.

"More than a foot rub and some food?" I asked with a smile. Her hesitation told me everything I needed to know.

"Sorry. I'm just tired." She reached behind her back and wiggled a pillow into place. Her eyes closed as she relaxed into my touch.

"Understandable." I slid my hands up to work on her tight calves. "What did you mean before? When you asked if I knew?"

One eye popped open, as if she wanted to see my reaction. "The cello. Diana thinks it's the key to my magic."

I considered for a moment before shrugging. "That makes sense to me."

Both eyes opened now. "It does?"

"From the first moment I saw you play, I felt magic." My thumb stroked down her leg. "But I didn't *know*. This was…a wedding present."

"Another one? How many priceless cellos do you own?" she drawled, but I felt her spike of nervous energy. "I'm not sure you can top a Stradivarius."

I released her legs and stood, pausing to tuck a pillow beneath her tired feet. "This one doesn't belong to me."

Her head tilted, a puzzled look on her face. I walked over and picked up the case. "The case is new," I explained to her as I brought it to her.

Thea swung her feet to the floor as I laid the cello case on the floor and knelt to carefully undo its clasps. She moved her head, trying to see around me as I opened the lid, but I blocked her view. "It's a gift, remember? Stop trying to peek."

Thea huffed and sat back on the sofa. Her arms were crossed when I turned to present it to her, but they slackened when she saw the cello I held.

"Julian…" Her voice broke, her eyes skimming across it, across its once damaged and now repaired body. "That's *my* cello."

I placed it carefully in her hands as tears streaked down her face. I swallowed against the knot in my throat, against emotions that I wasn't sure belonged to me or to her. "It took me a while to find a luthier skilled enough to repair it."

Her fingers trembled slightly as she ran them gently over its neck, and I felt her settle, felt peace overcome her.

When she finally spoke, her words were soft. "Thank you."

"I thought you might want it back. Although the Stradivarius is still yours," I added, allowing a bit of my satisfaction to slip through.

"I didn't know I missed it," she admitted as she studied it, studied the place where it was repaired like she was greeting an old friend.

I gripped her knees. "It's part of you," I said, and her eyes shot to mine at the gruffness in my voice. I cleared my throat carefully. "It's okay to miss your old life. It's okay for it to still be part of you. I never wanted part of you, Thea. I wanted all of you. This moment, the future, and your past. Every single piece."

She blew out a shaky breath. "I was…scared—scared that finding out the truth about what I am would take music from me."

"I never wanted to take you away from this." I tipped my head to the cello.

Love sparkled in her eyes as she gazed into mine, the warmth of our bond radiating through me as she smiled. "You didn't take me away from it. You gave it back to me."

CHAPTER FORTY-SEVEN

Thea

I had never gone this long without playing cello, and it showed. Even when my mother was in the hospital, I'd taken a moment to play on the odd days I left to shower and gather new supplies. Diana flinched as I missed a note, the sound like a banshee shriek to my ears, too. My arm fell away, bow at my side, and I sucked in a shaky breath.

"I'm sorry." I'd lost count of the number of times I'd uttered those words this afternoon.

"Stop apologizing." She reached for her cup of tea and took a sip. Watery winter light seeped through the windows, brighter from the snow falling throughout the city. But the inside of Diana's flat was cozy due to the crackling stove and the piles of books and sheet music scattered everywhere. It was a far cry from the penthouse I'd been staying in, and it *should* make me feel relaxed. "There's no need to be sorry. We all have off days."

I doubted Diana James ever had off days.

I was sorry, though. Between Diana's performance schedule with the Philharmonic and the brevity of our trip, I didn't have time to waste. If the key to my magic lay in my music, I needed to play, not shred her poor eardrums.

"Am I making you nervous?" she asked when I didn't continue. That would be a good excuse, but I shook my head. I already knew that wasn't the case, because I'd been putting Julian through the same torture in our hotel suite for the last forty-eight hours. "I think I forgot how to play."

Diana placed her cup on the table, pity softening her dark eyes. "You haven't forgotten. It's part of you and was long before you discovered your power. Let it be about playing, not magic. Play something from memory."

She was right. I'd been so focused on finding the key to my magic that I'd forgotten the joy I felt when I held my cello. I hadn't been focusing on the music much. I took a deep breath, closed my eyes, and lifted my bow once more. I didn't think about what piece. I just began. The first note was shaky, but with the second, something unlocked. My fingers found their way, music filling the room.

I was lost to it, to this piece that had always consumed me. The music carried me to a place beyond the worries and fears that had been clouding my mind. The notes wove around me, telling a story that was both familiar and new. For a moment, I forgot everything outside the music. Nothing else existed, and as the last note faded away, I opened my eyes to find Diana smiling.

I let out a breath as I saw the golden threads shimmering in the air around me.

"Is that..."

She nodded. "Magic." Her grin widened. "Told you so."

It was...beautiful, even as it slowly faded before my eyes. The notes were thin and delicate, crossing and intersecting. Before they could disappear entirely, I reached out, my cello resting safely between my legs. I expected the notes to vanish, but they were soft and strong like the silk of a web. Light flooded my skin, warm and comforting, as they dissolved into my flesh—then all around me, there was music. Aching, pulsing notes without rhythm or reason.

I shut my eyes against it, fading into that terrible melody.

Magic bloomed inside me, snaking into my veins to rouse the

power there. It ignited with a sudden, painful flare in my chest and flooded through me. It ravaged and cleaved until I thought my heart might crack in half. I clutched the neck of my cello to steady myself as I fought the urge to vomit.

Diana's voice cut through the air. "Thea! Release it!"

Then there were hands on my shoulders. Diana's magic grounded me, siphoning mine until my eyes snapped open. Music thundered around us, the colors of the room blindingly bright as the world spun out beneath my feet.

Not the carefully composed Schubert I'd played moments ago. This clashed and circled, rising in sharp piercing notes before falling into hell itself. The music was the air and the earth, the fire and the sun. It was the skin that hung on my bones and the light that stabbed my eyes. It was everything. It was primal and timeless.

It tore through the room. The windows rattled. Picture frames crashed to the floor and shattered. Diana yanked the cello from my hands, but the music continued, twining around me like serpents, hissing and writhing and squeezing the air from my lungs.

Diana's hands were on me again, her voice almost lost in the fury. "Thea! You are in control!"

Control.

But I couldn't control it. It was primal and raw, power that existed before the world was born. Power that would be here long after its death. I was nothing—*nothing*—compared to it. But I reached inside myself, searching...searching...

And then, beneath the maelstrom thundering inside me—a flap of wings, a rustle of dark magic that roared awake. Shadows fell through the room, darkness smothering the savage magic. My hands folded over my chest as my mate's magic eclipsed mine, shielding me.

Diana released me and collapsed into a chair. Neither of us spoke as that dark magic dissolved like smoke in the wind.

I panted, shaking my head. "I'm—"

"Don't say you're sorry," she cut me off. "Your magic is new. Unstable. It will take time."

"I don't have time." My voice split on the words, and fear swelled in my throat. I swallowed. "I don't know if I'm ready for this, Diana."

"No one is ever truly ready for power. Not those who seek it nor those who crave it."

"I've never wanted it," I admitted in a whisper.

"And that is why you will master it," she said fiercely, "and you will have help. Tell me. Was that Julian's magic?"

I managed a quick nod. As if answering her, his magic wrapped itself in a soothing midnight caress around my heart. Guarding. Protecting. Alert but calm. He thought his magic was something to fear but how could I fear that?

"Interesting. That is death magic. Your soul knows both the Song of Life and Death. That's normal for a siren, but to harness death... May I ask a rather personal question?"

"You've seen the ugly side of my magic. You might as well." I rubbed at the hollow lingering ache in my chest.

"Are you tethered to him?"

I nodded.

"Then you have free access to his magic." She thought for a moment. "He might even be able to draw on yours if he will open his mind to it. Your tether allows for it."

"I'm sorry," I said, realizing my mistake. "We *were* tethered. When we died, it was broken."

Her head tilted. "Why would you believe that?"

"A tether is broken only by death," I repeated what I'd been told.

"A tether is linked to the *soul*. If the soul lives..." She snorted, reaching for her teacup. It rattled slightly in its saucer as she brought it to her lips and sipped thoughtfully. "The tether a vampire fears is not a true tether—that is a *leash*. Vampires coopted the term, perverted it just like they did with *our* familiars. Most witches believe vampires are incapable of love, if you'll excuse me for saying so. I've met many that made me believe it."

"That's not true of all vampires." It wasn't true of Julian.

"You've shown me that, but it's important to understand that a tether is bonding magic. It's some of the oldest magic that exists, so old that even the curse could not contain it entirely and even death cannot sever bonding magic. Its entire existence centers on mates. But although a leash is also bonding magic, it is something else, something dark. Since there is no return from true death, I suppose in a way the leash is broken. But if the soul were resurrected…" She loosed a heavy sigh. "That is why the curse had to be broken. '*And magic slept while the world lay dying, cursed until it fed on darkness to survive.*'"

I raised an eyebrow.

"That is from our grimoire. Magic had to survive by any means necessary," she explained. "There is darker magic in the world now because of the curse."

"But why pervert the tether? Why turn it into a leash?" The bond should be beautiful. My own bond with my mate proved it could be.

"Witches believe vampires are responsible for the curse," Diana murmured. "Perhaps that was magic's revenge for their attempts to control it. Perhaps magic was so desperate to survive, so close to the brink of extinction, that it bound creatures together and forced them to protect each other above all else."

I swallowed. Could vampires really have been the ones to put magic to sleep? If that was true, wouldn't Sabine know, or Dominic? They'd been alive for thousands of years, alive when the curse took hold. They were powerful and respected. They had to know.

"But a human can be leashed," I pointed out.

She shook her head with a sad smile. "Too many creatures forget that all living creatures have magic in their veins, even humans."

"But now that the curse has been broken, there won't be any more leashes?" I wasn't certain I wanted her to answer me.

"Our tether changed after we died."

"Magic is awake. Everything is different. My family's grimoire speaks of the tether between mates, the true tether that existed before the curse."

"How old is your grimoire?" I blurted out. If it existed before the curse…

"Old." Another snort.

"You told me there was a spell in it to find your true mate."

"You remember." Approval rang in her voice. "A mate is a true gift. One that has been long forgotten and dismissed. And that bond—that tether—doesn't simply anchor you. It balances you. A *true* partnership. It will help you learn to use your magic. It will help you learn how not to fear it."

Could it? I thought of the beating dark magic, of the male that commanded it. Yes, yes, it could.

"You cannot fear your magic to wield it, but you must respect it," Diana told me.

"How do I do that?" I asked as the doorbell rang.

"Face it. Embrace it." She stood, moving toward the corridor. "Give it its rightful space in your life."

She disappeared into the hall, leaving me to sort through the thoughts swimming in my head. I was so lost to them that I almost didn't feel him enter.

Almost.

The vigilant darkness settled as he made his way to me, a devil-may-care grin pasted on his face, his hands shoved into his pockets. He looked every bit the part of the powerful vampire—except his eyes.

They scanned the room, his pupils a black disc ringed with a sliver of a blue sky. "Finished?" he asked in a rough voice.

I rose to my feet. "You felt it, didn't you?"

A moment of hesitation before a quick jerk of confirmation. "Should I come back later?"

It sounded like the question physically pained him, like he was fighting the urge to sweep me away to safety and was barely winning against it.

"I'm ready." I crossed to him, popping onto my toes to offer him my lips.

Relief dilated his eyes until they were breathtaking, electrifying blue again.

"I'm sorry if I scared you." I had no idea how much he'd felt, how much of his answering magic had come from the grain of it I carried inside my soul, and how much he'd managed to somehow send to me.

As long as you are okay. His eyes assessed me, his hands sweeping over my shoulders as he confirmed what he saw. I was in one piece.

"I am," I whispered. I sucked in a deep breath and turned toward Diana, who was placing my cello in its case. "Thank you."

"It was my pleasure." She carried my case to me. "If you aren't busy this evening, I could arrange for tickets to this evening's performance—for both of you."

My stomach sank as quickly as a stone dropped in water. Tonight.

"That is a generous offer," Julian said smoothly. "Unfortunately, we are engaged elsewhere, but believe me, I think we'd both rather see you play."

"The offer stands if you find yourself in London soon." She smiled warmly at me, then took a step closer and offered her hand. Julian tensed next to me, but I took it, bracing myself for that sharp spark of magic. But hers met mine like a friend's embrace.

"Magic is a gift," she reminded me, squeezing my hand. "Don't forget that."

"I won't," I promised.

She saw us to the door, standing to wave us off as Julian helped me into the Range Rover, the new vehicle chosen to easily transport my cello. When he slid into the driver's seat, he slipped off his gloves. Turning, he fiddled with my seat belt.

"You're sure you're fine?" He brushed a finger down my cheek. "If you aren't up for tonight, we can cancel."

"I'm looking forward to this evening." Not quite a lie. Diana was right. The first step to respecting my magic was to embrace it, to embrace the magical world and all its great and terrible beauty.

Julian chuckled as he hit the ignition. "Five minutes with the fae will change your mind."

CHAPTER FORTY-EIGHT

Julian

Two hours later, I knocked on the bedroom door.

"I'm almost ready," Thea called.

I leaned against the frame and reached out with my mind, caressing the bond between us. *Do you need any help? I'm very good at zipping. And unzipping.*

That would be counterproductive. No zipping required...or unzipping. At least she sounded amused.

How unfortunate. I'll have the car pulled around.

Meet you down there in five?

I'll be the one in the tux.

Her answering purr made me reconsider our plans for the evening.

Go, old man.

An eternity later, I checked my Rolex and swept the lobby for a third time. London was fae territory, which meant Thea was likely safer here than at her own court, but the fae could be unpredictable—like Bain's unexpected check-in a few days ago. But there was no sign of the fae prince or his ilk.

"Mr. Rousseaux, your car is waiting." The valet approached me, key fob in hand, and froze. I followed the line of his attention...to Thea.

The world stopped spinning.

Words failed me, my heart stuttering as I beheld her. Her gown was a shimmering skin of liquid gold, beaded with thousands of delicate crystals that sparkled in the light. It whispered over her skin, catching at her curves, and pooled at her feet. I swallowed as I followed the dip of its neckline to the curve of her breasts before forcing my gaze up. Her hair was swept up in a knot of fire to reveal her slender neck and the diamond collar I'd given her. She paused to tug her silk gloves to her elbows, completely unaware that every soul in the lobby was watching her. Looking up, her eyes met mine, and her smile nearly undid me. Everything faded away. Only her. Only the whisper of her heart in my own chest, each beat an answer, a promise.

I crossed to her, never breaking eye contact, and whipped my jacket off.

She grinned as she stepped into its cocoon. "Sorry, I was so stressed that I was running late I forgot my coat."

My tongue was thick, words difficult. "Never apologize. It's my honor to serve you."

Her teeth caught her lip, eyes glinting, and for the second time tonight, I considered throwing her over my shoulder and hauling her back to bed. But before I could, she slipped her arm through mine. "You clean up well."

"You're a Goddess." I led her to where the flabbergasted valet waited, keys still in hand. She snorted, but I gripped her hand in my own. "It's true, Thea. You're stunning."

As if to back me up, the valet stammered his well wishes, cheeks turning pink when Thea smiled at him.

"He couldn't even speak," I murmured to her as we stepped into the night.

"Maybe he was looking at you," she said as I opened her car door.

My laughter clouded in the winter air as I circled to the driver's side.

"Is the court far?" she asked as I worked my way through the congested streets of Westminster.

"Yes and no."

"Oh good, a cryptic answer," she teased. "Do vampires ever respond directly?"

"I see your attitude matches your hair this evening. That will make things interesting."

She fell silent, and I found myself stealing glances at her. She chewed on her lower lip. "Should I be more...docile? Around the fae, I mean."

"I assumed," I sat drily and took her hand. "But the answer is no...always no. I never want you to be anything but what you are." Her hand squeezed mine. "To answer your other question. The entrance to the court is nearby, but the court itself lies in the Otherworld."

"Otherworld? Like my court?"

I smiled at hearing her call it her court. I would support whatever decision she made regarding the crown, but no matter her choice, she would always be a queen. "It's hard to explain. The Otherworld is bound to their magic. Fae magic is different, and they guard its secrets from other creatures."

"So it would be impolite to ask?" Her eyes drifted to the window. "Is there anything I need to do? Bow? Kiss signet rings?"

I barked a laugh. "You are a queen. Even the fae will recognize that. They may bow to you. There is only one thing I would caution. Do not accept any invitation, any offer, any gift."

She turned to me, her eyebrows raised. "Why?"

"The fae love to bargain, to bind others by favors and gifts in exchange for their souls," I warned her. "We are invited guests, so accepting food and drink is safe and expected, but refuse anything else."

Her hand clutched mine so tightly I knew she understood the stakes.

"Here we are," I announced as we neared a small valet stand set up a few hundred feet from the club.

Thea leaned forward, her eyes scanning the nightclub and the line of people huddled behind velvet ropes to get in. "Brimstone," she read the sign over the door before glancing at me. "I think we're overdressed."

"We'll be using the private entrance," I said as the parking attendant opened my door.

"Sir, this is—"

"We're guests of the family," I cut him off.

His eyes rounded as he nodded and took my keys. "Anthony can show you the way," he offered, gesturing to the burly man helping Thea out of the Range Rover.

I loosed a small growl that made Anthony take a step back. "I know the way."

Thea rolled her eyes at me as I took her hand. "He was doing his job."

"He's fae," I said under my breath.

Her head whipped around to stare at him. "He looks human!"

"Glamour."

"Are they all...fae?" She looked toward the line of people waiting to get inside.

"Them? No. But the family wouldn't let a human guard their private entrance, even ones enslaved to them," I explained, wrapping an arm around her shoulders and leading her toward an unmarked black door.

"*Enslaved*?" She took off my jacket and passed it to me. I put it on, frowning as she shivered in the night air.

"Never bargain with a fae," I reminded her, "and Thea? Hold on."

She pressed close to my side as I opened the door, her head craning to peer into the inky blackness. I pulled her closer as we stepped through it—fell through it. At least, that's what it felt like. I expected the plunging sensation as the Otherworld swallowed us. Thea's scream cut through the dark, her fingers clutching my shoulder.

It's okay. I repeated it to her over and over. At least our thoughts could be heard over the roaring absent void. I ran my hands down her back in long, soothing strokes until the world reknit around us in a tapestry of gold and crimson. When the last strands settled in place, Thea lurched forward and retched on a finely woven rug.

Right in front of Bain and his retinue. He stared, his mouth twisting with distaste, but I ignored him, leaning down to help my mate.

"It will pass," I whispered to her. "I should have warned you better."

She wiped at her mouth, shooting me a glare. "You think?"

Thea rose up and froze as she took in Bain—his sloped, pointed ears beneath the carefully combed silver hair, the tattoos peeking out from beneath his shirt collar down to the ones covering his hands— their brutality at odds with his polished, formal appearance—and gulped.

I stepped closer to her, but she didn't shrink from his curious gaze.

As soon as she was steady on her feet an attendant rushed forward, silver platter in hand. She held it out, displaying several small cups of red liquid. "This will help," she said shyly.

Thea glanced at me, a question in her eyes.

"It's safe," Bain interjected before I could tell her the same. "We have no interest in poisoning a queen."

Thea regarded him with wariness. "What about trapping one?"

Bain stared for a moment, his silver-blue gaze unreadable, before he threw his head back and laughed. "At least, you warned her about *that*," he said to me, waving a hand at the platter. "No price. No bargain. Simply something to soothe your nerves. We would not wish you to be uncomfortable."

I nodded once to Thea, keeping my hand on the small of her back. She picked up a cup and took a small sip, her eyebrows shooting up when she tasted it. Her hand pressed to her stomach. "I feel...fine."

Bain inclined his head. "And now allow us to welcome you to the Infernal Court, Your Majesty."

Behind him, everyone bowed. Another attendant scurried forward and knelt before her.

"A gift," Bain explained, and Thea stiffened until he added, "to celebrate your ascension." I regarded Bain for a moment and he sighed. "*Freely* given. A gift of good faith."

Thea didn't move. Neither did I.

"It has been a long time since my court welcomed a queen." He gestured to the box. "It is a sign of respect without expectation."

Finally, I nodded.

Thea accepted the box and opened it. Her face betrayed nothing as she took in the pendant. It was crafted of gold and silver with a large black stone as fathomless as the space between our world and theirs. It seemed to swallow the light, as endless as the night.

"It was crafted here," Bain said as she studied it. "You will not find its equal in your world."

"I'm sure." She closed the lid softly and passed it to me. I tucked it in my jacket, surprised by the lightness of the box.

"Thank you for hosting us." Thea smiled at him, and perhaps it was the effect of the fae magic surrounding us, but she shifted before our eyes. Her skin glowed like polished moonstone, her hair flickered under the chandelier's light, and raw power radiated off her. A few of the fae attendants gasped at the subtle transformation, but Bain smirked.

"We have prepared some entertainment for you," he said as he swept an arm toward the corridor, "and we are so interested to hear news of *your* court."

I took Thea's hand, and we followed him into the bowels of the Infernal Court.

Are you really okay? I kept my gaze forward, allowing no sign of my concern to show. I wouldn't undermine Thea in front of them.

I am. Her words danced in my head. *I might need to ask for some of that to help with morning sickness.*

Thea... Did I really need to remind her a bargain was a bad idea?

Just kidding!

I didn't laugh. I doubted I would until we left the Otherworld. Tonight was a means to an end, but even so, I couldn't help wondering why the fae were so eager to meet my queen.

A feast had been prepared for us, platters of ripe fruit and soft cheeses, trays of roasted meats followed by decadent desserts. Miniature chocolate cakes shaped like hearts, drizzled with gold and garnished with silver. I smiled when she reached for a second one.

"Your queen has an appetite," Bain remarked at my side.

"I do," Thea crooned and reached for a third.

He blinked once, his nostrils flaring, before a smile lit upon his face. "I believe I understand."

I casually angled my body between the prince and my mate.

"You're a lucky male," Bain said, smirking at my protective stance. He leaned closer so that only I might hear over the strange music being played. "Your queen is a rare beauty and her power...astonishing. Congratulations on your joining...and your heir."

I held his eyes, allowing my dark magic to shadow them. "Thank you."

"No need to posture, Julian." He picked up a cake and popped it into his mouth, chewing it slowly and swallowing. "We have no quarrel with you, nor any interest in starting a fight with *Le Regine*, but we are curious."

"We?" I glanced around the room. "You and your servants?"

No one else in Bain's family had joined us. No one else had been invited to eat or enjoy the entertainment. It was...odd.

"We did not wish to overwhelm her." He tipped his head to Thea. "My family can be challenging."

She laughed, reaching for her water. "Have you met *his* family?"

Bain's shoulders shook with silent laughter. "True, but there are other reasons I've kept you to myself." He traced a finger around the rim of his goblet. "We've heard rumors that the curse that caged your magic has lifted."

Should we tell him? Thea asked.

I didn't look away from Bain, but I slipped my hand under the table and placed it on her knee. *He already knows. Keeping it from him won't do us any favors.*

"The rumors are true," Thea murmured. "It's been a shock to most of us."

Those silver eyes narrowed. "There are other rumors that a siren has risen to power, that she was the one who broke the curse." He looked to me. "I confess that seeing your queen, I'm beginning to believe it. Is it true? Is she…?"

"I'm right here," Thea said in a clear voice. "You can ask me."

I bit back a smile.

Too much?

I love when you're imperious.

"I apologize if my question offended you." Bain dipped his head, looking anything but sorry. He had ruled the Infernal Court long enough to know how to play the courtier, even from the throne.

She shrugged, her pale skin catching in the dim light. "It didn't. I am a siren."

Bain's haughty mask slipped, and he blinked. "And the Vampire Council has allowed this?"

"I don't answer to the Council." She stared back at him.

He snorted and picked up his wineglass. "They must *love* you."

"And your magic?" Thea pointed to the room around us. "It wasn't affected by the curse?"

Careful.

"The fae have never hoarded our magic—never sought to control it."

A laugh escaped me, and Thea glared at me. "I'm sorry," I said quickly, "but you don't *share* it, either."

"It is *our* magic," he said coldly. "Another creature could never wield it, even one as powerful as your mate."

"And it's different." Thea hurried forward with a sharp glance in my direction. "That's why it wasn't affected."

"We believe magic is a gift that chooses its recipient." His eyes flicked to me. "Perhaps your kind's greed enabled the curse to hold all these years."

"You think vampires were behind the curse?" Thea blurted out.

He nodded slowly. "I do, and if I were you, *siren* queen, I would be very careful which vampires you trust."

I tensed, but Thea picked up another chocolate cake. "Tell me something I don't know."

CHAPTER FORTY-NINE

Thea

The moment we stepped from our gondola onto the court's dock, a voice boomed through the space. "Where is she?"

"I think that's our welcoming committee," Julian said.

My eyes slid to him and found his smile grim. I'd expected there to be fallout with my sister-queens—braced myself for it—but now, as their power trembled around us, I wondered if returning to Venice was a mistake.

Though it wasn't Mariana or Zina who appeared first in the stone courtyard. It was Aurelia. She wore her usual leather pants and corset, but she'd foregone the cloak and sword. Instead, twin daggers were strapped to her thighs. Flat rage radiated from her, her scowl etching deeper when I smiled a hello.

I think she's pissed.

Lysander tried to warn you. My mate sounded amused, and I elbowed him.

He's the one who wouldn't let her come.

I'm sure he'll pay for that later. Julian laced his fingers tightly through mine. *But we don't know if we can trust her.*

I nodded, even though I'd seen the truth in Lysander's eyes—the battle he'd waged with himself over that choice. Aurelia crossed to us, her cold eyes flicking between us. "At least you're in one piece."

Julian's hand tightened on me, and I knew without hearing his thoughts that he was thinking of what had happened on the boat—how close we'd come to that not being true.

I sucked in a steadying breath. "Aurelia, please, hear me out."

"You don't have to explain yourself to me. I'm duty-bound to protect you." Each word sliced from her like shards of ice.

I took a step away from Julian, releasing his hand. He might not trust her, but I believed what she said. Aurelia might serve the court, but if there was a threat here, it wasn't her.

Are you sure about that?

I ignored my mate's insight. We would get nowhere if we refused to trust anyone, and I couldn't stop thinking about what Bain had said. Somehow I knew he was right. The real threat had to be a vampire...or vampires. And Aurelia was mortal. "It wasn't my intention to scare you."

"I'm not the one you should be worried about. *Le Regine* needs to speak with you. Now."

"I am *Le Regine*, too," I reminded her, determined to remain calm, even as I felt my magic twitching beneath my skin. "And I need a minute."

Our eyes locked and held. This was my first test. Mariana and Zina had demanded the audience, not my bodyguard. I didn't owe an explanation to the queens. Not if they were equals. But I had left Aurelia without explanation. I had undermined her duty and betrayed her trust. She had every right to be pissed at me, even if I stood by my actions and was "above" her in station.

"*Please* tell the queens I will meet them shortly," I added.

Aurelia's gaze flicked to Julian. "You've returned."

"My place is at my mate's side." He betrayed no hint of emotion as he spoke. Even through our bond, I couldn't get a read on him. He was as silent as death, and I wondered if being back here—being so close to the source of our magic—stoked his dark power.

Aurelia's hands moved to her daggers, her eyes narrow slits. "Your place is where *Le Regine* commands it to be, *il flagello*."

Julian snorted, looking unfazed. "My allegiance is to the one I love, not to some relic of my past."

Her fingers curled over the dagger hilts, but she didn't make a move toward him. "I'm sure you believe that, *vampire*. You may be powerful, but you are not invincible."

"Enough." I stepped forward. "Your warning is heeded. We will be more considerate of our actions—*both* of us."

Aurelia's gaze snapped to me. Her fingers loosened, but her eyes burned as she took in the meaning of my words. "I will deliver your message." She left without another word, her steps echoing ominously in the courtyard.

Once Aurelia had stalked out of sight, Julian turned to me, his hands settling on my shoulders. He searched my face. "Are you okay?"

I nodded, even though I wasn't sure.

"Are you sure you trust her?"

"I trust her sense of duty." I snuggled against his strong chest. Once we met with the queens, we likely wouldn't have a moment's peace. Not with The Third Rite looming and the wedding following that.

He slid his hands around me, drawing me closer, as if he'd been thinking the same thing. "Just be careful. We don't know what kind of game the queens are playing."

"I know." I took a deep breath, closing my eyes to linger in the stolen moment. "Let's get this over with."

Magic thrummed around me as we made our way to the throne room. My awareness of it was sharper than before, and maybe with time, I could wield it like Diana thought. But the heightened perception also served to remind me that I was back at court, that I'd returned to my crown and my throne, and that soon the Council would know that I was alive. If they didn't already.

We found my sister-queens waiting on their thrones, and I stifled a surprised smile, half wondering if they'd been waiting there for my return. Mariana smiled, but Zina's eyes narrowed, her look of disdain a perfect complement to Aurelia's fury.

At least there was one friendly face in the room.

"We're pleased that you have returned to us." Mariana stood, her pale blue gown swishing across the floor as she came to greet us. When we met, she leaned to kiss my cheeks and whispered, "Congratulations."

I didn't have time to ask her what she meant.

"This is no time to congratulate her," Zina stormed. "She left the confines of the city. She could have been killed."

Does she know?

Next to me, Julian expanded, darkness rippling from him.

"They are to be married." Mariana whirled around in a blur of chiffon.

I breathed an inward sigh of relief. The wedding was the least of my concerns. It was simply a matter of showing up on the right day in a white dress.

What a lovely picture you paint. Julian's face was stony, betraying none of the wicked amusement in that one word.

We're already mates.

How am I the romantic one?

That was a good question. One I didn't have time to consider as Zina continued.

"That is another matter." She rose, lifting her regal chin. "There has been no coronation and no agreement that they can be married."

"The only people who needed to agree have." I whipped a finger from Julian to myself. "It's not a big deal."

"Not a big deal?" Zina's eyebrows shot up. "The banns were published three days ago!"

My confidence slipped. "Banns?"

Julian grumbled a curse under his breath. "It's tradition—an archaic tradition," he added to me. "It just means our intention to marry has been publicly announced."

I waited for one of them to explain why that was a big deal. When they didn't, I shrugged. "Everyone knows that we're engaged—and mates. I don't see what the problem is—humans announce engagements in newspapers all the time."

"The problem"—Zina slinked from the dais and made her way toward us, each step as graceful as a panther—"is that the banns are published to allow the marriage to be disputed. As you can imagine, we've done nothing but field complaints!"

"About...our marriage? Why?" I blurted out.

"You may have proclaimed him King Consort," she spat back at me, "but there are few eager to see you upend a thousand years of tradition!"

"They don't have to come." I smiled at her. "Problem solved. Unless you plan to cave to some whining."

Mariana bit back a smile. "I don't think the disputes have merit. It will be up to your families to decide if there is an issue."

That should have been the end of it, but Zina continued in a rage. "And then there is the matter of your mortality. Leaving Venice was reckless. There is a reason why *Le Regine* accept the gift of immortality."

"You mean accept being turned into a vampire," I corrected her.

Julian squeezed my hand. *Don't tell them about the Council.*

I knew why he wanted to keep it a secret, knew why he was warning me not to tell them about that the Vampire Council had tried to assassinate me for being a siren. We couldn't trust the queens. One of them could have informed the Council about my decision to leave Venice. Until we knew for certain, it was better to keep that information to ourselves.

Zina stepped closer, a finger flung in my direction. "You—" Her words died on her lips, her nostrils flaring as she swept surprised eyes down me.

I think she—

"Thea can't be turned," Julian drawled, "because she's pregnant."

Her eyes bugged out of her head.

Mariana moved to her side. "Then more congratulations are in order," she said softly. "A blessing."

Zina stilled, not looking at the queen at her side but directly at me. I braced myself for her anger, her disbelief, but she shook her head and looked at Julian. "You stupid fool."

He smirked, but inside me, darkness rustled, his magic rumbling awake. "If I had a nickel for every time I heard that."

"This is why you're rushing to marry," she seethed.

"That was his mother's idea."

Zina drew back like I'd smacked her. "Sabine Rousseaux would never sanction your marriage to…"

"Careful," Mariana hissed. "She is your sister."

I was past caring. At least the gloves were finally coming off. Plus, I had a better parting shot. "Who do you think published the banns?" I asked her.

She glanced to Julian for confirmation.

"She's planning our wedding as we speak." He tugged me a few steps back. "Which means we have to cut this meeting short. We need to meet with her and prepare for The Third Rite."

Mariana looked like she was holding back laughter as Aurelia stomped toward the door, following us. Her shoulders squared as she reached the door and opened it for us.

We stepped through it as Zina called, "You'll both regret this."

CHAPTER FIFTY

Lysander

"What are you doing here?" Lia's sharp voice shattered the library's quiet.

I slammed my book shut and slid it onto the shelf. Her scent filled the air around me, tart and ripe and baiting. A memory of her lips, her body moving with mine, flashed to my mind. She would never let me get that close to her again. Not after I'd left her here.

I turned to face her, bracing myself, but there was no adequate preparation for seeing her. She was dressed for this evening, for whatever devilry the Vampire Council had concocted for The Third Rite. Black lace draped her shoulders like spilled ink on a perfect canvas. The gown found every soft, generous curve before pooling at her feet. But Lia didn't pale in that darkness. Not with her strength and fire, with all of her talk of duty. She commanded it. Her hair was freed from its usual braid, falling over her shoulders in a soft curtain. The lift of her brows, the tilt of her nose, the scar bisecting her brow, and the bow of her lips were the same as the memory of that kiss. Her velvet eyes smoldered under her dark lashes, not with the barely restrained hunger I felt, but rage.

I swallowed. "Research."

Lia's eyes flicked over my shoulder to the bookshelf behind me.

"Researching or hiding?"

"Who would I be hiding from?" I taunted as I lounged against the shelves, daring her to admit that she hadn't stumbled on me by accident. That I wasn't hiding. She was seeking.

She snorted and crossed her arms over her chest. "Would you like a list? The queens? There are even rumors that the Rousseaux family is on the wrong side of the Vampire Council."

I gritted my teeth. I knew why she was angry, and that understanding made me pause. But something about the way she held herself, the set of her jaw, stopped me. "I came to attend The Third Rite."

"To protect Thea, you mean?" she shot back. "Because she's carrying your brother's child."

"Believe me," I drawled, "Thea does not need me to protect her. I'm here because my mother has made it clear that all her sons have to attend."

Lia blinked, and her breath hitched, her breasts rising as she held it. It took considerable amount of effort not to stare, but I hauled my gaze up, flicking up my brows.

Her throat slid, and my eyes tracked the movement, studying the faint veins pulsing in her slender neck. "Why?"

"She's been dismissed from the Vampire Council." I straightened and started across the room. "I think it's a last-ditch effort to find us all suitable matches. She'd love to marry us off before our family stock falls further."

"Marry?"

Did I imagine her eyes dimming at that revelation? Or was that wishful thinking? Leaning in close enough to see the amber flecks in her irises, I studied her full mouth before returning my attention to those crushing eyes. "Jealous?"

She shrugged even as I caught her shiver slightly. "Why would I be jealous?"

"Because you'll miss stalking me in the library," I said with equal casualness.

"I'm not here because of you." The accompanying huff belied

the truth, and we both knew it. In fairness, if I knew where she hung out—when she wasn't checking up on me—I'd be inclined to do the same.

I smirked nonetheless. "Why are you here?"

"I live here," she said through gritted teeth, still not stepping back, still not putting distance between us.

"In the library?" I lashed my tongue over my lower lip, and her eyes followed the movement. "Or were you looking for *me*?"

My words snapped something, and she bolted backward, away from me, away from her lips. The distance did nothing but make the tension stretch taut between us. She sucked in a ragged breath. "The Court is full of *vampires*." Her lip curled at the thought. "I needed somewhere quiet."

"Is that why you're dressed for The Third Rite?" I asked, stepping closer, needing to be closer.

Her eyes flicked up to mine, dark and molten like the lingering ashes of a fire. "It's my duty. I'm not there to participate."

"You'll draw attention wearing this," I warned in a whisper, fiddling with the lace cap of her sleeve. "Are you sure you aren't looking for a match?"

She shuddered, as if she felt the fingers on her skin, not on her gown, but her eyes remained locked on mine. "Is that what you're looking for?"

"Is that an invitation?" I asked, my breath warming the skin of her neck.

"No," she breathed, but her eyes fluttered shut, betraying the lie in her words.

My lips ghosted across her throat. So soft. How soft was the rest of her? I groaned. "Liar."

"I'm not interested in a male who hides behind books," she hissed even as her head fell back, exposing more of that glorious throat.

I licked the column, along the scar that ran along—the scar that sent my guts clenching as I wondered who had touched her, hurt her, scarred her. If I ever found out…they would *suffer*. "I'm not hiding,"

I snarled, breathing her in. I took her chin and guided her face to mine. My nose brushed hers, and our breathing synced. "I'm right the fuck here, Lia."

"You don't know me," she murmured, those molten eyes never leaving mine. "If you did…"

"Show me." She tried to look away, but I gripped her chin more tightly. "Do you think you can scare me?"

"I know I can."

"Try," I dared her.

Her teeth sank into her lower lip and then parted, poised to speak. The door to the library creaked open, and we startled apart as Julian entered the room, holding two shallow black boxes.

"There you are." His eyes skirted from me to her, to the distance between us, to the blush staining her cheeks. "Am I interrupting?"

Yes, you dick. But I shrugged and tossed him a casual grin. "Lia stumbled upon me in the library. Quite *accidentally*. I was explaining to her that I was helping you and Thea with something."

Hurt flashed through her eyes. "What are you searching for? You can't still be searching for information on the curse."

Julian met my eyes and finally nodded his permission to tell her.

"The queen-killer," I whispered.

"Why?" Horror coated her face.

"Because we think it killed Ginerva, and if it exists, Thea isn't safe," Julian cut in.

Lia shook her head. "The queens hid it after her death for their own safety."

"Is it what killed her?"

Lia's eyes pinched at the corners. "I don't know. Zina found her. They believed her death was a result of the curse's chokehold on magic."

"But her death destabilized magic," I said.

"Or it was the first sign that the curse was slowly poisoning magic."

If that was true…

"Don't go looking for that weapon," she warned us. "It will only be a threat to Thea, and too many people want her dead."

A low growl slipped from Julian, but she shrugged.

"It's the truth. I need to go," she announced, moving toward the door, her gown rustling across the floor behind her. She paused and sneered at Julian. "The Third Rite will be starting soon. Shouldn't you be with Thea?"

"We were told to arrive separately. Perhaps you can stick close to her."

They sized each other up for a second—the two people most desperate to protect Thea in the world. Finally, Lia gave him a curt nod before vanishing out the door.

Julian lifted his brows as he held out a box. "I was told to deliver this to you." He looked over his shoulder. "I see that's going...well."

"Shut the fuck up. It was going fine until you interrupted us." I swiped the box from his hands.

"Fine?" He chuckled at my choice of words. "I wasn't sure if she was going to kill you or mount you." A snarl slipped out of me, and he held up a hand. "Sorry. I forgot that you two—"

"Don't say it." The only thing worse than fighting the desire I felt for Lia would be admitting to it.

He nodded, heading toward the nearest table and the stack of books I'd left piled on it. "Find anything?" He flipped one open, the casual gesture at odds with the heaviness in his voice.

"Not yet." I tucked the box under my arm and joined him. "It's strange. This is considered one of the most comprehensive magical libraries in the world. There are grimoires here that date back eight thousand years and ones that were collected in the last decade, but there isn't a single mention of the curse after it happened. All references to it are ancient."

Julian jerked his attention from the book. "None?"

"None, and no mentions of the queen-killer. I was beginning to think it was a myth, but..."

"Aurelia seemed scared when we brought it up. How is that possible there are no references to the curse or the weapon?"

"It isn't," I said grimly. "Someone is censoring the collection.

It's the only thing that makes sense."

"Then the fae are right." He slammed the book shut.

"The fae?" I waited for him to explain what the hell that meant.

"It was something Bain said to Thea during our lovely visit." He grimaced as he recalled his mandatory meeting with the prince. "He told her he thinks vampires are behind the curse."

"But the curse affected vampires. It affected our population." I stumbled over the words even as everything became clearer.

"I'm glad you'll be there tonight," he said, his words thick. "Even if Thea is immortal..."

The queen-killer still existed, and whatever magic darkened that weapon would kill her—kill them both.

"I understand." I clapped a hand on his shoulder. He didn't have to voice the fear that haunted him. She was immortal but not invincible. It would take more to kill her, but killing her meant getting around her bodyguard... I shut my mind to the thought.

Lia could handle herself, and if she found out I was worrying about her, she'd have my balls.

"I also can't find a reference to any vampire-eating monsters," I told him. "Whatever is preying on the Mordicum might predate our records."

His forehead wrinkled, his eyes straying to the books and scrolls on the table. "Nothing."

I shook my head.

"Then let's hope they're toying with us."

"Do we want to take that chance?" I asked.

"I don't think we have a choice. We have enough problems without adding a monster to our list." He shrugged. "Thea is safe here. The wards guarding the court will keep a monster out."

"We leave innocent vampires to die?"

"No, we just tackle one problem at a time."

"I should get ready for this party," I grumbled, reaching for the box he'd delivered. "Is this a present or..."

"I suppose we might as well find out." Julian popped open the lid, swearing when he saw what was inside.

That boded well. I opened mine, my brows nudging together as I stared at the simple white mask inside. Under it was an invitation printed on thick vellum. I plucked it free. "Wear the mask and find yourself at the Midnight Carnival," I read, turning it over to find the other side blank. "Well, that's cryptic." I tossed the card into the box and reached for the mask. "What the hell is this about?"

Julian's jaw tensed as he stared at his own mask. "Nothing good."

CHAPTER FIFTY-ONE

Thea

Pregnancy was...fun. I clung to the toilet like a life preserver, the porcelain cool against my fevered skin as I shook from the heaving. It hit every evening like clockwork. I didn't know why they called it morning sickness, but I was thankful it kept to a schedule. I practiced cello around the same time. When my nausea inevitably hit, I was alone. Julian's concern over how I felt was sweet, but I didn't need an audience.

"Should you go to this stupid Rite?"

I jerked up to find Aurelia watching me from the doorway to the bathroom. "I'm fine." I pushed myself off the ground to prove it, hoping she didn't note my shaky legs.

Her hawkish eyes pierced me. "I can see that."

"Why are you here?" I asked gently as I flushed and started to the sink to brush my teeth. She'd been avoiding me since our return yesterday. Turning the tap, I lifted my eyes to wait for her answer—and froze. She was dressed for the evening, her glossy hair loose over her shoulders, her lips painted red, her gown... "You look stunning."

I meant it. The black gown and the lines of kohl sharpening her eyes honed her brutal beauty rather than softened it.

She shrugged, but I spied color creep onto her cheeks. "The sooner tonight is over, the better."

Finally, something we agreed on. I cupped water in my palms and washed my mouth, patting it dry with a soft towel, then turned to her. "I suppose I'm supposed to be ready by now."

"Should you go?" she pressed, eyes skirting to the toilet she'd just caught me throwing up in.

"Don't worry. It happens every night, but I'm always fine after."

"Still...does Julian know?" Her voice strained on his name. She'd had mixed feelings regarding my mate before we'd run off to the island. Now, I suspected they'd settled firmly into negative territory. That she was bringing him up told me exactly how concerned Aurelia was, even if she struggled to show it.

"He knows, and I suspect he feels it through our bond, but he respects that I don't want him hovering over me the whole time." He would if I let him. Beautiful, frustrating, *overprotective* vampire. I headed into the bedroom. "I should find something to wear."

"You haven't picked a dress?" she asked as I followed her.

"Just because I *am going* this evening doesn't mean I'm looking forward to it. Attendance is mandatory. Sabine needs us there. Not going might send the wrong message." The message that the Council's attack had intimidated me. Screw that. "I assume the closet will have something for me. Isn't that the point of having a magical wardrobe?" I opened it and found a variety of simple dresses, flowing tops and matching pants, all in various shades of cream and beige. Not a gown in sight. I pushed the hangers apart, my fingers lingering on the buttery soft fabric of the outfits. But all the gowns it had presented me with upon my earlier arrival had vanished.

"It seems your closet agrees with me." Aurelia folded her arms over her chest, a haughty smile playing on her crimson lips. "You should stay home, resting and comfortable."

"I'll just wear this." I plucked the most formal option—a set of ivory pants and a wispy matching top. I frowned as I studied it. It was the best I could do. I imagined Sabine's face when I showed up in the outfit. It might be worth it to be comfortable, a luxury not afforded by the first two Rites.

Aurelia groaned, striding across the room. She picked up a black box and brought it to me. "It won't matter once you put this on."

Bracing myself, I flipped open the box and found a white mask and an invitation that I read to her. "You're invited to the Midnight Carnival."

"One of our oldest traditions in Venice," she explained. "It seems the Vampire Council made it a little more...interesting."

I picked up the mask and turned it over. There was nothing unusual about it. It was plain, boring even. I placed it on my dresser and opened the top drawer. "I'm not certain this will do much to—"

Aurelia gasped, doubling over and clutching her ears. She struggled to raise her head. "What. Is. In. There?"

I ransacked my drawer, tossing underwear to the side until my fingers landed on a velvet jewelry box—the pendant Bain had given me in London. I picked it up, and Aurelia cried out, the sound pure pain. I shoved it back inside, piling panties on top of it before slamming the drawer closed.

Aurelia took a stumbling step and collapsed onto the small bench at the foot of the bed. "What—what was that?"

"A present from the prince of the Infernal Court." I backed against the drawer, shielding her from what lay inside it.

Her mouth drooped as a single pained word fell from her lips. "*Fae.*"

I nodded, my mouth going dry. Bain had promised the necklace was nothing more than a gift, but the way she had reacted suggested otherwise. "He said it was a present between our courts."

"Maybe," she admitted, "but it's full of dark magic—dark *fae* magic. The Infernal Court is one of four courts, and they are the most evil of the bunch."

Evil. They had been civilized for our visit, but what lay beneath that carefully coiffed facade?

"I don't feel anything from it." I hadn't dared wear it yet. After seeing her reaction, I doubted I ever would.

"You wouldn't... Only fae can feel that magic."

"But..." My head tilted, my eyes widening as understanding hit me. "*You*?"

Her chin rose, pointing at me in defiance. "Half," she confessed.

I aimed toward the bed, needing to sit down. I studied her more closely. "You don't look fae."

"My mother was a witch. My father was a...bastard."

"We have that in common."

She swallowed. "But..." She snapped her fingers. I startled at the gesture. Bain had done the same in London. The surrounding air glimmered, and her features shifted. Her scar remained, her eyes still dark as night, but her face... She looked as though the Gods had crafted her, each angle precise and perfect, her cheekbones regal, her lips full and sensual, and her ears...

"I wear a glamour." She snapped her fingers, and that otherworldly beauty dulled. "It's better if people don't know."

"Do Mariana and Zina know?"

Her eyes flickered. "No. Ginerva took me in—gave me a home. She swore me to secrecy and held mine. My mother died giving birth to me, and my father..."

"Bastard," I said for her.

"It turns out no one wants a half-breed around. Ginerva was more open-minded than most. She taught me how to control my fae magic, how to hide it."

"But you know about the courts?"

"A precaution," she admitted. "Toward the end of her life, Ginerva became suspicious of everyone. She taught about the courts. She even summoned another fae to secretly teach me how to travel to the Otherworld. I think she planned to release me of my vow to her, to the court. The Otherworld would have been safer for me, even if they hate half-breeds as much as this world hates fae. She died before..."

The truth hit me. Ginerva had guarded Aurelia, protected her, and given her sanctuary from a world that didn't want her. And

Aurelia had loved Ginerva. Not simply as her queen or her charge but something much deeper than that. Any doubt I had that I could trust Aurelia vanished. She'd had nothing to do with Ginerva's death. I was certain of that now. Did that loyalty extend to the other queens?

"But it doesn't matter," she said. "Everyone who attends the Midnight Carnival must wear a mask, and when I put one of those on…" A ragged breath sawed through her as she looked to where I'd left mine.

"What?"

"The Rite is a masquerade," she explained, "unlike any ever concocted. I overheard Mariana speaking of it earlier. The mask will transform you into your true self." She laughed, the sound so hollow it echoed through the room. "The perfect costume."

The person who most of us hid from the rest of the world—revealed. No hiding behind charm or decorum or wealth. My stomach churned, and I almost ran to the bathroom as I considered the Rite's purpose. The creatures that might prowl the carnival. The truths the Rite would lay bare. The secrets they would expose.

"You don't have to go," I said to her. "If you think the mask will reveal—"

"It will." Her voice cracked, betraying her brittle nerves. I might not know Aurelia well, but it was clear it rattled her. "Since magic reawakened, it's been harder to keep my glamour." She squared her shoulders and looked me dead in the eyes. "But if you go, I go."

I heard what she didn't say running in the undercurrent of those words. She had failed one queen. She would not fail another.

I couldn't fault her for that. Not when I knew what it was like to fear losing someone—a fear I'd lived with most of my life. A fear I'd felt again in recent days as the wedding neared, as I faced taking the next step into the future and away from my past. I nodded, a plan forming in my mind, but there was something else. "If I asked you to help me with something, would you?"

"Right now?"

I shook my head. "It can wait until after The Rite." I licked my lower lip, scrounging up the courage to ask for something that felt impossible. "With everything happening, I need to stay at court. But the wedding is coming up, and…"

"Cold feet?" She lifted a brow.

"No! But I want… I want my mother there. She's in the city. There's a safe house for sirens in *Cannaregio*."

"I'm assuming the vampires don't know about this?"

"Julian does," I admitted, "but no one else. I need someone who can find her. The house is warded against vampires, and even if I sent Jacqueline or Lysander"—she flinched at the sound of his name—"they might not find it."

"So you want me to find her?"

I swallowed, trying to ignore the knot of hopeful fear in my throat. "Yes. I want her at the wedding… I *need* her to be there."

She considered for a moment before inclining her head. "I will seek her out and tell her."

It was the most I could ask. Mom might refuse to attend. Even with a siren on the throne, it was dangerous. But I suspected it wasn't fear that might stop her. She didn't approve of Julian, of my mate being a vampire, and while she might have accepted the facts, she didn't have to support me.

"About tonight," I continued. "Don't wear a mask."

She huffed. "I'm not sure that's an option."

"Don't wear that one. We'll find you another. Will anyone know that it's not one of the enchanted ones?"

She hesitated. "I'm not sure."

"Then it doesn't hurt to try, and if they force the issue, we'll leave the party."

"You said yourself that you need to be there," she pointed out.

"Yes, but I have a good excuse to duck out." I patted my stomach. I wasn't eager to announce my pregnancy to every magical creature in the city, especially when so many of them wanted me dead. Considering everyone we met picked up the changes in my scent, I didn't have a choice. But once they knew, we would all be in danger. Myself, Julian, and our child. The Council had already tried to assassinate me. Still, they couldn't touch me in Venice. It was a small comfort. "But we should try."

She nodded, but she remained silent as I changed into the soft ivory pants and top. The clothes felt amazing, especially given the way my body seemed to sway between overheating and freezing, thanks to my changing hormones. I prayed that whatever magic the mask inflicted wouldn't change that. I didn't bother to put on makeup or do my hair. There was a pretty decent chance none of that would matter once I put on the mask. If it knew me at all, I hoped it just transformed my clothes into a pair of jeans and knotted my hair into a messy bun—that was the skin *I* would feel comfortable wearing.

"We should go soon," Aurelia announced to me.

"Wait." I rummaged inside the closet, willing whatever magic listening to my desires to hear me. I tried to reach onto the top shelf and discovered I was too short. I guess the magic hadn't considered that. The magic, apparently offended, responded, and another shelf appeared, along with what I was looking for.

The mask, composed of layer upon layer of delicate rose petals, matched Aurelia's crimson lips. Its silhouette was lined with silk thorns along the edge that curved to cover half her face and that full mouth. Not the scarred side. No, it would show that, and I wondered if the magic knew what she needed as well. Not to hide from a past she had no say in but to embrace who she was *now*.

I passed it to her, grimacing once before placing it over her face. "I'm not sure it reveals my true self."

I thought it did, perhaps. The rose was beautiful and delicate, a pretty distraction from its dangerous thorns—so like the woman in the glamour before me. I said nothing.

She adjusted it on her face and bit her lip. "About what I told you…can we keep it to ourselves?"

"Of course." She deserved that respect, and my heart hurt to wonder how few had shown it to her.

"If some people knew…" Her eyes faded into some distant place, and I wondered if she wasn't worrying about people so much as one person in particular.

Once again, I kept my mouth shut. Things were complicated enough for everyone. If she needed to talk through her feelings, I would listen, but I wouldn't pry.

"Do you want to put this on now?" She pointed to the mask.

I stared at it for a second, my stomach churning in a way that had nothing to do with morning sickness. "I think if I'm going to face my true self, I'd rather do it in private."

And then take a minute to digest whatever it showed me.

"Should I...?"

"No. Stay." Alone, I might not work up the courage.

My fingers trembled as I picked up the mask and raised it to my face. Magic knit around me, its strands forming a glittering cocoon. Heat kissed my skin as the spell wove its enchantment. A pang of panic rocketed through me when smoke flooded my nostrils, choking my throat with its acridness before depositing the taste of ash and sulfur on my tongue. Something was on fire. No. Not something. *Me.* I was on fire. I was burning. Magic licked down my body in living flame, and I twisted against its hold as Aurelia shouted my name.

This wasn't the time to panic. I needed to think, which was hard to do while burning alive. Closing my eyes, I listened until I heard it. Smooth notes spilled into my ears, calming me despite the magical inferno that engulfed me, and with a deep breath, I gave into its stranglehold—gave into the music and trusted it.

The final notes rang out like bells in the dark, clear and bright, and I opened my eyes to find Aurelia staring.

CHAPTER FIFTY-TWO

Julian

The carnival began long before midnight and would undoubtedly continue until dawn. Most of the guests had arrived and donned their own masks by the time we made our way into the courtyard. The night was a swirl of creatures, some from myth, some of the earth. Globes of light hung in midair, illuminating the shadows below, and the wind carried the salty brine of the lagoons on the air to mix with the thick scent of the court's roses. Nude servers dusted in gold powder offered canapés and cocktails and even their bodies, judging by the bite marks on a few we passed. A ring hung overhead, a male and female twisting and contorting their bodies as one in ways that suggested the evening's debauchery was only beginning.

But the real entertainment was the guests themselves. At their heart, each remained a vampire or a familiar, but tonight they'd been transformed into creatures both elegant and primal, feral and beautiful. Under their masks and beneath magical guise, they might do anything they pleased.

"This could get interesting," Lysander muttered to me as we passed a group clad in downy capes, their masks and clothing pure as the driven snow.

I wondered what bloodlines they hailed from that they remained so innocent amidst the creatures stalking the carnival. We shared a look. "Lambs to the slaughter, it seems. Maybe you should…"

A growl rumbled from my brother, and I held back a smile. With his fur cloak rippling in the moonlight, he moved like the predator the mask had unveiled. It had contorted his features into a beast, his dark hair now untamed and streaked with more silver.

"It fits you." It suited his broad shoulders and warrior build, suited his ability to move between our family—*our* pack—and his quiet life hunting through ruins.

"I look like a bloody *werewolf*," he bit out.

I said nothing, didn't dare, because it was not entirely *untrue*. He was a bit of a lone wolf, though.

"Do you see anyone?" Lysander scanned the crowd, looking for signs of our family. Everyone should be here by now. Just Benedict remained in London, maneuvering relations with other magical factions in case we needed allies.

I was only looking for one person. Thea hadn't entered yet. I would know her as soon as I saw her. I tried not to think of what she would see in me, though. Of what the mask had revealed.

I hadn't dared look in the mirror at my metamorphosis, not when I spied the leather clothing that clung to me like rough scales or when the velvet draped over my shoulders fanned out like silken wings. I was darkness incarnate. I was the beast that prowled beneath my flesh. Death. Vengeance. The forgotten Prince of the Underworld reborn.

"I think that's Sebastian and Thoren. What the fuck are they wearing?" Lysander frowned, and I followed his gaze to find my brothers, both of whom were clad in ordinary brocade capes, gilded masks perched over their eyes.

"Halloween came early, huh?" Sebastian saddled over to us, Thoren close behind.

"You aren't wearing the mask." Lysander pointed an accusing finger at his own. "How the hell did you get out of this?"

Sebastian shrugged, his smug smile on full display under his ordinary Venetian carnival mask. "Thoren is a master of negotiation."

"How?" Lysander gritted his teeth, looking at Thoren for answers.

"I pointed out that it might be a good idea if some of us kept our heads this evening," Thoren said in a calm voice that held none of the mocking undertone Sebastian's had, even if his lips twitched. Thoren scanned Lysander. "We can't all run around acting like wolves."

"You two couldn't have negotiated on our behalf?" Lysander closed his eyes beneath his lupine mask. "Bastards."

I frowned. "What about me? If anyone needs to keep their head, it's the one with a pregnant mate."

"You're both taking The Rites," Sebastian said. "You don't have a choice."

"And why aren't you?" Lysander crossed his arms.

"You're really getting into the role, huh?" Sebastian rolled his shoulders. "Mother only seemed interested in making sure you two participated. She said since Julian is spoken for, you should—"

Lysander growled, a bit too convincingly. Maybe Thoren was onto something. "You're next in line."

"She seemed to think it was your turn." Thoren winked at him.

I thought Lysander might actually rip his head off, but he aimed his quiet fury at Thoren. "And you?"

A brow arched over Thoren's mask. "I asked nicely."

I bit back a laugh as Lysander cursed them both.

"Chill." Sebastian's hands dug into his pockets. "I'm sure Aurelia will be here. Maybe she'll be wearing a red hood and looking for a big, bad—"

Lysander curled his lip, a feral snarl cutting our brother off mid-sentence. "I don't know what you are talking about."

Sebastian snorted. "I have eyes, brother. *Big* ones."

"*Seb.*" Warning laced Thoren's voice. "We should patrol."

Sebastian grimaced. "You were serious about that part?"

"C'mon. If you behave, I'll let you check out that blood orgy in the ballroom." Thoren grabbed Sebastian's shoulder and prodded him forward, tilting his head in apology to us before they both vanished into the crowd.

We watched them go, Lysander muttering under his breath about fairness and duty.

"Now you know how I felt last October," I told him as we wove our way through the guests.

"At least you got a mate out of it." The crowd parted before us, whispers following us. Not that any of them knew who we were under these masks, but their magic had done its job. Ahead, a cluster of females in Grecian gowns, each mask a near-identical face, turned to analyze the crowd, searching for prey. The one in the center turned to her sisters and murmured in their ears. All three turned curious eyes in our direction.

One stepped forward, her gaze roving over us with interest. "Wolf," she purred, resting a hand on Lysander's chest, "have you ever fucked a Goddess? How about three?" When he didn't respond, her eyes skipped to me. "Your dragon friend is welcome to have a turn, too."

A low growl rumbled in Lysander's throat, his fangs snapping at her. She stumbled a step, careening into her sisters. They soothed her as we continued.

"You could have just said, 'No, thank you.'" I couldn't keep the amusement from my voice.

"You're mated," he said, the words rough and guttural.

"They were more interested in you," I pressed. "All *three* of them."

That earned me a snarl, but I laughed. I didn't tell him I thought Sebastian was on to something. Lysander was already down. Why kick him? Whatever was happening between him and Thea's bodyguard was his own business. Still... "If you need to talk about it, I've been in your shoes."

His mouth twisted as he shook his head. "Thea *wanted* you."

I clapped a hand on his shoulder to tell him I understood and dropped it.

"We'll have better luck from the center of the courtyard." He changed the subject as he aimed us away from the perimeter toward those mingling in the middle of the space. Even amongst vampires, we stood nearly a full head taller than everyone in the room, so looking out over the crowd might help us spot Thea.

Unfortunately, someone else was holding court at the heart of the party. We shared a look and cut our way through the crowd.

CHAPTER FIFTY-THREE

Jacqueline

"Are you planning to be a wallflower all night?"

I turned to find Camila at my side, and...words failed me. The mask had chosen well, transforming her black hair to raven feathers. It covered her eyes only but did nothing to suppress that shrewd, assessing gaze. Her gown consisted of two panels of black lace that covered her breasts and joined at the waist to fall between her legs, allowing her toned legs to slide free with each movement. The wings of her cloak offered a little modesty, but not much.

She met my gaze for a moment, holding it, before her eyes dropped to my mouth and lingered. "You're beautiful."

I shook my head. My transformation paled compared to hers. My features feline under the mask's magic, my gown silver white and specked with spots. Not a simple house cat. A leopard, swift and cunning, but perhaps no match for a raven.

Would I ever catch her?

"You are." Her tone left no room for argument.

I swallowed, a throb building between my legs. Gods, I wanted her. I would always want her. But... "You've been avoiding me."

I hadn't seen her since we returned to Venice.

"I've been occupied." Restless energy overcame her, and I knew what she'd been doing.

"Did you find him?"

"He left the house. There was no sign of him there and no clue where he went."

She would not rest until she confronted Willem—until she ended him. I couldn't blame her.

"I have to do this," she whispered. "I wish I could explain it to you."

I would never understand, not fully. We both knew that. But looking into her eyes, I realized something. "You don't have to." I swallowed against the raw ache in my throat. "I'm not going anywhere."

Camila's tongue swept over her lips, her eyes shadowing, words poised on that mouth I found myself ready to kiss.

"Jacqueline!"

I tensed at the familiar voice. We shared a look, and Camila turned to leave. I grabbed her hand. "Don't. Stay."

She paused before inclining her head and tugging from my grasp. She would stay but on her terms. We moved apart, and I plastered a smile on my face as we turned to face my mother.

"Camila," my mother greeted her from behind a fox mask. "I've heard you are the matriarch of the Rousseaux family now. Congratulations. It was time someone challenged Sabine."

My smile faltered. "Careful, Mother. You'll give me ideas."

"Don't make empty threats." Her eyes pinned me, dared me to prove her wrong.

I forced my anger deeper. Our relationship was strained, and with the enemies at our door, at my chosen family's door, I didn't need to make another one. "Where is Jessica? Or have you finally given up on your ludicrous plan?"

"Have you decided to take her place?" she cut back. When I remained silent, she rolled her eyes. "This is why I don't fear your threats. You never follow through on any of your promises."

Something snapped inside me. "Something I learned from *you*."

"I have never made you a single promise—"

"Exactly. You have never followed through, never cared for anyone but yourself and your privilege and your reputation."

"You could do with caring about your reputation," she started.

"Fuck. That." The words came out a snarl, more animal than human. Maybe it was the mask. Maybe it was just that I'd given up.

Her nostrils flared. "I suppose that answers my question. Since you refuse to make a match—"

"She already has," Camila snapped.

Then her mouth was on mine. I melted into the kiss, forgetting where I was, what I'd been arguing over moments ago. There was only her. Only us. She broke it too quickly, a smile whispering on her lips before she pulled away to reveal my mother's shocked face.

"You... Her..." Her head whipped from me to Camila and back. "How long?"

Camila twined her hand with mine. "Centuries."

"But you were married."

"And now I'm not."

I shot Camila a look that said *debatable*. But maybe...maybe part of her drive to find Willem—to end him—was about us, too. About finally freeing herself from that forced vow and giving us the chance we never had.

"Will Sabine support this?" My mother sniffed. "She'll want grandchildren, and you two..."

"She's already got one on the way," Camila said. I squeezed her hand, reminding her that wasn't public knowledge yet. Although when Thea finally made her appearance... I didn't think the mask could disguise her enough to smother the unmistakable scent of her pregnancy.

"And you two intend to take The Rites *together*?"

I wasn't sure she was processing this. I barely was.

"We do," Camila answered.

My heart soared, but I grabbed hold of it, willing it to stay firmly in my chest. Camila loved to get a rise out of people. To play games. She'd witnessed my mother's cruelty and decided to screw with her. What else could I believe? Yes, she'd told me she loved me before.

Yes, I couldn't deny this breathing, aching need I felt for her. But that didn't mean any of this was real.

"Well, I...will tell your father." Mother paused and looked at me. "And I will let Jessica decide if she wants to continue with The Rites."

It was more than I could have hoped for. "All I ask is that it's *her* choice."

"Keep your side of the bargain, and it will be."

My joy plunked inside me, heavy as a stone, but I nodded.

She studied us once more, like she suspected this was a trick, before disappearing into the party. I spun toward Camila. "Thank you." There were too many emotions, too many questions, too much hope, but I needed to know her intentions. "You saved her."

"I wasn't trying to save your sister." She tucked a strand of hair behind my ear. "I was trying to save *you*. She was just a bonus."

"Will you go along with it?" I asked. Her eyes pinched together, confusion muddying their bright blue. "Until The Rites are over?"

Realization hit her, and her smile wilted. "Go along with it?"

"You are married, and you have children."

"I see." Her frown deepened, and she took a step away.

I grabbed her hand. "Camila...I understand your priorities, but maybe someday, when *you're* ready, maybe then, we..."

"Are *you* ready?" she asked quietly.

My heart was pounding so hard I thought it might crack me open and spill out at her feet. "I have been ready since the first time I kissed you."

Shadows filled her eyes, the past returning to both of us. It had rained that day, keeping us from going on the horseback ride we'd been promised. I'd been sullen, annoyed that my day was ruined. Camila had tried to make me laugh, hadn't stopped trying until she succeeded. I couldn't even remember over what now. But I recalled the way her eyes had sparkled when she triumphed. She hadn't pulled away when I'd brought my mouth to hers.

I had known then my life would never be the same.

She moved closer, reaching toward me, and I tensed. "What are you doing?"

"Stop." Not a demand. A request. Her palm cupped my cheek. "I'm doing what I should have done during my first social season." This time, when our lips met, there was no urgency, only a gentle invitation. I saw it, then—her, our future, everything I thought I'd lost—and accepted. Her tongue brushed my lips, a soft entreaty, and I opened myself to her. She took the kiss deeper, tasting and exploring, until we broke apart, breathless and needy.

"Take me to bed," she blurted out.

I laughed softly. "Here?"

"Smart-ass." Her finger moved to trace the lines of my lips. Each movement deepened my need. She watched, her eyes shy and curious. The eyes that had found mine after that first kiss. "I've had lovers since Willem," she explained in a quiet voice.

I smiled at her confession. "I didn't exactly save myself for you, either."

She groaned, shaking her head. "Other *male* lovers. I've never... You're the only person I've ever truly wanted."

It was an effort not to find the nearest wall and claim her. She had waited for me, wanted me, never given up on me. Even when I'd thought she was gone, when I convinced myself I'd turned an innocent flirtation into something more, when I had struggled with wanting her, loving her.

"I have been in love with you for two hundred years," I told her. "No one else. You are all I have ever wanted."

"I meant it." She cleared her throat, peeking at me through her mask. "I want to take the Rites with you."

The tension between us lifted, and in its place a thread remained. A connection. A lifeline.

"I think..." she said slowly, her chest heaving slightly. "I think we're mates."

A smile broke across me. "I know we are." I brushed a kiss over her lips. "Or we will be by tonight."

"Tonight?" she whimpered, her eyes bright with the same gnawing hunger.

I brought our clasped hands to my mouth and kissed her knuckles. My thighs clamping together as I imagined taking her gloves off, pressing my palm to hers. "Tonight," I said firmly, as much for my benefit as hers. "Someone told my mother we would take The Rites together."

She shook her head. "Me and my big mouth."

I gave her a look that promised I had plans for that mouth. Then I pulled her toward the party, toward The Rite, toward our future.

Neither of us looked back.

CHAPTER FIFTY-FOUR

Julian

"Oh, for fuck's sake." I sighed as I beheld my mother. The spell's choice fit her a little *too* well. A plume of peacock feathers rose from the center of her mask, matching the ones layered into a skirt that trailed behind her. Her laugh carried through the space with ease. Our father stood quietly by her side, his own mask transforming his golden hair into a lion's mane.

"Someone's recovered from being kicked off the Council," Lysander muttered.

I wasn't as certain. My mother knew how to attract an audience. As we approached, our father tipped his head in our direction. She glanced, assessing us with a shrewd gaze at odds with the part she was playing, before beckoning us to join them.

"My sons," she announced to the others as we joined them. "My eldest has mated to the new queen, but Lysander is available." She shot a meaningful look at the females assembled nearby.

My brother bristled. "I'm only here until the wedding is over. I'm afraid The Rites will have to wait."

I could have sworn her feathers ruffled, but she laughed it off, murmuring farewells before sweeping away, her fingers digging into my arm and dragging me along.

"Where is your mate?" she demanded.

"We came separately." My frustration mounted at the reminder of Thea's absence.

"Her place is here. The Council will see—"

"She's got morning sickness," I whispered furiously.

Her jaw tensed. "A good excuse to some."

"That *excuse* is your grandchild," I reminded her. "And why are you so eager to dangle Thea in front of the Council?" After what they had done, I was having a hard enough time not seeking each of them out and turning tonight's festivities into a bloodbath.

Malice glittered in her eyes. "The Council needs a reminder of *our* power."

"Our? Don't you mean *her* power?" I gritted my teeth.

"She's a member of this family now—"

"I thought I was disowned," I pointed out.

"Don't be ridiculous. You are a Rousseaux."

I smirked. "Soon, I'll be a Melbourne." If looks could kill... I baited her anyway. "You wouldn't ask a female to abandon her name."

"She should take the name with clout," she hissed under her breath. "And as for you, it's the twenty-first century. You needn't be so old-fashioned. Thea becoming a Rousseaux sends an important message."

"I'll leave that for my mate to decide. We don't need to prove our power to anyone. Ours or *hers*," I added before Mother had an aneurysm. "The Council acted because they knew that."

"This is about more than magic," she said, her hand still clenching my arm. "It's about politics, alliances, and control. Don't underestimate them. We need to send the Council a message. Thea's presence will remind them of that."

"My mate is not a pawn." I yanked my arm from her.

"No, she is not. She is a queen, and they will watch her every move, starting tonight," she hissed.

"As delightful as this conversation is, people are beginning to stare," Lysander drawled.

She straightened instantly, suddenly aware of the attention on us, and preened like the creature the mask had made her. Looking to my brother with a courtier's smile, she muttered through her curved lips, "And you will begin looking for your own match."

"Like hell, I will," he said darkly. "I'm not interested in taking a wife."

"Liar," she said, her voice low. "Don't think I haven't noticed the tension between you and that handmaiden. Let me be clear, that is not a suitable match."

"Neither was mine." I came to my brother's defense. "And now you're singing her praises."

Before the argument could continue, a ripple went through the crowd. The people surrounding us turned, whispering and gasping, and I knew without looking who they were staring at. I knew it like the beating of my own heart, like the skin that clung to my bones, the blood that ran through my veins. A tendril of golden magic wrapped around my heart and tugged. My frustration faded away. Next to me, Lysander's eyes were wide. He tilted his head, wonder written over his features. Even my mother fell silent.

The entire party had stopped, and as if they knew, despite our masks, despite the enchantments imprisoning us, they had made a path that led directly to *her*.

Mask or no, she was a queen—and every soul here answered to the magic in her blood.

Thea's transformation revealed what I'd always known—since that first moment when I'd scented her in San Francisco. She was temptation and eternity and raw, primal power.

A phoenix. Even if death touched her, she would rise again stronger than before. Unbreakable. Unyielding. Absolutely fucking untouchable.

To all but me.

Her silk gown wrapped around her petite torso, feathers in shades of orange and crimson fluttering on her shoulders, the swell of her breasts, around her hips—and they were on fire. Flames wreathed her, licking harmlessly over her moonstone skin up to where her golden mask obscured everything but her sensual mouth and her emerald eyes. They met mine, and those perfect lips parted in a smile that belonged only to me—a smile that promised only I could touch that power, feel it under my fingertips, share it as we fulfilled that sacred call of our mating bond.

Which I would do as soon as fucking possible.

She showed no sign of fear as I approached, no horror at the creature the mask unveiled, and I knew what I had to do.

CHAPTER FIFTY-FIVE

Thea

He was death incarnate. Julian had always looked comfortable in the shadows, in the night. Tonight, he owned them. The lines of his black mask were brutal, cut to mimic the sharp, sculpted lines of his beautiful face. Pools of endless onyx stared from behind it. There was no hint of blue in his eyes. As he moved, light snagged on his leather clothing. On the scales. Behind him, his cloak fanned into great, veined wings.

This was the beast that lived inside my own soul, the terrible, beautiful monster that belonged to me. His magic bellowed in my blood, crying out to him in need—as if it sensed the urgency building inside me.

To touch him.

To claim him.

To show every soul here exactly who Julian Rousseaux belonged to.

Me.

His gaze never wavered from mine. Each step filled me with longing, power in his every movement. My opposite. My completion. My equal in every way. My mate.

All around me, creatures stopped to stare, sensing the

connection between us, but I didn't care. Let them feel it. Envy it. Covet it. Julian was mine, and I was his.

The mating bond thrummed between us when he reached me. Those endless eyes never left mine as he dropped to one knee before me.

"My queen." His words seared through me, intimate even despite this public display of loyalty.

I reached for him, and his hand grasped mine, his touch pulsing through our gloves. He lifted it to his forehead and pressed it there once before bringing it to his chest and then up to his kiss. My breath hitched, my gown no longer the only part of me on fire.

I barely processed the figures moving behind him until they, too, kneeled, heads bowed. Julian's brothers. His father. And soon others followed. Not all. But *many*.

So much for incognito.

I held my head high, drank in the power flowing through me, allowed myself to feel it—to become it. Across the courtyard, Sabine's gaze met mine. Her head tilted slightly, the closest to a show of fealty she was going to give me. I inclined my head back.

Queens shared power, and regardless of my rather strained relationship with my future mother-in-law, I knew it was the only way forward. Not to hide from our magic—to share it.

I dropped my attention to Julian, whose sinful grin radiated pride, and spoke in a clear, loud voice. "Your place is by my side, mate."

I rather like being on my knees for you.

Heat rushed through me, and it had nothing to do with my dress. Later, I would allow him to show me just how much he liked it.

Julian rose, his family following a beat later. Our fingers twined together automatically, as if they knew that's where they belonged.

"Goddess," he growled under his breath, and my toes curled.

We moved in step through the party, nodding hellos but not stopping to speak to anyone else. Not while our magic roared through us, the mating urge growing increasingly irresistible. My eyes lifted to find Julian watching me.

I'm not sure how long I can keep my hands off of you. The words brushed through me, a gentle request laced with need. His mask hid it, but I felt it. Maybe since my body demanded the same.

Don't.

His teeth sank into his lower lip, a fang flashing. *Careful, my love, or I will show everyone here who I belong to.*

Don't you mean who I belong to?

His hand tightened around mine as he picked up the pace, no longer playing the part of the king surveying his subjects. He was on a mission. My pulse raced as we surged through the crowd, out of the courtyard, into the halls of the court.

The spectacle continued inside, but the atmosphere shifted. The courtyard was only a show, a nod to propriety and politics with a hint of sensual deviance. *This* was the Midnight Carnival.

Black silk draped from the cavernous ceilings twined with enormous vines, giant leaves fanning from them. Once a palace. Now a sensual paradise. The hallway was empty, but music pulsed in the distance, its beat nearly matching the throb at my core. The sound beckoned us forward past candelabras spilling wax on the marble floor, urged us toward that hypnotic rhythm.

Julian paused. "I think that's the blood orgy Sebastian mentioned."

His body angled, turning in the opposite direction, away from the carnival toward our quarters.

"Julian, The Rite." I stayed in place.

"We don't have to prove anything." He drew me closer, unfazed by the flames that reached toward him. If he felt them, he said nothing.

I freed the desire inside me, let it shine from my eyes. "Who said anything about proving something? You are mine to do with as I please."

A smirk cocked his tempting lips. "And what would please you, my queen?"

"I came to take The Rite. I should see everything."

Julian stilled. He was the picture of an avenging God, crafted from onyx under his dark mask. "You want to take part in the blood orgy?"

Each word was strained, said with such care, and I knew that if I said yes, he would find some way to grant that desire, even with his mating instinct currently in overdrive.

"I want to see," I clarified, brushing the back of my hand over his scaled mask. "Only you can touch me...taste me."

The abyss of his eyes deepened, even as he shook his head. "Not...not while you're..."

I resisted the urge to sigh. I could push him, but I wouldn't. Not with him working so hard to check that primal instinct to protect and shield me and my child. Instead, I curled my lip. "Then maybe *I* will taste."

He stared for a moment.

I planted a hand on my hips and tapped into that power I'd felt in the courtyard. "I'm not the innocent human you met in San Francisco. A blood orgy doesn't scare me."

Finally, he tilted his head and extended his arm. "Then lead the way."

• • •

If I'd thought the propriety ended in the hall, the debauchery began in the ballroom. Julian gripped my hand as we entered it, and I immediately understood why. Sumptuous couches, chairs, and stools—all upholstered in deep velvet—dotted the room, and bodies covered every single one. Naked bodies. Writhing bodies. The only protection their masks. Vampires and familiars, some feeding, some...

"It's really an orgy." I blinked. I'd glimpsed some hedonism in San Francisco, but this...

People were still getting to know each other at the beginning of the season, Julian's amused voice echoed in my mind.

I gulped and nodded. *Well, they* know *each other now.*

He snorted. *Hardly. Some might, but the mask gives most of them a free pass to do as they please.*

Don't you mean who *they please?* Flesh was everywhere I looked, and it wasn't merely coupling going on. I heated as I stared at a group of five creatures entangled in a mass of limbs and sweat. One shifted to reveal a sixth party. I squeaked and turned against Julian's shoulder when I saw the male's face.

I see Thoren let Sebastian find the blood orgy. Julian gripped my waist and steered us away from his brother's private party.

I did not need to see that.

I've been telling him the same thing for centuries. It would be nice if he ever listened.

I laughed, smothering the sound with my hand so we didn't interrupt anyone around us.

You're very polite.

As we wandered through the room, the warmth inside me built. I wasn't embarrassed, but I was not quite turned on, either. *Why is* this *The Rite?*

Julian tilted his head, continuing our silent conversation. *This isn't. It's just a natural byproduct of giving a bunch of supernatural creatures a mask to hide behind.*

But they did this in San Francisco.

Some did. Many abstained or didn't come at all. Tonight, even the most reserved among us might dabble in things they'd never considered.

I see that.

As for why the mask is The Rite, I think it strips away the pretenses we hide behind. I told you before that vampires marry for life. At this point, some of us have made matches. If you're lying to your potential partner about who you are…

The mask revealed the truth.

Do you like what the mask revealed to you about me? The question spilled from me.

He stopped and turned, lifting my masked face to his. *There is nothing the mask could reveal, that* you *could reveal, that would make me love you less. But it chose well. It suits you.*

Yours suits you, too.

A beat. *It doesn't...scare you?*

I traced the lines of his mask, shaking my head. *You are the dark beast that guards my heart. I've felt you there, and now I can see you. You are beautiful.*

His head bowed, and I stepped closer.

Do you want to leave?

He lifted his face to mine. *If you want to stay, if you want to...*

I knew he meant it. If I wanted to stay, if I wanted to experiment, he would leash himself. He would accept it. My need ratcheted to crisis levels.

Tempting. I bit back a laugh and slipped my hand back into his. *But I'd rather have you all to myself. Now.*

So impatient. He aimed us toward the door opposite the one we'd entered through. *I have an idea...*

That leads to the throne room.

The smile that flashed under his mask told me he already knew. I shivered.

As we approached it, someone called to us. "It's off-limits. Warded."

I merely grinned at the concerned male and slipped past with my mate.

"Good thing I'm with the queen," he said as we stepped inside and the orgy next door silenced. It seemed the ward shielded the room from people and noise. Not even the thumping bass of the ballroom's music breached it.

"You've got me alone. What are you going to do with me?" I challenged him.

It was the wrong thing to say—or maybe the right thing—because I found myself over his shoulder. Julian hauled me toward the dais and deposited me on my throne. The flames of my dress brushed across its arms but didn't catch. Before I could protest, he dropped to one knee, then the other.

He grinned up at me, wicked intent gleaming in his black eyes. "Since I first saw you claim this, I have fantasized about this moment." He rucked my skirt up. "Now I finally have my chance."

The rough leather of his gloves gripped my thighs and yanked me to the edge of the seat, he growled approval at finding me bare.

Not a conscious choice. The magic had created every stitch I was wearing. I tried not to think of why it had left panties out. It probably had something to do with the ballroom next door.

He kissed my inner thigh, his mouth trailing to where I ached for him. My fingers clutched the arms of the throne as he teased me, nipping at my skin.

"My queen," he growled when his taunting lips reached the apex of my thighs and dragged his tongue up my center, roaring with approval at my taste.

I arced against that silken tongue and the pleasure it promised. Julian moved, allowing the scales of his mask to graze my swollen core, and I cried out his name.

Each lash sent me bucking against his wicked, tireless tongue. I threaded my hands through his hair, my legs coiling over his broad shoulders as he wound me closer to release with each stroke.

But I didn't want him on his knees. He belonged on the throne with me. My mate. My equal.

I need you inside me.

His mouth clamped down, sucking lightly but not releasing me altogether.

Please.

Julian lifted his head, ink-black eyes boring into me, into my very soul, and he slowly untangled himself from me. His hands went to his leather pants as he rose, freeing himself in one swift motion.

"How will you have me?" His voice was pure midnight.

I stood on trembling legs, my sex aching for release. "With me."

He swept his cloak from his shoulders before sinking into the throne. His arms sprawled lazily over the arms, his cock jutting proudly from his undone pants. I bit my lip as I drank him in, savored the primal, brutal masculinity rolling from him.

He lifted one hand and beckoned me with his finger. "I'm at your service."

I lifted my skirt to my waist, its flames dancing harmlessly over my skin, and crawled onto his lap. Julian's hand moved between my legs, angling his cock until it nudged against my entrance, his thumb coaxing the pulse above it in slow, languid circles.

I moaned at the unholy combination, my eyes shutting to everything but the sensation as I speared myself on him.

Julian welcomed me with a low, possessive snarl and hooked an arm around my neck, drawing me closer. I smelled myself on his lips and didn't blush. Not when my scent belonged there, belonged on every inch of his body. His cock plunged deeper, as if he could fuse our beings into one. I gasped as he filled me, as I claimed what was mine, what had always been, what would always be mine.

But I needed more. I reached for his mask and it gave way, transforming back into its simple white shell. The rest of the spell lingered as I stared into his eyes, flames wreathing my body and wrapping around him. I ran my fingers down the leather scales that covered his hard chest as I rode him on the throne. My knees knocked into its arms, but I didn't care. Not with his gaze boring into mine, claiming my soul while I claimed his body.

The hand around my neck moved down, drawing my mask off. We would not hide behind them. Not as we laid ourselves bare to one another, each thrust, each surge a vow that we belonged to each other, not for life but for eternity.

I wanted all of him. The hidden parts. The dark parts. The damaged bits still healing from the past. I wanted my love, my mate, my *king*.

And so I took him.

CHAPTER FIFTY-SIX

Thea

One climax led into another, pleasure rising and cresting in relentless waves fueled by the magic clinging to our skin. The need was insatiable, as overwhelming as the days following our mating bond. I rode Julian until I was near collapse. Finally, he hauled me into his arms. I whimpered with need, clutching him until my body calmed.

I nuzzled into his neck. "I'm starting to understand what was going on in the ballroom."

He barked a laugh, kissing my sweat-slick forehead. "The masks…"

I nodded, tilting my face up to his. "I like this Rite."

"I'd say we passed it." He grinned, and the world stopped spinning. There was only him—only us—and this never-ending hunger.

"And circled back and passed it a couple more times." I pulled gently from his arms, stretching mine over my head with a yawn.

"You're tired." It wasn't a question. He scooped me up. "I'm taking you to bed."

"About damn time."

"To sleep," he added.

"Protective vampires," I grumbled under my breath, but his mouth twitched. "Should we put back on our masks? Just in case..."

Most of the party had seen my entrance earlier and knew that I was the phoenix, but I didn't want to risk drawing extra attention by being the only ones not wearing masks. Julian must have agreed because he placed me on my feet and went to retrieve them.

I smoothed my skirt into place, admiring the way his body moved in his leather armor.

"Ready?" he asked, handing me my mask. I nodded and we raised them to our faces as one. The effect was instant.

Flames erupted along my skin, the heat at my core urging me toward the darkness rippling from Julian. Only it could quench my need. His jaw tensed, a fang tugging at his full lower lip, and I knew he felt it, too.

"Now, I really have to take you to bed," he said darkly.

I had a better idea. Or a more immediately gratifying one, at least.

"Or—" A scream cut me off. Followed by more. Sheer terror shattered through the wards that isolated us from the ballroom. Vampires and familiars fled inside, and Julian shoved me behind him.

I gripped his arms, uttering a single angry protest that was swallowed by the panic surrounding us.

Sebastian rushed toward us, his mask askew, his hands fastening the button of his pants, and yelled one word: "Run."

The only other exit from the throne room led into the queens' private chambers, and whatever wards protected them from intrusion held. Creatures piled up at the door, tearing at each other, trying to break it down.

"I can unbind the wards—" My words died on my lips as a figure flew through the oak doors and slammed to the stone floor before us. The vampires closest to us froze from terror or fear of the monster's attention as the air filled with the scent of festering flesh, of rot and decay. Blood stained the feathered wings that wrapped around the massive beast. It was three times Julian's size with those wings tucked around it. I didn't want to see them splay open, didn't want it to lift its gruesome head.

"Thea," he whispered. "Get through that door."

The demon unfurled those massive wings. Black eyes peered at us, two slits flared where its nose should be, and beneath that, not a mouth but a wide round hole layered with circles of jagged, razor-sharp teeth. It lifted its head and bellowed in an unearthly howl, calling its brethren in hell. Four spindly arms hung at its side. One shot out, slicing through the air with an audible whip that ruffled my hair, and snagged the vampire next to me. Blood rushed to my head, drowning out the captive vampire's screams as the demon lifted him in one smooth motion—and bit off his head. The decapitated body hit the floor with a sickening thud.

I doubled over, covering my mouth as I gagged.

Thea…

I didn't dare speak aloud, didn't dare draw attention to us.

I have to help them.

I braced for an argument. Instead, he tipped his head just once. *Go now.*

I stayed put. Fighting through the screaming horde would only make what I needed to do harder. I stilled, closing my eyes, and imagined that door and the thick woven bands of magic that protected it. I didn't have time to will my magic to unknot the ward, so I did the only thing I could think of. The beast roared as the first note of magic sounded and my music filled the air. Not the lovely golden light that I called each day with my cello, but a clashing, chaotic symphony that ripped at the magic guarding the room, rending and tearing until the spell guarding the door fell away. The escaping creatures barreled through it.

One paused, turning his golden head toward us. Sebastian took a step in our direction, but I held up a hand, my mouth forming a single silent command, "*Go.*"

You need to go, too, Julian begged silently.

I didn't budge. *Not a chance. Ride or die.*

The demon roared, its wide sucker of a mouth widening to show an endless swirl of stumped, stained teeth. The slits above them flared, scenting the air, as if trying to decipher what creature dared to use magic in its presence.

I can kill it.

I would. I had to, but I swayed on my feet. Julian moved, catching me before I collapsed.

"The song of death," I murmured. "I just have to find it."

But his movement attracted attention, and the demon advanced on us, scraping its hoofed feet along the stone, the sound vibrating in my bones.

"There's no time." He dragged me back toward that door, angling his body between me and the approaching monster.

"We won't make it." I strained, searching for that deadly melody.

Our eyes locked, and I knew what he was planning a moment before he said, "*You* will."

He lifted me off my feet and launched into a run that blurred the world. Behind us, the plodding footsteps picked up. I writhed against Julian's hold. He couldn't make me leave him here. He planned to sacrifice himself, but I wouldn't let him.

Before we reached the exit, three vampires stepped through, blocking it, their hooded cloaks drawn to hide their faces. The one in the center yelled something in Latin in a high, female voice.

The demon stopped. Its wings lowered as it turned to her and settled like an obedient dog, and for one moment, I thought we were saved. Julian started toward the door again, determined to get me out.

The female lowered her hood to reveal a maskless face, the others following.

"Selah," I whispered, and I knew before her mouth curled into a cruel smile that the Council wasn't here to save me.

"Get out of my way," Julian snarled.

Her laugh skittered down my spine. "But I went to so much trouble summoning our friend."

I squirmed free of Julian's grasp, but he wrapped one arm around my waist, as if readying to make another run for it.

"You unleashed the monster." She didn't so much as flinch at my accusation. "It wasn't enough to get Sabine off the Council."

"Not while you draw breath, *siren*." She spat the word at me, and my mate bristled.

I've got this, I told him.

I reached inside myself for that dark song, reached inside myself to will death on her—and found nothing.

Selah laughed at me. "An unfortunate side effect of the masks. I added a rather nasty spell. It siphons your magic to show your true nature, and you wasted the last of your magic helping all those innocents escape. That's why you'll never be a queen. Those creatures were peasants, nobodies, and you chose them over your own survival."

Footsteps sounded behind us. I didn't dare turn from Selah to see if it was help or more Council members coming to end us.

"That choice is what makes her a queen." Death coated Julian's voice.

Then Sabine appeared at our side, not a hair out of place, her face as unimpressed as ever, and a sword in her hand. "Selah." She made the name sound like a curse. "I suspected you were the one behind the attempt on my daughter's life."

"Daughter?" Selah laughed as she repeated the word. "I told the others that you sympathized with her."

Wait, does she mean me?

I think she does.

I swept the rest of the room while they argued and nearly collapsed with relief as I became aware of the others: Lysander snaking his way toward us, along the wall, Aurelia at his back; Mariana and Zina whispering frantically; Jacqueline urging Camila back out the door. Of the masked vampire that blocked their path.

Sebastian had gone for help. The rest of our family would arrive soon. Even a death-God was no match for the Rousseauxs.

Sabine pivoted, drawing my attention to her as she turned that detached look on the demon. "Is that the creature that's been terrorizing the poor Switches? The one the Mordicum fears?" She shrugged. "It isn't much."

"Only you could be unimpressed by a ten-thousand-year-old death-God, Sabine." Selah scoffed. "Perhaps I'll let it eat you next."

Sabine's head tilted to her, a bemused smile turning up her lips. "Oh, I think *not*."

"You think you can stand against it?" Selah swept her hand toward her monster. "Be my guest."

Sabine didn't move. "That's always been your problem. You think too highly of yourself, of your *pure blood*. I know exactly what I'm capable of. *I* can't stop it, but it can't stand against the power of three queens—not in their throne room."

She slashed a look of warning at Julian, then nodded to me.

I took a step toward the demon, and his grip slackened and fell away. Fear washed through me. Not mine. *Julian's*. My whole being screamed at me to turn to him, reassure him, but I knew it wouldn't matter. Not until the beast was gone. My sister-queens moved closer. Selah's mouth opened, managing a single Latin word before her voice cut off. She gripped her throat, wild eyes turning on every soul in the room, looking for who had magically muted her.

I didn't care whose magic it was. It had been enough to stop her unleashing the death-God.

"Call to the magic," she told us. "It will send this thing back to hell."

The death-God rose to its feet as we approached, bellowing, its blood-soaked wings flapping as if it might dare escape. But it didn't move—couldn't move thanks to Selah's command. Power wound through the air with a mighty wind that cut off its protests, beat against it, forcing its wings down. The beast began to fight, its instinct for survival overcoming its leash. I focused my magic around it, plucking at the notes of the world to construct a cage of blinding light around it. A rush of water rose from the stones.

Selah ran toward us, but Sabine caught her.

"Watch," Sabine hissed to the mute traitor.

I blocked them out, concentrating on the cage I'd built.

The air howled as our magic gathered and combined, and

it battered into each of us. I fought to stay on my feet, fought to keep my eyes on the death-God, even as exhaustion threatened to overcome me. Mariana reached for my hand, Zina taking her other, and magic flowed between us like a conduit.

Next to me, Mariana chanted an incantation, and a pit yawned open at the demon's hooves and sucked its legs into the abyss. Four spindly arms shot forward, grappling for purchase and finding none. Its howl shattered through the room as hell reclaimed it. The beast's arms scrambled against the stone, its great wings flapping, as the pit dragged it down. But it was no use. With one final bellow of rage, the Underworld swallowed it.

The room instantly calmed, our magic fading. I stumbled a step, and Julian was instantly at my side, his breath ragged as he pressed a kiss to my forehead.

"What are we going to do about them?" I managed a single nod toward Selah and her cronies.

"Leave that to me." Sabine faced Selah and lifted her weapon. "Any last words?"

A choked protest spilled from Selah's mouth, her voice returned but incoherent. I searched for a reason to put a stop to this, but I didn't know if I lacked the energy or the mercy. Maybe I didn't care.

No one intervened.

"It appears we're all in agreement." Sabine's sword swung, and Selah's head toppled to the floor. My mother flicked the blood from her blade and looked to the two male Council members, frozen in open-mouthed shock.

"Tell the Council that if they have a complaint about my family, they should direct it toward me." She pointed the sword at them. "Now, do *you* have a complaint?"

They trembled, backing away, shaking their heads.

She pursed her lips. "Get out of my sight. That's one problem down." Her face remained grim as she looked to the door—and the male filling it. "Now, what are we going to do about you, *Willem*?"

Julian aimed toward him, breaking into a sprint that spelled violence, and stopped two steps before Willem.

"You," Julian seethed. "I've waited for this day."

Willem pulled off his mask and tossed it to the ground, then wagged a single finger. "What are you waiting for?"

Julian lunged and connected with a hard wall of air. His head snapped back as his body arched off the ground. Willem flicked his wrist once, and I screamed.

CHAPTER FIFTY-SEVEN

Julian

Magic flung me against the stone, knocking the air from my lungs. I rolled over, coughing, to discover what felt like a few broken ribs, a broken ankle, and nothing more—no permanent damage done to anything but my pride. I lifted my head, pushing my bruised body up with my palms as Willem strode into the throne room, smirking down at me. "Don't get up."

"Fuck you," I snarled. I would rip him apart with my bare hands, tear his head—and that smug face—from his neck.

His eyes narrowed. "As I'm the only creature in this room with undrained magic, I would be more respectful," he said, "especially since you're bedding my daughter."

"I'm not your daughter," Thea said in a lofty voice. Sweat glinted on her brow, her breathing still uneven from defeating the demon, but she didn't back down from Willem. "And I have enough magic left to kill you."

Good girl.

Her gaze flicked to me. *I'm making this up as I go.*

I could have lived without knowing that. It had been hard enough to watch her drain herself to defeat the death-God. She needed to rest, not to face her bastard father.

"Were you part of this? Part of Selah's plan?" Sabine asked.

His eyebrows lifted. "Selah? The Council? Their power is *nothing*. Why do you think they cursed magic?"

My mother paused to digest this. We all did. "The Council?"

"Does it sting to realize they manipulated you? All of these years playing their games and you didn't even know?"

She glared at him. "Do you just like to hear yourself talk? Is that why you're here?"

"Truth hurts," he taunted. "I came for what's mine."

Blood roared, pounding in my veins as he looked at Thea. She stiffened but didn't back down, didn't drop her regal chin. Willem chuckled and turned away from her toward...Camila.

Jacqueline moved to shield her, and I seized the opportunity to crawl to Thea's feet. She dropped beside me, her eyes searching my injuries, her hands soothing over the already-healing bruises, the bones in my leg beginning to mend.

I'm fine.

Still, concern lined her face as she helped me to my feet.

Willem ignored us. Lifting his hand, he beckoned my sister. "Wife."

"I'm not your wife," Camila said through gritted teeth, but it wasn't hatred simmering in her words. Her body trembled, and I realized with horror that it was restraint. Jacqueline grabbed her arm, as if she realized it, too.

"I don't remember agreeing to a divorce." He tutted. "You can fight it all you want, but ask your brother what happens when you ignore your tether."

"What?" Thea gasped.

Even my mother's face blanched, her sword wobbling in her grip.

Willem threw her a look. "I'd put that down if you want your daughter to walk out of here alive."

"I'm not tethered," Camila said as beads of sweat poured over her forehead. Jacqueline wrapped her arms around her, physically restraining her against that tethering urge. Camila tried to turn into it, struggling to raise her hand to touch Jacqueline's face. "I died…"

"And why would that matter? You came back to life," he pointed out.

"But that's not…" My mother spun to me. "Your tether. It broke upon your deaths?"

Thea's chest heaved, her eyes apologetic as she looked at me. "I thought so, but…"

In London? It wasn't just the mating bond?

She nodded, apology written in her eyes. *Diana said a tether is linked to the soul. I never considered…*

"Let me be clear, you lay one hand on any of my children, and I will make you suffer in ways the world has never seen," Sabine snarled.

His shoulders shook with suppressed laughter as he circled the room. "I don't have to lay a finger on Camila. One command and she'll do anything I say. Gut herself. Jump from the roof. Kill that lovely companion who clings to her." He paused and regarded Jacqueline. "Is she the one…the one that kept you from ever giving in and truly loving me despite my orders?"

"Why would I have ever loved you?" Camila snarled.

"*Come. Here.*" The demand roared from his lips, and Camila lurched against Jacqueline's hold. When my best friend didn't release her, Camila screamed in agony.

"Let her go," I said to Jacqueline, the words little more than a hoarse whisper, and I took a step, burying a wince at the splintering pain in my healing ankle. "You can't fight it. If you do…"

I had not forgotten the price of fighting a tether. Resisting was as dangerous as complying. *If Willem thinks he's leaving here with her…*

Thea's hand found mine, our fingers twining tightly together. *We have to do something.*

My mate was right, but we had to wait for the right moment. Jacqueline sobbed as she released Camila, and Mariana moved swiftly to Jacqueline's side, murmuring quiet words in her ears.

Camila fought every step of the way, and when she reached him, she hurled herself at his feet. He bent and lifted her chin with his index finger. "If I wanted to kill you, I could have done that decades ago. Do you think the Mordicum found you? Saved you? I let you go because you were useless to me."

Hatred sparked in Camila's eyes. "I could say the same."

"So you are behind the Mordicum." Our mother shook her head, studying the blade of her sword like she was deciding on whether to run him through or take his head as well.

"I'm a fan of their work," he corrected her. "A patron, of sorts."

"But they aren't pureblooded," I said. "You wouldn't even marry a familiar."

"I never said I accepted them, but at least they act like vampires." He spat the word at me, glancing at Thea. "And as your mate's existence proves, I've become more open-minded. But that is neither here nor there. I only want one thing, and then we can go our separate ways."

I angled my body in front of Thea.

"I'm not here for your mate, especially now that you've…" He wrinkled his nose. "I can see that my experiment failed. She remains a siren. Keep her and your child."

I didn't shift from my protective stance.

"Stand up," he ordered my twin. She bellowed with rage as she rose. Willem gripped her chin, bringing his face a breath from hers. "Since Thea turned out to be a disappointment, I'm here for our pureblood children. Where are they? Where are Hadrian and Laurel?"

Camila went utterly still, save for the muscle that tightened in her jaw. It beat against his hold as she lied, "They died in your fire."

"That's not what you told our friends in the Mordicum." He tutted at her. "Tell me the truth."

"I don't know."

Not a lie, but the truth. Thea's face whipped up to mine. *Your mother was right. She knew not to tell Camila.*

It's better if you don't admit that to her.

"Someone knows." His hand slid from her face and yanked her body against him, bringing his blade to her throat. "Sabine? Julian?"

Camila's wide eyes locked with mine, and she mouthed a single word.

Don't.

My gaze slid to my mother's. Willem caught the movement.

"Perhaps a little more motivation," he seethed. "Thea, come here."

Ice filtered into my blood. I stepped in front of my mate. He would have to go through me.

Willem narrowed his gaze at me. "I'm her sire. She answers to *me.*"

Thea placed a hand on my shoulder, but I refused to move. I would stop her. He'd used their shared blood to abduct her before. I wouldn't let him within an inch of her.

"Come to me," he demanded, but she didn't try to move around me.

"I answer to no man," she said in a cool, clear voice.

Surprise lit his eyes. He hadn't expected her refusal. "I'm sure your mate appreciates that."

"I do, actually. I've never gotten off on controlling the weak." I shrugged. "Unlike some."

Golden magic filled my chest, Thea's magic warming with approval, even as she remained placid at my side.

His face twisted with rage. "Where are my children?" He pressed the blade harder into Camila's throat, drawing blood. "One of you knows."

When no one answered, his lips lowered to Camila's ear. "Even now, they won't choose you. Help you. You've always been unwanted. You can never count on anyone."

I barely felt Thea shift next to me.

Get ready.

I didn't dare look at her, didn't dare give away our secret language. *Ready for what?*

She didn't answer me.

Thea?

Darting a step forward, Thea blurted out, "I can take you to them. Just don't hurt her."

What are you doing? I kept my face trained on Willem. I didn't trust myself to move, to betray her lie, but was I supposed to sit here while my mate lured him away?

Willem pursed his lips. "My sources say she hasn't been very nice to you. Are you sure you don't want me to kill her before we go? You can thank me later."

"And you can go to hell!"

It happened so quickly that I didn't even see the movement. A torrent of wind tore through the room, battering against us, its center aimed at Willem. I fought against it, trying to reach Thea—to shield her. But the power...was coming from her.

Lightning lashed as Zina moved toward the center of the room. The source... We were near the source, and even with their magic depleted, they could always draw from it. Maybe even draw from one another's powers.

Willem stumbled, and my mother closed on him with two steps, sweeping her blade across his shoulder. He yowled, dropping his blade, and Camila shot into Jacqueline's arms. He clutched his bloody wound as the wind died to a soft whistle. "You'll pay for that."

"You're outmatched." Thea panted, her eyes wild, satisfaction pulling her lips back to bare her fangs.

"And you're drained," he crooned. "I hope it was worth it, because I won't rest until—" His words cut off. Willem grabbed for his throat, his lips turning blue as water gurgled from him.

"I'm not," Mariana said, stepping forward, one hand outstretched as she called forth her own power. She walked calmly to him and picked up his fallen sword. Magic glimmered around her, its brilliance near blinding, and she lifted it and took his head. Willem's body swayed before toppling before her, his head rolling to his side. "I hope you don't mind."

Thea took a single step...and collapsed. I caught her in my

arms, her body sagging boneless in my arms. Zina followed. Only Mariana remained on her feet, quickly racing toward her sister, dropping to her side.

I sank to the stone floor, gathering my mate in my arms. "Thea," I whispered. Her heartbeat was faint, but I heard it and the baby's.

"We used too much power, but they'll recover." Mariana closed her eyes, sighing with gratitude, then peeked out at us. "Unlike that one."

Footsteps raced into the room, my father and brothers joining us along with a dozen court guards.

"What the hell happened—" My father's voice cut off as he spotted Willem's body. "He's dead."

"Yes," Camila choked out, burying her head in Jacqueline's shoulder. "I'm free, free..." Her words shook my family from their shock, and they turned, questions pouring from them until their gazes fell on the queen in my arms.

"Gods," Lysander swore as Aurelia rushed toward us.

"She's unconscious, but she'll be all right." I wanted to believe that—chose to believe that.

"Let me help," Aurelia offered.

But I wouldn't let Thea go. "I can do it."

My ankle groaned as I pushed to my feet, but I ignored it. Holding Thea close to my chest, I surveyed the room. Jacqueline held Camila, running soothing, loving strokes down her face as she sobbed. Both of my parents hovered nearby, looking slightly taken aback by what was now obvious as my best friend and my twin held each other. Thoren ordered my brothers to check the perimeter. One attack in a night was bad luck. Two... I nodded my thanks to him, exhaustion seeping into my bones. All around us, bodies littered the floor, the vampires the demon had killed along with Selah and Willem. Blood pooled, its copper tang seeping in the air.

This was a mess. There would be fallout from the Council, and while the demon had been handled, the Mordicum still posed a threat, if we believed Willem's confession.

"We'll handle it," Mariana assured me from where she tended

Zina, soft eyes urging me to relax. "Thea needs to rest. Stay with her. It will help."

I nodded, carrying my mate away from the horror she had faced, wondering if mine was only beginning.

CHAPTER FIFTY-EIGHT

Thea

I woke in my bed, limbs tight and aching. My bedroom was dark, the curtains closed to seal out whether the sun or moon shimmered over the lagoon outside. Julian slept in a chair beside me. His leather clothing was gone, his muscled chest and the serpentine mark he bore back on display. I'd never realized how peaceful he looked when he slept. The permanent worry line between his eyes was relaxed. His carved, sensual lips parted as he breathed softly. There was a dark dusting of stubble on his chin.

I didn't wish to wake him, but his eyes opened anyway, as if he felt the bond between us awakening. He rubbed a palm over his jaw up to his bleary eyes, which focused on me slowly, and then snapped open.

"You're awake." The relief in his voice was palpable.

I bit my lip to keep from frowning. I zeroed in on that stubble—days' worth. Did I want to know how long I'd been out?

He offered a small nod, as if to confirm my fears.

Bolting up in bed, my hand flew to my stomach. I was no longer in my fiery Rite dress. I wore a buttery-soft nightgown, its touch soothing against my palm. Later, I'd thank him for changing me out of my party clothes.

"As far as I can tell, the baby's fine. His heartbeat is strong," he said swiftly at the fear on my face. He rose, picking up a glass of water, and handed it to me.

I loosed a sigh and smiled. I took a few sips, quenching my parched mouth. "*His*?"

"Or hers." He shrugged, as if to say he didn't mind either way. The important thing was the heartbeat itself. Julian took the empty glass. "Another?"

I shook my head. Julian deposited it on the nightstand and sat next to me, the mattress shifting under his weight. He took my hand, his touch soothing some last ragged remnant, and I relaxed against the headboard.

"What happened?" I asked him. My memories jarred through me, coming in flashes, perhaps from the adrenaline or maybe fragmented from calling on so much magic.

"The three of you killed him." He confirmed the most important question. "But it drained you. Zina as well. You were the first to wake up. You've been asleep for nearly a week."

I blinked as this processed. "A *week*? But the wedding…"

"Is tomorrow. Or it's supposed to be." His smile was strained as his blue eyes took me apart, as if he couldn't quite believe I was real. "All that really matters is how you're feeling. The wedding can wait." A pause. "How *are* you feeling?"

Physically, I felt fine. A little sore from the days I'd spent in bed. I tapped deeper and found my magic there, at its center, the kernel of Julian's dark power. And if he said the baby was fine…I should be, too. How I felt emotionally was a different story. My soul felt wrung out, taken from my body and twisted like a wet rag.

A squeeze of my hand sent my attention to Julian, who wore a look of strained patience.

"It's strange. I'm not sorry that my father is dead." I didn't quite know how to explain it. "But something about it still feels…wrong." I shook my head, feeling like the innocent, stupid mortal Julian had first met. "I should be happy. He was a monster."

"He was," Julian said darkly, brushing his thumb over the

back of my hand in soothing circles, "but that doesn't mean it's not complicated. And it doesn't make you stupid if you don't celebrate his death. You don't have to rationalize your feelings. You just have to feel them."

He was right, but the weight on my chest—that uneasy, queasy feeling—didn't lift. I turned my attention to other issues. "And the Council?"

They couldn't be happy that Selah was dead.

"They're not, but they're acting like they're horrified." His mouth twisted. "Admitting one of them actively slaughtered our kind hasn't gone over well. The Council is dealing with the fallout."

"At least they're preoccupied."

He snorted. It was a *small* mercy.

I wanted to linger here with him forever, never wanted to release his hand, but my body had other ideas. "I need the bathroom," I said apologetically.

He cursed under his breath. "I should have seen to that."

"I can see to it myself," I promised him as I rose.

"Are you hungry?" he asked. My stomach answered him, and he chuckled. "That's a stupid question. I'll get you something to eat."

Before he could turn to leave, I grabbed his hand. "Julian, about the wedding—"

"It can wait," he cut me off, something unreadable occupying his eyes for a moment before it left.

I shook my head. "I don't want to wait."

A grin tugged at his mouth, but he didn't give into it. "There's someone you should talk to first."

"Someone?" I lifted my brows.

"Aurelia tracked down your mother. She said you asked her to." His voice was quiet, tentative, and my heart clenched. Then it began to pound. "Maybe you should talk to her before you make any decisions."

"She's here?" My mouth went dry.

He nodded. "I'll find her and get you some food."

Before I could tell him that nothing would change my mind

about him, about marrying him, he disappeared into the adjoining sitting room.

As I cleaned up and brushed my teeth, there was a pit in my stomach that had nothing to do with morning sickness. The last time I'd seen my mother, everything was different between us. With her glamour lifted, and along with it the lies and the secrets she'd kept from me, I had wanted explanations. I hadn't been ready to forgive her. She hadn't even asked me for forgiveness. Maybe that was why, even now, I wasn't sure that I *could* forgive her. But even if I was still angry, I couldn't help seeing things in an entirely different perspective.

Lifting my nightgown, I studied myself in the mirror. There was still no sign of my pregnancy. I turned, checking every angle. But even if I couldn't see it and had yet to hear or feel it myself, I knew the baby was there from the love I felt. And maybe it was that love—that unconditional, unbreakable love I felt—that helped me understand why my mother had made all those terrible choices. Understanding didn't forgive it. It only helped me believe she'd acted out of love.

I emerged from the bedroom and froze. My mother stood near the bed, a tray of food in her hands. Our eyes met, tension like a stretched band between us. One wrong move and it would snap. She was as beautiful as the day we met in *Cannaregio*. Her copper hair was knotted in a bun at the nape of her neck, accentuating the sharp curve of her cheekbones and setting off her green eyes.

The same color as my own. Would the baby have those eyes?

"I'd ask if you wanted to take this into the other room—to an actual table—but *your mate* insists you get back in bed," she called over her shoulder, and I knew Julian remained there in case this meeting went poorly.

"He's a worrywart," I said loud enough for him to hear as I climbed into bed, bracing several pillows behind my back.

I'll leave you two. Let me know...

Love swelled in my heart, and I sent back the promise that I would. I knew how much it cost him to leave me here. Not because she was here—we both knew my mother would never harm me—but because his fear had yet to calm after recent events. And despite all of that, he knew that I needed this moment with my mother. Alone.

She carried the tray over and placed it next to me on the bed, on it a huge plate of pasta smothered in rich *Bolognese*. Its rich tomato-garlic scent wafted tendrils of escaping steam to my nose, and I groaned, stomach roaring.

"Julian asked what you would like." Emotion laced her words.

"My favorite." We shared a brief, shy smile.

"I'm glad. I…" She cleared her throat.

I reached for her hand, ignoring the jolt of magic that passed between us. "Not everything has changed. I'm still me."

She studied me for a second, looking for proof, but what she said was, "You're pregnant."

I stilled, the racing of my heart drowning out my hunger, drowning out everything. "Can you sense it?"

"Julian told me." Each word careful, delicate, like she was waiting for confirmation from my own lips. It must have been written on my face along with something else, because she added, "He didn't want it to be a surprise…for me. I think he wanted to give me time to adjust to the news, so I didn't upset you."

That was possibly sweet, but I'd still be having words with him later. "He should have let me tell you."

She swallowed. "So it's true."

"Yes." I forced myself to reach for my fork. I didn't look at her as I spooled pasta onto it. But my heart continued to pound, my hand shaking as I brought the first bite to my mouth.

She'd made me choose when she found out about Julian, disappeared from my life, and emerged as someone else entirely. As much as I wanted to believe the woman I'd known was still in there somewhere, I didn't dare hope. Because if it came to it again—if she disapproved of my child like she had of my mate—I didn't think I could forgive that.

Slowly, she stood. I swallowed my food, unsure what to say, what to do, if she left the room, but then she leaned over and kissed my forehead. "No wonder you look exhausted. The first few weeks are the hardest." She brushed back my hair, nodding to the food. "Eat as much as you can. If your pregnancy is anything like mine, you won't keep much of it down."

I stared up at her, at the concern and quiet joy and love shining down at me, and heat prickled my eyes. It turned to tears, and suddenly, I was telling her everything. The parts I had left out before and the things that had happened since. At some point, she'd taken a seat again. Not in the chair, but next to me, the tray shoved out of the way so she could run soothing hands over my shoulder, down my back.

When I ran out of words, her arm wrapped around my shoulder and she tucked me against her. She drew a shuddering breath. "I'm sorry I wasn't there."

I sniffed, swiping at my eyes. "I needed you."

She held me tighter. "I had to make choices, Thea. Not all of them were the right ones." She peered down at me. "It killed me to let you go, to let you enter this world, to hope you were ready to face your destiny."

"You told me to choose." I couldn't hide the accusation hiding there or the pain it still caused me.

Her eyes closed, but she nodded. "Because I knew you would make the *right* choice."

"But…I chose Julian."

"Exactly," she murmured. "You have never made decisions out of fear, only love. I knew then that he was worth fighting for—even if I'm not thrilled to have a vampire for a son-in-law."

"About that…" I screwed up my courage. "I know the wedding is going to be full of vampires, and I understand if you don't feel safe, but I'd like you to be there."

Tears lined her eyes. "You couldn't keep me away, and I'll be fine. I'm surrounded by vampires now."

That was a good point.

"It's tomorrow," I warned her, screwing up my face with what I hope said, *Surprise!*

She laughed. "I'll be ready. Are you?"

It was a question I didn't have to ask myself. My smile answered for me, toppling when it hit me that I'd had little to no say in the plans. "Yes, although I have no idea what I'm wearing," I told her with a laugh. "Hopefully Julian's best friend picked the dress and not his mother."

Mom pushed my tray back toward me. "Eat before it gets cold, and you can tell me all about them."

Maybe it was the magic of my quarters, but the pasta was still piping hot. I ate until I was full, laughing with my mother until my heart was as well.

It was late when we heard a tentative knock at the door. I knew who was on the other side, knew it like I knew my own soul, but it still amazed me. *He* still amazed me.

My mother smiled at me, at that look of wonder on my face. "I'll see you tomorrow."

I grabbed her hand. "Would you walk me down the aisle tomorrow?"

Her throat slid as she nodded. She squeezed my hand once and released it, crossing to open the door for Julian.

He filled the doorframe, hands braced on either side, fully clothed now but sexy as hell. "Am I interrupting?"

Despite our conversation, my mother shrank back a step. I couldn't blame the reaction. Not with the dark energy that radiated from Julian, not with his divine, lethal beauty.

She collected herself. "I was just leaving."

He moved to the side to allow her to pass.

She paused and looked at me. "I can help you get ready tomorrow, if you like?"

I didn't trust myself to speak, so I merely nodded.

"I'll show you out," Julian offered, if a bit stiffly.

I pushed out of bed, carrying the food tray into the living area. I'd just returned to the bedroom when Julian strode in behind me.

He stopped, his lips drooping into a frown. "You're out of bed."

"I'm fine." I resisted the urge to roll my eyes.

"It's not that." He aimed for me, hooking an arm around my waist and drawing me into his hard, broad chest. "I've just been looking forward to getting into bed with you."

"Oh." I leaned into him, filling my lungs with his scent—cloves and spices drifting in a midnight garden. "I've been in bed all day."

He tipped my face up with his finger. "I'm open to the chair, the desk, the wall—any flat surface, really."

"So open-minded," I teased, but my ribbing came out breathless, pulsing with the need I felt.

Julian didn't move. "Your mother is coming to the wedding."

Not exactly a question, but I nodded. "Is that a problem?"

"No." His forehead wrinkled. "Of course not. It's just a good sign."

"It is." A smile burst onto my face, one only for him, for us, for our future. "I told her everything. About the baby. About the island. My magic. I think we're going to be okay."

His shoulders sagged under whatever weight he'd been carrying. "Thank the Gods." He winked at me. "I need someone else I can trust to worry about you two as much as I do."

I couldn't understand it. It seemed impossible that I could fall more in love with him, but every moment, every second, every breath proved me wrong.

His throat bobbed, eyes darkening. "It's the same for me, you know."

"I can't wait to marry you." The words slipped from me, and his smile chased even the shadows from his eyes. "Technically, I think you're not supposed to see me the night before the wedding."

As if to prove how little he cared about that tradition, he scooped me off my feet. His mouth found mine, the kiss slow and languid, a reminder that we had eternity before us. Julian laid me on the bed, tucking a pillow under my head before he stripped his clothes off.

"I'm not worried about bad luck." He climbed onto the bed, urging my legs apart, then kneeling between them. His hands rucked my silk nightgown to my hips. Gripping my thighs as he moved closer, he lifted me until he was seated at my entrance. "The wedding is a chance to show you off." He pushed in an inch, and my fingers twisted in the sheets. "All that I am belongs to you." Another inch and I moaned. "I have for a very long time."

On the final word, he sheathed himself in me entirely, and I cried out his name. My nipples pebbled, the silk rasping against them. My skin tightened and grew feverish. Every inch of me came alive and centered on where he filled me. But despite the need that wrapped around both of us, he moved slowly, each thrust unhurried. My body answered his rhythm, my legs coiling around his waist, his fingers digging into the flesh of my hips.

He belonged to me, this God kneeling between my legs. And I belonged to him in ways that I was only beginning to discover.

There would be time later to allow that desperate need to claim possess us, but for now, I watched him, savored the masculine assurance on his face as he worked me toward an unhurried climax.

"What about your name?" I breathed, my eyes rolling a little as he hit a spot so deep inside me I nearly fell apart.

He stilled for a moment, and I rolled my hips, urging him to continue. His gaze heated, burning with an emotion I felt ignite in my chest. "*My* name? You want to take my name?"

I resisted the urge to turn into the pillow, to bite down on it to hold in my moans. "Yes," I managed. "I belong to you, too."

Love shattered through me, his dark magic rustling awake. "It will be a scandal."

"Even better." I flashed him a grin, the most I could manage with him so deep inside me, so deep that I felt him in my soul.

The blue of his eyes flared, one bright flash, before they settled into midnight. "Thea Rousseaux."

"Yes." I gasped, reaching for him. Julian shifted his weight, hands twining with mine as he pinned them beside our heads. "*Our* family name."

His eyes burned into mine as he processed what I meant. That the life we were building wouldn't be alone. That I'd chosen not only him but his family. That his duty was my own. That it was my privilege to share his bed, his life, his name.

Even if I would never get enough of stolen moments like this where we belonged to only each other.

CHAPTER FIFTY-NINE

Julian

"Last chance to run." Sebastian knocked into me. Turning his back to the guests, he swiped a flask from his breast pocket.

I rolled my eyes but took a swig before passing it to Lysander. "Why would I run?"

Lysander laughed and clapped a hand on my shoulder. "You're in so much trouble."

It was pointless trying to explain it to him. He wouldn't understand unless he was the one standing in my place. Maybe someday he would. My throat tightened, and I realized, looking at my brothers, that I hoped they all would—that they would all find the joy I'd found in my mate's arms. As for getting married, there was only one concern preoccupying me.

"What is taking so long?" I grumbled. I didn't want to run. I wanted to be married.

"Jacqueline's getting her ready. That will take a while—and you know there will be a big entrance." Sebastian pointed at the room around us for emphasis, the dreamlike decor proof that, thanks to my best friend and my mother, this wedding would be well-remembered for centuries to come.

The courtyard had been transformed into a fairytale. The red roses that climbed the walls were now white, their leaves and vines dusted silver. Their powdery scent floated on the air, and faint lights sparkled between the flowers, an enchantment of some type that looked a bit like fireflies dancing. Chairs lined the space in neat lines, frosted ivy and candles draped at every aisle seat, and down the center, an ivory carpet blanketed with pure, white petals.

"It's over the top," Sebastian said, leaning against the floral arch, dripping with more roses and lush peonies in full bloom that rose over our heads. His gloved fingers toyed with some of the frosted ivy twined through it with a sigh.

"I dare you to tell Jacqueline that," I said to him.

Sebastian held up his hands. "I don't have a death wish."

"I don't know. It's pretty hard to rile her up at the moment," Lysander said meaningfully. "Apparently, mating puts you in a very good mood."

Sebastian snorted, hitching his thumb at me. "He tried to take off my head over it once."

"I hadn't actually sealed the mating bond yet," I reminded him. "I was in a great mood after I did."

His look told me he had doubts.

But it was hard to doubt the glow that Jacqueline and Camila had worn when I saw them last night while Thea spoke with her mother. It had been the first I'd seen them since the attack, having refused to leave Thea's side until she woke. Their shared scent had been a momentary shock but a good one. My sister and best friend were spoken for now...

"I need to find mates for all of you," I threatened, shoving my hands into my pockets.

Sebastian's laugh earned him the attention of every nearby guest, but Lysander barely managed a smile.

Time for a new subject.

"Hadrian and Laurel look uncomfortable." Lysander nodded to where our niece and nephew sat in the front row. Celia hovered nearby, tasked with monitoring them.

"I think they're handling it pretty fucking well," I muttered.

That had been the second surprise of last night. My mother had kept her word, sending for Camila's children after Willem's death. According to my twin, Sabine had been vague on exactly where she'd been keeping them safe, saying they'd been at a very private academy, sent there by their parents until they hit maturity. I had no idea what private school could handle adolescent vampires, but no one wanted to question Sabine's generosity.

In return, my sister had graciously announced Sabine could be the family matriarch again.

"Looks like it's showtime," Lysander said as the priest made his way toward us.

There had been some debate as to whether a queen or the clergy should preside over the ceremony, but with Zina still unconscious, Mariana had opted to stay with her. I doubted Thea would mind.

"I'm told we're ready to begin." The priest tipped his head in greeting to us. "Will your other brothers stand with you?"

My eyes scanned the crowd past his shoulders until they landed on Benedict and Thoren. "They're serving as ushers."

Not entirely a lie. They were helping guests to their seats, but having them stationed toward the back for the ceremony seemed a smart decision. I'd managed to convince my mother to keep the guest list slightly more intimate than she would have liked, but we weren't taking any chances. With Willem and Selah gone, an attack seemed unlikely. Though one of the queens was out of commission, which left the court vulnerable.

The priest moved to stand behind us as the string quartet began to play. Guests looked at each other with slight confusion as the melody became apparent.

"Interesting choice," Lysander muttered.

I smiled, knowing instantly that Thea had chosen the piece. She'd been playing it the first time we saw each other, but even then, *Death and the Maiden* fit. When my parents appeared at the end of the aisle, the music shifted to a more traditional choice. The crowd murmured as they made their way to their seats. They always had that effect on people. My father in his tuxedo with his classic Roman looks, my mother as beautiful as the young priestess she'd been thousands of years ago. She wore black, which I tried not to take as a statement on her feelings regarding my marriage, but her gown wasn't cut to intimidate. Instead, its elegantly draped silhouette was understated.

They smiled at me as they took their seats on my side of the aisle, Dad winking at me.

Camila followed, smirking at me. Thea requesting her as a bridesmaid was a surprise, but I was pleased. She carried a bouquet of white peonies, her blush-colored gown accentuating the contrast of her dark hair and pale skin. Guests gasped as she passed, the glow she wore unmistakable.

Her mate beamed as she came down the aisle, looking utterly smug. Whether because she was basking in her new mating bond or finally marrying me off, I didn't know. But her smile when she reached me held the answer.

"About damn time," she muttered as she moved to her place as Thea's maid of honor.

"I could say the same," I shot back under my breath.

The processional music faded into the bridal march and the guests stood. I stopped breathing at the first glimpse of her.

Thea stepped to the end of the aisle, a simple spray of lilies of the valley clasped in her bare hands, her mother at her side. A hush fell over the crowd. Gold combs held her hair behind her ears, and it curled down her back in a sheet of fire. She wore no veil, but a delicate gold crown rose into a crescent moon dotted with moonstone. Her gown curved over the swell of her breasts and swept off her shoulders into airy chiffon that wafted over her slender arms to the elbow where it draped into lacy bell sleeves. The bodice nipped her waist, embroidered with shimmering silver thread.

She existed outside of time, each step a passing century, as she made her way through my lifetimes toward our shared eternity.

I only tore my eyes from her to look at her mother. Kelly stared for a moment, a million demands in her green eyes, and I nodded a silent vow to meet them all—to love her daughter, cherish her, place her above myself. Not a duty, but an honor. She returned the gesture and turned to kiss Thea's cheek.

Then my mate was by my side. The priest spoke, and we turned automatically to face each other as the ceremony began. I was only dimly aware of what was being said, too absorbed in her.

You are so beautiful.

She flushed, the color creeping down her neck, her décolletage, and drawing attention to the pearly scars that marred her skin.

I swallowed, the sight of my marks on her nearly my undoing. *You didn't cover your scars.*

Your mother suggested we glamour them, and I suggested she fuck off. She lifted one brow, her eyes glittering.

I bit back a smile.

What about our other scandal? Did you tell the priest?

I nodded once.

Our vows were simple. We'd opted for the traditional ones, leaving out the "to obey" bit per both our preferences. When she slid the ring on my finger and mine on hers, I realized I'd been wrong. The wedding hadn't been about showing her off. It had been about that one simple act, the promise of our love given shape. I was never taking mine off.

Ready? Her lips twitched as the priest began his final proclamation. *You're such a rebel.*

"I now present to you Julian and Thea Rousseaux. You may kiss the bride."

The collective gasp of the crowd made her grin. Behind us, Sebastian twisted his laugh at our boldness into a coughing fit. I didn't bother looking to see everyone else's reaction.

I only had eyes for my wife.

One step brought us together, and she was in my arms. *Mine*, my lips promised. *Yours*, hers answered. The world faded away, giving us one perfect moment.

When I finally pulled away, applause erupted around us, but I only saw Thea and her shining eyes, saw the love in them.

"For eternity," I murmured against her lips.

She brushed her mouth to mine. "Longer."

CHAPTER SIXTY

Thea

As soon as the ceremony was over and we'd received what felt like endless well-wishes, the reception began. Since most of the guests were vampires, we'd skipped a formal dinner, opting for a large spread of dishes and drinks. There were silver trays filled with imported cheeses, earthy from the caves where they were aged, and meats expertly cured in Prague and delivered this morning. Nestled between them were bowls of fruit so ripe their scent called across the room. And there was an astonishing variety of desserts—chocolate truffles, cream tarts, delicate *Viennoiserie* dusted with sugar and strawberries, petite cakes cloaked in pastel frosting, and, at the center, a towering wedding cake, piped with delicate sugar blossoms. Servers passed glasses of champagne mixed with what I suspected was blood.

But it was the music—an eight-piece orchestra—that had beckoned me onto the dance floor and into my husband's arms. Guests mingled, pausing to murmur more congratulations, but Julian hadn't let go of me for an hour. I knew this because two of his brothers, his father, and Jacqueline had all grumbled at him for hogging the bride. I nuzzled against his firm chest, completely content to let him keep doing just that.

"You might have to give me up eventually," I warned him when I saw Sabine's narrowed eyes on us. "I think your mother wants a dance."

"It's our wedding."

I tipped my face up to drink in his. "And she's been waiting almost a thousand years for it."

"You make a good point. Why do you have to do that?" He sighed and spun us away from the dance floor.

Sabine didn't smile as we approached. She was standing with Camila and two vampires I didn't recognize, tension stringing between them.

"Finally going to acknowledge the rest of the world," Camila teased.

I blinked. I'd never seen her in a good mood. *She's happy.*

Mating does that to you.

I still can't believe it.

But the joy written across her face couldn't be denied.

"I came to ask our mother for a dance." He forced a smile, and I resisted the urge to elbow him.

"Don't look so thrilled." Sabine offered her hand, clad in an elegant silk glove that continued to her elbow.

He shot me a suffering look as he swept her onto the dance floor.

I was about to find my own mother, who was probably hiding from all the damn vampires, when Camila stopped me. "Thea, I want you to meet my children, Hadrian and Laurel."

I stared at them for a moment, seeing what I hadn't before. Hadrian, Camila's oldest, was the mirror image of his father—*our* father. My mouth fell open, and I quickly shut it.

Camila seemed to realize that at the same time as I did. "And your half siblings."

This was awkward.

But Hadrian stepped forward, hand outstretched. "Mother caught us up on everything. It's a little weird, isn't it? You're our sister and now our aunt."

He might look like our father, but instead of finding cruel sharpness in his eyes, his were soft, crinkling warmly at the edges. I shook his hand, laughing. What else could we do?

"That sounds slightly more scandalous than it should," I admitted.

His sister remained silent next to him. She was younger, her face still carrying the soft lines of youth, but she looked like her mother and her grandmother, her eyes the same piercing shade of blue and her ink-black hair hanging in a glossy sheet past her shoulders.

I smiled at her, and she responded with a tentative grin. Hadrian took charge, leading small talk into stories of his time at the academy they'd attended during their separation from Camila, who remained silent while he spoke. Tears glistened in her eyes as he recounted a ridiculous story that involved being trapped in a tower by a werewolf.

As if sensing her mate's emotions, Jacqueline appeared, kissing my cheek before wrapping an arm around Camila's waist.

"Where have you been?" Camila eyed her. "We still haven't danced."

"Seeing to the champagne toast. Everything needs to be perfect."

"It already is," I told her and meant it. "Although I suppose I'll be skipping the toast."

"At least when I was pregnant you could still drink," Camila said wistfully.

"You drank while you were pregnant with us?" Hadrian sounded shocked.

"It was the turn of the century—the last turn of the century," she reminded him, but he remained horrified.

A dozen servers made their way through the crowd with flutes of champagne, undoubtedly the good stuff and thankfully without blood. One paused to offer us glasses. I'd just waved it away with a sigh when Lysander appeared.

"Have you seen Aurelia?" he asked me.

"She's probably hiding with my mom." I shrugged, and a wave of nausea hit me. I pressed a hand to my forehead. "What time is it?"

He glanced at his Rolex. "Just past five thirty."

"And it's still early, so don't think you're going to sneak away, too," Jacqueline said, sipping her champagne.

"It's not that…" I trailed away as a second one hit, covering my mouth until it passed. "I need to use the facilities."

Her eyes widened. "Oh. Let me take you."

I started to refuse until my stomach cramped so badly I doubled over.

Jacqueline steadied me, leading me away from the party.

"What about the toast?" Camila called after us.

"Don't wait," I croaked.

"Tell Jules where I took her." She rubbed soothing circles on my back. "Are you okay?"

"It happens every evening," I confessed. "I'd hoped for a reprieve, but…" I swallowed hard to keep from vomiting on her very expensive shoes. "It won't last long."

"Good, because that cake is going to be divine." She grinned.

I dashed the last few steps into the restroom, Jacqueline joining me.

Sweat clung to my skin, and I slumped against the tile to cool myself. Jacqueline shut the door as I slid to the ground in a crumpled mass of silk and tulle. Was it too much to ask for a break on my wedding day?

Another wave of nausea roiled through me, adding chills that made my skin clammier. I tucked my knees into my chest and focused on breathing, but nothing calmed my lurching, twisting stomach.

"You look miserable." Jacqueline held my hair back. "Is there anything I can do?"

I tried to take a few deep breaths, but the haze of nausea was turning into a full-blown storm. Not only was I not getting a pass, but I felt worse than ever. I scrounged up a smile that I hoped alleviated her concern. "Will you hate me if I say I need to lie down?"

"You're the bride. Everything can wait for you." She helped me to my feet.

"Tell Julian where I am, and that I'm fine and to stop worrying."

Because he would. I might be able to sneak away for a few minutes, but I knew how it would look to have both the bride and groom disappear. My legs shook under me, reminding me that I might get sick again at any moment.

"Yeah, good luck with that," she said drily. "I should see you to your room."

I swallowed the acid in my throat. "I'm fine. I know that a quarter of those guests are security in tuxedos."

Her grin told me I was right. "We just thought it might be nice to avoid bloodshed today."

"Believe me, I appreciate the gesture. I'm sure I won't be long." The churning in my stomach suggested otherwise, but I kept that to myself. I'd get over the worst of it, clean myself up, and make my way back to the reception. There was cake waiting for me, after all.

I reached for the door, and it opened on its own. Quinn squealed as she came into view and threw her arms around me. I'd spotted her in the crowd earlier but lost track of her. She pulled back, still clutching my shoulders. "I saw you sneak off. I can't believe you're married. When we met in San Francisco, I thought…" She trailed away when she got a good look at me. "Oh no, what's wrong? It's a little late for cold feet."

"Nothing." I forced a tired smile. I was genuinely happy to see her. I just hoped I didn't throw up on her. "Just a little morning sickness."

She shrieked, causing Jacqueline to flinch. Quinn clapped a hand over her mouth. "Sorry. I'd heard the rumors, but I thought it might be gossip."

"I better get back," Jacqueline murmured, casting one final look at me. "Are you sure you don't want me to come along?"

"I'm fine." I shooed her away. "Go tell my husband where I am before he freaks out."

She gave me a thumbs-up and disappeared deeper into the court.

"I need to take a nap," I admitted to Quinn.

She grabbed my hand and squeezed it. "Of course. Maybe we

can catch up later."

"Definitely," I promised.

She bit her lip. "You sure you don't want company?"

"I think I just need quiet, but thank you. I'll be fine in a few minutes."

Quinn looked unconvinced, but she leaned in for another quick hug and didn't press the issue.

But as I wove through the halls, I couldn't soothe the pit in my stomach. I felt...wrong. It didn't feel like morning sickness. More like being plunged into the icy, fiery depths of hell.

The empty corridors were a welcome relief, given my condition. I wanted today to be about me and Julian, and while it was the happiest day of my life, I didn't know half the people here. I guess that's what happened when the groom's family's guest list stretched back millennia.

I reached my quarters as Aurelia flew down the hall. "Thank the Gods." She gripped my arm. "I need you to come with me, *now*."

The chill that snaked through me had nothing to do with my nausea. "What's wrong?"

Her eyes met mine. "It's Zina. I think... Just come."

That was the pit in my stomach. Not morning sickness, but an intuition. I was connected to the other queens. If something happened to one of them...

"Where is she?"

"The throne room."

What was she doing in there? Questions would have to wait as I tried to keep up with Aurelia's furious pace. The adrenaline pounding through me overwhelmed the nausea, but my legs were much shorter than hers. I lost sight of her as she rounded the corner.

I stopped on the threshold of the throne room. Icy air blasted through the open door, so cold that my breath fogged. A copper tang filled the air. My fangs protracted, recognizing the scent before my brain did. Blood. Lots of blood, from the smell. Dread curled around me, settling in that yawning pit in my belly. Something was very wrong.

I took one step and hesitated. Maybe I should wait for Julian.

"She's in here," Aurelia called from inside the room.

If the blood I smelled came from her, I didn't have time to run for help. I reached out with my mind.

I'm in the throne room!

It felt like shouting down a tunnel. We rarely used our bond to communicate when we were apart, but I had to try.

When I entered, my eyes landed on the empty thrones first. Aurelia crouched, a body sprawled at her feet. She lifted her stricken face to mine, revealing her bloodstained hands.

CHAPTER SIXTY-ONE

Thea

My courage faltered for a moment, but I forced myself forward. My knees buckled as I reached the body. Zina. Her glassy eyes stared at the ceiling, her silver hair now muddy crimson from the blood pooling under her. She was still beautiful, even in death, but her skin was ashen, as if her magic had drained out with her blood. My eyes lingered on her wound, on the angry red slash, the flesh pulled back to expose muscle and bone. It was vicious but calculated.

"How?" I asked, already afraid of the answer. She was a queen. She should have healed, and if she didn't...

Aurelia's mouth thinned with anger. "She was attacked. It was a trap."

And if she had been attacked...

"We need to find Julian and Mariana," I said, the words rough and uneven. "And we need to get out of here."

But even as I spoke, I knew it was too late.

Aurelia did, too, because she lowered her head and wept.

"Come on." I bent and placed a hand on her shoulder, urging her to her feet. "We need to go. Whoever did this might still be here."

Her body shook, the sounds of her grief intensifying until it pealed from her, shrill as a bell. The sound jarred that instinct inside me, and I took a step back even before she lifted her face.

No longer Aurelia's.

"Mariana?" I whispered.

Her blood-red lips curved into a smile that sent a warning as sharp as a missed note through my veins. I ran for the door, reaching it just as it slammed shut.

I pounded on it with fists, with magic, with every bit of will I could summon, knowing what waited behind me. But it held, locked in place by the terrible magic that permeated the throne room.

"Oh, Thea," Mariana crooned, "stop trying to escape. We both know you aren't going anywhere." She rose, tossing a disgusted look at Zina's body as she stepped over and swept toward me. From the folds of her skirt, she lifted a dagger crusted in blood. "Every spell must have a counterbalance," she reminded me as she lifted it. "Meet the queen-killer."

"Where's Aurelia?" I sounded surprisingly calm, but Mariana's smile grew more hideous.

"Probably with the others." The hand holding her dagger dropped to her side. "You should hear what I did to them."

My composure cracked. "The others?"

"Your friends, your family, and all the simpering magical snobs they invited here. They're all dead, even your precious mate."

I couldn't breathe. My lungs fought to fill with air, but nothing happened. "You're lying."

She had to be. If Julian was dead, I would know. I would feel it.

She laughed, the sound like shattering glass. "Okay, I'm exaggerating, but they might as well be. This time, they will stay asleep." Her face lit up at my slackened jaw. "All those weeks you've had Lysander looking for the origins of the curse that put magic to sleep. You were so busy looking for answers, so convinced the important piece was who was behind the curse, that you never considered someone might be hiding it for a different reason."

"To use it," I said numbly. Mariana's confession had gutted me, hollowed me out. I didn't know how I was still standing.

"Yes, but this time, we did a better job. There is no breaking it this time around. It was a potent spell. We had to deliver it directly as a potion. It held us up for weeks wondering how we were going to get a bunch of suspicious vampires and familiars to ingest a potion. Even at those stupid Rites some of them won't ingest anything. The older and more paranoid ones. Granted, they were wise to be cautious. Then the perfect opportunity presented itself. Your lovely little wedding. Jacqueline didn't bat an eye when I suggested a toast, practically drooled when I insisted she let me order two cases of Cristal. And the best part was that I knew you wouldn't drink it."

"Because I'm pregnant." I covered my womb with my hand as another staggering stab of pain wrenched through me. The baby…

"Yes." She shimmied with delight. "When I heard about the wedding, I knew our time had arrived. But I didn't want to put you to sleep—couldn't do it. I needed you awake for this part. Then you told me you were pregnant, and I knew you'd refused to drink, thanks to your human past. I couldn't have planned it better."

"But…you were nice to me."

"Much nicer than Zina." She nodded. "In truth, I don't hate you. Not completely. You've done me more than a few favors." She toyed with the dagger, pressing her finger into its tip. "You've paved the way for our bid to take the throne."

Our. We. I'd been so distracted that I hadn't connected the clues in her words. She wasn't doing this alone. Of course she wasn't.

"When you made Julian take the throne, proclaimed him King-Consort…" She shivered, a dreamy smile on her face. "When we ascend, no one will fight it. Not after you already broke it."

"Who?" The word sank from my lips, even though I already knew the answer. There was only one person who corrupted this thoroughly, charmed this easily.

"I think you already know the answer." Willem stepped from the shadows, whatever glamour covering him evaporating.

"How?" I breathed. "You were *beheaded*."

"So much magic wasted on a mind that still thinks like a

human." Mariana laughed. "It was a simple illusion. No one argued when I offered our people to clean up the mess or they would have realized the truth."

Willem's lips curled into a cruel smile. "Never let someone else do your dirty work, daughter."

"I'm not your daughter. I never was," I snarled.

"He doesn't care," Mariana said, stepping closer to him. "What a king he will make. When we ascend the thrones—"

"There are three of them," I reminded her. "And if you think I'm going to join you, you're as deluded as he is."

She flew forward, only making it a step before Willem caught her and held her back. "You don't deserve that throne, but don't worry, we won't need you for long." She looked affectionately at Willem, placing a hand on her stomach. "We've been working on that. Soon our child will join us, and then we won't need you."

"Can't stop sticking your cock where it doesn't belong, can you?" I bit out to him.

He smirked. "You get that fiery spirit from me, you know."

"I get it from my mother."

"Ungrateful bitch." Mariana hurled the words at me, her hand brandishing the dagger in my direction. "You don't deserve to be his daughter and yet—"

"Darling," Willem said softly. "She is a means to an end, but why don't you give me that dagger before you forget?"

"Fine." Her pouting was short-lived, utter adoration replacing it as she looked to him, passed the dagger to him.

He took it.

And plunged it into her chest.

I cried out, instinct propelling me toward her as another sickening surge hit me. Blood spilled from her lips, her eyes never leaving his, as her legs folded and she fell to the stone floor with a sickening crack. The room went silent, as if the air had been sucked from it, and then it roared back to life with a force that sent me to my knees.

There was no one to help. I didn't have to check her body for a pulse. She was dead. The ground trembled as if it had felt the queen's death, too.

I fell forward to my hands, struggling to lift my head. "She loved you! Is there no one you won't betray?"

"She was volatile and weak." He wiped the blade on the hem of his shirt. "There is no place for weakness on the thrones."

"I will never join you," I panted out. I felt like I was being crushed. Magic itself lashed out in grief over the two lost queens.

"Thea, I don't need you to join me." He *tsked*, moving closer with that deadly blade. "You're a lovely girl but a bit too noncompliant for my taste."

"If you think anyone else would join you…" I shook my head, shifting back on my heels, but even as I said it, I knew I was wrong. There were vampires that would join him. Maybe even familiars.

"Do you think I haven't considered who will join me on the thrones? Oh, Thea, I thought you were smarter than that… Perhaps you do take after your mother."

I stared at him for a moment as a final piece clicked into place. He didn't need me on the thrones. Not when he had… "Hadrian and Laurel." I closed my eyes, trying to ignore the trembling world around me. "That's why you faked your death. You knew that Sabine would never reveal their location until you were dead."

It all made sense.

"And thanks to your wedding, they were delivered right to me as planned. Congratulations, by the way. At least you won't be married long enough to wish you'd never said yes."

My fingers curled into fists as I stood there, my chest rising and falling with each deep breath I took. The anger was building inside me, a storm rolling into the sky. Julian was alive, and that meant his magic was still inside me, that light and dark, life and death were mine to command. I listened for that terrible music. I might not walk out of here, but I would die fighting.

"Now, Thea." He crouched in front of me and pressed the tip of the dagger under my chin. I didn't dare move, but I didn't need to move to call my magic. I just had to hear it. "I know that look in your eyes. Don't get any ideas. I wouldn't want you to do anything you might regret."

"I wouldn't regret it," I seethed.

"Well, first, there is the matter of your mate and all those magical creatures. Right now, they're asleep but alive. It would be very easy for me to end them." He tilted his head, arrogance glinting in his dark eyes.

But I wasn't stupid. "You're going to kill them anyway." There was a chance I could save them. "Someone will be able to break your curse."

"Actually," he drew out the word, "that was always the issue with the original curse. They tied its power to love, blind to the fact that even a vampire might love what they feared, given enough time. I chose something more permanent. As long as the thrones remain, so will the spell on your mate. You might be willing to give up your crown to save him, but what other creature would make that sacrifice?"

"I'll find someone."

"Someone the throne will accept. Magic chose you because you are powerful. Whatever weak soul you might dupe won't ascend the throne."

"Your problem is that you mistake goodness for weakness. Maybe some creatures are like you, but there are many who aren't." I would find them. I didn't care how long it took. I just had to walk out of here with my own life.

"I was worried you'd say that." He stood and walked to the door. "So I made sure I had a backup plan."

I couldn't hide my horror as he opened it to reveal my mother standing there.

For one terrible moment, I believed she had betrayed me. Then I saw her confused eyes. She looked from me to my father, her fists clenched at her sides.

"Come to me." Willem snapped his fingers.

"I'm not—" The words died in my throat as my mother took a lurching, defiant step forward. "Mom?"

Her eyes closed as she took another step and then another,

blindly walking to him like she was on a lead.

"Hasn't your mother ever told you why she was so against you taking a vampire as a mate, taking him to bed?" Willem released a high, cruel laugh. "Your mother knew what would happen to you. She knew that you would be tethered—just like she was."

That was why she hated vampires, why she'd refused to give Julian a chance. She'd fallen victim to one before, and she'd known what would happen if I, too, lost my virginity to one.

"No." It slipped from my mouth, and I found myself moving toward her. I would stop this. I couldn't let her go to him. Not while he held that blood-soaked dagger. I reached for her arm, and Willem clucked his tongue.

"I wouldn't do that if I were you. You remember what happened when Julian tried to resist his tether."

"I'd rather die fighting you than die at your hands," she seethed.

"Why die at all?" He shrugged. "As long as Thea plays along, there is no need for further bloodshed."

"Is that why you killed Zina? Because she wouldn't go along with it?" I shook my head.

"Naturally."

"And Mariana?" I asked through gritted teeth. "She would have done anything you wanted."

His mouth curled into a smile. "And she did. But I had no use for her and no interest in an ambitious woman sitting at my side."

My mother reached him, and he wrapped a hand around her throat but didn't squeeze. A gentle threat to remind us that we were at his mercy. With his strength, he could snap her neck like a twig. I was still learning how to summon my magic. Even if I could call it forth easily, I was no match for his vampire reflexes.

I didn't dare move another inch. "What do you want from me?"

"I want you to give up your throne."

It was such a simple request that for a minute all I could do was stare. I didn't want the throne, didn't want the politics or the power. I'd told Julian as much. While my crown offered me some protection, it also painted a target on my back. I could easily give it up. I could hand it over and be done with the whole mess.

But it wasn't that easy, because Willem did want the power—had already done terrible things to claim it. I had no doubt he would do even worse if he tapped the power of the *Rio Oscuro*.

"I can release them from the spell when it is accomplished." He dangled the promise like bait. "You can have your mate back, go off and have your family, and be done with this business. I know you never wanted the throne."

And that was precisely why the throne had chosen me. Because I didn't want it.

I lifted my chin so I was staring directly into his black eyes. "What makes you think you can claim the throne? *It* chooses."

Those dark eyes rolled. "A lovely fairytale. I'm sure you believe you were chosen. Why wouldn't you? Mariana had a vision, after all. Convenient, no?"

My eyes flicked to her lifeless body. Had it all been a ploy? But if it was...

"And lucky for you, she did, because you were dead. Your mate was dead. The throne gave your life back."

"It...chose me." But my tongue tripped in my mouth.

"Do you want to know the truth?" He peered at me, his eyes assessing something only he could see. "*Le Regine*, the thrones, the curse—all of this was an attempt to control magic and dictate who had access to it. As a queen, you are bound to the throne. *You* serve *it*. The throne was simply a well that was tapped, and the myth of the three queens was created to serve one purpose: to limit magic. Anyone can control this resource. The thrones are simply a conduit controlled by vampires—a way to keep other creatures from having access to the *Rio*'s magic."

"Then why do you need me?" I demanded.

"Because your bond with the throne can only be broken in one of two ways. You can either voluntarily relinquish the crown...or you can die." He tipped his head toward the bodies. "Zina would never have given up her power."

"And you think I will?"

He smirked. "I think you don't want to watch your mother die."

"Don't," my mother said, her jaw clenched. "You can never let him have that power."

"Still bitter?" He snorted.

"Me?" She raised a brow. "I got away from you."

"Is that what you think?" He shook his head. "I had no interest in raising our daughter—not when I knew I could find her when she was ready. Why waste my time?"

My mother's eyes blinked rapidly as she processed this. "But I hid her from you."

"A waste of time," he crooned, "and a costly one. I hear you made yourself quite ill using all that fae magic."

"Fae?" I blurted out.

She didn't look at me. She didn't speak. Not because he had her pinned. No, his grip was too loose for that. She could easily slip out of his hold.

"Only powerful magic could have shielded the two of you for that long, especially from my tether," he explained to me, his eyes pointed at her. "A fae glamour could be bargained for, but their magic is different than our own. It was eating you alive. Was it worth it?"

"To protect her from you? Yes."

"You're a fool," he said in a low voice.

"You're a monster."

He didn't deny it. "Although I'm curious about the terms of your bargain. What did you agree to? Will they come for both of you someday?"

"They will never touch her. As for the rest, it's none of your business," she snapped, and I choked back a sob. Bain had said the same—that the fae could not touch me. I'd thought it was a bargain with the queens, but it was my mother's agreement—her sacrifice.

"What did you promise them?" I begged her.

"Myself," she said simply. "I bargained my life to protect yours. I agreed that when you reached twenty-five or you married, I would return to his court and serve him."

My mouth went dry, all thoughts eddying from my head. I wouldn't be twenty-five for a few more years, but now I was married. If I had known, I could have used the next couple of years to find a way out of the agreement. "Why didn't you tell me?"

"You can't break a fae bargain," she said softly, knowing what I'd just realized: that my wedding to Julian today meant the fae would call in their bargain soon. "You've sacrificed enough for me. I won't take any more of your happiness. This day was always going to come."

"How touching. I'm glad you two have made amends."

"Shut up," I snarled.

"You would do well to remember I hold her life in my hands—bargain or no. The fae won't care if she's dead."

"I will never give up the throne," I warned him. I couldn't. I knew what he was capable of, and I had to keep him from tapping into the world's most powerful well of magic.

"Do not delude yourself, Thea. I *will* kill you both." He leveled a gaze so cold at me that it turned my blood to ice. "So you will do exactly as I say—or everyone you have ever loved, including your unborn child, will be dead within the hour."

CHAPTER SIXTY-TWO

Lysander

It felt like I'd been looking for Lia for hours. I assumed she would stick close to the celebration, but something had been off since my return to court. She was acting strangely, and I couldn't decide if she was avoiding me. We'd come close to crossing a line the last time we were alone. I had barely seen her since.

I finally found her on a balcony on the far side of the queens' private quarters—one of the few that offered a glimpse beyond the court into the city that existed outside the *Rio Oscuro's* magical veil. Despite the winter chill in the air, she wore nothing over her silk gown. Nothing to cover her bare shoulders. I considered slipping off my jacket, but I suspected she would refuse it.

Maybe even think of it as an insult.

It had taken effort not to stare at her during the wedding when she'd entered in that pale cream dress, its silk fabric flowing over her curves in a way that told me what lay under was even better than what I'd imagined in my dreams. I allowed myself a moment to appreciate her now. Out of her usual leather, there was a softness to her that took me aback. Maybe because I suspected very little about Lia was soft. Or maybe because I knew a few parts of her were—parts I couldn't stop thinking about.

"There you are." I stepped onto the balcony. "I've been looking for you."

She didn't turn toward me, even as her shoulders tightened. Instead, she stared across the Grand Canal in the direction of the bustling Rialto Bridge. "Why?"

That was a very good question. One I wasn't sure she wanted me to answer. Hell, one I wasn't sure I wanted to answer. I stepped to her side, keeping enough distance that there was no risk of touching her, of stoking that smoldering flame between us. "I like your company."

Maybe it was too honest of an answer, but it was better than admitting I couldn't stay away. No matter how hard I tried—and I was fucking trying.

She snorted but still didn't look at me. "Try again."

I couldn't come up with a safe response, so I switched tactics. "Why are you out here? The party is in there."

"I've never been one for parties." Her grip tightened on the stone railing. "And Thea doesn't need me to protect her." She continued to watch the bridge as flurries began to fall around us. "So many tourists, even with the weather."

"Humans love Venice." I glanced at her bare shoulders again. "Are you cold?"

She shook her head. "I'm not that fragile." She paused. "Why do they love it?"

It took me a second to realize we were back to talking about the tourists. "Venice is beautiful. There are few cities like it in the world." I shrugged. "A human once told me that without the cars and traffic, it feels like a place where magic could exist. Maybe they can sense the truth."

Even humans had a little magic in their blood, after all.

"I guess I wouldn't know about other places."

I didn't miss the bitter current in her words. I could almost taste it in my own mouth. "Would you ever leave?"

"I try not to ask myself that. It's...easier."

Easier because she couldn't leave. "What if Thea left?"

Her head finally whipped in my direction. "She's leaving again?"

"No!" I'd fucked that up. "It was just hypothetical."

"My service is bound to the throne itself. I cannot leave the city."

"That…sucks."

Her lips curved slightly. Not quite a smile but close. "Yes, it does, but if I could leave…I would."

Somehow I knew that, because whether either of us liked to admit it or not, we were similar. "I've never been able to stay in one place too long. I guess I'm always searching for something."

"Sounds nice."

I swiveled and leaned against the railing. "Sometimes."

"And the other times?"

I stared past her, not daring to utter the truth—to admit what I'd realized since coming here.

Lonely.

It was fucking lonely.

Even with my crew around me.

"What are you searching for?" she asked.

"I don't know."

"That sounds pretty pointless," she said drily.

I barked a laugh. "Maybe it is. But it's something to do, and I've got a lot of time on my hands."

Her eyes went distant, and she fell silent again, as though my words had triggered her.

I couldn't take my eyes off her. "Sometimes, you don't realize what you're searching for until you find it."

We stared at each other, knowing we were again at the edge of that precipice, so dangerously close to falling into whatever this was between us.

"We should get back to the wedding." She straightened and took a step toward the door, away from that perilous edge. "I don't want Thea to worry."

I followed Lia inside without a word. How long could we keep dancing around this?

We remained silent as we made our way back to the courtyard, but as soon as we stepped out of the queens' quarters, Lia paused. "Lysander, there's something—"

The color drained from her face.

"What is it?" I grabbed her shoulders, feeling a flicker of magic even through my calfskin gloves.

"Something's wrong," she moaned, lifting wide eyes to mine. "We need to find Thea. Now."

We didn't waste any time as we cut through the corridors that led to the public grounds of the court. But with each step I took, I began to feel it, too. It began like a trickle of dread that quickly morphed into a low, persistent queasiness.

Before we reached the courtyard, a female stumbled inside, panic-stricken. She took one look at me and lunged in our direction. Out of nowhere, Lia produced a knife.

"You're Julian's brother, right?" the woman said. She didn't wait for confirmation before she grabbed my arm and tugged me ahead.

I didn't budge. "And who are you?"

"Quinn. I'm a friend of Thea's. We met in San Francisco." She kept pulling on me. "Something's wrong. Come on."

Lia and I exchanged a glance as we followed her.

"Where were you hiding that?" I tipped my head to her knife, wanting to know where the hell she'd been hiding that one, given her dress left nothing to the imagination.

"Not the time," Lia snapped.

"I was just wondering if you had another one."

"What's going on?" I turned my attention back to Quinn.

She was shaking too hard to answer me. I moved twice as fast as the others, my dread deepening as I did. Something was very wrong. Each step I took was a struggle, as though some primal instinct wanted me to stop.

But I didn't stop. I pushed forward. Though nothing could have prepared me for what I found.

Bodies littered the ground, and for one horrible moment, I thought they were dead. But there was no blood. No signs of violence. I moved to the vampire closest to me and knelt to check for a pulse.

"They're alive," Quinn said as she reached me, Lia beside her. "But they're…"

"Asleep," I finished for her. Standing, I scanned the room, my eyes pausing as I spotted my parents and my brothers. Jacqueline and Camila. Even Julian.

But not—

"Where's Thea?" Aurelia asked before I could.

"I don't see her." I turned on Quinn. "What the hell happened?"

She hugged herself, still shaking. "There was a toast, and a few minutes later, everyone just passed out. I think it was the champagne."

"Why do you think that?" My eyes narrowed. She said she was a friend of Thea's, but how could I trust her when she was the only one unaffected?

"I don't like champagne. I didn't drink it. Everyone else did." She wrinkled her nose.

Thea wouldn't have, not with being pregnant. So where was she?

"We need to find Thea." I nodded at Lia.

"She went back to her rooms," Quinn told us. "She said she wasn't feeling well."

I prayed that was the result of morning sickness and not whatever had poisoned everyone here.

Across from me, Lia swayed on her feet and clutched her stomach. I shot to her, placing a steadying hand on her back. "What is it?"

"Something is wrong." She gripped my arm frantically. "We need to get to the throne room."

My eyebrows shot up. "The throne room?"

She jerked her head. "Yes. It's the magic. We have to hurry."

"Come with us," I ordered Quinn.

"Try to stop me," she said even as her lip trembled. At least she was brave.

I forced myself to go slowly enough that I didn't lose them. I wouldn't risk going ahead and leaving them behind. My heart stuttered when we spotted the open throne room door.

"Stick together," Lia ordered us as we approached it. She took one step through the door and halted.

I cursed as I took in the bodies on the ground, blood seeping into the stones.

"Gods," Lia breathed. A curse or a prayer. Maybe both.

"Lysander!" Thea cried, and my eyes turned to her in relief. She was alive, in one piece as far as I could tell.

But next to her... My relief leaked from me as I took in Willem, and next to him, Thea's mother, with a knife held to her own throat.

"How the fuck did you three get in here?" Willem growled.

"I don't like champagne," Quinn's voice cut through the air.

"Me neither," I said.

But he wasn't looking at her or me. He was looking at Lia in a way that made me want to rip him apart.

He pointed a finger at her. "And you?"

She didn't say a word.

"Lia," I said her name under my breath.

"No, something else protected you." His mouth curled into a cruel smile. "Why don't you come out and play?" He snapped his fingers, and Lia doubled over, hands clutching the sides of her head.

"Lia!" I moved to her side, reached for her, but she jerked away from me, even as her face lifted to mine—*her* face but *not* her face. Any doubt I had that she was the most beautiful female I'd ever seen vanished. Her human features smoothed into immortal skin, a faint light glowed in her eyes, and as she dropped her trembling hands, I saw her ears, and every thought eddied from my head, save one.

Fae.

CHAPTER SIXTY-THREE

Thea

"Fae." Willem spat the word at Aurelia.

Lysander moved away from her, his face slack with shock. I didn't dare move. Not with that knife pressed to my mother's throat. The air was still. None of us even drew a breath, save for Aurelia. She shook, trembling from whatever magic had ripped away her magic.

Willem strode toward her, laughing. "Perhaps she's come to call in her bargain with you, Kelly. Our daughter has fulfilled the terms of your agreement. Your new fae master should be along to collect you." He turned toward me. "Do you have any idea what the fae will do to her? They're much crueler than vampires. You can't even imagine—"

A strangled cry cut him off. Blood bubbled from his mouth, the sharp end of the dagger protruding through his throat. He stumbled a step, revealing my mother, panting from the effort of her surprise attack.

"You always loved to hear yourself talk," she snarled.

He reached for the dagger, his fingers grappling for the blade as my mother collapsed behind him. Her body arched from the stone floor, and I rushed toward her as Lysander tackled Willem. They were a blur of blood and motion. I knelt next to my mom, trying to soothe the spasms racking her body. Aurelia and Quinn joined me, shielding us both from the savage battle happening between Lysander and my father.

"What do I do?" I begged them. "It's his tether. She disobeyed him." She'd fought that primal connection, and I knew what the cost would be. Julian had died fighting his tether. I couldn't lose her. Not after what she'd given up for me. Not after things were finally healing between us. Looking to Aurelia, I said, "Make a bargain with her. Save her."

Aurelia dropped into a crouch beside us, tears glistening in her eyes. "I'm not that powerful. I'm only half fae. I'm sorry."

I turned to Quinn, the silent sorrow on her face telling me what I couldn't bring myself to face. There was nothing to be done. Not in this life. I held my mom closer as my last hope evaporated. "I'll find you," I promised her, sobbing. "I can bring you back."

She lifted a trembling hand to my face, managing to shake her head a little. "No. Do not go where I am going. Do not risk your child. Being your mother was my greatest honor. I'm so proud of the woman you've become. Trust yourself." Her voice was barely a whisper. "Let me go, Thea. Save your magic to finish him."

Her eyes glazed over as her breathing became a faint rattle in her chest.

"No." I looked at Aurelia. "Take her to the Otherworld."

"Thea—" Quinn cut in, but I ignored her.

"Snap your fingers!" I demanded. "Take her to the fae."

Willem hadn't been able to control her magic. If fae magic was that powerful, another bargain might be the only thing that saved her now.

"You don't understand. I am bound to the court, not only by a vow, but to the throne itself," Aurelia said. "Even if I could—"

"Then I will make a bargain with you," I cut her off. "I will release you if you take her to your people. Ginerva taught you about your magic. I know you can do it."

Aurelia turned to where Lysander and Willem struggled,

something unreadable on her face. Then she nodded. Only once. She grabbed my mother's hand, snapped her fingers, and they disappeared.

A hollow pang rang through my chest. I might not see either of them again. I wouldn't blame Aurelia if she never came back here. Next to me, Quinn rose and offered me her hand.

I stared at it.

"Let's finish him," she said. "For your mom."

I took it, hauling myself to my feet. She was right, even if I had no clue how to do that. Even the knife—the queen-killer—hadn't been enough to take him down.

"Enough." My voice boomed through the room.

A second later, Lysander flew against the wall, hitting it with a bone-splitting crack. He groaned as he slid to the floor and didn't get back up.

"Help him," I told Quinn, who rushed to his side.

Willem appeared before me, dagger lodged in his throat. His lip curled as he reached up and yanked it free. He flicked the blood on the ground and lifted it in my direction. But he didn't lunge. He didn't make a move.

Why? He could kill me and take my throne. That was his plan the whole time.

Lysander lifted his head, managing to croak a few words. "His magic. He can't call it." He lifted a bloody hand to his throat, and I realized what he was telling me.

Willem used spells. Old magic stolen from the grimoires of witches his family had taken over the years. But he was still a vampire—still stronger and faster than I was. He could end me easily, even without his magic. Unless...he couldn't kill me.

I was the only surviving queen, the last one linked to the magic that flowed through the water of Venice. The magic flowed through me.

I was queen. Not him. He could lust after my power. He could try to claim it, but magic had chosen me. It had deemed me worthy. I had not asked for it, but I could no longer fear it. Because even before the throne, my magic had been with me. It was a part of me. It had always been there. I'd found it in my music long before I knew what I was or who I would become. It was inside me. It was mine. I was magic.

I listened for its song. Magic's notes sang through the air, high and bright around me, low and foreboding in the shadows. Life and death caught up in their endless dance. I opened myself to those dark notes, called them forth. Quinn cried out as darkness wove around me, blocking out the light, blocking out the entire room until it shrank away like a memory, leaving only him and me.

Willem's eyes locked with mine as the shadows swirled.

"If you had your voice, would you beg?" I asked him. I shook my head, feeling my throat slide. "I spent my whole life wanting to meet my father. What a disappointment you were."

I lifted one finger and twisted, conducting the dreadful symphony around us. The notes were brittle, jagged things that climbed up and then fell down again, a venomous melody of discordant keys. Darkness curled around his neck, creating a garrote. He opened his mouth, his eyes bulging from the pressure, and the shadows shot down his throat. Willem gagged, clutching at his throat, trying to find the words to save himself. But nothing could save him now. I wouldn't allow it. I didn't look away as death sang its final lullaby. I watched as it claimed him, watched as he paid for his sins.

He didn't suffer enough.

When his body crumpled to the floor, I closed my eyes and let that terrible music fade back into the shadows of the world. When I opened my eyes, not a trace remained.

The world rumbled beneath me as magic died.

I felt magic unspool around me, heard its broken melody faintly. Aurelia had told me that with two queens, they had barely managed to maintain control over the *Rio Oscuro* and had nearly lost the source of magic altogether. Now I was the only thing standing in the way of its total destruction—and I wasn't strong enough. Not after calling on my power to end Willem. Not with so little mastery of my own magic.

A faint warmth spread through me as I thought of my mother's final words: *Trust yourself.* But how? I'd caused all of this. I pulled in a deep breath, let it out, and listened.

I had to try.

I had to save them.

Closing my eyes, I focused on the song of the magic, using it like a lifeline to guide me. Its muted notes ebbed away, the sound of fading magic, but soon I heard a gentle swell of notes carrying the vibrancy of life, the air in my lungs, the earth beneath my feet. Magic called out to me, like the remnant of a dream, like a whisper. A new resonance hummed through my bones, and when I looked at my friends, I not only heard magic.

I saw it.

Golden threads wove around Quinn. She cast worried eyes on me before turning her attention back to Lysander's wounds. And as I watched, the threads of magic settled around her head like a halo.

A crown.

Three crowns to bind.

I dashed to her and dropped to my feet before Lysander. "The prophecy you found in that grimoire. What did it say?"

He grimaced as he pushed up, his dark hair sticking to his bloody face. "About the queens?"

I nodded as the ground shook beneath us. I lurched forward, the stone floor stinging as my palms grappled across it.

"Three crowns to bind," he repeated from memory. "Three thrones to choose. Three queens to sacrifice. Ever as three bound. Ever as three free."

"What does it mean?" Quinn called as the ancient walls groaned around us.

"I think the thrones are choosing you. It might be our only chance to stop the source from collapsing."

"Me?" But even as she spoke, the golden light glowed more brightly around her head.

"Yes, two queens will be enough to stop it."

"But what about the others? The spell?" Lysander asked.

"Will you take the crown and give it back?" I asked Quinn. "The spell will bind everyone until three queens release the enchantment binding the thrones to the source." *Ever as three bound. Ever as three free.*

"Yes, but..." She trailed away, and I knew what she was thinking.

Two queens weren't enough to break the spell, holding everyone else, holding Julian. We needed a third. Another queen willing to both take the throne and give it up to wake them. I turned to him, searching for a sign that thrones would choose him—begging for magic to show this one mercy.

There were none.

"You could try," I said despite the lack of sign. Maybe it would be enough.

"I've never shown any sign of magic," he warned us.

"We have to try," Quinn decided, and he didn't protest.

I looked at him. "If we can take the thrones, we stand a chance."

We made our way to the thrones, and Quinn paused at the dais. "That one," she said, her voice full of awe as she looked toward Mariana's throne. "It's pulling me."

I gave her an encouraging smile, the world rocking beneath our feet. A fissure cracked along the stone floor, and I shouted, "Hurry."

Quinn climbed the platform quickly, wasting no time. My heart in my throat, I turned to Lysander. A muscle worked in his jaw, and he shook his head slightly.

Before we could ascend the dais, music swelled around us, notes joining as magic healed. Quinn's dark eyes widened as a blinding light settled over her, and a crown of seashells appeared on her black hair. The air stilled, the enchantment placated for the moment.

But it wasn't enough. Only three queens could stop this.

I looked at Lysander and whispered, "Try."

He took a deep breath and walked toward Zina's vacant throne. There was a moment of hesitation, his solemn face quiet with prayer before he sat.

Nothing happened.

I strained to hear the magic, listening for any change, listening for its powerful symphony, but it remained the same. Calmed but not whole. Tears clawed up my throat and found my eyes. I blinked them back furiously.

"I'm sorry." Lysander's head fell forward, but not before I caught a glimpse of defeat shadowing his eyes.

"We'll find a way." Magic was stable. There were others in the city that had not come to the wedding. I knew it. I just had to find one we could trust.

Beneath the dais, a seam split open, inky water spilling out in poisoned waves like blood from an opened vein. The salt of the sea mingled with the fresh air and filled my lungs. My mouth watered, my stomach churning at its thick briny aroma. Magic was coming apart at the seams, and I had no way to stop it.

"It didn't work," Quinn cried, clutching her chair with white knuckles. "The spells are putting too much strain on the source. I can feel it."

That's why Willem had waited for us all to be here. He'd known that his plan would only work if three magical beings ascended the thrones. I looked at the bodies scattered on the floor. Mariana and Zina had died from the dagger, its curse stealing not only their lives but their magic.

"We have to—"

The roof caved in, cutting me off. Lysander threw himself over me, shielding me from the falling debris.

There wasn't time. We were going to lose. If only...

A loud crack sounded in the room, and I braced myself for impact, but Lysander drew up, shouting something. Lifting my head, I discovered Aurelia standing near the thrones.

"What are you doing here?" I shouted. "My mother—"

"Is safe." She forced a grim smile. "I thought you might need me."

I stared at her elegant pointed ears, at that unearthly beauty she no longer dimmed. Lysander gawked beside me, seeing her again for the first time.

Fae. She was fae. And while I'd been warned against their

magic, I knew better. I could trust Aurelia and her magic. As if to prove my suspicions correct, silver strands of light wove around her head, anointing her. Magic was fighting to survive. I would fight along with it until my last breath.

"Take the throne!" Her eyes widened as her lips pursed to say no. But I shook my head. "There's no time. Trust me. Take the throne."

Aurelia leaped onto the dais, carefully avoiding Lysander's pained gaze. She wasted no time taking the seat. The air shimmered around her, and she let out a small shriek as a crown of jagged obsidian shards appeared on her head.

It took effort not to collapse with relief as the world quieted entirely. Lysander knelt beside me, bowing his head in reverence.

"What the hell are you doing?" Aurelia asked, eyes still wide and fearful. "Get up."

He didn't look at her as he rose. Instead, he turned to me.

"What now?" he asked.

I bit my lip, hoping I was right, hoping I'd understood the cryptic prophecy correctly. I walked toward my throne slowly and took it. The weight of my crown dropped onto my head. It felt heavier than normal. Perhaps because it bore not only the weight of my responsibility but my entire future as well.

Standing, I turned to the new queens and lifted it from my head. "Ever as three bound. Ever as three free." I swallowed back the fear that threatened to choke me. "If we return the magic, we'll be free. Everyone will be free."

Quinn rose. "And vampires will no longer control the source?" She grinned, her shoulders slumping in relief. "Sounds good to me."

I looked to Aurelia. She didn't move. Instead, she stared at me. "We give up the crowns?"

Panic seized my chest, but I managed a nod.

"But..." Her eyes searched mine. "What if you're wrong? What if the source needs the queens? What if..."

I understood her fear. I felt it, too. It was a gamble based on a riddle found in an old book. "My father believed it," I said slowly, "so much so that he tied his curse to these thrones. He believed no queen would ever give up that much power." I paused and lifted my chin. "I believe we are better than that."

She considered for the longest second of my life before standing.

Lysander moved to the side, his gaze cast away as Aurelia moved to my left. Quinn joined me at my right. We walked to the edge of the dais, staring at the black water lapping from the chasm in the stone.

They took off their crowns.

Ever as three…

"Together," I murmured. In unison, we threw the crowns into the water. I reached for their hands and waited.

CHAPTER SIXTY-FOUR

Julian

The world returned with startling clarity, vivid and overwhelming, even for my vampire senses. I sat up, wincing, and looked around, meeting the confused eyes of everyone surrounding me. Even my mother's face was drawn in shock, as if seeing everything for the first time. The colors were brighter, tinged in a golden light, even though the night sky sheltered us. Smells crowded my nostrils: the thick perfume of the wedding flowers, the scent of spilled champagne, the musty brine of Venice. Someone moved, and my head whipped toward them with predatory instinct, the sound so crisp and loud that it was disconcerting. And under my skin, in my veins, magic roared.

"What happened?" I asked my mother. She shook her head, her eyes searching the room for clues. It was like we'd been shaken from a deep sleep and had emerged into a new life. I placed my hand on the stone to push up and caught sight of my wedding band. A new fear overtook my confusion. "Where's Thea?"

My mother's mouth opened, but someone else called out to me. "I'm here!"

I nearly collapsed with relief, but when I lifted my head to track her, my heart stopped. Thea rushed toward me, her wedding gown soaked with blood, her hair tangled in wild waves over her shoulders. I jumped to my feet and moved in long, fast strides, meeting her halfway.

"You're okay," she sobbed, running her hands over my chest, repeating those two words like she needed to say it to believe it.

I gripped her shoulders, looking for the origin of the blood but not finding a scratch. As soon as I was satisfied, I crushed her to my chest as my heart slowed to a more normal rhythm. "Thea…"

She didn't need me to ask. Instead, she clung to me and repeated the entire story. I listened with numb shock, torn between my relief that she was safe and my horror at what she'd endured.

"There's something else," she whispered. "To break the curse, we had to sacrifice our crowns. It was the only way to free you."

"Sacrifice?"

"We gave magic back to the earth." She pulled back enough to study my face, her eyes darting around us. I knew why, and my arms tightened around her.

"I can feel it." The throttle on magic was gone. It flowed freely now through all of us. I'd never known magic unbound from the queens. It was life itself down to the very atoms of my being. It was everywhere and all things. Something only beginning but never-ending. "Everything is different."

"Not everything." She placed a reassuring hand on my chest. The magic between us remained. Our souls were still one, our lives still bound in immortality.

I gazed down at her, at my wife, at my mate, and managed a smile. "Not that."

But before I could cross that threshold of joy, Lysander approached. Aurelia trailed him, her shoulders tense. I searched for proof of what Thea had told me, but any trace of fae was hidden again. Aurelia kept her hands balled into fists at her sides, her knuckles white as she stayed a step behind. I raised an eyebrow at Thea.

"Some of the Vampire Council want an audience," Lysander told us in a low voice. "Mom is trying to distract them, but…"

"It's fine," Thea cut in. "The sooner we get this over with, the better."

"You don't have to justify what you did," I said.

"I'm an expert on justifying myself to the Council," she deadpanned, leaning her weight against me. "And it's better if I tell them."

I inclined my head. "Whatever you wish." It was her decision.

Lysander glanced at Aurelia. "What about her?"

Thea and I shared a look, and she asked slowly, "What about her?"

"Are you going to tell them the truth?"

Aurelia flinched, her eyes darting around like she wanted to escape, but she didn't move.

Thea shook her head. "I don't think it's necessary. If Aurelia doesn't want them to know about her involvement, that's up to her. Quinn won't say anything." She leveled a hard gaze at my brother. I pitied his ability to withstand her glittering emerald eyes. "Will you?"

"No," he said in a tone made firm by the ice coating it. "It's none of my business what she is."

"Lysander," I said gently, reaching for his shoulder, but he shrugged it off.

"I need some air." He strode toward the doorway that led to the canal.

Aurelia watched him leave, her face contorting with a feeling I knew all too well. Pain mixed with longing. She finally tore her eyes away. "I should have expected that," she said bitterly.

"We won't say anything, either," Thea promised, and I nodded. "Your secret is safe with us." She hesitated. "About my mother…"

"I took her to the Hallow Court. From what Ginerva taught me, they were most likely to help her," Aurelia explained. "They did. As far as the bargain she made, I don't know. I will check on her later."

"Thank you." Thea grabbed her hand and squeezed it. "I owe you."

"No, you freed me. Our bargain is fulfilled." Her eyes strayed in the direction Lysander had exited. "Now I'm free to live my own life." She didn't sound happy about that. She smiled, but it didn't reach her eyes. "If you don't need me at the Council audience, I think I'd like to be alone."

"Of course." Thea watched her leave, sighing as Aurelia disappeared inside. "Should I go after her?"

"Give her space," I murmured, drawing her back into my arms. "Give them both space."

"Lysander is being a dick," she said flatly. "I'm...surprised."

"So is she. But they need to sort this out on their own."

Thea scowled but finally agreed. "And we'll have to find my mother *again*."

"We will," I swore. "The Hallow Court is one of the light courts. She is safe. I'll have Benedict reach out."

"Thank you." Something drew her attention over my shoulder.

I turned to find my mother approaching, followed by the remaining Council members.

"I guess it's time to face the music."

"We need to speak with you." Sabine sighed as she appraised Thea's bloody wedding dress. "That gown was from Paris."

"Priorities," I muttered.

"Careful. I'm the head of the family again," she reminded us, "since it seems you are both now Rousseauxs."

Is it too late to take your name? I kept my face straight as sent the question to Thea's mind.

She bit back a grin. "If the Council wants to speak with me, we should do it now. It's my wedding night. I have other plans."

My mother sighed, but a slight smile played on her lips. "At least you married a radical."

• • •

Two hours later, the arguments showed no sign of ceasing. Thea had told them what had happened and the decision she'd made, casually leaving out Aurelia's involvement and revising the facts to shoulder any perceived blame. We'd gathered in the throne room, and my mate had insisted that anyone who wanted to be present could attend. She sat on her now-powerless throne with me by her side, trying to hide her yawns as everyone continued to bicker.

"It was not a decision for you to make," Marcus said when Thea finished speaking. "Without the power of *Le Regine*—"

"You were all cursed. I had to make a decision," she cut him off. *Good girl.*

"It may have been possible to break the curse without such drastic action. As it is, magic is now defenseless."

"Defenseless?" she repeated. "You were defenseless—all of you—and it was my call to make. It was my crown to give up."

"But in doing so—"

"No. It was my decision to make." Thea rose to her feet. "And I have made it. Magic should flow freely. Magic is for everyone. It's not something to be controlled. This is how it should be, how it was before *Le Regine*. The curse needed to be broken. Magic shouldn't be controlled or hoarded. All creatures should have access to magic."

"Idealistic fool," Marcus snapped. "There are creatures that must be controlled. If you were truly meant to be a queen, you would understand that."

Thea's face hardened into steely resolve. "I didn't ask to be made queen. I never wanted this responsibility. But magic chose me. It was suffocating. It was dying. The Council needs to adapt to this new reality, to work with other creatures to ensure it's used responsibly, and to represent what all vampires want. This isn't an ending. It's an opportunity. We can be better. The world is changing, and we must change along with it. Or we are all doomed."

The room fell silent, but my mother inclined her head ever so slightly. A show of respect for Thea's bravery.

"We will discuss this and find a new way forward," Sabine announced. "Will you be staying in Venice?"

Thea looked at me and raised an eyebrow.

Up to you.

"We're going on a honeymoon," Thea decided, "and after that, we'll let you know."

She didn't wait for a response before she grabbed my hand and aimed us out of the throne room. We both knew the Council would try to keep us here. As soon as we were in the corridor, I asked, "Where are we going on this honeymoon?"

"Anywhere but here," she said drily.

"Okay, but hear me out. Why don't we start now? It's still our wedding night."

"What did you have in mind?" she purred.

I swept her into my arms, carrying her toward our quarters. "Let me show you."

• • •

Moonlight seeped through the windows, lighting her skin with a soft glow. I traced a finger down her bare abdomen, marveling at the slight swell that was finally showing. Thea's hand combed through my hair, and she smiled lazily at me. "That was an excellent start to the honeymoon."

"I concur," I said, continuing my exploration of her flesh.

"Do you think I did the right thing?" she asked softly.

I pressed a kiss to her stomach and sat up. "You didn't have a choice."

"There is always a choice."

"Sometimes there is no *right* choice, but I think you made the best one. I would have done the same." It was likely a small consolation, but she shook her head as if to say it wasn't. I smiled.

"I made the one I could live with, but I'm afraid others won't see it that way." She sighed. "I chose you. I never wanted power. I only wanted you."

"I'm here," I reminded her, "and I'll always be here. We'll face whatever comes together."

"Where are we going to go?" she asked, reaching for me.

"Paris? San Francisco? Name the place. I promised you the world."

"You already gave me the world," she murmured, "when you

gave me your heart." We stared at each other, need deepening in her eyes. "I just want to live. I want to play cello and make babies and love you for at least the next hundred years."

"Only one hundred?"

She wrinkled her nose. "For the rest of my life."

"That's a very long time."

Her hand found my chest, found the mark that had not vanished when she gave up her throne. It had changed—like us. Above the crescent moon, rays of light haloed it. She traced her fingernail along one. "What changed it?"

Somehow I was certain of my answer. "You did."

"But I gave back the crown, the throne, the power."

"No, Thea, the power was always yours," I said softly, curling my hand around hers and holding it against my heart. "This belongs to us now. Our *lives* belong to us now."

And we were the sun and moon, night and day, darkness and light.

Death and life.

Unbroken and unending.

Her eyes met mine, full of light and hope and promise. "Wherever we go, my home is at your side."

"As is mine." Lowering my mouth to hers, we sealed that final vow. Shifting my weight, I moved between her legs, our bodies pressing together, seeking the promise of each other. A low groan escaped my lips as I slid inside her. She moaned as we joined, her fingers sinking into my shoulders as we moved.

"Promise me it will always be like this." She gasped as her legs tightened around me.

I kissed her in response, pulling away only far enough to whisper my answer, "It will be—for eternity."

ACKNOWLEDGMENTS

When I set out to write Thea and Julian's story, I expected it to be one book. I should have known that a story as epic as theirs would need more. Thank you for coming along on this journey—a journey that is only just beginning.

Huge thanks to Louise Fury, my badass agent and biggest cheerleader. To the team at The Fury Agency, thank you for looking out for me and bringing my books to new readers all over the world.

Thank you to Liz Pelletier and the entire Entangled team for being behind Filthy Rich Vampires! Thanks to Yezanira Venecia, Jessica Turner, Heather Riccio, Lydia Sharp, Curtis Svehlak, Brittany Zimmerman, Angela Melamud, and so many more for all of your hard work.

Thank you to the team at Tantor for bringing FRV to audio! Thank you to Dialogue Books for bringing FRV to the UK, to the teams at Blanvalet for bringing them to Germany right from the start, and Wydawnictwo Kobiece for taking a chance on my vampire lovers! Thank you all!

I am so blessed to be surrounded by talented authors who inspire me every day to keep writing. Special thanks to Cora, Robyn, Kim, and Rebecca for being there when I needed to cry or scream. A huge thanks to my reader group, Geneva Lee's Loves, for being like my book family.

Huge thanks to the team at Vella for giving me a chance to tell this story since the beginning!

And to my family for giving me both a reason to write down these crazy stories and the support and love to do so. Thank you to my older kids, James and Sydney, for brainstorming sessions about magic, and to my little one, Sophie, for being an endless source of it. And thank you to Josh for being my mate, my tether, and my #1 fan.

Filthy Rich Vampires: For Eternity is a steamy romance full of extravagance and an ending that will leave you on the edge of your seat. However, the story includes elements that might not be suitable for all readers. Violence, familial estrangement, blood rituals, beheadings, mind-altering substance use, and death are shown on the page, with sexual assault and discussions of cancer in the backstory. Readers who may be sensitive to these elements, please take note.

*Don't miss the exciting new books
Entangled has to offer.*

Follow us!

 @EntangledPublishing

 @Entangled_Publishing

 @EntangledPub

AMARA
an imprint of Entangled Publishing LLC